DATE DUE

SE 1 2 0			
AG 0 1 09			

DEMCO 38-297

The WOAD to WUIN

Also by Peter David

Sir Apropos of Nothing

The WOAD to WUIN

SIR APROPOS of NOTHING
Book Two

PETER DAVID

POCKET BOOKS

NEW YORK   LONDON   TORONTO   SYDNEY   SINGAPORE

POCKET BOOKS, a division of Simon & Schuster, Inc.
1230 Avenue of the Americas, New York, NY 10020

Copyright © 2002 by Second Age, Inc.

All rights reserved, including the right to reproduce
this book or portions thereof in any form whatsoever.
For information address Pocket Books, 1230 Avenue
of the Americas, New York, NY 10020

Library of Congress Control Number: 2002105146

ISBN: 0-7434-4830-8

First Pocket Books hardcover printing August 2002

10 9 8 7 6 5 4 3 2 1

POCKET and colophon are registered trademarks of
Simon & Schuster, Inc.

For information regarding special discounts for bulk purchases,
please contact Simon & Schuster Special Sales at 1-800-456-6798 or
business@simonandschuster.com

Map drawn by Paul J. Pugliese
Map concept by Kathleen O'Shea David

Printed in the U.S.A.

Acknowledgments

The author wishes to thank Kathleen O'Shea David for her craftsmanship in producing the maps for both the original *Sir Apropos of Nothing* and this, the sequel.

Also, he wishes to thank Albert Alfaro of Imaginarium Galleries for his creation of the Drabits, a species of whom Mordant is a vocal member when he is so inclined. You can own your own drabit if you encounter them at various Renfaires (including the one in Tuxedo, New York) or by going to *www.animatedpuppets.com*, or phone them at (570) 420-9817. Tell them Apropos sent you. This will not get you a discount on future purchases. Might get the author one, though.

And finally, he thanks John Ordover and Scott Shannon at Pocket Books for their belief in what has now become a series, agent Andy Zack for putting the deal together, and all those who have opted to spend some hours with our struggling antihero, and looks forward to seeing you all here this time next year for *Tong Lashing*.

To Kathleen . . .
my partner on the long and winding woad . . . uh . . . road

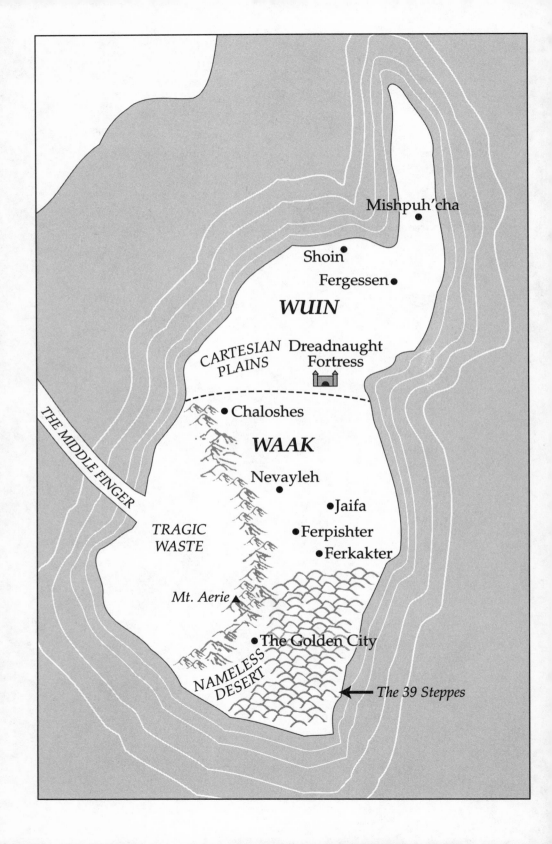

BOOK ONE
Fate Accompli

Chapter 1

The One Thing

*I*t is important you understand that I do not like taking people's lives. I have done it several times but derived no pleasure from it. Furthermore it has always been in self-defense, and, as suspect as it may sound, it has usually come about as a result of someone inadvertently throwing themselves on some sort of sharp implement I happened to be pointing in his, her, or its direction. I have never, however, been the sort to start a fight when it could be avoided . . . or, for that matter, failed to run from it if remotely possible. Anyone who has read my previous chronicles of my "adventures," of which this is a continuation, is already rather painfully aware of that.

So you will understand the distress I felt when I was standing there in the middle of an otherwise lovely glade, on a fairly crisp and yet invigorating day, staring in dismay at the hairy-footed dwarf that I had unintentionally killed. A death which would unexpectedly thrust me—in every sense of the word—into an escapade that was alternately the most exhilarating, and most terrifying, that I had ever experienced. And considering what I had experienced previous to that point, that is saying some.

For those who are new to what can only in the broadest and most ironic terms be referred to as my hero's journey, I shall tell you as simply as possible what you need to know in order to understand me. (Indeed, I should observe that if you are interested in my life, you may very well lack sufficient brain power to comprehend all but the most minimal of explanations.)

My name is Apropos, occasionally referred to as "Apropos of Nothing" due to my lowly birth and lack of . . . well . . . anything, really, that could be considered valuable. Of late I was dubbed Sir Apropos, still of Nothing, an honor which—for reasons I won't go into here—did not quite work out. Suffice to say that one whose patrimony consists of a group of knights raping my tavern wench mother, providing me an existence of endless betrayal and deprivation which served to give me a somewhat cynical, shall we say, view of the world . . . well, one such as that does not end up living happily ever after. I was foolish enough to briefly entertain the notion, and paid severely for that unbecoming naïveté by winding up tossed in a dungeon barely twenty-four hours after being knighted, which was something of a record at the court of King Runcible in the state of Isteria.

Once I managed to escape the dungeon through means literally too ludicrous to go into here, I hit the road in the company of a rather vexing young sorceress (or "weaver," as her type is also known, short for "magic weaver") who called herself "Sharee," which may or may not have been her true name.

I never found out whether Runcible sent his knights after me to bring me back. On the one hand, his pride was no doubt hurt; on the other hand, he and his queen—and certainly his daughter—might have been well-pleased to be rid of me. If they had been determined to hunt me down, it likely would not have been all that difficult. My ears tended to stick out a bit too much, and my flaming red hair was long and unruly. My nose was crooked from having been broken several times, and although my eyes were a remarkably pleasing shade of gray, the rest of my hodgepodge of features invariably overwhelmed them. Furthermore I was lame of right leg, and got about with the aid of a sizable walking staff that also served as a formidable weapon. In short, I was easy to spot and difficult to disguise.

Sharee was less distinctive. She dressed customarily in black, with ebony hair cut short and curled around her ears, and her rather prominent chin perpetually out thrust as if she were challenging the world to take its best shot at her. There were times when it seemed to me that her prime reason for existence was harassing me and taking great pleasure in the bizarre vagaries of my life. Still, in some ways she was the truest friend I had ever encountered, if one defined *friend* as "perpetual irritant."

Just in case Runcible's knights did happen to be following us, we retreated west and later north, to take refuge in the Tucker Forest. This was not done without a certain degree of trepidation on my part. The Tucker Forest was a nesting area for a particularly vicious group of cutthroat monstrosities called the Harpers Bizarre, with whom I had considerable bad blood. I would far have preferred to take refuge in the Elderwoods of my youth, but the only way to get there was either along roads too heavily traveled for my comfort, or across the Screaming Gorge of Eternal Madness, about which the less said the better. Besides, Sharee seemed rather confident that if difficulties arose, her weather-related magiks could dispose of the Harpers with alacrity, and so the Tucker Forest became our temporary haven while we waited for the name Apropos to fade into the furthest recesses of royal memory.

Fortunately I had considerable proficiency in forestry, one of the few true talents I possessed other than evasion, self-preservation, and rank cowardice. I had developed the forestry skills in my youth, and they had not faded in time as I grew to young manhood. I was reaching the end of my teens when we took up temporary refuge in the Tucker Forest. We found a cave in which to reside, well hidden from casual observation either from ground level (i.e., thieves) or from overhead (i.e., the Harpers Bizarre). We figured we would spend a couple of days there and then work our way farther west in order to distance ourselves more from Runcible's men. I spent time hunting, catching small game, while Sharee preferred to alternate between meditating and acting as if she had something far better to do with her time than remain with me.

Occasionally, though, we had mild fun together. For instance, I commented to her that I would be interested in learning some magic. In response, she started teaching me card tricks. Not real magic at all, and I was quite irritated with her at first. But in short order, I actually derived some genuine amusement from it. I was a fairly quick learner, and also picked up some easy sleight-of-hand, including misdirection and the ability to apparently pluck a card out of the air. Not much of a trick to the latter, really. Simply keep your hand straight, hold the upper corners of the card securely on the back of your hand, between your fingers, and then snap it quickly forward. The card seems to have come out of nowhere. As noted, not genuine magic, but sometimes we measure the quality of life's passage by just how much of an assortment of mindless pastimes we develop to entertain ourselves through it.

In terms of hunting, at first I stuck to small animals. But I tired quickly of a steady diet of rabbit and squirrel. So I redesigned and reconfigured the traps for bigger bait, hoping to snag a small deer or perhaps even a straying unicorn. Immortal or not, such creatures could still die from a quickly snapped neck, and such were my traps intended for. Naturally I set them nowhere near the roads that occasional travelers might use, lest an unfortunate accident occur.

Yet it happened anyway.

I was moving through the forest one day with my customary stealth. It may sound boastful or vainglorious, but when I elect not to be detected in the woods, it is nigh unto impossible to find me. It is one of the few instances, outside of swimming, where my lame leg does not deter me. Stealth does not arise from speed, but from economy of motion. A high-speed marathon would leave me hopelessly abandoned, but if you were seeking someone to move at a snail's pace for days on end, I was your man.

Approaching one of my more crafty noose traps, I suddenly heard a startled and truncated yelp from ahead. It was definitely of a human variety of noise. It took me a moment to realize whence the sound had come—namely from my trap—and but a moment more to grasp, with horror, the likely significance of it.

Disdaining silence, I practically crashed through the under-brush, hoping there was time to salvage the situation. 'Twas not to be. Instead I came upon a scene utterly dismaying . . . and yet also utterly fascinating in a perverse way, and I do mean perverse.

The small pile of food which had served as bait within the snare now lay scattered about. The noose was drawn taut, dangling about three and a half feet in the air. And suspended from the noose itself, its feet clear of the ground by a good six inches, was the aforementioned dwarf.

It was a damned odd-looking thing. Its head was slumped to one side. It was round, with features that looked fairly squashed, as if someone had sat on its face. Its arms were the disproportionate length so common to its kind, but its legs were longer and less bow-shaped than one customarily saw in such creatures. Its feet were odder still. At first I thought it was wearing hairy slippers of some sort, but then realized that it was barefoot and simply had the most hirsute pedal extremities of any creature I'd ever seen that didn't also possess a tail.

It also sported an extremely sizable bulge in its loins which even its loose-fitting breeches couldn't obscure. I'd never been present at a hanging, but had heard that the victims of such incidents usually had themselves a fairly healthy protuberance at the moment of death, which had always struck me as somewhat puzzling. If any-thing could be deemed a sure killer of arousal, it was having your neck snapped. But here was I, first-hand witness to the phenome-non, and so knew it to be true. Who would have thought?

I still felt some measure of guilt for the passing creature's untimely demise, but there wasn't much I could do about it after the fact. So instead I proceeded to do the most reasonable thing one could under the circumstances: I checked him over for valuables. I didn't bother to cut him down; gruesome as his situation was, it was easier to inspect him while he was upright. While his most noticeable bulge began to diminish, I happily relieved him of another—a fairly decent purse hanging on his belt which I quickly discovered was filled with gold coins the like of which I'd never seen. Still, as opposed to coins unique to specific realms with different faces of monarchs etched in the surfaces, gold was definitely gold no matter whose countenance adorned it.

Then I spotted something twinkling on the brush just beneath the dwarf's dangling feet, shining and winking at me in the rays of the setting sun. I reached down and picked it up. It appeared to be some sort of golden ring, but it was much too large for ordinary wear. I could easily fit three of my fingers into the thing. An earring perhaps, but there was no clasp for it to fasten on. It felt rather warm, and I turned it over and over in my hands, inspecting it carefully. It was then I noticed some sort of writing on the inside. It was not easy to make out and, confusingly, the letters seemed to be fading along with the dissipating warmth. But what it read was:

One thing to rule them all.

I didn't know to whom "them all" referred, or what the one thing might be, so really I was somewhat ignorant of the purpose of the ring. Would that I had remained that way.

It was at that point that I heard something coming toward me through the woods. From the sound of it, it appeared to be a group of men, at least half a dozen. They were making no attempt to move quietly; a deaf man could have heard them coming. Unfortunately they were between me and the cave.

Without thinking, I shoved the ring in my pocket and quickly sought, and found, refuge amongst the underbrush. As I mentioned earlier, when I am endeavoring to hide in a forest, I am almost impossible to detect. I drew my cape around me and huddled low, unmoving in the lengthening shadows of the forest.

The men arrived in short order, and a more motley assortment one could not have imagined. The one who seemed to be the leader was a strong, fox-faced, handsome-looking man. With him was an astounding array of . . . hell, I'm not sure what they were. A couple more hairy-footed dwarfs, a few trolls, some other freakish-looking individuals. I had absolutely no idea where they could have come from; none of their ilk had ever passed through any of the regions in which I'd resided.

They saw at once the dangling dwarf, and oh, the moaning and caterwauling that they sent up then, I cannot begin to tell you. In catching the names they were tossing around, it appeared that the deceased one was called Bubo, and the tall man was Walker. The others had an assortment of staggeringly annoying monikers that were impossible to keep straight: Hodge and Podge, Hoi and Paloi, Hither and Thither, Tutti and Fruitti, So On and So Forth, etc. It was rather cloying, and I could only be thankful I wasn't traveling with the group as I would likely have beaten myself to death after two days rather than die slowly of excessive cleverness.

The tall one called Walker was standing directly in front of Bubo, obscuring him from my sight, and then he turned and looked grimly at the others. "The ring is not here," he said.

There were gasps and lamentations and growls of "Death to the thief!" which naturally didn't sit all that well with me.

"The body is still warm," said Walker. "The thief cannot have gotten far." Now, I have to admit, I bridled a bit at the word thief. Not that I wasn't one, you understand, but in this particular circumstance, it wasn't as if the deceased had any use for his possessions anymore. I figured I was as entitled to what he was carrying upon him as anyone else. "Spread out. Find him," Walker continued.

Moving in smooth coordination, they headed out in all directions. I didn't breathe. One of the dwarfs came within two feet of me but passed me by without noticing me hunkered down in the brush.

I waited what seemed an interminable time there, my legs getting numb, my arms feeling like lead weights. Night had almost fallen when I finally chanced to rise, my sharp hearing convincing me that I was alone.

Except . . .

In a sense, I wasn't.

I felt an extremely odd tingling in my loins. My little soldier was standing at attention, and he wasn't little. Furthermore, I felt some sort of foreign object down there. Even though I knew I was alone, I still glanced right and left to ensure privacy, then reached down into my breeches to see what was up. Well . . . what else was up, beside the obvious.

To my utter astonishment, I discovered the ring, nestled securely at the base of my member. Apparently I'd had a hole in my pocket, and as if it had a life of its own, the ring had worked its way through and nestled into my loins, wrapping itself around my privates as if it were destined to be there. I pulled on the ring in an endeavor to remove it. It wouldn't come off. I tried again and again, as forceful as I could be while still retaining some delicacy, as I'm sure you can well imagine.

It didn't budge. Here I had been wondering how one could possibly sport such a sizable ring, and now I had inadvertently discovered the answer. Furthermore I was so swollen that it didn't appear capable of being removed until the tumescence went away. Which it did not seem inclined to do. And out there, exposed in the woods, I felt rather too self-conscious to "relieve myself" of the pressure.

I was utterly mortified, but I had nowhere else to go as I headed back to the cave. Fortunately I had my great cape with me, so I would be able to draw it around myself and hide the noticeable bulge, for I certainly did not need Sharee laughing at my predicament. My hope was that if I simply ignored the thing, it would go away. And certainly spending time with Sharee would increase that likelihood, for if I'd had any remaining interest in the opposite sex after my rather disastrous history of liaisons, the weaver was more than capable of putting it to rest.

I hoped that she might not be in the cave when I arrived, just so I had a few minutes to get myself settled with the cape still around me. Such was not to be, however, for there she was, tending a small fire and looking up at me expectantly. "Did you bring food?" she inquired.

"Bad luck trapping," I said, which was true enough. Hungry we might have been, but I didn't think we were hungry enough to eat a dwarf. I settled down some feet away from her, adjusting the cape. My loins did not seem to be calming. Instead, in Sharee's presence, there appeared to be even more excitement than before. And I thought, *Oh, my friend, are you barking up the wrong tree. If there is anyone who is not at all interested, it is—*

She was upon me in a flash.

I could not believe it. One minute she was sitting there, looking at me oddly, and the next she was on top of me with such force that I slammed my head against the cave wall. Her hand went straight to the place I'd been trying to keep hidden, as if she knew what was going to be there. Her eyes were wild with a fiery light, and she was smothering me with kisses even as she started pulling both of our clothes off in her eagerness.

Now . . .

I'm not stupid.

I figured out what was going on in pretty short order. I didn't for a moment think that suddenly I had acquired so sensual, so commanding a personality that Sharee felt compelled to savage me in every carnal way imaginable. Obviously it was the ring. The damned thing was enchanted somehow, and it was an enchantment that no one—even a skilled weatherweaver such as Sharee—was able to resist. She was not in her right mind. Under the circumstances, I would have been a cad, a bounder, and an utter rot-ter to take advantage of the situation. And if you think that I failed to do so, then clearly you have not been paying attention.

Truthfully, although I was not exactly resistant to the concept, I'm not sure I could have kept her off me even had I desired to. She was unstoppable, and thanks to the ring, I was more than up to the challenge.

And later I was up to it again. And again.

And again.

All through the night.

I lost count. By the time the morning came, my head was swimming with exhaustion, my belly practically in pain from lack of nourishment. But my suddenly very public private was still fresh as ever, and Sharee just as enthusiastic. I let her have her way with me again, this time so bone weary that I didn't even move. I just lay there, splayed on the cave floor, and thought about bathing in freezing water.

Finally Sharee fell asleep, and I knew beyond question that I had to get the hell out of there.

Apparently realizing that the joy ride was over, my seemingly insatiable rod slumped a bit, but not enough for me to pull the ring off. Quickly I dressed and bolted from the cave. I figured that Sharee would be waiting for me when, or if, I got back.

I was ravenously hungry at that point. Perhaps Sharee could live on love, but I did not share that capacity. I moved quickly through the woods, counting on my staff—my wooden one, not the betraying member in my breeches—for more support than even my lame leg usually required. Animals seemed to be giving me wide berth, however, and the few nuts and leaves I could safely eat off the trees were hardly enough to keep me going, particularly after the evening of ardor I had spent.

I made my way to the main east/west road which ran through the upper section of the Tucker Forest and cut east. I knew there was an inn along the way. It wasn't much, but I figured that at least they'd have some sort of minimal food there, and I could replenish myself. I also needed to distance myself from Sharee for a time. I assuredly couldn't go back to sleeping in the cave with her; the woman obviously would not leave me alone. Not as long as I had this Significant Other to deal with.

I felt it stirring with renewed life as I approached the inn, and drew my cape even more tightly around myself. Fortunately enough it was a brisk morning, so no one would question why I was keeping myself so covered up.

Once inside, I took a table toward the back, in a corner, with the intention of keeping entirely to myself. The innkeeper, a dyspeptic- looking fellow, glanced at me suspiciously. I held up the money, jingled it slightly, and that seemed enough to satisfy him. He moved away as the serving girl approached me. I'll admit she was a comely thing, which is what made what happened next somewhat tolerable.

"A stein of mead," I told her, "and do you have any decent mutton?"

She looked me up and down. Even though I was covered up, I suddenly felt as if her gaze was boring right to where I didn't want it to go. I crossed my legs, cleared my throat, and started to repeat the question.

"Upstairs," she interrupted. "First door on the right. Now."

"But . . . I haven't eaten."

She brought her face toward mine, and her breath was warm and pleasant. "I'll be your appetizer . . . and your main course . . . and your dessert . . ."

Oh, my gods. "Miss . . . I . . . that is to say . . ."

"Upstairs, now," and there was iron in her voice, "or I'll take you right here."

She meant it. I could see it in her eyes, hear it in her tone, she was quite serious.

I went upstairs, to the room she indicated. There was a bed there with a lumpy mattress. Ten seconds later she was there, and the waitress provided room service.

Five minutes later the waitress's mother burst in on us, shocked and appalled. She threw her sobbing daughter out, slammed the door behind her, faced me, and I knew then what was coming.

I was worried that the tavern keeper was the husband, and figured that he'd be upstairs in short order with an ax . . . or, worse, love in his eyes. But such was not the case; they were simply a mother and daughter who worked at the tavern.

And they had friends.

Lots of friends.

Now I have to tell you, a situation like this had, at one time, been one of my fantasies. I grew up in a tavern, saw whores in action. And I had always wondered what it would be like to be so in demand that people—women, in my case—would throw themselves at me by the cartload, and even be willing to pay me, just for the privilege of melding their bodies with mine.

Well, no one was offering me money, although I have no doubt that I could have fleeced them for all they were worth. I likely would have, too, had any of them given me the chance to talk.

Apparently there was a village nearby, and all I can surmise from the parade of female flesh that marched in and out of my room was that the menfolk were not doing their job. The women came to me in all shapes, all sizes, young and old, pretty and . . . less so. I tried to keep a smile on my face, tell myself that this was the price of fame. I literally, however, lost track of time. Day and night became meaningless to me. Oh, I was fed, at least. The tavern wench kept bringing me food. At one point the innkeeper stuck his head in, grinned, and said, "Keep at it, my lad! That's the ticket!" as if he was my best friend in the world. I managed a meager wave and realized that he was probably charging the women admission. He was making *my money*. It didn't seem fair, and if any part of me had been able to rise from the bed aside from the one part of me that appeared inexhaustible, I would have done something about it.

I tried to leave, several times. They wouldn't let me. Finally they tied me to the bed. There are worse ways to pass one's hours, but none come readily to mind.

* * *

I have no idea when Walker and his people showed up. It could have been a day later, a week later. I was floating in a haze of exhaustion and numbness. All I knew was that there was a thumping up the stairs, and the door burst open. For a moment I thought it was a mob of angry husbands, come either to chop me to bits or—for all I knew—have their way with me. Then I squinted as I recognized that improbably heroic face. I was nude from the waist down, obviously. I couldn't remember a time anymore when I'd worn breeches. He took one look, turned to others crowding in, and said firmly, "He has the ring."

There was certainly no use denying it. "You want it? Take it," I mumbled in exhaustion.

Walker stomped in, tossing a blanket over me. Producing a blade, he severed the bonds holding my hands to the bedframe. "It is not ours to take. I will not ask how you came by it; the past no longer matters. Thanks to the ring, you are now the possessor of the One Thing Which Rules Them All."

"The One Thing being . . ." and I pointed to my happy soldier.

"Yes." He nodded, and the others mimicked the nod. "That thing."

"And 'them all' would be . . . women."

"Yes," Walker said once more. "What you possess is a ring, forged in the—"

I held up my hands and rose from the bed, fumbling about for my breeches. "No. Don't tell me."

"But you should know," said Walker.

"Yes, it's a really good story," one of the dwarfs said, in a slightly whiny tone.

"I don't care!" I insisted. "It probably involves some powerful magic user somewhere, and dark forces, and evil hordes wanting it back. Right?"

"Well . . . essentially, yes," Walker admitted, looking a bit uncomfortable.

"Fine. Save it. And get them out of here." I pointed at the cluster of women that was already assembling, seeming rather distressed over the prospect of my possible departure. "All I want to know is how to get rid of the thing."

"You must toss it," said Walker solemnly, "into the Flaming Nether Regions. Only there will it be melted, its threat ended for all time."

I knew the Flaming Nether Regions well enough. I had once been squire to a knight, Sir Umbrage, who hailed from thereabouts.

You may be wondering why I did not question the interest this mixed bag of meddlers might have had in the ring. I shall make it plain: Clearly they were heroes. Bubo, previous possessor of this lovely trinket, had probably been as much in demand as I was. Walker's people had obviously been serving to keep women away from him . . . or perhaps him away from women . . . while they escorted him to the Flaming Nether Regions. They were in the midst of some great quest, into which I had been unwillingly—and unwittingly—drawn. I like neither heroes nor quests, because becoming involved with either invariably gets people killed. I have no patience for adventures, even though I perpetually seem to find myself in the middle of them, and the sooner I depart their vicinity, the better. Far from dauntless, I am easily daunted. I want nothing but to make money, have some fame, fortune, and fun, and survive to die of old age in my bed.

In short, I'm just like you. Look down your nose at me at your peril, for it is yourself you very likely judge.

So I had no interest in what had brought them to this point in time. I simply said, "Take me there."

We set off.

There was much trouble along the way.

I could go into detail, of course. I could tell you about the dark warriors who set upon us, the flaming black hailstones, the totally unexpected return assault of the Harpers Bizarre, who apparently were now under the command of a great and powerful weaver, the rampaging fishlike killer creature called the Orcuh, and much,

much more. But it was not a pleasant period, just about everyone in the group was killed, I spent the entire time with a raging tumescence in my breeches, and one of the dwarfs—Thither, I think it was—kept eyeing me in a manner I found most disturbing. I was frankly relieved when the Orcuh stepped on him.

So you'll pardon me if I simply say, again, that there was much trouble along the way, until finally only an exhausted Walker and myself were left to stand on the edge of the formidable precipice overlooking the Flaming Nether Regions.

Far, far below raged the Regions. A continuous lava flow, the origin of which no one knew, flames licking upward with formidable intensity, and smoke billowing, making it extremely difficult to see more than a foot or so down.

"All right," I said to Walker. "Now what?" I had my hand discreetly around the ring, trying to pull it off, thinking that now that it had reached its inevitable destiny, the damned thing would go without a struggle. Unfortunately I was as hard, and the ring as stubborn, as ever.

"You throw the ring in," said Walker matter-of-factly.

"Yes, well, small problem. The ring doesn't appear to be cooperating."

"That does not surprise me."

"Well, it surprises me!" I retorted, wiping sweat from my brow. "You made it sound simple! Get to the Flaming Nether Regions, toss the ring in, we're done! How do I remove it?"

"The ring will only detach itself," said Walker, "when the bearer's heart stops."

"*What?*" I felt all the remaining blood in my body that wasn't elsewhere pounding in my temples. "You mean when I die?" I now realized that, obviously, when Bubo had died, the ring had fallen through his leggings and onto the ground where I'd found it. "You couldn't think to mention that *earlier?* I'm supposed to *kill* myself? That doesn't leave much of an upside for *me!*"

"There is . . . an alternative," Walker said.

"Good! Excellent! What is it?" Relief was flooding through me.

Walker produced a very sharp-looking knife. "Cut it off."

I took the knife, turning it over in my hand. Yes, indeed, very sharp. "And this will cut through the ring?" I said doubtfully.

"No, nothing can cut through the ring."

As I said, I'm not stupid. I quickly realized where this was going. I fought down rising panic. "So my choice, you're saying to me . . . is either death . . . or a life not worth living."

"Think of it this way," Walker said, trying to sound commiserating. "Certainly in the past days, you've received a lifetime's worth of attention to your member. Is that not enough?"

"No! Most certainly not! And I—"

"*Mine!*"

The cackling, unexpected voice caught us both unawares. We turned, standing there on the edge of the gorge, and I couldn't believe what I was seeing.

Bubo was approaching us, his head still at that bizarre angle from when the noose had snapped his neck. He did not, however, appear to realize that he was deceased. His skin was the color of curdled milk and shared some of the same aroma. His eyes were wide and solid black, his teeth rotting in his head. As he approached, his hands were spasming, as if he was trying to clutch something with them. "My precious! Mine!" he cried out, sounding like a screeching baby bird.

"Stay back!" Walker said to me. "He wants the ring!"

"If he can get it off me with an option other than what you've offered, he can have it!"

"No! Don't you understand? If the dark weaver who forged the ring gets it back, no woman in the world will be safe!"

"I'll buy them all locked chastity belts! It will work out fine!" I was tugging at the stubborn ring. "Here! Your old friend wants you back! Go! Go!"

"Undead thing," Walker said defiantly, facing the creature which had been Bubo. "You do not frighten me." He started to pull his sword.

Bubo didn't wait. He leaped through the air as if he weighed nothing, landed squarely on Walker's shoulders and gripped Walker's head with his feet. With a quick twist of his hips, he snapped Walker's neck. Walker's dead body collapsed like a sack of potatoes, his sword still only half drawn.

I started to back up, but there wasn't far to go. "Stay back!" I shouted hollowly, holding my walking staff threateningly. There was a vicious blade in one end of it, but I doubted such a thing would be of use against something already dead. "Stay back, or I'll . . . I'll . . ."

In truth, I had no idea what I would do. Bubo, however, did not wait to find out. With a scream he leaped across the intervening distance, howling, "Give it back to me! My pretty! My pretty ring! My precious, mine!" Either he didn't realize where we were or, in his undead and obsessed state, he simply didn't care. He slammed into me, knocking my walking staff from my hands, driving me back, and suddenly there was nothing below me but the yawning gorge of flame and death.

We tumbled, falling through the smoke, but barely a few feet below, there was a rocky ledge extending that I hadn't seen before. I struck it, rolled off, grabbed it with my desperate hands, and hung there.

Bubo was holding on to my left leg.

I tried to kick him off with my right, but that was my lame leg, and I had little strength in it. Bubo didn't even seem to notice. Instead he clambered up my leg, and—gods help me—shoved his hand into my breeches, his cold, clammy palm wrapping around the still unbudging ring, my protuberance now his only means of support.

"*Mine!*" he howled, holding on to it. "*Mine! Mine!*"

It was too much.

My brain shut down.

My heart stopped.

I died.

For an instant.

The next thing I knew, I was slammed back to life. The world whirling around me, I realized that I had fallen, but fallen onto yet another outcropping of rock. The smoke had hidden the fact that the cliff face was not exactly smooth.

I heard screaming below me, and looked over the edge of the rock formation which had proven my salvation. Bubo had been less fortunate. My death, however brief, had been sufficient for the ring to slip free, and Bubo with it. I saw him spiraling down, down toward the flame, screaming and shouting, *"I have it! I have my precious back!"* tumbling end over end, probably not even aware of what was happening. I heard his shouting continue, all the way down, and then there was a sudden roar of flame as Bubo and the ring hit the lava below. Somewhere—in my own imaginings, most likely—I could swear I heard a deep, pained voice of anger roaring in fury as the ring melted in the fiery furnace of the Flaming Nether Regions . . . which was, I suppose, only fitting.

It took me quite some time to climb, hand over careful hand, back up to the edge of the cliff from which I had tumbled. Walker was lying there, dead as a stump. I checked him over, pulled some valuables off him, and kicked his body over the edge. I had no more need of it than he did, and saw no reason to leave it lying about.

Tired, bone-weary, I had nowhere else to go and so started heading back to the cave. I didn't know whether Sharee would be waiting there or not, and at that moment I didn't especially care. I just wanted somewhere that I could collapse.

The journey back to the Tucker Forest was considerably less adventurous than when I had been heading toward the Flaming Nether Regions. I could only conclude that whatever beasties and vile creatures had taken an interest in my sojourn while I was in possession of the ring, they now simply did not care since it was no longer on my person. That really does summarize why I am the last individual that you'd want to have along on a quest. No matter what the object was that we might have managed to acquire, as soon as someone threatened my life over it, I would not hesitate to hand it over to them. There were very few riches or treasures—or anything, really—that I would consider worth dying for. Oh, I might try to trick my way out of the proceedings, but if a sword is to my throat or it seems as if I'm going to have to fight overwhelming odds in order to hold on to whatever it is, then to hell with it.

But I couldn't help but wonder, as I trudged along, why it was that I found myself pulled into these sorts of escapades. Not only was I not an audacious soul by nature, but I was in fact the opposite. The fewer quests for me, the better I liked it.

Why, you may ask, was I so reluctant to engage in adventures?

Simple answer: fear of getting killed.

And why not? That's what it all gets down to in the end, isn't it? In my life I had survived mad bird creatures of several varieties, warlords, crazed kings of the frozen north, unicorn stampedes, and a lethal attack by the greatest hero in the land. I had managed to keep my head safely attached to my body mostly through strategy and a little luck . . . all right, a lot of luck. But how long was I reasonably supposed to think that my good fortune would hold up? It could not possibly do so forever . . . and I didn't want to be around when it did finally run out.

This is actually rather beside the point, but I thought I'd make the observation: Have you ever noticed that, after someone has died, those who survived him suddenly become self-proclaimed experts on what the deceased would have liked to see? "Poor John would have liked an oaken coffin." "Ah yes, Timothy, he would have wanted me to have his favorite sword with the perfect balance." "Definitely, poor Brian, he would have liked nothing better than for us all to get drunk, steal his body, quarter it, and deliver it to four syphilitic prostitutes at each corner of the kingdom, because that was just the kind of joke-enjoying jackanapes that Brian always was, and it would have given him a right good giggle."

As for me, I never presume to postulate what the dearly departed would have wanted because I am quite reasonably sure that, in the final analysis, they all would have wanted the same thing . . . namely, to keep on living. What happens to me while I'm alive is of the utmost importance. What happens to me after I'm deceased, I absolutely could not give a damn about. And I very much suspect that every dead person out there would concur. I don't see much leeway. If there's an afterlife, then the departed are either too busy romping through heaven's grove or suffering eternal torment to care about what's going on in the world left behind, and if there is no afterlife, then obviously the entire thing is moot. "So and So would want it that way." The amount of hubris such a comment requires is truly staggering, but still everyone says it and everyone does it. And yet those same individuals would look down their noses at me just because I'm rude enough to want to postpone, for as long as possible, that inevitable time when my survivors will have the opportunity to say, "Let's sever his head and use it for a quick game of Kickabout, because Apropos would have wanted it that way."

Pardon my written wanderings. Although I am writing of the days of my youth, I am rather somewhat older now . . . a staggering circumstance considering I never thought I would last this long, or at all. The mornings are much hotter and the nights much colder these days, and my attentions prone to occasional waywardness. I would be most obliged if you would forgive an old reprobate his shortcomings.

So . . . as I made my way back to the cave over many days, I continued to ponder my odd situation. Truly, it was a curiosity. There were those who would have craved adventure in their lives, but wound up living and dying in relative quiet. I, on the other hand, who would not mind in the least being left alone, invariably found myself in a world of trouble sooner or later. Life, it seems, does love its little ironies . . . or perversions, as the case may be.

When I drew within range of the cave, I tried to get a feeling whether Sharee was still there, or if she had set out on her own. I also noticed, as I drew closer, that the sky in the area was darkening. This struck me as not the best omen in the world, for Sharee was a weatherweaver, and yes, it was possible that the approaching inclement weather was simply a normal happenstance. However it was also possible that she was in a foul mood, and that mood was being reflected in the skies above. I don't wish to sound self-centered or self-absorbed. After all, here I was commenting on the unwarranted hubris of others but a short time ago, and yet I now write of how I was concerned that the weather itself related to me. That would seem utterly ridiculous if there were not a better than even chance of it being true in this instance.

In case I have not mentioned this before, I have this annoying habit of being right considerably more often than I am wrong, particularly when it comes to surmising potential catastrophes rolling in my direction. But by that point I was bone-weary, footsore, and more than willing to risk whatever anger the young enchantress might have had brewing within her than having to face yet another evening on my own.

To this day, I question why I bothered. I must have had some reason that I sought her company. I could have gone off about my business, never seen her again. Perhaps it was that she was simply someone to talk to, and I—like most creatures—sought the company of others. Or it's more likely that by keeping someone around with whom I could converse, I could spend that much less time dwelling upon my own thoughts. The more time I spent with others, the less time I needed to spend with myself.

As it turned out, the decision was taken out of my hands.

I approached the cave, drawing my cloak more tightly around me as the weather kicked up fiercely. "Sharee!" I called her name, trying to shout above the harsh winds that enveloped me.

If there was one thing that was highly attuned within me, it was a sense of imminent danger. As a result, I was already in motion when the lightning bolt struck the tree that was a mere foot to my left. It was a thin tree, and the lightning split the trunk as I scrambled about on the dirt, trying to get away. For an instant I thought that it was purely coincidental, and then I realized the foolishness of that notion. When one associates with a weatherweaver, and when one has even the slightest reason to think that the weaver might be put out for some reason, any bolt of lightning is automatically suspicious . . . particularly one that misses you by as narrow a margin as that one had.

The air itself smelled burnt, and the hair was raised in my nostrils and on the back of my neck. Remembering that lightning tends to strike higher points, I elected to remain flat on my belly as I called out, "Sharee! Are you in there? Did you do that?"

At first there was no movement, and then slowly I saw her shadow approaching the front of the cave. She appeared then, and it seemed as if shadows were stretching from her, consuming the entirety of the entrance. Even though it was midday, the sky surrounding us was black as pitch. The winds were blowing the clouds about fiercely. I fancied I could see images in the clouds, dragons and ogres and monsters of all shape and stripe. Every single one of them seemed irritated with me.

"Sharee—?" I prompted.

"Of course I did that," she said impatiently.

"Do we have a problem?"

"*A problem?!*" She seemed dumbfounded that I could not comprehend what it was that she was so angry about. "You have the temerity to ask me that? Do you think I'm a fool? Do you think me oblivious?"

"I confess to some ignorance on my part," I admitted. "I'm not sure exactly why you would be—"

"*You had your way with me, you pig!*"

"Ah. That," I said slowly.

"Yes, that! What did you *think* I was upset about?" Her hands started to quiver and crackle with barely contained fury. Even though the lines in the air that weavers draw together to create their spells remained largely invisible to me, I could still perceive that she was gathering threads together to mount some new attack.

Suddenly I felt a bit ill-used. "Excuse me!" I called out, and I even stood, pushing myself to standing using my staff. This was potentially a suicidal move, but I believed that if I didn't show strength, I was likely a goner anyway. "*Excuse* me. But it's not as if you gave me a good deal of choice, you know!" She flushed furiously, which didn't stop me from speaking. "I had my way with you? It seemed from my position—namely horizontal—that you were far more intent in having *your* way with *me*. You didn't care in the least about my feelings."

Apparently that was the wrong approach to take, because clouds rushed together abruptly, and I barely had any warning before the air was alive once again with lightning. I whirled, my lame right leg almost collapsing beneath me, only my staff providing support as the air crackled and exploded with heat and light. When it subsided, I blinked furiously against it to recapture my sight. The first thing I noticed as the flash blinding began to fade was that the trailing corner of my cloak was blackened. That's how near a thing it had been.

"Your feelings? *Your feelings?*" she raged. "You don't have any feelings, you heartless monster! That you would go to such lengths . . . that you would seek out some sort of charm or spell to seduce me—"

"Is *that* what you think happened?" I said incredulously. "Believe it or not, Sharee, not everything in the world that occurs is about you. Yes, yes, there was ensorcellment, I won't lie to you about that. But it was not as you describe it."

"Oh?" She did not sound particularly inclined to believe me. "Then describe to me what did happen, then. Tell me the truth of it."

I opened my mouth, and then closed it without a sound emerging.

I didn't want to tell her. Really, can you blame me? The entire affair was possibly the single most humiliating that I had ever experienced. I couldn't even figure out where to start, because there really wasn't much of any starting place that would make me look good, and she'd want to know the details, and gods, the conclusion of the whole business . . . .

"No answer. Lying bastard. Can't even come up with an accept-able mendacity? You're losing your touch, Apropos. The simple fact is that you use people. That's what you do. It is your gift. You use them for whatever purpose it pleases you, and then you discard them while laughing up your sleeve at your superiority."

I said nothing. There was nothing I could say. It was too ridicu-lous, too humiliating. I suppose I should not have cared what Sharee thought of me, but unfortunately, I did. And I realized in that moment that I would rather have her think me a bastard, a manipulator, a cretin . . . anything other than an object of utter, degrading ridicule. A miserable fool who was helpless as he was used by a plethora of women and then engaged in an adventure so farcical that he'd almost had to part company with his manhood in order to conclude it.

There was silence then save for the rumbling of thunder, which was still near enough and sufficiently threatening to keep me all too aware of my vulnerability. Then I heard her say, "Go away. Go away before I kill you where you stand."

Well, with an invitation like that, I didn't have to be told twice. I turned and went off into the woods without another word.

Several weeks later curiosity overtook my better instinct, and I made my way back to the cave. She was gone. There was no sign that the cave was inhabited, or indeed ever had been.

I did not know where she had got to, and I suppose I should have considered myself lucky to be quit of her.

I wasn't. Despite the relief I should have felt, instead I was filled with regret that this state of affairs had arisen to drive us apart in such a manner, and—even though I had been ill-used, even though I was merely a victim of circumstance and falsely accused—well, Sharee and I had been through a bit together. I had risked myself to save her on one occasion, and she in turn had made sacrifices in order to rescue me on another. The truth was that I was saddened our time together ended in such a manner, and wished that somehow there might be some way that I could make things right.

A general rule of thumb that I shall impart to you herewith: When it comes to the affairs of wizards, never wish that you could have prolonged exposure to them rather than counting your lucky stars when they depart your life. For sure as hell the gods will hear you and take perverse pleasure in granting your request . . . as they did with me.

Chapter 2

Fear and Loathing at Bugger Hall

*I*t's always being "written" somewhere. Have you noticed that?

Any number of times in my somewhat tortured and torturous career—the details of which I have been endeavoring to chronicle in an honest fashion, which would certainly serve as contrast to how I lived most of my life—I encountered situations or scenarios that had been "foreseen" by someone. Sometimes they existed woven into tapestries by Farweavers: magi whose special gift was to pictorialize the future. More often, they were written down as vague predictions of things to come. Sometimes they were in free verse, other times they rhymed, but there was a particular and peculiar consistency to them in that they were of absolutely no use ahead of time. Only afterward, once lives had been lost, blood had been spilled, screams of torture had been unleashed to the heavens . . . only then could one look back and say, "Ahhhh . . . all right. That's what it meant."

I have never, ever understood the mindset of prognosticators who felt compelled to engage in such foolishness. If they truly have the foreknowledge to perceive that which is going to happen, why can they not simply tell us in clear, coherent manner just what it is that's going to occur? Why must they hang shadows and riddles upon it? What sort of perverse pleasure do they derive tormenting people who—as of the time of their predictions—likely are not even yet born? "When the rising sun of the eighth house is nigh, then will the high tower collapse upon the running river." Hell, half the time you don't even know for certain if they're even referring to you at all.

The only explanation upon which I have been able to settle is that forecasters and Farweavers walk a fine line between one of the oldest disputes between man and his gods.

On the one hand, we humans tell ourselves that we are blessed with free will. We make our decisions and live or die by them. When faced with forks of destiny, it is we and we alone who decide which road to walk.

On the other hand, whenever anything goes wrong, we cross our arms, rest our hands upon opposite shoulders and—lacking any better explanation to the contrary—shake our heads and sigh, "It's the will of the gods." "The gods wished it so." "The gods move in mysterious ways."

Of course they move in mysterious ways. They have to keep it mysterious, because if they tried to explain it, anyone with the education of a pustule would be able to say, "But that makes no sense at all!" To which the gods would stammer and hem and haw and have to admit that not only are they not remotely omnipotent, but they in fact have less of a clue how the universe really works than any of us do.

One simply cannot have it both ways. We cannot tell ourselves that we are the choosers of our own destiny if we simultaneously ascribe to all-powerful beings the options of diverting those paths anytime they choose. If that is the universe in which we live, then one has to wonder what the point of anything is. It makes no sense to strive for heroic ideals or endeavor to pursue some sort of unique path to glory if the gods can impose their own agenda at any time.

The entire question also sends one into spirals of quandary about such things as predestination. If it is possible to predict some things in detail, then we must further assume that it is possible to predict *all* things. Should that be the case, then absolutely nothing that we do matters, because it's already been decided somehow, somewhere, that we're going to do it or not do it. Don't feel like getting out of bed one morning? It matters not; it is written that you won't. Your mate looked at you cross-eyed and so you felt like killing her? Might as well. The law doesn't matter, because higher laws—the laws of gods—dictate whether you will or not.

In short, if you analyze the relationships of gods to men, you are forced to one of two conclusions:

There are gods, in which case the aspirations of men don't matter. So why bother?

There are no gods, in which case we are alone in the universe, there is neither heaven nor hell, and this miserable endless hardship of a life is all we get with no hope of eternal reward for the pure and eternal damnation for the wicked. So why bother?

As you might surmise, I am simply endless fun at parties and other such gatherings.

Believe it or not, all of the foregoing will actually turn out to be pertinent to matters as they will turn out in this narrative. First, though, it becomes necessary to explain to you how I came to be the owner of Bugger Hall.

With Sharee gone, I once again took up residence in the cave, and for quite some time I lived out my pleasant fantasy of being left alone. I stayed in the forest, foraged for what I needed, and every so often if I desired a change of pace, I would rob someone. I am no highwayman; although I did learn the trade, I have no stomach to accost wayward travelers and attempt to relieve them of their possessions. I hardly strike a frightening figure; even if I wore as terrifying a mask as I could obtain for effect, I'm still clearly lame of leg, and a limping master criminal simply does not have the desired effect upon potential victims. I could have rigged traps, but the Tucker Forest has no reputation for being haunted (unlike the Elderwoods of my youth), so such endeavors might well have prompted my victims to search the woods and perhaps turn me up.

So instead I simply went for the line of least resistance. The forest was quite large, not really passable in one day except if riding the fleetest of horses. So when travelers would camp for the night and fall asleep, I would sneak upon them and help myself to their riches, and occasionally a flagon of wine or whatever drink they had upon them in a skin. By the time they awoke hours later, I was long gone. And since I would always drop pebbles and such into coin purses to replace the weight, the chances were that most of them did not even know they'd been robbed until it was too late and they were long out of the forest. I would then bring the coins back to the cave and bury them, safe from prying eyes.

So between the occasional forays into thievery and the search for game in order to keep my belly full, the time passed in a most uneventful fashion. I could not have been happier . . . save for those times when I was insanely bored.

How typical of the human animal, is it not? To obtain a desired goal, and then to become annoyed with it once it is in your possession. Yes indeed, a pretty enigmatic and contradictory bunch, we humans.

Months went by in this manner, one season rolling into another. The cave was nicely cool during the summer months, but in the winter I nearly froze there, and one evening when the cold simply became too intolerable, I set out through the forest just so the movement would keep me warm.

By this point enough time had passed that I was utterly convinced the soldiers of King Runcible would either never find me, or else weren't actually looking for me in the first place. Thus emboldened, I set out. Once getting to the main road, I headed west this time. I had no idea what lay in that direction, but I knew that going east had the potential for disaster. For all I knew, all the women with whom I'd been involved, the young and the old, the glorious and the wretched castoffs, all of them might well be waiting for me. They would all be sharing Sharee's opinion of me and would probably beat me to death with shovels if given the opportunity.

When I started out it was broad daylight, but a full day of travel brought me toward evening with not much in the way of respite in sight. Finding no lodging, I clambered up into a tree to provide me protection from any predators—the animal kind or, even worse, the human kind—and found a secure place in the upper boughs. It was hardly comfortable, but I'd certainly had worse as I drew my cloak tightly around me and slept fitfully. Upon the rise of the sun, and blessedly no advent of snow, I descended and set out once again. With the cold weather rolling in, though, game was becoming scarce, and my belly was protesting its emptiness to me under the assumption that simply registering a complaint would be sufficient for me to attend to it.

By midday, with hunger pains sharper than ever and the bark of the trees on either side of the road looking better and better, I became aware of activity up ahead. Traffic in the roadway began to pick up with merchants and others discernible ahead of me. In time the blessed smell of cooking meat reached my twitching nostrils, telling me that food and, hopefully, lodging was to be had yonder.

Sure enough, a structure loomed as I turned the corner of the road. It was not terribly huge, perhaps slightly larger than the average tavern. However the owner of the place clearly had aspirations to something greater than a mere tavern, for the sign which hung outside read, "Bugger Hall." I couldn't help but think that "Hall" was a rather pretentious name for someplace as unprepossessing as that which lay ahead of me, but I wasn't about to let the proprietor's self-aggrandizement deter me from getting some rest and sustenance.

I opened the front door and was almost knocked over by the

blast of noise and raucous laughter that erupted from within. The Hall was packed. I had to admit, I was impressed. Whoever was running the place was doing a hell of a business.

It took me a few moments to maneuver my way over to an empty table, my lame leg making its usual contribution to my inelegance. Those who bothered to afford me a glance did so with haughty sneers before hunkering back down over their drinks. Once I was seated, a serving wench approached me and eyed me contemptuously, no doubt considering me a pauper and vagabond. I couldn't entirely blame her. I must have been a sight, bedraggled as I was. But I also knew that I had the wherewithal to pay for whatever I desired, and as soon as I raised up my purse and jingled it slightly, she knew it as well. From then on I was served in a most expeditious manner, and spoke very generously of the tip I planned to leave her for her attention. In point of fact, the tip I was going to leave her was "Don't give patrons contemptuous glances," since I had no intention of sharing my money with her. But she certainly didn't have to know that.

The wench refilled my mug with mead, and I would have liked nothing better than to enjoy the burning sensation of the liquid cascading down my gullet. At that moment, however, there was a roar of combined laughter and frustration near me. I glanced over my shoulder and observed that there were four men engaged in a very serious game of cards. The laugher was a wide man with a flattened face, piglike nose, and a beard that looked like a bird's nest. He pounded loudly on the table as he scooped up assorted glittering coins. The sovs and dukes which comprised the pot winked at me invitingly as the pig-nosed man grinned and gathered them into a sack. "Gentlemen!" he boomed with the air of someone who loved winning more than life itself. "It has been a pleasure, as always!"

Believe it or not, he rose and began bowing. As he swept his arm down as part of the bow, the breeze created by his sizable arm caused a few cards to scatter off the tabletop. A couple of them sailed into my lap, and I looked down at them with curiosity. At king of swords and a viceroy of cups. How jolly. Well, perhaps such a lucky draw might indicate that my luck would be changing in short order.

The theatricality of the winner did nothing to cheer the mood of the losers. They were staring forlornly at the tabletop in front of them which had once held their respective riches. The bearded man, still bowing, was a bit too obsessed with his own smugness. I figured that he had probably cheated. Men who are that insufferably pleased with themselves after a card game are generally in that state of mind because they're not only happy they won, but they're tickled that they managed to pull something over on someone.

For no reason that I can readily explain to you—other than that one who has nothing tends to hold zealously on to anything that he acquires, no matter how nominally useless—I tucked the cards under my tunic as I shook my head slightly in disgust at his behavior and turned away. Apparently my disapproval registered upon him. It's a measure of the pettiness of the man that he gave a damn what some stranger passing through thought of him. "You!" he called.

I looked around, despairing of the possibility that there was another "You!" that he might be addressing. Or perhaps he had simply shouted out "Hew!" because he wanted an employee to go out and chop some wood. Admittedly the former was wishful thinking, and the latter was just too stupid to be contemplated, but you'll be amazed at the desperate lengths the thought process will go so as not to have to deal with the inevitable.

"You!" he said again, this time a step closer to me.

Tapping myself on the chest, I inquired with as much innocence as I could muster, "Are you addressing me, sir?"

"I saw you shaking your head at me, young pup! You did so as if you were expressing disgust!" His face was darkening, although he didn't seem entirely angry. Instead it was as if he was enjoying the art of the bluster. But he was built far too powerfully for me to simply dismiss him as some sort of poseur. If I angered him, there was no question but that he would make things extremely miserable for me.

"I merely shook my head in incredulity, sir, that the gods so blessed you with such winning prowess," I said cautiously.

"And what is that supposed to mean? What are you implying . . . ?"

"Nothing, sir." I tried to sound as humble as possible. I simply did not need to get drawn into trouble with this idiot.

But he was not going to let it go. Perhaps he thought I needed a lesson, or maybe he just wanted to show off to his friends. And then there was the outside chance that he was simply an asshole. Whatever the reason, he pulled back a chair opposite me, the legs dragging loudly across the floor, and he dropped into it so that he was not quite on eye level with me. "Do you know who I am?" he demanded. I shook my head. "I am Bugger! Owner and operator of Bugger Hall!"

"A pleasure to meet you."

"You," and he stabbed a meaty finger at me, "do not sound pleased."

"I am sorry that you haven't found my pleasure sufficiently pleasing," I told him, almost tripping over the bizarre wording that the sentence had required.

"I believe I know why you do not sound pleased! It is because," and his face darkened. It seemed he was going to be able to work himself into a lather without my contributing a damned thing to the process other than just sitting there and staring at him with incredulity. "It is because . . . you think I have cheated!"

The smell of mead was wafting off his breath fairly thickly at that point. For a moment I entertained the notion of trying to hold a small flame within range of his mouth. The alcohol content on his breath would likely ignite it, his head would be burned to a crisp, and I wouldn't have to deal with this fool anymore. But I had no flame handy, not even a candle. "I have no reason to think that, sir," I assured him. That wasn't quite true. Not only did I have my suspicions, but the simple truth is that I suspect everyone of cheating. It's the advisable way to live your life. There are two types of people in this world: People who have betrayed you, and people who have not betrayed you . . . yet. The former require close scrutiny, the latter even more so. So really, you can't go wrong expecting the worst of people. If nothing else, it will greatly lessen the chances of you being smashed in the head with an urn filled with your mother's ashes and having your life savings stolen. And I speak from personal experience in the matter.

His gaze was fastened upon my hip. At first I thought he was trying to appraise my endowments through my breeches, and I wasn't certain whether to be flattered or nervous or both. But then I realized that the true object of his desire was the large purse I had hanging from my belt. Sure enough, he said, "How about a quick hand of Naipes, then? You have a fairly decent amount of money there, I would say."

"Yes," I allowed, "a healthy sum. But I'm not interested in wagering it."

"Oh, come on!" growled Bugger, wavering slightly in his seat. If he'd had two sober bones in his body to rub together, he would have desisted in this foolishness, but such was not the case. "Play me, if you be a man."

I smiled wanly. "And don't think I'm not ever-so-pleased that you're concerned about my manhood, but I don't care to . . ."

"I'll give you two-to-one odds." And before I could speak, he amended it, "Make it four to one . . . no, five to one! Five-to-one odds!" That was actually a rather interesting offer, and for a moment the aspect of my character that called for caution and staying out of potential fiascoes was fully at war with my greed and avarice. But before I could say yea or nay . . . and I have to admit, I was leaning toward yea. . . he promptly said, "All right, ten-to-one odds, damn you, on one go-around of Naipes! You drive a hard bargain! But, har har, no man alive can be saying no to odds such as these, harrrr!"

I wondered precisely at what point he had started talking like a pirate, but it didn't matter. What mattered was that my mental mathematics—dubious in quality as they so often were—were still sufficient to assure me that even the winnings he had amassed were not equal to ten times what I had in my purse. I pointed this deficit out to him, thinking that it would draw an end to the matter.

I saw from the momentary surprise in his drunken eyes that he had indeed been caught off guard. What I did not count on, however, was the snickering and jostling from those sitting nearby, clearly rather pleased that old Bugger had gotten himself into something of a fix. But this gave him only a few moment's pause, and then with a grin that bordered on the demented, he sneered at me and said, "All right, then. One hand . . . and I'll put up this entire place against the contents of your purse!"

"But . . . I don't want the place," I said. The entire conversation had tripped over into the unreal.

But even my lack of interest didn't daunt him. *"What?"* he fairly roared. "No interest in Bugger Hall! Do you have any idea of the proud history of this place?" He stood then, his chair toppling back, and I thought for a moment that he was going to produce a sword out of somewhere and attack me with it. But apparently he just wanted some declaiming room. "This place," he informed me, "has been in my family for four generations! Every generation it would be handed down, from a father Bugger to a little Bugger, being passed along . . ."

"Not unlike the clap," I muttered.

Fortunately he didn't hear me. Instead he thumped the table loudly and shouted, "That is just how confident I am that I will defeat you, you little toad! You . . . you worm! You gutless wonder! You—"

"All right, all right!" I said in exasperation. "As you will, then. Deal the cards. One hand, winner take all!"

There was a ragged cheer from the onlookers, who were probably thrilled just to see an end to this pointless confrontation. But my mind was unclouded, and I was looking around the place and seeing the potential. It was packed. It looked to be an extremely profitable enterprise, and I wouldn't mind in the least coming into possession of it.

Removing my purse, I thumped the small sack into the middle of the table with a most satisfying jingle of coins. The sound of its weight drew appreciative "ooohs" from the crowd. They knew I was not some mere charlatan. But they also knew, or at least suspected, that whatever money I had upon me, I wasn't going to remain in possession of it for long.

Naturally they didn't know me very well.

For one of the few times in my life, I actually played the hand that I was dealt. Mine was good. His was better. He slapped down his combination of tens and kings, two in cups and two in wands, which surpassed what I was holding. Not even bothering to display the faces, I slapped down the cards in disgust.

The thing was, I had kept my money close to me. I suspected—and turned out to be correct—that he would reach over to scoop up his winnings. This he most obligingly did, just as I slipped my hand into my tunic and pulled out what I'd secreted in there. "Hold it!" I snapped at him, catching him completely off guard, his look of triumph giving way to confusion as I snagged his left wrist with my hand. Since I was reaching diagonally across him, it immobilized him for a moment, trapping his arm crosswise across his chest. "What the hell is this up your arm!" I demanded, maintaining my grasp on his left wrist with my left and, and reaching over with my right hand toward his loose sleeve. I moved so quickly, so deftly, that no one saw the cards already tucked into my fingers. Even if they'd been in a position to, their gazes would have instead been upon the exact place that I'd just told them to be, namely on Bugger's arm.

With an ever-so-slight flip of my fingers, it suddenly appeared as if I was extracting two cards from Bugger's sleeve. The king of swords and viceroy of cups were right there in my hand, and I had made the maneuver so quickly that it occurred to no one that the cards were already in my possession.

Well, I amend that. It certainly occurred to Bugger, who let out a yelp of anger and alarm . . . the anger because he realized that he was being had, and the alarm because he intuited just as quickly that he was going to have a hard time making anyone believe it. This was particularly the case when someone has just made a killing at cards, and those he was playing are especially open to hearing accusations of cheating. That would naturally invalidate the game, and restore some measure of pride to those who had taken the beating.

"It's a trick!" Bugger shouted.

"Bloody well right it's a trick!" snapped back one of the men whose money had been cleaned out in the game. "And we know who's been pulling it, and the gods only know for how long you've been perpetrating such shenanigans!"

Now they were converging upon him. "For years now we've put up with your winning all the time!" one of them snapped at him.

"All the time? What 'all the time'? I was the main loser last week!"

"Aha! Proof! You did that deliberately just to throw us off the scent!"

Bugger was unable to come up with any sort of reasonable response to such a preposterous train of logic. I simply sat back and smiled, secure in my knowledge of human nature and human idiocy. Finally he found his voice to point at me with quavering finger and say, "But he . . . he . . . you're not going to listen to him . . . ?!"

"He's not saying anything!" was the response. "He's simply the one who caught you red-handed! You're damning yourself with your own protests!" They were converging upon Bugger from all sides. He backed up, trying to get some distance from them, and instead bumped into one of the larger specimens standing directly behind him. The shortest of the group approached him, looking up at Bugger, his face twisted in fury. "For ages now, we've listened to your bragging and your self-aggrandizing, and the way in which you boast about your achievements! It's always 'Bugger this' and 'Bugger that' and 'Bugger some other damned thing!' And now you're revealed for the cheater and thief that you've always been!"

"No! No, I—!"

They didn't want to hear another word of it. Instead they came at him, grabbing him by the arms and legs, pinning him. Bugger struggled mightily, for he was larger than any one of them. But even he couldn't overcome the lot of them, no matter how much he pulled and pushed and shoved.

"Kill him!" they shouted. "Kill the cheater!" "Kill the thief!" It was, I must say, a pleasant diversion to hear such things being shouted and not be the subject of them. But then another of them cried out, "Burn his damned hall down!" and that did not sit particularly well with me.

Immediately gripping my staff to propel me, I was on my feet. There was now such a din, such a commotion what with one man yelling over another about what to do with the "cheater," that I knew I was going to have problems making myself heard. Nevertheless, I endeavored to do so, pounding the table in front of me with the base of my staff while bellowing, *"Gentlemen! Gentlemen!"* over and over again. Short of dousing them with water, that's the most effective way to gain the attention of a mob. If nothing else, certainly being called "Gentlemen" was such a novel experience for the crowd of reprobates and loafers that it couldn't help but capture their interest. My mind was racing in the customary way it had when I was confronted with a situation and had not the slightest clue what was going to pop out of my mouth in an attempt to deal with it. It's a quite stimulating way to live, really, provided it doesn't kill you along the way.

"Gentlemen," I said once more, this time in the quieter but still commanding voice which I could effect when the situation called for it. "Gentlemen . . . there have got to be more generous and humane ways to deal with this predicament than simply killing him. After all, how will you possibly get your money back if you take him outside and beat him to death . . . as pleasurable an experience as that might be?"

Considering they were an angry mob, they were rather attentive. The only one who seemed ready to tear me apart was Bugger, and I suppose I couldn't blame him, since he and I knew that I had set him up. Understand: I was certain that he had, in fact, been cheating, and so this was simply some belated justice catching up with him. And in the off chance that he'd never cheated at cards, well . . . I'm sure he did something wrong in his life at some point, so on that basis this was deserved.

The largest and loudest of the men looked me up and down. "What are you suggesting?" he inquired.

My right leg may have been lame, but my mental limbs were extraordinarily strong from a lifetime of sprinting ahead of others. So when I was asked, in a rather challenging fashion, what was going through my head, I was ready. Bugger's attention was fixed upon me with an odd combination of curiosity, anger, and fear. He knew perfectly well I had put him in this fix, that no one was believing otherwise, and that—like it or not—his continued health was entirely dependent upon the next words out of my mouth.

"Bugger put his place up as a bet on our game . . . the game which we now know he used to cheat me." I saw him struggle for a moment in mute protest, but then he wisely collected himself. I was the last person in the place that he wanted to offend at that moment. The knowledge no doubt gnawed at him, but there was nothing he could do. I continued, "Let us say, for the sake of argument, that he acknowledges his transgression and turns this hall over to me."

Bugger paled considerably at that. His captors looked confused. "Let us say that he does. How will that possibly be of benefit to us?" asked one of them.

"You come here to drink, for the most part. Do you not?"

Nods of heads.

"All right. Then this is what I propose." I leaned back against a chair, trying to look casual, when the fact was that my leg was tiring just a bit. "As the new owner of Bugger Hall—a name that I would maintain out of respect and deference to its proud heritage—I would institute a new policy in which . . . from the hours of five to six in the afternoon . . . all drinks herein, and hereinafter, would be half the normal price. In that savings, between the normal amount and the half price, all the money that you have lost to this swindler would be reclaimed over time."

There were still glimmers of suspicion, since what I was suggesting didn't provide immediate restitution, or the satisfaction that derives from a solid bloodletting. But there was an undeniable attractiveness to the proposition. As if to make sure there was no room for confusion, the largest one said slowly, "So, from now until doomsday, every day we would be able to get half-price drinks . . . for one hour?"

"Exactly. Happy?"

There is always that moment, that uncertain instant, between the time when you have given your best attempt at fast-talking someone, and when you learn whether your target has snapped up the bait. That interval is simultaneously the most daunting and the most exhilarating time of any swindle.

Then I saw the spreading smiles, and the glinting eyes of men who valued their ability to leaven their dreary lives with mead, and knew that I had fashioned a bargain. Heads nodded, and there was chuckling and looks of approval, and so it was that I acquired the watering hole known as Bugger Hall.

The wenches who worked the place didn't particularly care one way or the other. To them it was simply a job, and the identity of whoever was paying them their pitiful wages was of little or no consequence.

This came as greatly unhappy news to Bugger, who had been laboring under the mistaken impression that his employees owed him some debt of loyalty. It was a rather sad thing to see, really, him standing there in the middle of the place that bore his name, suddenly an outsider. "You . . . you . . . !" was all he managed to stammer out. That was all right with me. I was very much used to people being seized with paroxysms of fury in trying to address me. Usually if they didn't throw a punch in the first ten seconds or so, none would be forthcoming.

"Now listen carefully," I said in a low voice, keeping a smile plastered on my face. "The gentlemen whom you 'cheated' are right over there, patting themselves on the back because of what they believe to be a deal well done. It is very much not to your advantage to say or do anything that is going to get them worked up. Face the fact that I very likely saved your life just now—"

"A life," he snarled, "that would not have been in danger in the first place if not for you!" He came toward me, probably with the intention of breaking my neck. Not wanting to give him the opportunity to take such potentially catastrophic actions, I laid a hand on his shoulder just as he got within reach. Although my frame may not look like much, there is considerable strength in my arms, and that served me well enough as I pushed him forcefully down into the nearest chair. He looked rather surprised at being manhandled so, and I felt it was best to try and keep him in that temporary state of confusion. I dropped into a seat opposite him while the recently "cheated" customers made good on the last fifteen minutes of the hour of happiness that I had created. It was, at the moment, of no consequence to me at all, since I hadn't paid for the mead supply that they were consuming. But if I were going to be running the place, then sooner or later—the former, most likely—I would indeed have to be making my own arrangements with suppliers. That was where I felt Bugger might be of help.

"That's as may be," I allowed, admitting that his danger had been largely due to my own maneuvering. "But it would be best to deal with the reality of the situation. I have this place now. It need not be as disruptive to your life as you believe it, however."

His face darkened. "What are you talking about?"

I shrugged. "You've invested much time and effort into keeping the place running smoothly. I don't see why we can't come to some sort of an arrangement so that you can continue to do so."

He simply stared at me as if I were suddenly speaking in a foreign tongue, which was unfortunate considering that I did not think my meaning had been particularly obscure. "An arrangement. Are you suggesting . . . ?"

"That you stay here in my employ," I confirmed, head bobbing. "It is, after all, your family name. It has been, until now, your life. I merely wish to—"

"You merely wish," said Bugger, voice dripping with contempt, "to take all the benefits of being owner of the place without having to care in the least about the day-to-day operation. Here I've spent years, making a point of being hands-on with every aspect of Bugger Hall, to assure the continued quality. And the first thing you want to do is fob off responsibility to someone else."

"Not just someone else. To the man most qualified to get the job done. Certainly an understanding can be reached that—"

"Oh, I think an understanding is eminently reachable," he replied, but not in a tone that I liked. He leaned forward, and beneath the bushy growth upon his face, his mouth was twisted in a snarl. "Here is the understanding: I am a peaceful man by nature. A moral man. It is because of this peacefulness that—once the initial shock of anger has left me—your puny neck has not been snapped beneath these hands that could uproot a small tree." I took careful stock of the meaty fingers, and had the distinct impression that he was not just making idle boasts. "It is because of my morality," he continued, "that you will be able to sleep peacefully at night, secure in the knowledge that I will not come to you in the still of the darkness, shoving a pillow over your face and smothering the regrettable life out of you. For that matter I could, upon this very eve, torch this place so that you will be the proud owner of a large pile of ashes. The thought of taking such action, however, against the fine service establishment crafted by my ancestors, is anathema to me.

"However, understand this, flame hair: I will find a way to destroy you. It may not be today, or tomorrow, or this year, or even the next. But you have ruined my reputation with these, my most reliable customers. They would always look upon me as a cheater and a liar."

"And you're claiming that you never cheated at cards?" I asked skeptically.

He glowered and said nothing. At that moment I wasn't sure whether he wasn't responding because he knew that I had caught him out, or because he felt the question so contemptible that it wasn't worth his while to respond. Finally, in a voice so flat and without intonation that it was almost chilling, he said, "You have ruined my reputation. A man is only as good as what other men think of them . . . except, I suspect, for you, who is thought of more highly by some than he could possibly aspire to."

"Don't even begin to think you know of, or understand, my aspirations," I warned him.

He let the comment pass and instead leaned forward, peering out from beneath bushy eyebrows. "You took my business, but more . . . you took my pride. A man without pride is almost as dangerous as a man who has no reason to live."

"A man who has no reason to live," I retorted, "is a suicide, and therefore hardly a threat."

Smiling thinly, Bugger said, "If a suicide jumps off a cliff . . . he's certainly a threat to whomever he lands upon. If a suicide thrusts a sword through his chest . . . it would have tragic consequences for anyone who might be leaning against his back. There is no greater threat to the living than a man who has no concern of dying. And may the gods help the enemies of such a man."

I suddenly felt very dry in my throat, and the backs of my eyeballs hurt. Without further word, Bugger rose from his chair, strode toward the door, opened it, and exited his family business. Somehow I knew that he wouldn't give it a backward glance. I was right.

From around me there were cheers and congratulations to me on my new vocation. But I was receiving the approbation of fairly drunken men who were consuming my liquor at bargain prices. So their approval meant very, very little in the grand scheme of things. A man who developed romantic attachments to ten-year-old boys would doubtless have received three huzzahs upon his arrival, so undiscriminating was the crowd by that point.

I had won a small battle. I then prayed to the gods that it would not be as shortlived a victory as my others had been.

The gods answer all prayers.

In my case, the answer is invariably mocking laughter.

Chapter 3

The Vision Thing

*I*t is always a tragic circumstance for a truly inveterate cynic, such as myself, to own up to those moments in life when he is genuinely happy. Such admissions raise false hope in others that if a cynic has the capacity to enjoy some aspect of his existence, then true happiness and the loss of dreary cynicism is but a short step away.

I am not such an individual. I am one who has confidence in his trepidation. Being happy actually appeals to the cynic in me, because all during the time that I am pleased about something, I firmly believe that sooner or later it will be taken from me. A truth of the human condition is that people enjoy being right. That extends even to the conviction that all will turn out wrong. I like constancy in my universe, so to me happiness is a transitory state that exists primarily to make the sting of loss all the more poignant. I really don't think that anyone truly appreciates anything they have until it's gone.

So I tell you with clear conscience and never having had the slightest belief that all would end well, that the two years I spent operating Bugger Hall were a very happy time for me. Had things not ended as they had—and, indeed, as they invariably did for me—I would likely be there to this day. Managing the place was no trick for me at all. Indeed, I discovered I had a knack for it. And why not? I had spent the first fifteen or so years of my life growing up in a busy tavern called Strokers. I had absorbed all the ins and outs of running such an establishment, and although Strokers was a smaller operation than Bugger Hall, the principles were fundamentally the same.

True to my word—a rarity, I'll admit—I kept the hour of happiness. Indeed, it's my understanding that other drinking establishments began to imitate my initiative, by popular demand. I found that very amusing indeed.

Although I kept my ears open and made casual inquiries of guests every so often, I could find no trace or idea of what Bugger was up to since he had departed the walls of his establishment. This concerned me somewhat. The main reason I had offered him the position in the first place was that I was an advocate of the belief in keeping one's friends close and enemies even closer. But Bugger had been impolite enough not to cooperate with my stratagems, and so he was gone from my scrutiny. In that perverse sort of way I had that anticipated encroaching disaster lurking about every corner, I remained certain that Bugger would show up sooner or later. And when he did, whatever happened as consequence would have a most negative impact upon me.

This was not mere pessimism, I assure you. My personal history was rife with individuals who would disappear from my life, only to make return engagements. On some occasions those unexpected reappearances reaped great rewards for me, although invariably they were transient in nature. On other occasions I had encountered familiar faces in most unfamiliar and unfortunately timed arenas, and such meetings had always led straight to disaster.

So I had no doubt in my mind that Bugger and I would cross paths again at some point in the future. Just how soon it would be, and what sort of dire consequences it would entail for me, I could not even begin to guess. In fact, on some nights—particularly during inclement weather—I would sit alone in a corner, having mead brought to me steadily by my wenches, and try to anticipate all the absolutely worst moments that Bugger could make an unexpected return.

In truth, I thought about a lot of things during those two years. It became something of a habit with me, to sit alone and reflect upon my life. It wasn't as if I had been living it all that long. And yet, as I thought about it, it certainly seemed to me that for someone who had been in this world for barely two decades, I had managed to annoy an impressive number of people, many of them in high places.

Particularly when winter would come in, the days shortening as the nights lengthened, I would stare into the fire crackling in the hearth and think about all the people in my life that I had disappointed, or in whom I had misplaced my trust.

My mother, Madeline, a tavern wench and whore who was convinced that I had a great destiny ahead of me, and had her faith in me rewarded with a brutal death at the hands of an equally brutal assailant.

King Runcible of Isteria, who had taken an interest in me and chosen the unusual tactic of elevating a commoner to the position of squire . . . and eventually even to knighthood. His wife, Queen Beatrice, who had never been anything but kind to me . . . and their daughter, the Princess Entipy, whom I had first considered to be a fire-setting lunatic who worshipped the witch goddess Hecate, but later found her to be . . .

Well . . . just a lunatic, I suppose. At least, she had never started any fires in my presence, although for all I knew she had burned the castle down since I'd departed.

So there they were, the royal family of Isteria. They had honored me and loved me, and I had turned on them for reasons that were really very good ones. But they couldn't have known that, and the disappointment and anger was as keen to them as if my motivations were purely selfish and mean-spirited. I could still see Entipy framed in the window of the castle, a single candle burning in the window, betrayed by a man for whom she had let down her guard and had actually loved . . . or at least as close to love as a twisted little loon as that could come.

And then there had been Tacit. Tacit One-Eye, adventurer and hero, whose destiny I had usurped. He was my best friend in all the world, and I was directly responsible for him ending up a hollow remnant of his former self.

There was Astel, my first . . . well, hardly my first love, although she did relieve me of my virginity. She was also the first woman aside from my mother that I ever truly trusted . . . and I paid for that trust rather catastrophically.

On and on the list went, and in the end I could only think of two people in my life whom I had not genuinely disappointed. One was the dreaded Warlord Shank, a ruthless barbarian ruler whose engagement party I had wound up being a waiter at. And the other . . .

Well, the other was King Meander, the vagabond king. A self-made outcast from a frozen realm in the far north, Meander led a troop of loosely allied warriors collectively known as the Journeymen. They recognized no boundaries, went wherever they wished, whenever they wished. In a way, I envied them their freedom and sheer insouciance when it came to such things as nations' borders. I might very well have been inclined to join up with King Meander, for his rogue philosophy was appealing to mine own. There was something that prevented me from doing so, however. For there was a very distinct possibility that it was Meander who had killed my mother.

It was not possible to say for certain. King Meander was, among other things, not right in the head. I had occasion to ask him point blank about the deed, and he claimed not to remember. It was understandable, I suppose. The tale had it that Meander, some years back, had been trapped in a glacial cave during a days-long blizzard. His wife had been his only companion, and when both of them were starving, she took her own life so that he could have sustenance. And Meander had actually engaged in the forbidden and awful indulgence of feasting on his wife's flesh in order to survive.

There are legends that those who consume the bodies of their fellow humans are transformed into cursed monsters. That may have proven to be mere fancy from a physical point of view, but there was no denying the horrific damage done to Meander's mind and sanity. He claimed to have no recollection of one day carried over into the next, living purely in the moment since the past was so painful and the future so empty. So when Meander said he might well have killed my mother in some insane fit of depraved pique, or might not have done so . . . there was no way to determine. That was, to put it mildly, somewhat frustrating for me.

I could have endeavored to kill Meander regardless. Indeed, I was not the least bit squeamish over the notion of possibly depriving someone of their life unjustly. I wanted someone to suffer for my mother's slaying, and if Meander was the one, that would have been fine with me. If he did the deed, he would pay for it with his life. If he in fact was not responsible for her death, then in the afterlife he would certainly seek out the shade of the person who was responsible and even the score in Hell.

The reason I hesitated to directly confront and challenge Meander was quite simple: The man was wide as two trees and carried a gleaming sword that was the size of a small horse. If we had crossed blades, he could have carved me up like a holiday goose without expending any effort. I knew in my heart that my mother would not have rested any easier even if I had slain her slayer; so certainly there would be significantly less solace if I had wound up resting in pieces.

Even so . . .

Even so . . .

It gnawed at me. It bothered me. And further, it bothered me that it bothered me.

The triggering event may indeed have been my parting of the ways with Sharee. I should have been pleased to be quit of her. Keeping company with magic users is always an ill-advised activity. Yet I had hooked up with Sharee . . . had felt drawn to her, even had dreams about her which I was certain she had somehow planted in my sleeping mind (although naturally she denied any knowledge of it).

Probably what I found most attractive about Sharee was that she had no expectations of me. My mother, the king, the queen, the knights, Entipy, all of them anticipated that I would, or could, or should behave in a particular manner and accomplish certain things. My full time occupation for much of my life, I felt, had been confounding expectations others placed upon me, usually out of the sheer perversity of my fundamental nature. But Sharee attached no particular significance to me. Indeed, she seemed to spend most of her time making veiled insults. At the same time that she taunted and berated me, she also obviously enjoyed my company, which led me to conclude that she possessed that same spiritual perversity that I myself had.

So here was a woman who expected nothing of me, wanted nothing of me . . . and I had let her down. She had never built me up into anything whatsoever, and yet I had come crashing down in her eyes nevertheless.

How in hell, you may wonder, do you possibly let down someone who had no expectations of you at all? Well, now you understand my quandary. I spent many nights stewing over that little paradox, I can tell you, and as day rolled into night and back into day, and as year turned into year, I came no closer to solving it.

I had always prided myself on my selfishness, on my self-centeredness. It was an uncertain and constantly shifting world in which I lived, one that I had oftentimes manipulated in a most masterful fashion. I had managed to survive through boundless confidence, finding endless means by which to dodge trouble, watching out for my own best interests at all times, and not giving a damn what anyone thought of me. Yet this poxy bitch Sharee had introduced the seeds of doubt and concern, and such things could well prove fatal to someone like me.

I did not want to aspire to anything other than living a long life, making money, and dying peacefully of old age in my bed. The moment I gave the concerns and expectations of others precedence over my own, I could potentially be walking down the dark and dismal road of heroism. I had trod it before, albeit in sideways fashion, when I had usurped Tacit's role in what was clearly a grand adventure that the fates had designed for him. But to my credit (or, I suppose, lack thereof), there had been nothing heroic in the way I had gone about it, and my reasons had been suitably base and vile. So on that score my conscience was clear. Well . . . better to say that my lack of conscience was clear.

But . . . gods, the rage and hurt that had been in Sharee's face. It was even more profound, of greater depth than that which had been expressed by just about anyone in my life.

I wondered if she had put some sort of "guilt" spell upon me, but even I knew her skills did not lie in that direction. No, this was coming from within me, and I disliked the notion that there was anything within me. It was disconcerting. I had always been proud of my fundamental lack of depth. If I didn't lack depth . . . then who was I?

I really, truly started thinking about the future beyond the simple parameters of *would I live through it?* I found myself staring at the confines of Bugger Hall and thinking dangerous thoughts such as, *Is this all there is? Aren't there great things I might be accomplishing? Could there possibly be someone, somewhere, whose life I could improve? Or destroy? Either way. At least it would be an accomplishment. Something, any something, is better than nothing. And I should know, being Apropos of Nothing.*

But if I overreached myself, if I strove to be more than I was, I could very well wind up with nothing, including my life. More than anything, I wanted to survive . . . if for no other reason than I wanted to give as few people as possible the satisfaction of outliving me.

And so I pushed thoughts of the future out of my mind . . . until the evening when the future intruded upon me in a most calamitous manner.

It happened thus:

I would love to be able to tell you that there were all manner of signs and portents, giving me fair warning that my comfortable-if-pensive life was about to change dramatically. But the truth of the matter is that in most cases, such scene-setting is performed purely in hindsight. One may have, on any given day, vague concerns that something is going to go wrong. But then the day passes in a manner not dissimilar from any other day, and by the next morning the previous day's concerns are long forgotten. However, on the day upon which misfortune does occur, people can always be heard to mutter, "I knew it! I knew something was going amiss today! I knew it the moment the cow didn't give milk or the cock crowed early or I heard the sound of a child crying in the distance."

I, after spending a lifetime of pretending, am endeavoring to craft these recollections as truthfully as possible, and so I disclose to you that I was utterly blindsided. I did not see it coming at all. In retrospect, even if I had, I don't know that there would have been all that much that I could have done about it.

But I will tell you, again truthfully, that the moment the stranger came in, I had a misgiving about him.

We were in the dead of winter, that gloomy time that seems to stretch out unto infinity, when the summer months are long forgotten and the promise of spring a paltry and absurd notion. Customers tend to become more sullen around that time of year, and I found myself in the position of having to break up more fights than I would have liked to. It wasn't that I was concerned whether my customers split their respective skulls open or not. But I didn't need them bleeding all over the place or wrecking my furniture. Some tavern or hall owners hired brutes to calm things down. The problem with hiring brutes was that they usually wanted unlimited drinking privileges. As a result, either they drank themselves into a stupor and became functionally useless, or else they wound up starting as many fights as they stopped.

I opted for a two-pronged approach. First and foremost, I had a good eye for potential troublemakers, and if I spotted difficulty in the making, I would slip sleeping herbs into whatever they were drinking. I don't care how belligerent a man is; if he's unconscious, he can't cause much trouble. Second, for those occasions when things developed too quickly, I kept a crossbow behind the bar. I'd practiced with it over the months and become a fairly mean shot. If you needed an archer to man some parapets and try to hold off an invading army by targeting running soldiers at sixty yards, my skills would prove woefully inadequate. But give me a man standing with his back to me about ten paces away, and I could dispatch him with alacrity.

As I was saying, during this particular time of the year, I tended to scrutinize my customers even more carefully than usual, to intercept difficulties before they began. And when the stranger entered, whatever alarms that were present within my head, developed by long practice, began to sound.

By appearance, the stranger did not seem much to be concerned about. Not a young man, but of indeterminate age, he wore a full beard with gray encroaching upon the chin. He was cloaked and hooded, but was making no endeavor to hide his identity, for he pushed the hood back upon entering, to reveal a shiny pate so reflective that I fancied I would have been able to see my face in it if I gazed upon it long enough. More than that, however, he had a very nervous manner about him. He seemed tentative, uncertain. If I had to summarize him in one sentence, I would say that he came across as someone for whom the very act of living held untold terrors, and he continued doing so only out of some vague sense of obligation (although obligation to whom, I could not begin to guess.)

The hall was crowded that evening, as it was many of them, and yet the stranger glided through the throng without coming into contact with anyone. This was a bit of a relief, since casual brushings were the main cause of unexpected fights breaking out ("You touched me!" "I did no such thing." "Are you calling me a liar!?" And then, of course, festivities would commence). The stranger, however, not only kept to himself, but it was as if he was living within a world crafted solely for his own needs. I decided in very short order that he was either the most pitiable, or the most dangerous man that had ever set foot in my place.

There was an unoccupied table at the farthest end of the main room. It was not particularly popular since it was as far away from the fire as could possibly be, and there was also a stiff draft coming through, originating from a source that I had yet to locate despite extensive endeavors to do so. Yet he was drawn to that spot as if the cold and he were bosom companions. Once seated, he simply sat there, staring off into space. One of the wenches came over and chatted with him for a few moments. I gestured her over as she walked away from him, and when she came over to me, I said, "What did he want?"

"He said 'Ale, and keep it coming,'" she told me. "Thick, broad accent he has. I'd peg him as being from the far western lands."

This last was of no interest at all, but I nodded as if this made all the difference in the world to me. Then I asked, "Are you sure he has money to pay?"

She nodded. "He jangled a purse at me when I asked. I heard sovs clinking within right enough."

I hadn't taken my gaze from him. He was definitely an odd duck. Even my regulars, as in their cups as they were, sensed it. It was as if he drained energy from the room, or at least in his own little corner of it. They glanced at him with a mixture of annoyance and mild belligerence, but no one wanted to initiate problems with him, and so he was left alone. His presence, however, did serve to shut things down early. For the first time that I could recall in quite a while, most of the place had emptied out well before midnight.

Yet there the stranger remained. He seemed to me almost sadness incarnate, as if he was mourning not only for those things which he had lost, but those which he knew he was going to lose and was helpless to avoid it.

His boots were well worn; he had walked a great deal, obviously not having the money for a steed. His cloak, which obscured whatever he was wearing beneath, was rather threadbare. I could see places where holes were developing within. The wench, as had been her instruction, kept bringing him ale after ale. He did not down it or toss it back. Instead he drank very slowly and very steadily, as if pacing himself. I began to wonder if he was waiting for someone to show up . . . or, even more ominously, for something to happen.

Finally Bugger Hall was empty save for myself, the two wenches, and the stranger. "Mr. Poe," one of the wenches said in a low voice, "that one . . . he's beginning to make me nervous."

"Only beginning to?" I asked with dry irony. "I haven't liked the look of him from the moment I saw him." I scratched my chin thoughtfully, and then said, "Call it an evening, girls. I'll attend to this fellow."

"Thank you, Mr. Poe," they both echoed, and I could see their relief. They both obviously wanted to put some distance between themselves and this odd stranger. I couldn't blame them; I wouldn't have minded doing the same thing. But I didn't have that option. It was my place, after all. Furthermore, I was beginning to have a few suspicions. What if this fellow had shown up specifically looking for me? What if he was waiting for everyone to clear out so that he could approach me with some sort of offer?

For that matter, what if he wanted no witnesses so he could endeavor to dispatch me? Heaven knew I had enough enemies who would not hesitate to get rid of me, if they knew where I was and when I would be alone. The namesake of Bugger Hall was certainly one, and there were many others besides. I had tried to keep a low profile. I had let my beard grow out to a full, shaggy length, so much so that my face was practically hidden behind whiskers. When I walked about the tavern, I favored a simpler, unadorned cane instead of the elaborately carved walking staff. I was not necessarily the most inconspicuous of people, but even so I could minimize my exposure.

The wenches departed, bundling themselves against the cold and wishing me a good night. That left the hall empty save for me . . . and my guest. The fire was beginning to burn lower. He didn't seem to notice or care. Nor had he budged from his chair in the corner, even though more hospitable tables in the hall had opened up.

I started to walk toward him then, but stopped and went behind the bar. I pulled out the crossbow, which was already nocked. There were two arrows loaded in, each of the two triggers permitting the bolts to be fired individually. Setting aside my casual cane, I pulled out my more formidable walking staff. One could not be too careful. Still, I did not wish to appear as if I was attacking him, so instead I just walked casually toward him. I swung the crossbow easily in one hand, making no threatening move with it, but also making it quite obvious that I was prepared to do far more with it than just hold it.

He did not so much as afford me a glance. I stopped about two feet away and waited for him to say something. He did not oblige me.

So I sat down across from him at the table, while very casually—but noticeably—placing the crossbow loudly between us. There was nothing the least bit subtle about my message. But his lips simply thinned in amusement. Perhaps he found me funny . . . or ludicrous. I suppose, in some ways, I really couldn't blame him. Finally I said, "I'm getting ready to close up now. Are you departing or—?"

"Do you have rooms for let?" he inquired. His voice was rich and deep, but also possessed of that same pervasive melancholy.

"Yessss," I admitted slowly. "However, they are not free. They will require payment . . . in advance. Ten sovs."

"Ah." He sounded a bit sad to hear that, but it was sadness twinged with amusement. "A fair, if slightly exorbitant sum. However, I am confronted with a bit of a problem."

"That being . . . ?"

He looked at me full for the first time. There was a world of hurt in his eyes . . . as if he had seen things that were simply far too much for him to cope with. "I do not have the money for it, I fear. Not in advance . . . not at all."

Slowly what he was saying began to sink in.

"Are you saying . . . you are totally without funds?" When he nodded, I began to do some quick mental calculations as to just how much he owed me for the ale, and most definitely did not like the figures I was coming up with. "But . . . but my wench . . . she said you had a purse full of . . ."

He reached into the folds of his cloak. My hand strayed toward the trigger of the crossbow just in case he tried something. But he merely pulled out what was presumably the purse he had showed the wench. He tossed it over to me with a casual flip of his wrist. I caught it, felt it, and instantly knew that the wench had been had. "Chain-mail links," I said in annoyance.

He nodded, smiling wanly.

I let out a sigh of exasperation as I gently put the crossbow down on the floor, before I yielded to the temptation to use it— not in self-defense—but in a fit of pique. "So you have no way of paying for the . . . for however much you've had to drink."

"I did not say that," the stranger replied, sounding enigmatic.

Shifting in my chair, I asked, "So . . . you do have money, then?"

"Oh, no, no," and he chuckled as if the very idea was ridiculous. It was odd. For all that he'd been drinking, I couldn't smell any alcohol on his breath. "No, I don't have two sovs to rub together. But," and he glanced left and right as if worried that he was being watched, "I can tell you that there's more than one way to pay for something."

"I only know of the one, and it involves something jingling that isn't small pieces of armor."

He took no note of the sarcasm in my tone. "I can give you . . . information."

I wasn't certain I liked the sound of that. I began to wonder if he wasn't some sort of a herald of trouble. Perhaps one of the many people who wouldn't mind seeing my shoulders lonesome for my head was putting out feelers, trying to locate me, and this fellow knew of one of those attempts. "What sort of information?" I asked. "Who are you, anyway?"

"No names. Names have power."

I groaned, crossed my arms upon the table, and my head sagged down upon them. "You're a weaver of some sort, aren't you," I said, knowing the answer even before I asked.

"Of a sort. How did you—?"

"Because all you magic users are alike. You make a tremendous show of not telling anyone your true names, because 'true names have power.' How many times have I heard that old wheeze?"

"I don't know," he replied, sounding a bit perplexed.

I lifted my head and fixed an annoyed glare upon him. "It was a rhetorical question, you idiot."

"Ah. Sorry for the confusion," he said apologetically.

For a moment I wrestled with the notion of listening to what he had to say, as opposed to writing off the cost of the ale and just throwing the old fool bodily from my place. I certainly had no intention of having him stay to work off his debt. Like attracts like, and the last thing I wanted was to keep a magic user around for an extended period of time so that others of his ilk might show up and wreak havoc. More out of morbid curiosity than anything else, though, I asked, "And what sort of information would you have for me, then?"

"If I tell you, will my account be settled? I do not like to leave accounts unsettled, particularly at this time of my life."

I'd more or less written off the money anyway, so I shrugged and said, "Sure." Then I leaned back, interlacing my fingers and propping one elbow up on the back of the chair. I have to admit, he seemed rather pleased that I was going to listen to him. Gods knew the last time he'd had anyone he could really talk to. I fell much into the same category. In the past two years I had kept social contact to a minimum. Acquired no friends because I didn't want them. Even kept the wenches at a distance, although there had been times when they'd expressed interest in me. Once upon a time I would never have thought I could spend two solid years wrapped in chastity (unless one was actually referring to a girl named "Chastity"), but my experiences with the ring had . . . I don't know . . . temporarily burned me out on the opposite sex. That, and the burn I still felt in the back of my head every time I thought of Sharee's eyes upon me, and the way she'd looked at me with such venom. There might indeed come a time when I changed my mind, but for the time being, I'd been spending all my nights alone and not disliking it at all.

"I," said the stranger with a touch more self-importance than I thought appropriate to someone who was trying to weasel out of a bar tab, "am a Visionary."

"Indeed."

He cocked his head slightly. "Don't you know what that is?"

"Should I?"

"Well," he said, looking as if he was warming to his topic, "you've heard of prophecies, haven't you?"

"Yesssss," I said cautiously.

"How people are always saying, 'It is written that so and so will happen.' Well," and he leaned back and thumped himself on the chest, looking rather pleased with himself. He still didn't smell drunk, but he was acting it. He was also speaking louder than he'd been before. "I am the one who actually writes it."

"You mean you're like a farweaver?"

"No, not a weaver. Weavers operate via threads of the natural world. We Visionaries draw our magic from a different plane. Nor do I require tapestries. Words are my threads, pages my tapestries," and he moved his hands through the air as if he was scribbling. "And here's the amazing thing. I never actually know what I'm going to foresee . . . until I write it down. It just . . . just oozes out of me, like . . . like . . ."

"Pus?"

He actually laughed at that, which was odd considering I'd been trying to insult him. "Some would characterize it in that way, yes."

I shook my head and started to get up. He looked surprised and grabbed me by the forearm with unexpected strength. "You would walk away from me?"

"I would if you let go of my arm."

"But—"

"I'm supposed to be impressed by what you're telling me?" I demanded. "I know of your type, of your prophecies. You make everything so vague and incomprehensible, so caught up in your cleverness to obscure your meaning, that everything you predict is useless until after it happens! Either that or it's worded so broadly that people spend years arguing over precisely what you were talking about in the first place."

"Ah, but here's the difference between me and other Visionaries: I'm not very good at it."

I stared at him in disbelief. "And this is supposed to mollify me how, then? How can you possibly hope to be of service to me if you're now telling me that you are inadequate at the job to which you aspire?"

"Well, because I'm too literal minded, is why. I share your impatience with those who would be unclear or obscure in their meaning. As a result, I would make my predictions and simply upset people. A woman wants to hear, 'Love will change your life.' She doesn't want to hear, 'You're going to fall hopelessly in love with a man who will brutalize you for three years before dumping you for a girl half your age.' A man wants to hear, 'You will distinguish yourself in battle.' He doesn't want to hear, 'Men will marvel at how quickly you flee the foe, and you will be the subject of derision and scorn for the rest of your life as a result.' You see the problem?"

I hated to admit it, but the fellow made a degree of sense to me.

I have, as you know, some interest in the ways of destiny and fate. The notion that people simply could not deal with the truth of what awaited them certainly made as much sense as anything when trying to determine why prognostications were usually so oblique in their phrasings. I scratched my beard a moment in thought, then said slowly, "And you're saying that you can predict precisely what will happen to me.'"

"Oh, absolutely. But," and he raised a warning finger, "I must ask you not to hold me responsible for what you learn. I have to say, I'm very, very tired of people venting their frustration upon me just because their life isn't turning out the way they expect it to."

"Well, fortunately enough, I am so used to things not turning out the way I expect them, that I doubt you could tell me anything that would be of tremendous bother to me. I've spent my life expecting the worst, and occasionally being lulled into a false sense of security until such time as the worst occurs. So I assure you I won't be as faint of heart as some of your earlier clients."

"That's excellent!" he said, sounding genuinely chipper about it. "Just get me some parchment and writing implements, and I will be more than happy to accommodate you and settle accounts between us."

For someone who was fundamentally a bum, he certainly seemed rather obsessed with keeping accounts settled. In short order I had obtained a parchment and quill, and placed them before the Visionary. I watched with curiosity as he closed his eyes, leaning back a bit. His eyelids seemed to flutter a bit. His breathing slowed, and I could see that his hands were shaking ever so slightly. I had to admit, if he was some sort of fraud, he was certainly putting on a good show.

He had picked up the quill, dipped it into ink, and slowly he brought the point down, down, until it barely just tapped the parchment. And then the quill pen began to move quickly, so quickly that it almost seemed as if it had flown right out of his hand. Rather than someone who was writing furiously, he came across more like a horseman who was barely keeping control of his mount.

Faster and faster the quill point flew across the parchment, and each line it left behind was perfectly written. Three lines, four and five, and I frowned and craned my neck, trying to make out what it said. I was very proud of my ability to read, you understand. Many men my age, and quite a few who were older, were illiterate. But my mother, despite the calling to which she had fallen, had been well-educated . . . mostly by her mother, since her father had had very little patience with her from the beginning. And my mother had made a point of teaching me how to read as well, something that seemed an utter waste of time to Stroker, the oaf who owned the tavern in which I'd grown up. "He'll always be a nothing. Why are you making him a literate nothing?" he had demanded. Stroker always knew just what to say.

But now I was staring at the parchment and I couldn't make heads or tails of it. "What language is that?" I demanded finally.

"Runic," said the stranger, without even glancing up at me. He wrote another two lines and then, his hand trembling from the exertion, he slowly and delicately placed the pen down. He raised up the parchment, scanning the runes.

"Don't you know what you wrote?" I asked.

He shook his head. "No . . . no, I don't. Not until I . . ." Then he stopped and blinked like an owl in the daytime, and then blinked again, and then muttered, "My word," which didn't help me in the least, and "Oh, my word," which I liked even less than "My word."

"What sort of game is this?" I demanded. "Because I really don't have time—"

"Is your name Apropos?"

The question caught me off guard. The wenches, as you may have surmised from before, knew me simply as "Mr. Poe." It was the name I'd gone by since I'd arrived there, and I'd never felt inclined to give my full moniker to anyone. I reasoned that the fewer individuals who bandied my name around, the better and safer it would be for me. So when the Visionary inquired of me, I felt a sudden chill upon me. To a degree, this had almost been a simple, foolish game. The notion that this person could truly see what would happen to me . . . that my future and fate were that locked in . . . was contrary to everything I believed about myself. The moment when this little "game" of mine turned serious was similar to jousting with someone wherein you're using a wooden practice sword, and you suddenly discover that the other fellow is armed with a broadsword.

"Yes. Yes, it is," I admitted slowly. I tried to discern which symbols in the writing were the equivalent of Apropos, but quickly gave up. "How did you know?"

"I didn't. Not until I read this." He scanned the symbols, shaking his head. With each shake I felt more and more depressed, and I wasn't sure why. "Oh dear," he said, and then, "Oh, dear, oh, dear, oh—"

"Stop that!" I slammed my palm down on the table, causing him to jump. "You're making me nervous!"

"And you have every right to be," he said, staring fixedly at what he'd written. Either he was a remarkable actor, or he genuinely was seeing it for the first time, having written it while in some sort of trance. "Considering what's going to be happening . . ."

"What? What's going to be happening?"

The wind had been building up in intensity outside, and suddenly it blasted open the door. I jumped, startled, thinking for a moment that someone had burst in to interrupt us, or even threaten us. But there was no one there. The flames in the fireplace leaped upward as a result of the sudden air fanning them. For an instant the wind blew the parchment out of the stranger's hands, but he snatched it from the air and slapped it back down to the table. I, meantime, hobbled over to the door, threw a shoulder against it, and forced it shut. The wind still bucked and whinnied outside like a frustrated phantom horse, but I secured the door and then went back to my seat. My impatience was swelling. The haunted mood of the moment, being exacerbated as it was by the creepiness of the weather, wasn't helping any.

"All right . . . out with it," I said firmly, not wanting any more games.

He looked at me cautiously and said, "You know . . . it's not too late to go for something oblique."

"What?" I was having trouble processing through my brain precisely what he was saying.

Sounding very hopeful, like a recalcitrant child trying to get out of chores, he said, "I could fashion some sort of verse so that it's typically obscure. Speak in broad terms about what will happen—"

"No."

"I could do it in rhymed couplets? A limerick, perhaps. Or a nice—"

"No!"

"—haiku," he finished weakly.

"Bless you," I replied, unfamiliar at that time with the poetry form about which I would later learn during my sojourn across the continent of Chinpan. "Now, if you would be so kind," I continued, each word bitten off, "tell me what those damned runes say."

"Yes, well. . ." He cleared his throat (somewhat unnecessarily, I suspected). He hunched forward, studying the runes. "It says . . ." He paused a moment, looked at me hopefully, and said, "Last chance for vague rhymes so it will be like all the other—"

"Do you see this staff?" I asked him, holding up my walking staff slightly, although that was more for emphasis than out of any real concern that he wasn't seeing it. "I will either bash your head in, or shove it up your buttocks, or both, unless you tell me specifically what's going on."

"All right, all right. A quick question, though . . . do you have provisions?"

"What?" I had no idea what he was talking about.

"Handy. Provisions handy, for going on a trip."

"What . . . sort of pointless jest is this?" I asked him, but my voice reflected my uncertainty. He did not appear to be joking in the slightest. And indeed, my hesitancy seemed to anger him.

"If you wish to be unprepared when your fate befalls you, then by all means continue to sit there and stare at me, slack-jawed and confused like an imbecilic jackanapes," he said tartly. "If, on the other hand, you wish to have some measure of preparedness, then you will hie yourself to your larder and prepare, as expeditiously as possible, whatever you can carry for a lengthy journey during which time game will likely be scarce." When I didn't move, his face clouded so that his eyes seemed to gleam against it. "Well?"

That got me up and out of my chair. It is most amazing how cynicism and skepticism can quickly be set aside when even the intimation of a threat to one's life and limb is being suggested. Without another word I raided the larder, took everything that I could find and comfortably carry. Two skins of water, several legs of mutton, some hardtack, dried meats and vegetables. I wrestled with my priorities, for my lame leg did not lend itself to carrying heavy burdens for too extended a time. On the other hand, I didn't want to be caught short of supplies.

And part of my mind was scolding me. *He's having you off! This is some sort of game, and you are once again the butt of the joke! Have done with this nonsense, write off the ale he consumed as a cost of doing business and knowing for next time, and throw this oaf out into the cold!*

Yet I kept preparing rations. They always say it is better to be safe than sorry, and when it came to my safety, nothing took precedence. Not even the simple joy I would derive from booting the man out of my place.

Finally I had everything I could reasonably carry together and shoved into a carrying sack. It wasn't light, but it was bearable. Hauling it, and myself, back into the main room, I found the Visionary still seated there, looking just as perturbed as he had been earlier. I slid the sack off my shoulder, allowing it to thud to the floor, and then I mustered my annoyance and said, "All right,

Visionary, I've done as you instructed. And so help me, if this is a twisted jest on your part . . ."

"I jest about many things, Apropos," the Visionary said darkly, "but when it comes to my talent, nothing can sway me from the sacredness of my task. Is that," and he indicated the sack on the floor, "supplies?"

I blew air through my lips in annoyance. "No. It's my collection of eighth-century erotica."

"Really?" He seemed intrigued, raising an eyebrow.

"No, of course not!" I fairly exploded. "Yes, it's supplies. Now, let's get on with this!"

"Very well." He took a deep breath, and then looked at the text. "First . . . your old acquaintance, Denyys, will return quite shortly. After that, you—"

"Wait. Stop."

He looked at me quizzically. "According to this," and he tapped the parchment with a finger, "this may not be the best time to tell me to stop."

"All right, but according to this," and I imitatively tapped my finger on my head, "I don't have any recollection of an acquaintance named . . . what was it? Deh-NEE-us?"

"Well, you do."

"Well, I don't!" The fire of my suspicions as to the absurdity and duplicity involved were being greatly stoked. "I think I have some familiarity with my own life, Visionary, which this piece of paper of yours most obviously does not! I do not, and never have, known anyone named Denyys! So either you are a liar and poltroon, or else you're just incompetent!"

"How dare you!" he thundered, and it could have been my imagination, but it seemed as if the wind howled all the louder in accompanying protest. "My phrasing of my predictions aside, there is no Visionary greater than I! None!"

"Then I'm afraid that doesn't speak well of your brethren." To say I was unimpressed at that point would have been to understate it.

For a moment he seemed so flustered that I thought he wasn't going to be able to get another word out, which at that point would have suited me just fine. But then he took in several deep breaths and, though he had been half-risen to his feet, he now set himself back down again and steadied himself. "It is imperative that you listen to what I have to say, because your future may depend upon it."

"My future?" I scoffed. "Well, if I am to believe you, what I would do and not do on behalf of my future is utterly beside the point. It's all written down there, isn't it?"

"Some of it is, yes," he said flatly. "But how you react to, and anticipate, certain occurrences and happenings will very much dictate how you meet your fate. For instance, if I tell you that you will embark upon a long journey, I'm not telling you how many hands you will have attached to your body when you embark, am I. Whether you have two, or one, or none, very much depends upon how prepared you are to face your future. Now shall I continue?"

'Twas a waste of time, of that I was becoming more and more convinced, but I told myself that there was no harm in listening to the fool, even though in doing so I risked making myself as grand a fool as he. "Very well, then"—I sighed— "pray continue."

"Remember, I was the one who offered to give it to you in oblique fashion, just to avoid this sort of—"

"Will you get on with it!"

He looked back to the parchment, seemingly oddly pleased that I had lost my temper. It was as if he considered such impatience to be an indication that I was genuinely paying attention rather than dismissing him out of hand. This time I resolved not to interrupt him until he had finished all the nonsense.

"Your old friend, Denyys, will return," he said, and then fired me a quick glance, obviously to see if I was going to interrupt him yet again. When I simply sat there with a bland expression, he nodded once to himself in apparent satisfaction and continued, "Denyys will be pursued by armed men who desire to kill her. She will seek refuge with you. You will reluctantly provide her with said refuge. Armed men will then attack and destroy your tavern, but you will escape through previously unknown catacombs. . . ."

I broke my promise to myself, although I had not intended to. "*What?* Destroy this place? Catacombs? What catacombs? Aye, there's a wine cellar beneath our feet right enough, but they are no catacombs! And what armed men? What do they want with her? What—"

As if I hadn't spoken, he warned, "You will become a mere shadow of your former self while escaping to the Tragic Waste on the Road to Ruin. . . ." He frowned and took a closer look at the parchment. "I . . . think that's what it says. Although sometimes runic *R*'s can look like *W*'s. . . ."

I had had enough, and more than enough. "All right," I said, standing, propping myself up with my staff. "I said that I would listen, but there's only so much of a limit to my tolerance. You spin a pretty enough tale, Visionary, but let me tell you of some facts. Fact one," and I counted them off on my fingers, "Despite your assurances to the contrary, I do not known anyone named Denyys. Fact two, I am not in the habit of standing up to armed men if I don't have to. Fact three, if someone shows up seeking my aid against armed men, I can personally assure you that I will turn that individual over to the armed men without a second's hesitation. Fact four, there are no catacombs beneath Bugger Hall. And fact five, which should be the most salient to you, is this: I refuse to listen to any more of this drivel. Satisfy yourself that you have availed yourself of my ale with impunity, for I've no stomach to continue this nonsense, nor a desire to hear any more. . . ."

"You are in luck," spake the Visionary. He was looking with what seemed great sadness at the parchment, and I could see that his pointer finger, which he had been sliding along the letters to keep his place, had rested on the final words of the runes. "As it so happens, you are not going to have to hear any more."

With what I fancied to be my customary, hard-edged cynicism, I asked, "Oh, and why would that be? Do I lose my hearing? Does this rune here say 'deaf'?" And I pointed at one runic symbol at the very bottom of the page.

He stared up at me, and the fire from the hearth was reflected in his eyes, as if perdition itself was peering through to me, and he replied, "Ironically, you're close. It doesn't say 'deaf.' It says 'death.'"

And despite the absurdity of the pronouncement, nevertheless I pulled my hand away as if the paper had suddenly lit on fire.

Apparently because the entire thing simply was not sufficiently melodramatic, the front door once again burst open, propelled by the fury of the rising winds. Exceedingly annoyed, I made my way over to the door and placed my hand against it to close it. It was at that moment, my hand resting against the portal, that I heard an unmistakable sound.

There are many noises in this world, but very few highly individualistic ones. One such is a sword being drawn from a scabbard. Another was the one I heard just then: The sound of a bolt being discharged from a crossbow, from somewhere in the darkness most drear.

When it came to self-preservation, my reflexes were simply unparalleled. The second I heard that all too familiar noise, I knew there was no time to try and slam the door shut to intercept it. I had barely a split instant to react, which meant that I gave it no conscious thought whatsoever. Instead I pivoted on my good foot and turned myself sideways, leaning back from the doorway.

I barely saw the crossbow bolt as it streaked past me. It was little more than a slight blurring of air. I did, however, hear it, like a swarm of angry insects, and then I heard an ugly, thumping squish of a noise, like a knife slamming down into a melon. My head snapped around, and I saw the Visionary sitting there, half out of his seat, looking down in shock—but not, curiously, in surprise. The bolt was still quivering in his chest, and then he said, "Oh, my. This may hurt a bit," before he slid back down into his seat. Then he slumped to one side, and I could see that he was still breathing, but the blood was already begining to ooze from his chest and drip onto the word that he'd designated as "death" on the parchment.

I did not know what to attend to first. I turned away from the door, the wind still blasting through, chilled to my very bones for more reason than just the weather. For I knew that passing strange had transpired this night, and was still occurring, and I knew that I was being dragged into it against my will . . . provided I had any will. The wind suddenly took the parchment then, yanking it from beneath the still hand of the Visionary, and tossed it carelessly onto the fire, where the ends began to curl and blacken.

With a cry I reflexively made for it, forgetting about the open door, forgetting about everything except my fate as it was laid out on that piece of paper. I took several steps toward it, then paused, realizing that it would be useless to me. I couldn't read ancient runic. But then I further realized that I might be able to find someone else who could, and on that basis I should have it with me just in case. There might be further information of which I could make use. It was, however, too late. The paper was curling back upon itself, crackling and flaring up, and most of it was already scorched and unreadable even to someone who had the eye for it.

I spun, faced the fallen Visionary, dropped to one knee so as to be able to look him in the eyes. *"Your death!"* I practically shouted in his face. I knew that I was talking to a dying man, but naturally I was far more concerned about my welfare than his. "You foresaw your death, didn't you! Not mine, but yours!"

He didn't reply, unless you would count a throaty gurgle as a reply.

"What else? What else did you see?" I demanded to know. But I wasn't even getting gurgling. "Is it happening? All happening, right now? Where's this Denyys? Can I control my fate still? Am I a helpless pawn? *What is to become of me?!*" I wailed.

The door had been sitting open all that time, and suddenly my heart leaped as a figured cloaked in gray burst in. It spun without looking in my direction, the edges of its great cloak whirling

about, and with a grunt it shoved closed the door against the buf-
feting of the wind. The newcomer on this night of insanity—the
mysterious Denyys, perhaps?—turned to face me while simultaneously pushing back the hood of the cloak.

It was a female, her dark and disheveled hair framing her face.
She took exactly two steps and stopped in her tracks. I knew her.
And why shouldn't I have? She certainly knew me.

"Apropos?!" she cried out, not sounding particularly thrilled to
see me.

"Sharee," I said, my mouth twisted in a parody of a smile.

Chapter 4

Destiny's Bastard Stepchild

Of all the ale joints in all the towns in all the world, I had to wander into yours!" said Sharee with clear ire. The door suddenly rattled on its hinges, and Sharee jumped slightly in response to it, perhaps thinking that someone was trying to break through. As I'm sure you can imagine, the notion that someone might be endeavoring to smash down my door any moment was not a concept destined to give me much peace of mind. Upon realizing that there was nothing at the door save gusts, she appeared to take some small measure of relief . . . but not much.

"I assure you, Sharee, I am no more thrilled to see you than you are to see me," I informed her.

But clearly Sharee was in no mood to listen or trade borderline-witty repartee. Despite the passage of years, she looked precisely as I remembered her. I wondered if this involved some sort of sorcery, or if she just knew how to take care of herself. Her eyes flashing, she stepped forward and said briskly, "I need you to hide me."

Naturally I guffawed rather loudly. There was much I did not know at that point. I did not know whether this was actually "Denyys" I was seeing before me. Or mayhap this was simply an odd coincidence. "You can't be serious," I replied.

She looked over her shoulder fearfully, and that certainly struck me. *Fearfully.* That was not an emotion that came easily to Sharee, or Denyys, or whatever name she truly bore. When I had first encountered her, seemingly a lifetime ago, an angry mob had been about to burn her at a stake. In the face of imminent incineration, she had never once lost her composure. Indeed, she had treated those before her with outright contempt, as if she held their lives in her hands, rather than the other way around. So if there was something after her now that was actually cracking that infernal composure of hers, it must be a very considerable challenge and threat.

Naturally I wanted no part of it.

My response of "Get out of here" was uttered at the exact same moment that she said, "Of course I'm serious." She stood there then with her mouth open, clearly surprised by what I had said. She walked toward me, emotions warring in her face, the inclination to tell me to go to hell battling with the impulse to ask more insistently for my aid. But before she could say anything, her attention was suddenly caught by the slumped-over man at the table nearby. The fellow, you'll remember, who had an arrow in his chest.

Apparently forgetting me completely, she went over to him quickly and tilted his face so that it caught the glow from the fireplace. "I know him," she said. "I know this man. He's a Visionary. What is he doing here?"

"Bleeding, and I've no intention of joining him, thank you very much." I figured I couldn't have made it any clearer than that. "This assault is not your doing?"

"Don't be an ass," she retorted as she touched the base of his neck. Her eyes widened. "He's alive!"

"He won't be for long. Nor will I, quite possibly, if you stay."

Quickly Sharee turned away from him and advanced on me.

Involuntarily I took a step back and held my staff in a defensive posture. I wished at that moment that I was holding the crossbow, but it was out of reach on the floor, underneath a bench that had fallen over when I'd jumped up earlier. She took one scornful look at the staff and said, "What did he say to you? What did he tell you?"

"He said if I help you, this place is going to be destroyed! So you see," I explained in a surprisingly conversational manner, considering the circumstances, "why I'm being less than hospitable. Not that I thought I needed a reason for doing so when it involves someone who tried to blast me out of existence last time I saw her."

"You took *advantage* of me!"

"Oh, as if you didn't of me!"

"I wasn't in my right mind!"

"The stone against my back was as hard and cold as if you had been in your right mind, Sharee, and I've still got the scars to prove it."

She was five paces from me, and I swear she only took one step, but suddenly she was right there in front of me and she grabbed me by the front of my tunic. In a low, angry voice she said, "You have to help me, and you are going to help me."

"I'm going to help you out the front door! Who fired that arrow in here, anyway, if not you?"

"My pursuers. It was pure happenstance. The bolt went astray, but they aren't far behind, I can promise you that."

I wasn't intimidated by her proximity or the threat implicit in her nearness. The fact that I had seen fear in her face had humanized her for me to some degree. That, I suppose, and the fact that I'd seen her naked. That also helped. "Good, I'm glad they aren't far behind," I replied. "That means you'll be out of here that much sooner."

"Apropos . . ." she said, and there was a hoplessness to her tone as she stepped back, releasing the fistfuls of cloth she'd been grabbing. She looked as if she desperately wanted to convince me to help her, but hadn't the faintest idea how to go about it.

My ears were attuned for the slightest sound of pursuit. I didn't hear anything yet. But that in and of itself meant nothing. It could be that they simply valued stealth, and were approaching slowly and cannily since they had no idea just who or what was awaiting them in Bugger Hall. Certainly if I were in their situation, that's what I would be doing. Only fools come barreling in without thoroughly ascertaining just what it is that awaits them.

"I'm going to regret asking this, most likely," I admitted, "but my curiosity is up. Just what in the world did you do, and to whom, to land yourself in this degree of trouble?"

I suppose I should address the fact that neither of us were doing a damned thing to aid the bleeding Visionary. I would chalk that up to the fundamental pragmatism by which both Sharee and I operated. I knew the man was done for. She knew the man was done for. We'd seen the positioning of the bolt, we saw blood pouring out of him as if he were a wine casket with the spigot knocked off. Dwelling on it would have been pointless, and neither of us were of the temperament to stand with the fellow and give him hollow assurances that everything was going to be all right when, in fact, the minutes of life he had remaining to him could likely be counted on the fingers of two hands, if one alone didn't do the job. Matters of a far more pressing nature were seizing our attention.

Apparently the Visionary was sporting enough to comprehend this as well. His breathing slowed and he hummed some vague tune softly to himself, but otherwise he left us to our own problems. Since he'd obviously seen his own death foretold in his writings, at least he could take some small pleasure in the notion of a job well done.

"I . . . may have made some enemies," she said slowly. "One enemy in particular."

"I see. And does this fellow have a name?"

"Lord Beliquose."

The name meant absolutely nothing to me. "Should I know him?"

"He's a warrior chief, the captain of a squad of sellswords. He claims the title was given to him legitimately, but nobody knows for sure."

"I know for sure that I don't care," I informed her. "What did you do to this Beliquose?"

She shifted uncomfortably, once again looking back over her shoulder at the shut door. Any moment I half-expected a large booted foot to kick it open, and a brace of arrows to come hurtling in. "I . . . may have taken something for which he had developed a certain fondness."

I moaned quite loudly. "You stole something from him."

"I may have done."

"*Sharee*—!"

"Apropos, please!" she said with growing urgency. I knew she was hating the entire concept of seeking help from me, and I admit I derived some bleak pleasure from watching her grovel. "You have to help me!"

"I have to do no such thing! If I help you, your Lord Beliquose is going to come marching in here and bring the place down around my ears!"

She looked at the Visionary. "Did *he* tell you that?"

"Yes, if you must know, and I have no particular reason to doubt him. And even less reason to help you!"

Her face flushed, she snarled, "You owe me! You owe me, you pig, for what you did to me!"

"I owe you nothing save a quick boot to the backside! You have powers! If you're so worried, you do something about him!"

The moment I said it, I knew that I had inadvertently stumbled upon the true problem. Her lower lip quivered ever so slightly before she brought it under control, and she said tightly, "No, I don't. I have no powers. Or almost none. I call upon the storm, I get at most a slight brush of rain on my face. I summon lightning, and I receive less than what would be required to make a decent-sized spark. I call for the snow—"

"And nary a flake, yes, I comprehend the situation."

"Do you?" she demanded. Now she was pacing, her body catlike and tense. "I don't think you do. A weaver is what I am, Apropos. It's all that I am. If my abilities desert me for some reason . . ."

"Don't sell yourself short," I said in what was hardly designed to be a comforting tone. "Even if you aren't a weaver, you can fall back on being a colossal pain in the ass. . . ."

My voice trailed off then, for my ears had caught a sound that rose above the howling of the wind. It was a branch snapping in the manner that could only be a foot setting itself upon it. My voice a sharp whisper, I said, "Sharee! Get out of here! Now! I will defy this prediction! I will defy the fates! I spit in the face of my so-called destiny, and there's nothing that you can say or do that—"

She fumbled within the folds of her cloak and withdrew a jewel so large, so fiery, so impressive, that it caused my voice to dry up in my throat.

I got a chill just looking at the thing. At first I thought it was reflecting the flames within the hearth, but upon closer inspection I realized that it was generating its own inner fire of beauty. The thing was big as my fist, and was magnificently clear. I put out a hand before I even knew that I had done so, and without a word Sharee placed it in my open palm. I gazed at it wonderingly, angling it, examining the facets. I was no jeweler, but I certainly had an eye for valuable gems. One does not spend as much time as I have as a thief without developing a knack for being able to separate the quality jewelry from the dross. And this was as far from dross as I was from ever passing through the gates of heaven.

There were no flaws whatsoever. Not only was it the largest gem I had ever seen, but it was perfectly cut. "Where . . . where did you . . . ?" I managed to get out.

She didn't answer directly, which was certainly nothing unusual for weavers. Sometimes they could be counted on to answer every question you might have . . . save for the one you really, truly needed an answer for. "It's beautiful, isn't it."

I considered a smart-ass reply, but couldn't get my lips to produce the words. Instead I admitted, "Yes . . . yes, it is. It's . . . it's like nothing I've ever . . . it's . . ."

Conspiratorially, with yet another glance over her shoulder, she said very quickly, as if sensing that time was running out, "There's a mountain range with more like this. Hundreds more. Every one just as perfect. I'll bring you to it. More of a fortune than a hundred Apropos could spend in a thousand lifetimes."

"Where? What mountain range?" I asked suspiciously.

"If I just tell you, you might try to go without me. But I said I'll take you there. . . ."

The glitter of the diamond danced before my eyes. I had never seen such beauty. I felt as if my brain was going to explode just from trying to comprehend it, as if the thing was not made for mortal man to gaze upon.

My avarice bubbled to the surface, filling my mind, my heart and soul, until there was nothing in my consciousness save for the glitter of the jewel. The world was moving up and down slowly, and then I realized belatedly that I was nodding. I saw the smile on Sharee's face, and suddenly caught myself.

"No!" I said abruptly, shaking off the entrancing power of the gem as if it was the foggy vestiges of sleep. Her expression fell, and before she could react I started shoving her toward the door. "Leave me alone! Get out of here! This is how it starts! This is how it always starts! I let my avarice or thirst for fortune and glory send me on an insane path toward self-destruction. Sooner or later my luck will run out, and I'd just as soon it be later, thank you very much! If there are so many damned gems in the mountains, give this one back to Beliquose and go get some of those! Now go! Get out of here right n—"

She took two quick steps forward, sending me off-balance, and I would have fallen had I not gripped a table and saved myself. She pivoted and all the wheedling and cajoling was gone. Instead, in a voice just as hard as the gem she'd been palming, she said sharply, "If you force me into their hands, I'm just going to tell them you're my compatriot. That you were the one who came up with the entire scheme!"

"They won't believe you."

She nodded her head vigorously. "Oh, yes. Yes, they will. I can be very convincing, Apropos, as you well know, considering my lies once managed to save your life. Well, now they'll cost you your life, so you see that these things have a way of evening out."

For one of the few times in my existence, I was speechless. I had never so wanted to knock a woman's head off her shoulders as I did with Sharee at that moment. Because the horrific fact was that she might well be right. There was every possibility that she might be able to convince her pursuers that I was in league with her. Oh, there was a chance that she wouldn't. That they'd just grab her, thank me for my time, and take her off to do whatever the hell they wanted to do with her. But in weighing the risks that were before me, it was one that I had no desire to take.

The Visionary coughed. Considering he was dying, he was being quite considerate about not distracting us from our own imminent and very likely demises.

Trembling with suppressed rage, I snapped at her, "Over there!" I pointed to the bar. "Behind there, there's a trapdoor that leads to the cellar! Hurry! Hide yourself there, I'll . . . I'll think of something," I growled.

She did not wait for me to invite her. Instead, shoving the gem into the folds of her tunic, she dashed over to the bar and vaulted it, her cloak swirling around her like mist. She dropped behind the bar out of sight, and a moment later I heard the opening and then closing of the trapdoor, telling me that she'd secreted herself away. Quickly I licked the palms of my hand and ran them over my hair to smooth it down. My heart was racing and I did all that I could to calm it before it tore right out of my chest in its urgency. There was, after all, no reason to panic. I was not entirely without resources, and I did, after all, have a few tricks up my sleeve.

I moved quickly to the bar behind which Sharee had just disappeared. With Sharee's pursuers right outside, I didn't have any time to waste.

Now understand, I was not a weaver, nor did I have any interest in such a vocation. But I'd had all manner of individuals come through Bugger Hall at one time or another, and therefore had managed—over a period of time—to be prepared for just about anything. From behind the bar, I extracted a small box and opened it, trying not to rush even though there was a good deal of urgency in my situation. Inside the box was a piece of what appeared to be ordinary white chalk . . . except, if one looked closely, one would have seen runes etched into it. I could not comprehend the runes on the chalk any more than I could on the parchment that the Visionary had read from, but there wasn't time to worry about it. There was also a small, folded piece of paper in the box with a transliteration of what it said on the chalk. I took both of those and went straight to the threshold of the hall, drawing a quick line with the chalk while muttering the words as rapidly, but carefully, as I could. Then I went to the windows and did likewise. Once I had finished, I placed them back in the box, and then sat down on the far side of the main hall and waited. I glanced over at the Visionary. His head was flat on the table, his eyes glazed, drool coming from his mouth.

"Can I get you anything?" I inquired solicitously.

To my surprise, he responded, "Blanket . . . would be nice."

"Oh." I got up, went to a storage room, and returned with a blanket just as there was a loud and insistent thumping at the door. "We're closed!" I called as I tossed the blanket on the Visionary. He sighed peacefully, comfortable in his ebbing life. In a way, I hoped that I would face death with that degree of aplomb . . . rather than the way I would likely face it, which would involve a good deal of sobbing and profanity.

"YOU'LL OPEN FOR ME," came a voice from outside. It was deep and resonant, and obviously belonged to someone who was quite accustomed to being obeyed. I wasn't particularly anxious to meet the owner of that voice.

Quickly I grabbed up the crossbow that had fallen to the floor, glancing once more at the crossbow bolts to make sure they were in place. I steeled myself and, trying to sound relaxed and conversational, without a thing to hide, said, "I think you'll find yourself in error."

The door exploded inward. The wooden lock I had affixed to it snapped off and flew across the room, landing in the fireplace and causing a slight jump of the flames. The door hung open and therein stood one of the largest bruisers I had ever set eyes upon.

He was a barbarian if ever I'd seen one. He was dressed in black leathers, with one of his arms equal in size to both of mine. He filled the entirety of the doorway, and his cloak was billowing and lined with thick black fur, probably from some creature he had slain with his bare hands.

He wore a helmet that was also of sculpted leather. The helmet covered the entirety of his head, except for a narrow T-shaped space which allowed vision. His eyes glowered from within. Two curved horns extended from its forehead, almost making me wonder whether he wasn't some sort of demon creature himself.

I also couldn't help but notice the sword that was hanging at his left hip. Even in its scabbard, I could see that it was a broadsword. The hilt was the size of a small child. I didn't even want to think what the blade itself looked like. The breeze alone generated by a near miss from the thing could likely break one's spine.

I knew his type all too well. The type who was filled with unspeakable capacity for brutal savagery, yet at the same time looked down upon all civilized men because he considered us soft, weak, and unworthy.

Behind him, barely discernible to the human eye, were the shadows of others, poised against the forest, awaiting an order from him. I couldn't quite make out how many of them there were, but I knew I wanted them nowhere near.

"WHERE IS THE WEAVER?" he demanded, making no pretense of being there for any reason other than Sharee. The sheer volume of his demand almost caused my inner ear to collapse.

I arched my eyebrows, looking innocent. "Weaver?"

"BY CRUMM, DO NOT PLAY GAMES WITH US, LITTLE MAN." His fingers tightened into a fist. He didn't look especially happy. I could see the play of his muscles beneath the skin of his bare arms. I was suddenly glad he wasn't bare-chested. There was only so much inferiority I could reasonably be expected to deal with on any given evening. "WE KNOW THAT THE WEAVER IS HERE."

"Could you please . . . stop . . . shouting?" I asked.

He tilted his head slightly and looked at me with open curiosity. "SHOUTING? AM I SHOUTING?"

"Yes!"

"MY APOLOGIES! IS THIS ANY BETTER?"

"No! You don't sound any different!"

He shrugged. "WHERE I COME FROM, THIS IS CONSID-ERED NORMAL CONVERSATIONAL TONE. I'M AFRAID YOU'RE JUST GOING TO HAVE TO LIVE WITH IT, BY CRUMM!"

"Who the hell is Crumm?"

"HE IS THE GOD OF MY PEOPLE! A DARK AND BAR-REN GOD, WHO DOES NOT CARE FOR—"

"Actually, I stopped caring about the answer even before I finished asking the question. So you can just stop telling me." And I leveled the crossbow at him for emphasis.

He barely glanced at it. I don't think he cared if I held it or not. Considering the size of him, I could have discharged both bolts into him and he'd hardly have felt it. "GOOD! FOR I HAVE PLACES TO GO AND THINGS TO DO! SO HAND OVER THE WEAVER!"

"I have a Visionary here," I offered, trying to sound cooperative while the ringing in my ears from his volume subsided ever so slightly. "Will he do? You can have him, at least for a brief time." I indicated the Visionary who, by that point, had the blanket over him. "See? There he is."

"Don't mind me," the Visionary said helpfully, interrupting

himself for a moment with a thick cough. When he regained his breath, he continued, "I'm just dying."

"ALL RIGHT," said the barbarian, obviously not caring in the slightest. He turned his attention back to me. "DID YOU KILL THIS MAN WITH THE CROSSBOW YOU HOLD THERE?"

"No. You did," I said as judgmentally as I could. "Or one of your people did. Sent a bolt flying in here while you were chasing down . . ." I paused just in time and then finished, without the slightest indication that I'd changed what I was about to say, "whoever it was you were chasing down."

It was hard to tell with the way that the helmet cast the shadow upon him, but he seemed to smile ever-so-slightly. "WHAT IS YOUR NAME, LITTLE MAN?"

"They call me Poe, you great shouting oaf."

"POE . . . I AM LORD BELIQUOSE. STEP ASIDE OR I WILL KILL YOU." He did not even bother to draw his sword, allowing instead his hand to rest on the pommel in a very significant manner.

"Well, I am certainly not fool enough to ignore an offer such as that," I said gamely. I lowered the crossbow as if even the slightest thought of resisting was gone, and—stepping to one side—I gestured widely for him to enter, and tried not to smirk as I did so.

Confidently he endeavored to pass through the doorway . . . and slammed to a halt. What I could see of his features were clouded and confused, and he pushed against the empty space again and again, harder and harder, and it was all I could do not to laugh. Finally I gave in, allowing myself a contemptuous chortle as I watched his antics. He drew back a muscled arm and let fly with all his strength, and still the impact ended at the threshold.

"You're wasting your time, Milord," I said mockingly. "I applied a magical ward as a seal." The truth was that I had taken a bit of a risk. I had no idea what it was that had caused Sharee's abilities to malfunction, and for all I knew my petty magical talismans would likewise be ineffectual. Obviously, however, they were not, and for that I was most thankful, if I could just determine who precisely to thank.

"A SEALER WARD," he snarled. Clearly I had upset him. Even more clearly, I couldn't have given a damn.

"Exactly so, yes. Neither you nor any of your cronies will be able to penetrate it. You may have been able to break down the door since that was just outside the ward, but anything which you endeavor to send across the ward to injure me . . . well, you'll have no luck there."

I heard the thump of a crossbow. The bolt struck against the ward, hung there for a moment impotently, and then fell to the ground. I smiled once more, feeling rather pleased with myself. I may not have had a weaver's skills, but I could put a ward in place as well as the next fellow.

I saw the rest of his minions moving forward, watching me, glaring at me. A nasty-looking crew they were, most of them hooded and cloaked, looking like phantoms in the night. "The more, the merrier," I called out in good cheer. "You're all not invited to come in. So feel free to stand there with each other and look stupid . . . which you're all doing a bang-up job with, I should add."

"YOU'RE MAD," Beliquose informed me. "THAT YOU DARE SPEAK SO TO ME . . . TO ALL OF US . . ."

"I'm greatly saddened that you're so bothered by it. What a pity that you can't come in here and say that."

Suddenly from behind Beliquose there was an infuriated roar, and a she-creature spat up from hell charged one of the windows. Her hair was wild and matted, she was stooped over in such a way that she seemed more beast than human, and she had thick furs on her shoulders and arms, except I couldn't quite determine whether she was wearing them or she was genuinely hirsute. From a good four feet away she launched herself across the intervening space, obviously intending to smash in through a shuttered window. At the velocity with which she was traveling, I daresay that the shutters would not have slowed her if left to their own devices. It mattered not. The wards were just as effective upon the windows as upon the threshold. The creature rebounded, falling upon her back but coming up quickly in a roll and crouching, skittering back and forth like an oversize mastiff. She glowered at me from the darkness for a moment, then darted away. I was pleased there was no back entrance into the place.

"Taking the wife out for a stroll?" I inquired.

Lord Beliquose did not seemed particularly amused. "THAT IS MY HOUND. MY BLOODHOUND. HER NAME IS BICCE. SHE IS ONE OF MY MORE BELOVED SERVANTS, FOR SHE HAS NEVER FAILED ME. SHE HAS LED ME TO THIS PLACE, TO THE PLACE WHERE THE WEAVER HIDES. AND IF SHE INDICATES THAT THE WEAVER IS HERE WHILE YOU CLAIM OTHERWISE, I WILL NOT HESITATE IN CHOOSING WHOM TO BELIEVE."

I felt as if I was going to start bleeding out my ears thanks to his voice. "Your loyalty to your creature is almost as touching as her loyalty to you," I said, but the jocular tone of my voice was unrelated to the seriousness of the situation. If this creature was indeed a bloodhound—and I had every reason to believe her to be—then my normal talent for prevarication was going to avail me naught. The tracking ability of hounds was unmatched.

No one quite knew whence hounds had sprung. Some said they were virtually creatures of magic in and of themselves, while others claimed them to be a throwback race tracing their lineage back to the dawn of humanity. Whether they were more human than animal, it was impossible to say. But there were several things about hounds that I knew of a certainty. First, they were utterly loyal to their masters, and obviously that was Beliquose in this case. And second, once a bloodhound was on your trail, it was virtually impossible to shake them. Had I known that Beliquose had such a creature at his disposal, I would have taken Sharee's gem, shoved it into a private, unwizardly place, and sent her on her way without hesitation.

Except I believed Sharee when she said she would have named

me as co-conspirator, and barbarians such as Beliquose were noto-
rious for seizing upon any excuse to commit mayhem and
manslaughter. I was truly faced with the devil I knew (Sharee) versus the even larger devil I knew (Beliquose). And all the while I
was determined to try and thwart whatever so-called destiny was
reaching its ugly, tapering fingers for me.

So I stood there, trying to look nonchalant and in control of the
situation when such was most definitely not the case. Endeavoring
to force bravado, I called out, "The windows are even better protected than the entrances, Milord. It would do you well to heed
my advice and be on your way. It is entirely possible your weaver
may have been through here, which is what drew your bloodhound to this spot. But she has gone on her way. If you hurry, you
might find her yet, but—"

With a deadly edge to his voice, Beliquose said, "I NEVER
SAID THE WEAVER WAS A FEMALE. IF YOU HAVE NO
CLUE WHOM WE SEEK, HOW DID YOU KNOW HER
GENDER?"

Shit, I thought bleakly. I was losing my touch. I had spent two
years in relative safety, not having to worry that the slightest mis-
spoken word might lead to disaster. The easy life had made me
sloppy, and now I was in a spot as a result of it.

"You mentioned it earlier, actually," I said, trying to sound very
off-hand about it.

"NO, I MOST CERTAINLY DID NOT."

"I'm afraid, milord, that you most certainly did."

"ARE YOU CALLING ME A LIAR, YOU PISSANT?"

I shrugged, realizing that it would probably be better if I didn't
reply, but the lack of response was more than enough to set him
off. Beliquose suddenly threw himself with full force against the
ward, and I took a step back even though I knew intellectually that
he wouldn't be able to penetrate it. He struck it again and again,
perhaps out of sheer frustration more than anything else, and then
he yanked out his sword. Gods, the thing was a monster, even
more frightening than I would have thought. The edges were ser-

rated, and the blade was at least two full armlengths long. I suspected that I wouldn't be able to lift it even were I using both hands, but Beliquose gripped it in one hand and swung it with such force that sparks actually generated at the contact point. The ward held firm, but I was certain that the structure itself actually shook.

"WHAT WOULD YOU PROPOSE, LITTLE MAN?" he demanded. "THAT YOU KEEP THESE WARDS IN PLACE INDEFINITELY? WHAT MAKES YOU THINK I AM SIMPLY GOING TO GO AWAY? MY MINIONS AND I, WE CAN STAY HERE FOR AS LONG AS IT TAKES. WILL YOU TURN AWAY TRAVELERS AND CUSTOMERS OF EVERY STRIPE SIMPLY BECAUSE YOU WILL NOT LET US CROSS YOUR THRESHOLD? IN CASE YOU HAVE NOT REALIZED IT YET, YOU ARE UNDER SIEGE. YOUR ONLY HOPE FOR GETTING OUT OF THIS ALIVE IS TURNING SHAREE OVER TO US, NOW!"

And I realized that he was right. Everything had been happening too quickly, and it was now spiraling out of control. I had not had the time and luxury to develop a completely thought-out plan. I was just improvising, trying to last from one moment to the next. There was, I suppose, a certain irony to that, considering the circumstances. Here I'd had a Visionary tell me everything that was going to happen. One would have thought that, given all that, I'd be able to plan ahead. Instead I felt as if I was running like mad to catch up with the destiny that had been set out for me.

Well, to hell with that. This was clearly a hopeless situation, and if turning Sharee over to them was my only way out, then that's what I was going to do. Quickly I ran the Visionary's words through my memory, and realized that he'd said I would agree to help her . . . but that didn't mean I couldn't change my mind. And he'd said that I would escape into catacombs . . . but not "we." And he also predicted destruction of the tavern . . . but what if that happened at a date in the far future? What if it wasn't even this place?

This "hopeless situation" might, in fact, be a win/win scenario. I might be able to defy prophecies and portents by turning Sharee over to Beliquose, in which case I was indeed master of my own destiny. Or at the very least I had found loopholes that would enable me to salvage this horrific predicament. She might well try to implicate me, but I at least had a shot at fast-talking my way out of that. As for the gem . . . ah, well, that was a tragic state of affairs. More of those, hundreds of those, all there for the taking in some place that only she could lead me to.

I pictured myself walking around in such a glorious environment, chipping the gems out of their stony encasement and placing them into a sack filled with others like them. Acquiring in no time at all enough fortune to last me forever. A very pretty picture indeed.

And in taking the time to indulge in such reverie, I screwed myself.

Because at that moment, there was suddenly an ear-shattering smashing from the direction of the hearth. I spun just in time to see Bicce, all teeth and claws and fur, crash down squarely into the midst of the fireplace.

Naturally she promptly ignited.

With a roar like something spat up from perdition—which was, for all I knew, where she was born and bred—Bicce thrust out madly with her feet, shoving all the burning wood out of her way, clearing it so that she could move out. "BICCE, NO!" bellowed Beliquose, but since she was barely sentient even under the best of circumstances, she was hardly going to attend to her master's voice when she was on fire.

I was busy cursing myself out, even as I scrambled for liquid to try and extinguish the nearest log. (It had come to rest against a table leg, and the leg was starting to go up as well, flames licking at the underside of the table.) How, I wondered, could I have been so foolish as to forget to raise a sealer ward in the fireplace? I'd been concentrating purely on the common means of entrance, but it had never occurred to me that someone would be mad enough to scramble onto the roof of the hall and hurl themselves down a chimney into a burning hearth.

But Bicce was hardly a typical human, or a typical anything, really. At that moment she was rolling around furiously on the floor, trying to snuff out the flames that were devouring her fur. Her howls and yips were far more animalistic than anything else . . . although, to be fair, if even the more ordinary and articulate of humans was going up in flames, the chances were that they would probably sound not much different than the suffering Bicce.

My crossbow slung over my shoulder, I grabbed a bucket of water which had been drawn earlier for the purpose of washing down the floor, turned to wield it, and to my horror saw that the fire had spread. Not only was the table already a loss, but the fire had leaped to the curtains and carpet. The wind howling through the front door was stirring things up even more, and Beliquose was watching with frustration. He seemed, however, far more concerned about Bicce than he was about me.

I ran to the table and poured water all over, putting out part of it, but then flames leaped to the crossbeams in the ceiling, and my heart sank. If the ceiling was burning, then it was just a matter of time.

"BICCE! GET OUT OF THERE!" Beliquose shouted.

She would have been able to leave. The wards were designed to keep people out, not in. Bicce could have exited at any time. But she did not choose to do so. Instead she pounded at the flaming sections of her fur, and her head snapped around, her beady eyes focusing on me with pure hatred.

"Thanks for warning me about the bitch!" I snapped at the Visionary, suddenly seized with an urge to blame someone. The Visionary simply stared at me with glazed-over eyes. It was a race as to whether he would die from the bolt in his chest before the flames got to him.

"YOU'VE NO ONE TO BLAME FOR THIS BUT YOUR-SELF, LITTLE MAN!" called Beliquose. "STAY IN THERE

AND DIE IF YOU WANT! WE CAN ALWAYS GET THE JEWEL OUT OF THE ASHES OF YOUR FORMER HALL!"

Well, thank the gods Beliquose knew just what to say to make me feel ever so much better. I started to make for the bar, and then had the barest of warnings before Bicce unleashed an ear-splitting roar and leaped at me. In one motion I unslung the crossbow and fired both bolts. She was moving fast. One missed her, but the other struck her solidly in the shoulder and knocked her back. There wasn't time to reload; I tossed the crossbow aside and brought my staff to a defensive posture. There was a roar and a soft *splutch* sound simultaneously. Bicce, undaunted, had just yanked the bolt out of her shoulder, and didn't seem the least slowed by the wound. Indeed, I think I'd only succeeded in aggravating her.

I pivoted on my good left foot and faced her, bringing my staff up horizontally, and that was the only thing that saved me. Her jaws clamped onto the lower section of the staff and we went down in a tangle of arms and legs and claws . . . well, her claws. Would that I had some.

If she'd had more of a human drive to her mind than animal, it would have occurred to her to simply release the staff from her teeth and drive those deadly jaws forward toward my throat. But she didn't. Instead, like any animal, she refused to let go of something once she had a good grip on it. She swung her head this way and that, endeavoring to tear the staff out of my grasp. It was the only thing that was keeping those vicious teeth at bay, even as the claws—or at the very least, hard and pointed toenails—on her bare and hairy feet tore at my legs.

"THE MOMENT YOU DIE, THE WARDS LOSE THEIR EFFECT!" Beliquose shouted at me, and I knew he was right. Mystic wards are designed to protect the safety of those who dwell within and set them. But if the warder is deceased, then obviously he can no longer be harmed, and the charms forfeit their potency. "THEN I WILL COME IN THERE, TAKE YOUR BODY OUT, AND HAVE IT DRAWN AND QUARTERED, AND THEN I'LL TAKE THE

REMAINING BITS AND FEED IT TO PASSING WILD ANIMALS, BY CRUMM!"

This was enough to prompt me to make a mental note, even as I fought for my life, to speak to the makers of wards and tell them that plenty of harm could still be done to the deceased even after they'd passed (which made little difference to me, but it might matter to others who were more squeamish about such things), and they might want to try and develop a way to extend the lifetime of the spell. As it was, though, considering I had some sort of lupine monstrosity endeavoring to tear my throat out, I had greater concerns just then.

My walking staff was actually cleverly constructed to separate into two halves, transforming one potent staff into two equally nasty batons. I took that option now, yanking the upper section clear of the lower with a quick twist. Bicce saw the movement out of the corner of her eye, and she obviously tried to process the tactic in her brain even as she still, rather aptly, doggedly refused to let go of the lower half. That moment's hesitation on her part was all I needed as I slammed the base of the baton's upper section into the side of her head. The move startled her, and I pressed the slight advantage for all it was worth. Again and again I bashed the upper section of the staff against her, and then curled my left leg under her and shoved her clear of me. She tumbled backward, and now the entire place was filling with smoke.

From within the blackness, I heard thick coughing, and the aged voice of the Visionary called, "You are set now . . . upon your path . . . nothing can . . . alter it . . . you . . . poor devil . . . you know . . . I'm . . . I'm starting to feel . . . a little better . . . a bit . . . stronger. . . ."

At which point, with a snapping of wood and crashing of timbers, a section of the ceiling collapsed in upon him, and the Visionary vanished in fire and debris.

And Bicce let out an infuriated howl and came at me again, throwing aside the lower half of the staff which she'd just been chewing on. She was almost upon me, and then I clenched the triggering device on the upper section of the staff. On the head of the staff was a carving of a lion locked in combat with a dragon, and out of the dragon's open mouth snapped a vicious four-inch blade. It had saved my life on several previous occasions, and it did so now as well, as I swung the staff section in an arc and the blade caught Bicce squarely across the face. She let out a howl, clutching at her left eye and cheek, and I saw blood welling through her fingers. I couldn't have been happier if I'd managed to hack through her throat.

Her scream of pain was matched by that of Beliquose as he watched helplessly from the threshold. There was now fire everywhere, on the furniture, on the walls. I couldn't believe how quickly it had spread, and the smell of burning meat coming from the direction of the broiling Visionary did little to help matters.

Still, there was nothing so dangerous as a wounded animal, and I figured that Bicce would be no exception. For the moment I had the advantage, and I pressed it. Bicce swung blindly at me, distracted by pain and her impaired sight. I sidestepped her swipe, albeit just barely, and swung the staff blade forward and up. The intention had been to lay her open from belly to throat. In that I was unsuccessful, falling short by barely a quarter inch, but the blade still sliced up her front, and she screeched in agony. A heartbeat later her entire torso was soaked in blood.

I lunged forward, grabbing for the fallen lower section of my staff. I got my hands on it, slamming it into the upper half and making the staff whole again. At that moment my weak right leg twisted under me, and I went down to one knee.

Bicce seized the opportunity. Her legs coiled, she leaped straight at me, high and tight, her arms outstretched, and if she'd come into any sort of contact with me, she could have torn me to bits. My move was totally instinctive: I rocked back, thrusting upward with the staff, and the blade caught her in the chest, just below the heart, dammit. She cried out in agony, and for the first time actually sounded more human than animal, but I didn't take the time to consider it. Allowing the momentum to carry her, I swung the staff backward and over my head, toward the door. Bicce tumbled backward and off, and skidded over the threshold.

I used the staff to shove myself to my feet just as Bicce scrabbled around and attempted to leap back through the door. No go. She slammed full tilt into the ward again and fell back, clutching at her stabbed torso and ruined face. I saw then that her left eye was gone, and the entire left side of her face was completely covered in blood. Yes, I was just making friends everywhere.

My eyes were thick with tears from the smoke, and my lungs were starting to burn. I heard Beliquose shouting something else, but couldn't make any of it out, and I doubt it would have been of much use even had I understood every word. Miraculously the pack with provisions that I'd prepared was still leaning against the bar, unharmed. I grabbed the pack, slung it over my shoulder, and limped quickly to behind the bar. I grabbed the one other thing that I thought might be of use: my sword, which I also kept hidden behind the bar to deal with any rowdiness or emergencies. It was a hand-and-a-half sword, usable either as a one- or two-handed weapon. Also called a bastard sword, it had been given me under rather unusual circumstances, and although I detested the individual who'd presented me with it, nevertheless it was a fine weapon and not one I was about to abandon. Easing the pack to the floor, I strapped the sword hurriedly across my back, picked back up the pack, and yanked up the trapdoor. I started coughing violently from the smoke as I eased myself through the hole in the floor and pulled the trap overhead behind me. After all, I certainly didn't want debris falling through after me, and the longer we could convince Beliquose that we were burned corpses instead of escapees, the better off we might be.

I dropped down the short ladder to the cellar, and Sharee was waiting for me. Having managed to set aside the brief look of fear I'd seen on her face, instead she now sported that expression of disapproval which I knew all too well. I wondered whether she was truly disapproving, or instead had simply "put on" this particular face like a handy mask to hide whatever inner turmoil she might be experiencing. She was on the floor of the cellar, her back against the wall, and there were kegs of wine, ale, and mead near her. She saw my disheveled and ashen look and immediately said, "What were you doing up there? Burning the place down?"

"However did you guess?" I said sarcastically.

She looked me up and down with something that almost approached concern. "Are you all right?"

"All right?! This is all your fault! If not for you—!"

"My fault?" She'd been sitting on the floor, but now she scrambled to her feet and put her hands on her hips defiantly. "Excuse me, but you were the one claiming that, if you gave me aid, all manner of disaster would befall you!"

"So?"

"So you gave me aid. Therefore you brought this on yourself. If you set events into motion, I can hardly be faulted for that."

I couldn't quite believe it. What she might have been lacking in magiks and sorcerous ability, she more than made up for in sheer gall. My hands trembled. Not since my enforced time with the psychotic Princess Entipy had I so wanted to drive my fist into the face of a woman. I did not do so, of course, for the most obvious and fundamental of reasons: I was concerned she'd hit me back. Instead I settled for shaking a finger in her face and snapping, "We'll discuss this later."

"Provided we have a later."

It was a good point. The fire was raging out of control overhead, and the temperature was beginning to rise even down in the basement. Even though smoke had a tendency to rise, there was still enough seeping through to provide an immediate threat. Less immediate was the prospect of the entirety of the structure collapsing down upon us.

I studied the wall with a scrutiny that I'd never before employed. It certainly looked solid enough. Sharee, meantime, was beginning to notice that we were in a less-than-advantageous position. She had recaptured the aplomb I'd first encountered her displaying those many years ago. Obviously, despite the fact that Lord Beliquose had inspired some sort of concern within her, she continued to be utterly undaunted by the prospect of being burned alive. I could only conclude that either she was exceptionally brave or else she had her priorities totally out of whack.

"We can't stay here," she said.

"Brilliant observation." I was pulling all the kegs and such away from the walls, shoving them toward the middle of the cramped space.

"Any thoughts as to a way out? And what in the name of Hecate are you looking for?"

"I'm looking for a way out, and don't mention Hecate." I started thumping my fist on the walls, not remotely sure what I was looking for. It was damned near impossible to see in any event. Usually when I was in the cellar, I had the trapdoor opened and my vision aided by light from overhead. But now the trapdoor was shut to buy us whatever extra time we could, and consequently I could see almost nothing.

"What do you have against Hecate?"

"She's a witch goddess and Entipy worshipped her and I don't need such creatures invoked when I've got a burning tavern getting ready to collapse on my head. Damn it all!" I pounded the wall in frustration. "If only I could see—!"

I forced myself to calm, which was not an easy thing since I could feel the temperature climbing. Sweat was beginning to bead on my skin, and breathing was becoming a bit more of a challenge than it had been as the air became more heated.

Suddenly light flared up behind me, and I whirled, almost falling as I did so had I not braced myself with my staff. I had thought that flame had worked its way down to the basement and was about to torch all around us, but then I saw that Sharee was down on one knee, engaging in some sort of process on the floor. She had in front of her half a globe, and she was using a pestle to grind up something within it. Whatever it was, it was giving off a very impressive luminescence. I peered over her shoulder and couldn't quite believe it, for it seemed that whatever it was she was grinding up within . . . it was moving.

"What the hell . . . ?" I muttered.

"Glowworms," she said without looking up. "Pound them into a fine paste, and the slow discharge of their life force radiates light for up to twenty-hour hours."

"You're armed with shining slugs. Charming, and yet repulsive."

"Don't complain." She placed the upper portion of the globe atop the lower, and they interlocked with one another. The globe had dozens of holes in it, allowing light to seep through. "The time you spend bewailing this and that and the other thing could better be spent getting us out of here . . . provided you do indeed have a way."

The light was meager, but at least it was something. I continued to study the walls, running my hand along them, and the air became warmer and warmer. . . .

And then I felt it.

"Here," I said abruptly.

Sharee came in behind me, holding the globe high in an endeavor to see better. "Here what?"

"The wall is much cooler here." I pressed against the area, trying to determine exactly the length and width of the chilled area. "That would seem to indicate that there's something on the other side that would be of benefit."

"Such as . . . ?"

I fired her a look. "Whatever's there, it has to be better than here."

I felt around, probing, trying to keep my fear and desperation from mounting. I reached up toward the ceiling where it formed a juncture with the wall, pushing and pulling at the same time, not knowing what in the world I was endeavoring to find, but hoping I would know it when I found it.

"Apropos . . ." said Sharee warningly.

"I'm still looking."

"*Apropos!*"

I looked up. Flames were penetrating the area overhead. The smoke was becoming thicker, and every breath of air was more forced than the one before. Embers were falling all around us like snowflakes blossoming from hell. I heard cracking of timbers from overhead and a loud groaning as the structure of Bugger Hall bent in upon itself.

At that moment my questing fingers felt a small indentation that seemed man-made rather than a result of natural wear and tear. I pushed in, then through, not certain what I was aiming for, and then I felt a section of the wall move. Sharee gasped in surprise as the wall suddenly slid inward like a large door. It did not do so easily, but desperation lent strength to my not-particularly impressive body, and I pulled with all the might I possessed. Perhaps some sort of hinges took over, because the wall swung inward smoothly then and blackness lay before us. Thick waves of stink and stagnation billowed out from within, and I could see nothing that lay before us save Stygian darkness. But anything was better than dying . . . or, at least, so I was wont to tell myself in those days.

There was an even louder crack from above, and I shouted, "Come on!" as I threw my arms around Sharee, pushing her in ahead of me, and then thrust myself into the darkness right behind her as the structure over our heads collapsed. We stumbled into the darkness, flame and smoke billowing behind us. I turned and yanked on what seemed to be a natural outcropping from the rock, but might have been a manmade handle. In either event, the rock wall swung shut behind us, just as a ton of debris fell into the area we had recently vacated. I sagged against it, panting.

I knew instantly we were in some sort of caves. Catacombs, most likely, just as the old man had said. In the distance I heard dripping water, and there was a dankness in the air that was already working its way into my bones, but at that moment I was just happy to be alive.

The glowworms gave us some small measure of illumination, but not much against the impenetrable darkness that surrounded us. Just enough, it seemed, to prevent us from tripping over things and killing ourselves. Not that there might not be who-knew-what hiding in the darkness, ready to dispatch us itself.

Sharee held the glowworm globe up in front of her so I could see her face, and her eyes glittered in the darkness. "You pushed me in here first," she said.

"Yes."

"Was it because you were trying to make sure I was safe by getting me through before debris fell . . . which indeed it did? Or were you concerned there might be some sort of booby trap that would be triggered by the first person entering, and you sent me in first so I could take whatever might spring out at you?"

Naturally I drew myself up, gave her a stinging look of contempt, and said, "The former, of course. You insult me, Sharee."

"I didn't think it was possible to insult you, Apropos." She drew her cloak around herself, extended one arm from within its folds so that the globe was in front of us, and moved forward into the darkness.

Which was fine with me. After all, just because no booby traps had snapped upon us entering, didn't mean that there might not be more ahead, and better Sharee than me to encounter them first.

Besides, if Sharee was busy leading the way, I hoped she would not notice the magnificent gem that I had pickpocketed off her while I was shoving her into the darkness ahead of me. I had just lost my business; it seemed only fair that some manner of reparations be made, even if she was unaware of it.

Chapter 5

In the Shadow of Ba'da'boom

*I*t was quite an adjustment to go from the pounding noise which had enveloped us moments before to the almost frightening quiet that was our new environment. It was, in fact, more than quiet; it was a bleak stillness that was evocative, I imagined, of the grave. Naturally that was hardly a comparison that did much for my racing heart.

It was a cave, all right, but like nothing that I had ever encountered before. Heaven knew that I had hidden in caves enough times, but they were always small, puny things in comparison to this.

It seemed impossible to me that such environs could possibly occur in nature. Rock walls loomed ahead of us, but they were flat and narrow and seemed to exist primarily to provide different directions in which we could go. Three different points of entry appeared to lay before us. It was just as the Visionary had said: catacombs. A massive underground series of mazes designed to keep travelers lost for days, perhaps forever. It wasn't as if the notion of remaining in the burning tavern and facing the wrath of Beliquose was all that pleasant an option, but it was starting to look better in comparison.

In the darkness it was difficult to determine just how high the ceiling went. I picked up a stone, which was covered with slime, and threw it as hard as I could straight up, listening for an echo from when it hit. I heard nothing. I felt it, though, when the descending rock struck me in the forehead. I staggered slightly and rubbed the newly rising bump on my forehead.

Sharee looked pityingly at me. If she was at all disconcerted by our surroundings, she didn't show it. In fact, she actually seemed more in her element than she was before. Holding the glowworm sphere in front of us, she cautioned, "Stay close to me," and then added sharply, "but not too close."

"What's wrong, Sharee?" I demanded, but I spoke in a hushed tone for no reason that I could determine. "Worried that you won't be able to keep your hands off me?"

"If by that you mean away from your throat, that did occur to me, yes."

"Well, well . . . a far cry from the 'Help me, Apropos' I was getting just a short time ago."

She ignored the jibe, probably because she knew I was right, and she simply hated it when I was right. And since it was so rare that I had the indisputable high ground with her, I decided the smart thing to do was press it. Make her admit that she had been more than willing to set aside her distaste for me when it suited her purposes and preserved her scrawny neck.

But something about the place we were in stopped me from bothering with such comparatively trivial digressions. There seemed to be nothing but mud on the ground wherever I stepped, and I heard water dripping steadily from somewhere in the distance. Sharee was staring at the options for our forward progress, studying each one. For all I knew, we'd be damned the moment we set foot down the wrong one. Hell, there might not even be a correct one.

And as if the darkness and the dripping and the general chill in the air wasn't enough, I sensed something else as well.

Now again, I was not a magic user or weaver. But I had a sensitivity to such things, and that sensitivity was in full bloom at that point. There was something magical in the air, but not in any sort of romantic sense. Instead it was a blackness that went beyond the dearth of light. The place reeked of absence of love, and pity, and mercy, and it was as if something truly evil were hanging just beyond the next turn, ready to pounce upon us the moment we lowered our guard.

"Sharee," I said slowly, "what . . . is this place?"

"I'm not certain," she replied. Her nose was wrinkling as she sniffed the air. "I have my suspicions . . . but I'd rather not say."

"Why, because you're afraid you'll be wrong?"

"No," she said reasonably, "because I'm afraid I'll be right, and merely mentioning the names of the place and beings involved will set into motion—"

But before she could finish, I heard a noise which—even to this day—will sometimes cause me to awaken from my sleep bathed in a cold sweat. It was such a subtle, yet ominous, sound that I wasn't entirely certain at first whether it had been within the caverns . . . or within my head.

Sharee glanced around, as if trying to determine from where the noise was originating. "You heard it, too?" I asked her. "A sort of distant 'boom' sound? Like . . . like something hammering on a giant drum?" She looked at me briefly and gave me the slightest nod. Beyond that, she said nothing. Instead she just gestured toward the catacomb entrance to the right.

But I wasn't about to throw myself headlong into some situation that I couldn't even begin to understand. "Hold it, weaver," I said firmly. "I'm not going anywhere until I know where I'm headed."

"And what would you prefer?" she demanded, her hands on her hips. I was waiting for her to notice that the gem which she had been carrying was no longer in her possession, but apparently she was too distracted by our surroundings to take note of it. "To just stand there until the end of time?"

"Better that than the end of my time. It's not right for me to throw myself into danger until I have some comprehension of what I'm facing."

"You? You're going to speak to me of right and wrong?"

I took a step toward her and nearly slid in a patch of mud, preventing myself from falling only through the quick action of my staff. "Don't get holier-than-thou with me, weaver. You're the one who got me into this fix through your thievery. You know you were in the wrong. And you were terrified of what Beliquose would do to you if he caught you."

"I was not," Sharee said flatly.

I knew it was foolishness of me to press the matter, since the last thing I wanted to do was risk drawing attention to the gem, considering I was aware that she no longer had it on her person. Nonetheless I had thrown wide the door to the topic, and there was no use shutting that door now. "You most certainly were. I saw the fear in your face. Fear as I've never seen before upon you."

"Apropos," she replied, and there was something in her voice that sounded different from the usual arrogance and self-satisfaction to which I had become accustomed. There was a touch of genuine honesty. "Apropos . . . there is something about me you need to understand: I don't care what happens to me. I truly don't. I am not anxious for death, but I do not flinch from it. This makes me very much the opposite of you, since you elevate yourself and your interests above all others. . . ."

"Just because you're apathetic, Sharee, that doesn't make you a Samaritan. If you have a point, get to it."

"All right." She let out a slow, steady breath. "You say you saw fear on my face back in your tavern. Mayhap you did. But it was not fear for my fate should Beliquose get his hands on me. It was fear for the world . . . should he get the gem. You see . . ."

"Forget it," I said.

"What?" She seemed surprised. "But since you asked, I thought I'd—"

"No. I said forget it." I shook my head. "When is the world going to understand that I don't give a damn about various tales of heroics, curses, and derring-do? Beyond its value as something to sell in a marketplace, the specifics of the gem are of no consequence to me. The only thing that really concerns me is where the devil we are, and I maintain, Sharee, that I'm not going to budge from this spot until you tell me."

"Fine. Don't budge," she said with a shrug. "Stay here and rot."

"That's not going to happen," I told her confidently. She raised a bemused eyebrow, obviously mildly interested in the way I spoke with such conviction on that score. "I'm going to be traveling through these catacombs, and journey on the road to ruin. How's that for a cheerful future?"

"Are you now?"

"Yes."

"And you know this . . . how?"

"It was written," I said confidently. Now I still steadfastly wanted to believe that I was in control of my own destiny, that my fate was in my own hands. But Sharee and her kind set great store by such pronouncements, and she would be quite likely to hearken to any prognostications. Mystical and mysterious weavers might be, but if one knew the mindset properly, they could also be easily manipulated without their even being aware that that was what was happening.

Sharee proved no exception to this. "That Visionary? Did he foresee that?"

"Yes. And how interesting that while your powers seem to be deserting you, his were as strong as ever . . . to say nothing of the wards that I erected. . . ."

She waved dismissively. "My source of magiks is totally different from a Visionary's. His come from within, mine from without. And charms need not draw upon nature's threads since their uses are so specific and limited. So . . ." She took a step closer, and the nearness of her provided a small bit of warmth in the dankness. "The Visionary . . . did he make mention of me?"

"Only that you would set it into motion. Beyond that," and I shrugged. "So my fate is set. Yours, however, is fluid. If you want to better your chances of getting out of wherever this 'here' is, you'd be well-advised to keep as close to me, and in my good graces, as possible. So enough fencing and enough keeping of weaverly secrets. Tell me true, Sharee, what this place is, and we will travel it together. Or else I shall leave you to your own devices. And by the way, for someone who claims that she does not care what happens to her, you certainly took exception to what I did to you several years back, so save your posturing for those who know you less intimately than I."

I never saw the blur of her hand in the darkness, but the palm cracked smartly enough across my face. The stinging was sharp, but I didn't give her the satisfaction of putting my hand to my cheek and rubbing it.

Her voice low and angry, she said, "I swear, Apropos, if you ever speak of that again in that vile manner, I will strike you down."

She meant it. I knew she meant it. And somehow it seemed a rather unwise proposition to challenge her sincerity. Nevertheless, I remained where I was and exhibited no inclination to follow her.

Air hissed in a most irritated manner from between her teeth. "All right," she said finally, folding her arms beneath her cloak. "I had my suspicions, but that distant noise . . . that 'boom,' you heard it . . . ?" I nodded. She continued, "There are tales of caverns, underground caverns carved long ago by a particular species of troll called Rockmunchers. It was said that they staked out a specific area of mines and caverns and made it their home. As their name might suggest, they consumed rocks. It was their sustenance. What brought them to the attention of the surface was the fact that, as a result of their dietary habits, they excreted valuable minerals, including silver and gold."

I blinked in astonishment. "They shat gold, is what you're telling me?"

"In essence, yes." Despite the seriousness of the situation, a small smile played on her lips. "The problem is that humans caught wind of it . . . *don't start. Don't make the obvious pun.*"

"I wasn't going to," I lied.

"Because if you keep interrupting with smart remarks, we'll be here for eternity."

I bowed in a mocking manner. "You have my attention and my silence."

She looked at me warily, before continuing. "Wave after wave of humans descended into the realm of the trolls, hoping to get the Rockmunchers and enslave them. The Rockmunchers fought back, as you can well imagine. The result was a bloody slaughter, as the foolish humans destroyed the very creatures whom they would have exploited. But even more than that, they unleashed something terrible. For the Rockmunchers had a touch of magic to them, as all trolls and other creatures of legend do. And when one commits genocide against such a race, it allows for a great darkness to slip through and wreak havoc."

"What are you saying?" I asked slowly. "Are you saying this place, where we presently are . . . ?"

"It is, I believe, the stronghold of the Rockmunchers . . . or their former stronghold, I should say," she told me. She looked around warily. "They called it Ba'da'boom. That sound you heard, that we both heard . . . that was the sound of their war drums."

"You said they were dead," I reminded her.

"Yes."

The words hung there for a moment. "So are you now telling me," I said, trying to keep my voice steady and my dry heaves under control, "that some of them in fact survived? Or that we're hearing the vestiges of their shades, preparing to go to war against opponents?"

"Yes," she said again.

I felt ill. I had no stomach for human foes or genuine trolls if it could be at all avoided. To now find myself confronted with ghost trolls . . . it was madness. Utter madness.

"Forget it," I said firmly. "I'm staying here."

"There's no going back, Apropos," she reminded me. "The tavern collapsed behind us. You'll never dig yourself out, and besides, the door swung inward. With all the debris behind us, you'll never get it open."

Experimentally I pushed against it. She was right. It wasn't budging, and I realized that I could stay there for the rest of my life and keep on pushing without success. Even if I had proper tools to do the job, it would likely prove impossible.

"But we have to do something," I said, sounding far more whiny than I would have liked.

"I agree," she said readily. "And the 'something' we have to do is head forward."

"And if we encounter whatever remains of these Rockmunchers?"

"Then we deal with them, Apropos. We've no choice."

I most definitely did not like the prospect of having no choice. I felt as if the walls were closing in from all sides. My breath was coming in ragged gasps, and I could practically feel my heart smashing against my chest in an endeavor to get out. I licked my dry lips, looked this way and that in some vain hope that another exit would suddenly present itself, and clutched on to my staff so tightly that I nearly splintered it.

"Dammit, Apropos, be a man, for gods' sake," she snapped.

Sorry I'm not half the man as you, I wanted to say back to her, but somehow that didn't particularly seem much in the way of comebacks. So I settled for scowling fiercely at her, which I'm sure thoroughly intimidated her, and then I nodded and said, "All right. Let's be off with us."

Without hesitation she headed for the right-hand entrance into these catacombs, which had been carved out of solid, cavernous rock untold centuries ago by creatures who were either long dead or waiting in ambush for us, or both. I half suspected that she, in fact, hadn't the slightest clue which way, if any, was the best way to proceed. She just wanted to appear certain of things so that I would follow her. Not a bad plan, actually, considering my fractured and fearful state of mind just then.

For quite a while, nothing happened.

Oh, we still heard every so often the distant *boom, boom*. It did not occur steadily, but instead at odd times, and it made me start to wonder about the agency behind it. It might have been something living. On the other hand, it might indeed have been some sort of natural phenomenon. I couldn't imagine what . . . but something. It would sustain for brief periods, or sometimes even several minutes, before stopping once more.

We completely lost track of time as to how long we wandered in Ba'da'boom. Along the way, though, I found a particular type of mineral which seemed rather effective for leaving markings on the rock walls. The catacombs were as maze-like as we might have anticipated, but at every cross-juncture, I would place an arrow indicating which way we had gone. On a number of occasions this prevented us from going in circles, for if we reencountered one of my little arrows, we knew that we had already passed that way and would set off in another direction. In this manner we gradually made our way through the catacombs.

When we tired, we slept, albeit in shifts. When we hungered, we ate. There was, however, very little talking. I knew that Sharee still carried resentment toward me with the business of the ring. For my part, I couldn't really think of all that much that I wished to discuss with her. So we passed our time together in silence. Eventually we'd been wandering through Ba'da'boom for so long that I was having trouble remembering a time when the sun had shone upon my face. The one consolation I was able to take in all this was that there was no way the annoyingly loud Lord Beliquose could possibly be following us. Not even a bloodhound could track us now, I reasoned.

In time, I tired of the silent companionship. It happened during an occasion when we were sitting at a juncture point between two corridors. We were eating some of the rations that I had brought along. Water, fortunately enough, had not been a problem. We had gone through the water in the skins that I had brought, but we'd managed to find enough small rivers and natural water sources around us that we'd filled them as we went. I was beginning to feel somewhat bedraggled. I longed for a warm bath, and to cease feeling dirty and grimy. As I chewed on a tasteless piece of hardtack, a rat came scuttling up, its nasty eyes glittering in the darkness. When the repulsive little things had first encountered us in the caverns, I'd been nauseated and appalled by them. But there were so many other unnerving things I'd had to deal with that, by that point, rats had become almost incidental. The moment the thing was stationary, I swung my staff hard and crushed the creature's spine with the carved wooden head. The rat flopped about helplessly, screeching its death screams, and I hit it again in order to terminate the ungodly noise.

Sharee looked at the bloodied pulp of the creature with a face twisted in disgust.

"Don't turn your nose up at it, weaver," I said with more cheerfulness than even I felt. "If we're down here long enough and we run out of provisions, you're looking at a typical luncheon."

"Do you enjoy making people sick, Apropos?" she asked.

"I don't know. I've never given it much thought."

The glowworm globe was starting to burn low. She'd replenished it every so often, and I had no idea how many of the things she had squiggling about on her person. Nor did I know what they were eating to survive. Each other, possibly. I just hoped her supply of them didn't become depleted. The caverns were oppressive enough. Having to face them in utter blackness was more than even I could stomach. She shook a new supply of the worms into the now-open globe and proceeded to mash them down. As the light began to generate once more, she muttered something that I didn't quite catch. "What was that?"

"I was just wondering," she said, "what you *have* given much thought to."

"And what is that supposed to mean?"

"It means," and she sounded more sad than anything when she

said it, "have you ever given thought to doing something for people other than hurting them?"

I looked at her contemptuously. "Sharee . . . I've never gone looking for trouble, and I've never hurt anyone who didn't hurt me first. And on those occasions when I have endeavored to help people, it ended in nothing but disaster. So don't presume to know me, don't presume to judge me, and certainly don't presume to lecture me, because you know nothing about me."

"And what do you know about you?"

"All I need to."

"Apropos, no one in the world knows all they need to know about themselves. The first step to truly knowing yourself is to realize that you know nothing."

I snorted at that.

She leaned forward, and she seemed genuinely interested. "Tell me, Apropos . . . are you a good guy, or a bad guy?"

"I can't believe we're having this conversation."

"I'm the one who's having it, Apropos . . . and considering the pure revulsion I feel when I look at you because of what you did to me, you're fortunate I'm having it with you at all."

"To hell with you!" I snapped, standing up abruptly and promptly cracking my head nastily on a low overhanging rock. Unlike earlier when I had refused to rub my slapped cheek, this time I clutched my head with both hands and muttered a string of profanities. Sharee actually laughed, which annoyed the hell out of me, but also made me realize (in my distant, pained way) that I had never actually heard her laugh before. It was a not unpleasant sound. "I'm pleased you're amused," I said sourly.

"Apropos, listen . . ."

"No, *you* listen. You feel I victimized you. I feel I was the one who was victimized. But apparently I need to point out that I provided succor to you and got my hall burned down as a consequence. So however unjustly you feel you were treated, at the very least one would have to say we were even."

"You gave me succor because I forced you into it."

I grumbled something even I couldn't comprehend and sat back down, still rubbing my head in irritation.

Sharee took a quick drought of the water, using it sparingly since we had no idea how long we would be making our way underground, or how long the water supplies we found along the way would hold out. Then she reminded me, "You didn't answer my question."

"It's a ridiculous question."

"Whether you consider yourself good or evil is a ridiculous question?" she asked, looking at me askance.

"The most evil of men finds the best of reasons for what they do," I said, "while the most pious of men consume themselves with cleansing themselves of what they believe is evil. It's a nonsensical notion, a question best left to philosophers and clerics."

"And you are neither of those."

"No."

"Then what are you?"

I stared at the squashed rat. It was actually starting to look appetizing . . . certainly more appetizing than this conversation. "What am I?"

"Yes. What are you?"

"I was a tavern owner until you came along and wrecked it."

"Yes, and before that a knight, and before that a squire, and a thief before that," she rattled off. "But what . . . are . . . you?"

"I am whatever my next profession is, just as you are a weaver. What sort of . . ."

But she shook her head firmly. "No. I am a weaver because that is who I *am*. It is in my heart and soul. Were I a whore, I would still be a weaver. There are wenches slinging mead who will tell you that they are actors, and kings who would really consider themselves freelance sellswords who just happened to be wearing a crown. You have to decide what you are, Apropos, and once you know that, you truly can determine whether you're good or evil. Although I can tell you this"— she snorted disdainfully—"a tavern keeper you most certainly are not. That is not fit for you. Whatever you are, it is far greater than that."

"Again, this is nonsense. I still do not . . ." Then I stopped talking, and frowned, and turned the conversation over and around in my mind, and suddenly things seemed a good deal clearer to me.

"Apropos . . . ?" she prompted.

And suddenly I was upon her, grabbing her by the front of her tunic. She let out a gasp of surprise, which was exactly what I wanted, and I shoved her back against the rock wall. Not hard. I wasn't trying to hurt her. Frankly, if it came down to a serious battle of fists, she could probably have disposed of me rather ably. But I had caught her off guard, and that was all that I was trying to attain.

"You know something," I said.

"Are you mad? Get off—!"

"You've foreseen something somehow. Something that I'm supposed to be doing, something that could affect a sizable number of people. Something that will give me power. But you're not certain how I'm going to use it, and you're trying to figure it out now before we reach that point."

Her face was flushed, surprised, and she tried to look away from me. I shook her gaze back to my eyes. "That's it, isn't it."

"It's none of your concern," she said, and shoved my arms off her. I stepped back and her glare was like a shimmering beacon of hostility.

"Not my concern? This is *my life* you're holding up for examination."

"I thought you believed in defying whatever destiny has in store."

"Yes, I do believe that," I affirmed, "but you don't. And on that basis, I'm curious to know what it is that my answer would entail. Let us say that something significant were going to happen to me. Something was going to give me power over—for instance—life and death. Let's say that I was going to be 'evil,' or at least what you would judge evil to be. What of it? What is it to you?"

"Why, then," she said, "I would have to stop you."

"*Stop* me?" I scratched at my bearded chin. "Stop me how?"

"With the power of this," she said, and reaching into her cloak . . .

. . . she pulled out the gem. It glittered at me mockingly.

I blinked in surprise. Sharee, for her part, looked insufferably smug. "What, did you think I was unaware that you had removed it from me? Did you truly think me that stupid? If you wanted to carry it around instead of me, that was of no consequence to me. But do not think I couldn't take it back from you whenever I wished. I may not be a thief on your lofty level, Apropos, but I can hold my own. And this gem is my own. And now I'm holding it." She smirked and couldn't resist adding, "So there."

It was at that moment that I heard that steady *boom, boom* sound once more, enabling the underground realm called Ba'da'boom to live up to its name. I had become so accustomed to its on-again/off-again nature that I couldn't even say at that point how long this most recent pounding had gone on. All I knew, though, was that it was steadily getting on my nerves. As I slung my pack with our provisions over my shoulder, I bellowed in frustration, *"Will you cease that infernal booming?"*

Much to my surprise, it stopped.

Sharee and I exchanged looks of surprise.

Then it started once more, and it sounded louder. Even more alarming . . . for the first time it sounded nearer. Not only that, but—although it could have very well been my imagination—the shadows cast in the dim light of the glowworm globe seemed longer, more ominous. They seemed to be . . . reaching out to us somehow, and I could swear that they were moving in ways that did not remotely reflect what we ourselves were doing.

"Oh, bloody hell," Sharee whispered. "I . . . think we'd better evacuate."

At that moment I was so paralyzed with fear that the only thing that was going to be evacuated anytime soon was my bladder, and possibly my bowels. I knew that I needed something that would cause me instinctively to bolt, and with the thought came the deed. I suddenly lunged forward, snatched the glittering diamond from her still-outstretched hand, and ran.

"Hey!" yelled Sharee in aggravation, and then she was after me. This was, at least, something I could understand. Fear of assault by restless specters was so beyond my ken that it caused me to freeze on the spot. But fear of being apprehended by someone from whom I had stolen something, *that* was a state of affairs to which I was quite accustomed. Familiarity bred speed, and I moved as quickly as I could. The pack was bouncing up and down on my back against my sheathed sword, and I was balancing myself quite skillfully with my staff as I made my way handily. Sharee was right behind me, still calling out my name, sounding most frustrated about the entire state of affairs. She did not, however, think to stop and try and draw me back to her, which was fortunate, since she was holding the only light source.

I moved as quickly as I could, cutting left, right, left again with no particular pattern, or even rhyme or reason to my tactics. I tried to keep an eye out for wall markings I might have used to guide us, but it was entirely possible that I missed some since I was moving so quickly. Right, then left, then another left, then right. It was impossible for me to be certain, but I tried to find the routes that seemed to be the easier to navigate. Then again, for all I knew I was heading us straight into the open arms of whatever was coming at us from behind.

Suddenly the light dimmed out. "Sharee!" I called out, whirling to face her, wondering if she had somehow dropped the globe or some such, and was on the floor scrambling about, trying to retrieve it.

There was no sign of her.

I spat out a curse and shouted her name again, but oddly enough, profanities did very little to bring her to hand. To be specific, they didn't accomplish a damned thing, for curse as I might, she did not magically appear in response.

"Apropos!" I heard her call, and for a heartbeat I thought that somehow she had been rendered invisible. But then my budding hysteria quelled that perception as I realized she was calling me from somewhere, but it was distant. Or perhaps it was nearby. It was really impossible for me to tell, because the way her voice was echoing, she could be just about anywhere. Obviously I had done too good a job running from her, for I had managed to lose her. Now we both had a problem, but it was too late to rectify it. Fortunately enough, it was never too late to panic.

It's moments such as this that I would love to dazzle you with some previously unsuspected supply of bravery that I might have produced at that moment. But I think you very likely know me well enough by now to predict that my response to the peril of the situation was to scream Sharee's name over and over while sweating profusely and feeling that darkness was about to overwhelm me. My breath was coming in faster, more frantic gasps, and I was completely disoriented.

And, worst of all, I was in the dark.

Now the human ability to adapt to various environments has always been quite phenomenal. Along those lines my eyes had adjusted rather nicely over our extended stay in the cave to the meager light that the glowworms provided for us. But even that was gone now, and although I was able to discern the vaguest of shapes, that was the extent of it. Furthermore, it seemed as if every one of those shapes was moving ever so slightly, plus the constant and consistent *boom boom boom* had not eased up. I felt as if it was entering every aspect of my being, physical, mental, and spiritual. I was living and breathing the *boom*. I was becoming one with the *boom*. The poison of the crimes that had occurred here in the depths of Ba'da'boom was infecting me, and I had no way of flushing the toxins from me.

I heard other sounds then, aside from the incessant *boom*, turned and stumbled down another passageway, and then the blackness became absolute.

Absolute.

It is a cliché, I suppose, to say that one cannot see one's hand in front of one's face. And because it is such an overused statement, it diminishes the true horror of genuinely not being able to see one's hand in front of one's face. It's like being struck blind all at once. I knew I was waving my hand before my eyes, waggling my fingers, but they might as well have been totally disconnected from my body for all that my eyes assured me of their presence.

My legs trembled frantically, and I leaned blindly forward, hoping that I would come in contact with something to guide me. I would have used my walking stick as a cane the way that the blind do, but I needed that to lean on, for my right leg had not miraculously become whole. And with the ground uneven and invisible to me, I required everything I could get my hands on to prevent stumbling.

I reached out, out, and my questing palm found a wall. There seemed to be some sort of carving in it, letters. I had no idea what they said, nor did I wish to know.

I made my way haltingly along, with the constant *boom* near to driving me mad, and that was when I felt something sliding off the wall beneath my very hands. At first I thought that somehow my hand had slipped across some sort of . . . of slime growing on the rocky surface. But then I realized that there was no wetness at all. That the wall was dry to the touch . . . but cold, so very cold . . .

. . . and the wall was moving again, or part of the wall, the surface of the wall . . .

My mind began to splinter as I yanked my hand away with a shriek. Somewhere, far in the distance, I thought I heard Sharee call to me in response to my cry, but she might as well have been leagues away, a lifetime away.

Those other sounds I'd heard earlier came to me again, and I hadn't been able to identify them earlier, but now I could, even though they seemed incomprehensible. The darkness itself was moving. Those sounds I heard, underscored by the ceaseless *boom,* were the sounds of the shadows peeling themselves from the very walls.

I know it sounds insane, I know it is easier to say that these were the fevered imaginings of a terrified mind, but I knew at that moment with utter clarity that that was what was happening.

I ran. I no longer cared about trying to make my way carefully. Instead I simply began a mad dash, in a direction I did not know, to a destination I could not possibly find.

Naturally I fell almost immediately. My toe hit a rise and I went sprawling, managing to hold on to my staff only through a miracle of desperation. I fell heavily, smashing one of my elbows, and pain shot through it and up and into the roots of my teeth, it felt like. The darkness was actually undulating around me, and I staggered to my feet, each step agony. I didn't have to see or even feel my knees to know that they were bleeding. I sobbed pitifully, cursed the fates that had brought me to this hellish place, and the gods who had turned their backs on me, if they had ever cared about me in the first place.

And still I ran, and then I heard other noises, whispers, coming from all over, in front and behind and sideways. There was a *whoosh* through the air, and something that sounded as if it was being propelled by great wings, and something went through me. It was as if I were naked and being pounded by a chill north wind. It cut to my marrow and I cried out, because it was so painful and yet morbidly fascinating, all at the same time. And then it was gone, and something else came through, and there were voices in my head from everywhere, whispering to me, crying out to me in words I could not comprehend: *Gedowdaheer, Gedowdaheer!*

"Help me!" I screamed, wanting nothing more than to forget that I had ever entered the infernal place called Ba'da'boom.

I twisted, shrieked as the shadows sliced through me yet again, this time calling in icy tones, *Fuggedaboudit!*

My inner voice, which had steered me right (and wrong) on so many occasions, tried to tell me, *You're imagining it! There's nothing there! It's all in your mind!* But those sensible thoughts were drowned out by the overwhelming frenzy of fear that drove me, deeper and farther. I ran headlong, bounced off walls, stumbled again and again until I thought I no longer had any capacity for feeling left in any of my extremities, and still I kept moving.

And that was when I saw the light.

At the far end of the passage, ever so slightly, ever so little, the darkness looked a bit lighter than where I was. I was able to discern different surroundings, although I could not see for sure what they were.

The *boom* grew even louder then, and the shadows seemed as if they were becoming more substantial, pulling at me, trying to slow me down. Or it might have been the fatigue of my own limbs serving to impede me, but my mind was far too frenzied at that point to be able to distinguish. It seemed as if the *boom* had become so vast a thing that it was developing a physicality all its own. That it was manifesting as yet another obstruction which I literally had to force my way through. I cried out deep in my throat even as I shoved myself forward, feeling as if my body weight had tripled, and the rocky floor was angling upward. I stumbled again, hauled myself up, and the shadows cried out in infuriated unison as I propelled myself into some sort of large chamber.

It was an intersection of stony corridors, but far larger than any other that I'd encountered. It was as if a number of different paths had converged upon this one place, and yes, yes, there was light. It was meager, but it was there. It was sunlight, tiny, delicate rays of sunlight, penetrating through some sort of holes in a ceiling so high that I couldn't even begin to discern it.

The *boom* was now so overpowering, thudding so in the floor and walls and in my own head, that I no longer had the will to stand. Only my staff was keeping me up, and the shadows were coming together. In the minuscule light of the chamber, they had greater form now, or at least they did to me. They howled at me, berated me, leaped upon me, and blamed me for their hideous state of affairs, for their deaths, for the great evil that had been done to the creatures they were in life, and I have never, ever been as terrified as I was at that moment. I tried to turn away from them, to shield myself from them, but they were everywhere, just everywhere.

Instinctively I endeavored to get to the lighted areas, as pathetic illumination as that provided, but they strove mightily to keep me away, blocking me, pounding me down, seeping into me as killer frost gets into the bones to destroy someone by freezing them to death.

And something occurred to me at that moment.

I had no idea what put the notion into my head; desperation, most likely. With the *boom* overwhelming me, with the shadows of reality or of my mind threatening to leave me a gibbering wreck, I found enough strength to lunge toward the meager light and—as I did so—I yanked the glittering diamond from the place on my person where I'd secreted it. My arm was outstretched as far as it could go, and it was just enough as the gem caught the light that was coming from on high like the eye of one of the gods staring down at me.

I wasn't entirely sure what I was expecting to happen at that moment, but I could never have anticipated what did occur. The diamond—already a source of inner fire by its very nature—seemed to become scalding in my hand as the light suffused it. It reacted to the daylight in the way that flame reacts to air stoking it. It gobbled the light eagerly, like a starving child, and then sent it in all directions. A rainbow played against the far walls, and I heard something howling within my head. There is nothing quite as daunting as the death screams of those who are already dead.

I moved the diamond, tilted it this way and that, casting light everywhere I could within my field of vision, and the shadows seemed to fall back. There was angry hissing, and even though I could still feel the soul-numbing chill within me, there was the distinct sense that I had narrowly avoided an even more terrifying fate. *"Get back! Get back, you bastards! Soul suckers! I wasn't responsible for what happened to you, but by the gods, I'll take you down now, you hand servants of hell! Back! Back, I said! Back!"* Over and over I shouted these overwrought commands and many more.

And suddenly, from one of the passageways, something huge came at me, more solid than anything else, more terrifying than anything that I had seen. *"BACK!"* I bellowed.

It spoke to me then, in a confused female voice, and it said, "Apropos?! Gods, what's happened! Look at you!"

"Sharee?" I could barely get her name out. My tongue felt thick in my head. I was so overwhelmed by my fear that I totally forgot to preserve my detachment and disdainful air. Instead I lurched toward her and threw my arms around her, sobbing out my terror and what I'd gone through. What an idiot I must have sounded like to her at that moment. *"The shadows! The shadows wanted to kill me! They were coming off the walls! Keep them away! Keep them away!"*

It was dim enough that I couldn't see her face, which was fortunate, since I'm sure the mixture of contempt and pity she must have felt at that moment would be a sight I would have carried with me for the rest of my life. She didn't address my delusions or cries of what I had seen, but instead simply said, "Come with me. I found a way out."

"You did?!"

"Yes, I did. But give me the gem back. . . ."

"Here! Here!" I thrust it into her hands, and she took it and shoved it into a pouch in her cloak. "Take it! You've earned it! I don't want it! It's yours! It's yours!"

She led me out of the caverns of Ba'da'boom then, out into the daylight and safety from the shadows.

Within two minutes I'd managed to light-finger the gem off her and tuck it back into my pack.

Gratitude is fine as far as it goes, but riches go further still.

Chapter 6

Fate's Finger

Sharee was as good as her word. She had indeed stumbled upon a way out of the catacombs of Ba'da'boom, and when we first emerged from the place, I alternated between squinting against the now-blinding daylight and sobbing in piteous joy that we were out. (This was, of course, before I snatched back the diamond.)

In retrospect, I should have realized while still within, fighting the shadows that I was convinced had come to life to haunt and harass me, that we were getting nearer to the surface. It had been difficult to tell with the gradations of the subterranean paths we'd been following whether we were going down or up or staying level. But the holes that permitted some lifesaving rays of the sun to filter through should have been enough to make me realize that we were getting close to salvation.

We emerged from a hole in what appeared to be a solid rock wall. "It was the water," she told me. "I heard it. I heard the waves."

Waves indeed. We had come out onto a shoreline, and I recognized it instantly even though I had only seen it from a distance, while riding along one of the outer roads that circumvented the Elderwoods some years back. I was stunned that we were there. I mean I absolutely could not believe it. We had crossed, underground, on a diagonal, virtually the entire state of Isteria. I knew that time had lost all meaning while we were under there, but still . . . the notion that we had been traveling for so long was just shocking to me. "How many days were we down there?" I croaked out.

Sharee shook her head. She had no idea, either, and I could tell from the dazed expression on her face that she had been doing the same mental mathematics as I had been and was coming up with the same appalling conclusions.

A large beach stretched out before us. It was not sandy, but instead hardened and almost claylike in its composition. The sea that washed up against it was perfect and clear and azure blue, with nary so much as a whitecap in sight. The sea might have had a name attributed it to it by mariners, but we simple landfolk had always referred to it merely as the Nameless Sea.

The cliffside from which we had emerged stretched hundreds of feet into the air. There was probably a path that led down to the beach where we were standing, but I had no idea where it might be, and the cliff itself seem fairly unscalable. At least I knew that I wasn't going to be scaling it anytime soon. Even an experienced rock climber might have been daunted by the challenge, and I with my lame leg would simply not be remotely up to the task.

For that matter, even if we did manage to climb the cliff . . . where would we go? I was coming to the realization that such matters had to be considered. During our subterranean sojourn, I had been driven by only one concern: getting out. Now that we were out . . . where were we to head? We had given Beliquose the slip, obviously, but there was no Bugger Hall for me to return to. I was without employment or resources or anything beyond the pack on my back and some coins in my purse . . . enough to last a while, provided we stayed in Isteria . . . which no longer seemed possible. The only other thing I had going for me was . . .

I turned to Sharee. "Take me there," I said abruptly.

She looked at me in confusion for a moment, and then her face cleared. "Ah. There. You mean . . ."

"The mountain you told me about that had more of those diamonds. Hundreds of them, you said." I'm sure that my basic avarice was quite naked in the way that I asked. "You said you'd bring me there if I helped you. Well, I helped you. Bring me."

"We just got out from subterranea," she reminded me. "You can't be so anxious to find another place to spelunk around, can you?"

I couldn't answer the question immediately . . . mostly because I had no idea what *spelunk* meant, other than possibly the sound a pebble makes when dropped into a thick mug of ale.

Sharee, meantime, appeared to have lost interest in me. Instead she was padding across the beach, her face tilted up toward the sun, her arms outstretched, and she actually pirouetted in place if you can believe that. It was the most relaxed, the most joyous that I had ever seen her. It was as if she had forgotten that I was there . . . or, for that matter, had made the conscious decision to set aside her dour attitude for a brief time and celebrate the fact that we were both still alive and reasonably whole.

She made her way to the edge of the beach, and that was where the sand was. She removed her boots and let the sand sift between her toes. Then she suddenly started peeling off the rest of her clothes. She turned and saw my hesitation, and the annoyed frown returned.

"Like it or not, neither of us has anything the other hasn't seen," she said with grudging acknowledgment. "And I am anxious to wash off the last vestiges of that place. Do as you see fit." And without another word she shrugged off the last of her vestments and plunged naked into the water.

Well, a metaphorical gauntlet had been thrown down, and so naturally I had to follow suit. I stripped down and dashed into the water, and promptly started screaming. Paddling about, she turned in the water and looked at me quizzically. I, in the meantime, was madly backpedaling out and—the moment I had emerged—threw my cloak around me to cover my trembling nakedness.

"*Gods, woman, do you have ice water in your veins?!*" I cried out. "That water is freezing!"

"Well, it *is* winter," she reminded me. "Being a weatherweaver, extremes of temperature don't affect me as dramatically as they do you."

"*And you could not have mentioned that earlier?*"

She shrugged and backstroked around as I sat on the sand, wrapped up in my cloak. It had been my intention to wash out my clothes, but the thought of wearing such cold, sodden things was not particularly attractive. I only wished I had something clean to change into. But when I had hastily tossed together provisions, alternate clothing was not something I thought about. I made a mental note to remember that for the very next time I had to go on the run. And considering the way my life went, that could be just about any time.

I watched her paddle around, and she noticed me smiling at her. She halted, and I couldn't tell if she was treading water or whether her feet had found purchase beneath. "What is it?" she asked, head cocked.

"You just look . . . at peace."

"So?"

"So . . ." I shifted beneath the cloak. "So . . . what's that like? To be at peace?"

"What an odd question," she said, brushing back her hair which had fallen in her face. "You've never been at peace?"

"No."

"No?" She sounded skeptical. "What about the two years you spent running that tavern? You made it sound like you were fairly happy."

"That's not the same."

"How is it different?"

I wasn't entirely certain I could articulate it. "I suppose . . . because for one to be at peace, one has to be able to confine one's perceptions entirely to the moment. I never can. No matter what I'm doing, no matter how well things are going . . . I will always be thinking of it as transient and waiting for it all to be snatched away from me. And damn it, Sharee, don't look at me in that pitying manner! I will not be an object of pity!"

"Then don't say pitiful things."

"It's not pitiful!" I shifted in the sand and started digging small holes in it with my toes. I tried not to sound as if I was feeling sorry for myself, and was only partly successful. "Everything in my life, every time I've had anything of any substance, it's been snatched away from me. Never has there been a creature who was more aptly named than I: Apropos of Nothing."

"Now you truly *are* being self-pitying," she said disdainfully. "Everyone has suffered loss in their lives, Apropos. And yet they've managed not to be soured on life itself."

"They're not me."

"That much is certain." She appeared to give it thought, and then she said, "Try to take just this moment . . . what we're experiencing right here, right now. We've escaped from the caverns of Ba'da'boom. We've left Beliquose and his bloodhound far behind. We're alive, and perhaps you're a little cold . . ."

"A little?" I was trying not to let my teeth chatter.

"The point is . . . enjoy the peace of this moment. Go ahead," she said with a slight tone of challenge to her voice. "Just relax. Be at peace. Don't think of strife. Don't think of anything except pure peace."

"You're being ridiculous, but if it will quiet you . . ." I shrugged, then closed my eyes and considered all the blessings of fortune that had, at least, allowed us to survive to run away another day.

I thought of all the luck I'd had . . . not the bad luck, but the breaks that had allowed me to survive. After all, the fact that I was still alive was, in some respects, nothing short of miraculous considering all that I had experienced with nothing save my questionable wits and mild fighting abilities to defend me. Perhaps, I thought, Sharee was right. Perhaps if, rather than dwelling upon injuries and unhappiness of the past, I considered only the possibilities of the future in a positive light, why . . . peace could indeed be mine.

Suddenly an earsplitting howling tore the air. A single wolf, I thought, which might not be a problem, except the sound was more deep throated, and even more human in tone than a mere wolf. It was the "human" aspect that made me realize, even before I heard a depressingly familiar voice.

"THERE THEY ARE, THE THIEVING BASTARDS! AFTER THEM!"

The fact that he was such a great distance away did nothing to disguise the sudden presence of Lord Beliquose. Still covered by my cloak, I twisted around and looked in utter astonishment at the tops of the cliffs. Sure enough, there they were: Beliquose, and his beloved lapdog, Bicce, and his men . . . who, now that I could see them, appeared to be numbered about a dozen or so. A dozen sellswords and cutthroats no doubt, but their trade was less important than the fact that several of them had longbows and seemed to be sizing up the distance and the possibilities of making the shot. Beliquose and several of the others were on horseback. Bicce pitched back her head and uncorked another howl even more soulful, and frankly frightening, than the first.

"FIVE MINUTES!" Beliquose bellowed to his men. "FIVE MINUTES TO FIND A ROAD DOWN, AND IF NOT THAT, THEN WE CLIMB DOWN HAND OVER HAND!"

I would actually have paid serious sovs to watch them clinging batlike to the cliff's surface, except I had the sickening feeling they would be just inconsiderate enough to survive the descent.

I staggered to my feet, but, because I wasn't carrying my staff, I stumbled and fell into the pile of clothes Sharee had left behind. Sharee, meantime, was splashing out of the water, running for her clothes. By that point I had managed to stand and was in the process of pulling on my breeches. I also took the opportunity to shove the diamond into the inner pouch of my belt, having just lifted the gem off Sharee's clothes when I'd become entangled in them.

If Sharee noticed, which she might well have, she said nothing, for she was too busy getting dressed herself and probably reasoned she could just grab it back from me when the mood suited her. She might not have been entirely wrong on that score, either. Battles of wits with wizards are always ill-advised engagements. I was suited to it, having led an ill-advised life, but I do not recommend it for anyone who values their sanity.

"How the hell did they find us?" I snarled as I yanked my tunic over my head and grabbed for my cloak. "Don't tell me that damnable bloodhound was able to track us while we were underground?"

"That's exactly right," she said, adjusting her cloak.

"How? It's not as if she could have detected our scent!"

"Creatures such as that one have tracking abilities that go far beyond something as mundane as aromas. They track your very essence."

"Well, thank you for sharing that with me," I said in irritation.

"Any thoughts as to what we should do?"

"You're looking to me for advice?"

"Well, I'm feeling a bit tapped out at the moment." She was clearly annoyed as she looked up toward the tops of the cliffs. Beliquose's people were already spreading out, seeking some sort of quick way down. I hoped the damned cliff collapsed under them. That'd be bloody quick enough.

My mind raced, picturing the area where we were. I looked out at the sea, studying it, looked up at the sun.

"What are you up to?" she demanded.

"Checking what time it is. I think it's approaching low tide. All right. Come on."

"What difference does that make . . . ?"

"The difference between life and death. Come . . . walk this way."

I started heading northwest, along the edge of the beach. Then I stopped, turned, and saw that Sharee was limping behind me, favoring her right leg as I tend to do, especially when I'm tired. "What the hell are you doing?" I asked.

With a smirk, she reminded me, "You said 'Walk this way.'"

I stared at her blankly. "Is that supposed to be funny?"

"It was just a joke, Apropos," she said, sounding a bit defensive. "You said, 'Walk this way,' and started walking in an odd manner, so I thought it might be droll if I imitated it."

"Well, don't." Now even more conscious of my game leg than I usually was, I continued on my path. "Jokes are humorous things which bear repeating. Having someone who walks oddly saying 'Walk this way' and someone else then imitating that gait is not remotely humorous, and certainly no one could possibly find it amusing enough to repeat to someone else."

"You are much too sensitive." She followed me, making no more efforts to copy my manner of stride. "You still haven't told me. Where are we going?"

"The Middle Finger."

Although I was moving as quickly as I could, she easily drew alongside me, and now she thumped herself on the forehead with the base of her hand. "Of course! The Middle Finger. You realize, of course," she said in a cautionary tone, "that even if we make it across, we could wind up in worse shape than we are now. That puts us directly into the desert known as the Tragic Waste. I don't know that any has ever survived it."

"Beliquose, I suspect, means to kill us by this point. I doubt very much we will survive being killed."

"How do you know that's what he intends to do?" She stumbled, almost fell, but then righted herself.

"Because he's invested a lot of time and energy tracking us down. If I were him, I'd certainly kill us."

"If I were you, I'd kill myself," she retorted.

I could see that Beliquose's troops had spotted our movement. They were pacing us, up high in the cliffs. Suddenly very, very distant, I heard a twang, and then a single arrow cut through the air in a graceful arc, heading straight at us.

Now, I'm no warrior, certainly, even though I was given a knighthood. But I had training, and I'd learned a few things. And although I was hardly a gladiator, my mind was sharp enough to judge trajectory quite accurately. So when I saw the arrow aloft, I stayed exactly where I was, unflinching, while Sharee (I was pleased to see) ducked several feet back, right to the water's edge.

It plunged into the ground about thirty feet shy of us and just sat there, upright and quivering (which, by startling coincidence, happened to be my typical defensive posture).

"It wasn't an attack," I said coolly. "One of their archers wanted to see if we were within distance."

"And you knew we weren't?"

"Not even close," I assured her, disdainfully turning my back to the cliffs even as I heard another shot being launched. "As you can see, he doesn't have remotely enough range to . . ."

Then I staggered slightly, craned my neck around, and saw to my horror that an arrow had just thudded into the pack on my back.

"Oh, pus bucket," I muttered. I quickly unslung the pack, yanked the arrow out, threw it down, and then said, "Hurry. A moving target is harder to hit."

"Is that another lesson from your vast storehouse of military knowledge?" she asked sarcastically as we set off as quickly as my lame leg would let us.

I heard much whooping and hollering from the cliff as they pursued us. The unfortunate thing was that time was on their side. I wasn't sure how long it would take us to get to the Middle Finger. I was certain enough that we were heading in the right direction, but I didn't know how close we were. On the other hand, my familiarity with the cliff was extremely limited, and I was concerned that there might be a pathway down at practically any point. If that happened, and they managed to get down to our level, they'd cross the beach in no time and be upon us.

Sharee and I stopped talking, which was something of a blessing in and of itself. As occasionally happened in periods of stress, I tended to forget the lameness of my leg. The usual result is extreme pain and exhaustion after the crisis has passed, but for the duration of the emergency I can move quite quickly. I had been pursued by a herd of unicorns once, for instance, and was almost like the bloody wind on that occasion. Having a group of cutthroats and ruffians after me, led by a she-bitch from hell, wasn't quite as dire as a unicorn stampede, but it was damned close.

The sun moved across the sky in its reliable way. It was nice to know that there were two things I could count on at any given moment: that the sun would rise and set, and that my life would be spiraling down the crap hole.

"We're getting close," Sharee said abruptly.

I seized the occasion to stop briefly, leaning on my staff and gasping heavily. "How can you tell?"

"The sound of the ocean. Farther up ahead I can hear breakers crashing up against rock. The seas can get rather fierce around the Middle Finger."

"Have you crossed it?" I asked.

She shook her head. "No. But I've done a bit of sailing in my time, and the sailors taught me a great many things."

"I'll bet."

"What's *that* supposed to mean?"

Before I could respond, there was a sudden war whoop. I looked in concern in the direction of the cliffs, seeing what I already knew I was going to see.

Beliquose and his men had found a path.

It wasn't immediately evident to me, but I saw them disappearing one by one from sight. There were crevices and crannies along the way down, and one of them there must have formed a sort of natural stairway. I saw the horses being left behind, tethered up. Well, that made sense. There was no way the creatures would be able to make such a descent, and Beliquose probably felt that it wouldn't take long for him and his crew to attend to us and return for their beasts. And if someone was foolish enough to happen along and steal them, well . . . the tracking and scenting powers of Bicce would certainly more than make up for that.

The increasing urgency of our situation prodded us forward even more hastily. The sounds of the crashing surf were audible to me as well, and suddenly it just seemed to come out of nowhere.

"There, there!" cried out Sharee, pointing and jumping up and down just ahead of me. And she was right.

The thing was, the Middle Finger was so low down in the water that it wasn't easy to spot at first. The Middle Finger was one of five stony reefs which extended from the shore. Because of the way they were positioned, they bore a passing resemblance to the fingers of an outstretched human hand. The outer fingers (or, if you will, three fingers and thumb) extended relatively short distances and then came to an end. The Middle Finger, however, stretched off into the distance several miles. Standing on the shoreline, it was easy enough to see the distant shore to which the Middle Finger adjoined, serving as a natural bridge between the two.

The span, however, was not one that was easily crossed. As the tides ebbed and flowed, certain sections of it would become totally submerged. One minute you would be walking the Finger, and the next you'd find yourself up to your knees in choppy water, and then higher still, and a wave would knock you off your perch.

Farther out to sea the Middle Finger rose to a significantly higher level, well above the waterline so that—if one was able to reach that point—the rest of the journey could be made without being thrown into the unforgiving waves. The problem was, getting to that point. The pitfalls involved in a crossing, the endless hammering of the water, the high winds . . . these were more than enough to keep the bravest and most daring of men far off the Finger.

But foolhardy men will tread where the bravest of men will hesitate to go. And men who will cut and run rather than fight will go even farther if it means they have a chance of keeping their heads squarely upon their necks.

I glanced behind us and saw that Beliquose's men had almost gained access to the shore. Within minutes they would be hard after us and upon us. If they got to us before we got to the Finger, they could surround us, cut us off. Our only chance was to make it to the Middle Finger before they made it to us.

Desperation gave us speed that we would ordinarily not have possessed, and so it was that we were upon the Middle Finger well before Beliquose and his troops could reach us. The one other advantage we had, once upon the rocky extension, was that it was so narrow that Beliquose and his people would have had to come after us single file. That meant that, if heavens forbid it did come to a fight, it would be a succession of one-upon-one, rather than simply being overwhelmed by strength of numbers.

On the other hand, perhaps they didn't require strength of numbers. For as Sharee and I sprinted (but carefully, watching our footing) along the Middle Finger, arrows whispered through the air around us, like bees with vast amounts of attitude. I quickly realized, though, how curious the circumstance; they were not killing us. The arrows were falling around us, coming so close as to trim my beard, but not one of them thudded home. Considering the horrifying accuracy with which Beliquose's archers fired their bolts before, this sudden inability to strike a target seemed a touch suspicious to me.

Sure enough, the explanation came moments later when the very distinctive voice of Beliquose bellowed over to me.

"IT NEEDN'T BE THIS WAY, POE," he informed me.

It might be useful to illustrate for you, as a reminder, just what "this way" entailed at that moment.

Sharee and I were standing on a strip of rock barely wide enough for one person at a time. We were a good two hundred feet, perhaps more, from the shoreline, where Beliquose and his people were standing. The sun was shining, which was nice enough, and the day was cloudless. But one wouldn't have been able to tell it from where we were standing, for it was as if we were in the midst of a gathering storm. Although the water level itself was about, oh, three feet beneath us (albeit rising rapidly), that would have only mattered if the sea was calm. Instead waves were leaping up on either side of us, crashing high, surging about with such ferocity that it almost seemed to be a thing alive. The tide appeared to be rising, and the fierce seas were wasting no time in announcing their intentions to sweep us into the depths which lay dauntingly on either side of us.

So the prospect of matters being some "other way" was, I admit, an alluring one, however briefly. Not to mention the fact that Beliquose was somewhat difficult to ignore. Despite the hammering of the surf, I could hear him perfectly. The man's volume was unmatched by any phenomenon I'd ever experienced, and I'm someone who's been pursued by avalanches, so I know something about the matter. I thought that when I'd encountered him back at Bugger Hall, he'd been loud, but that apparently was as nothing compared to his true capabilities. I was beginning to suspect that, were he so inclined, at close range he could have made someone's eyes explode with little difficulty.

I stopped where I was and carefully turned to face him, not wanting to turn too quickly lest I send myself tumbling into the water. Sharee, who was just ahead of me, saw my hesitation and plucked at my sleeve. "Stop fooling around," she demanded.

I ignored her, cupped my hands around my mouth, and shouted, "How could it be different?"

"WHAT?" Beliquose called.

"How could it be different?"

"WHAT?"

I waved my arms in frustration over the fact that I obviously couldn't come close to projecting with his degree of amplification.

"This is nonsense!" raged Sharee, and now she was pulling me with even more insistence. "He's trying to trick you!"

"He is, or perhaps you are," I shot back.

"LISTEN TO ME, POE. ULTIMATELY, WE DON'T GIVE A DAMN ABOUT YOU," Beliquose was calling. "ALL WE WANT IS THE GEM! THE GEM, AND THE WEAVER, SO WE CAN PUNISH HER FOR HER THIEVERY! GIVE THOSE OVER TO US, AND YOU CAN WALK AWAY FROM THIS!"

"We can walk away from this now, Apropos!" she said insistently. "We just head in the opposite direction from them—"

"Shut up!" My thoughts were racing. Now that I was out of the darkness and the constant, oppressive feeling of despair that accompanied my stay in that labyrinth, my mind was emerging from a distant haze. I reached into my cloak and pulled out the gem. Her eyes widened and she reflexively checked her own person for it as it glittered mockingly in the sunlight. I noticed that the water seemed to be getting higher, and the safepoint above the waterline was still an uncomfortable distance. The wind buffeted me, and only my staff prevented me from tumbling into the water.

"*You bastard!*" she snarled at me upon realizing that it was no longer in her possession.

"THAT'S A LAD!" Beliquose called. I couldn't help but notice, though, that his archers were inching closer, and they were nocking arrows. They weren't going to fire yet, but they weren't taking for granted that I was about to have a change of heart.

I waved it in her face. "What's unique about this?" I demanded.

"What are you talking about?"

She covered it well, but I saw the slightest flicker in her eyes. Over the roar of the waves I said, "You said there were more like this! A mountain full!"

"*Yes!*"

"Then why *this particular* one?" I demanded. "Why do you care about this one gem? Why does *he* care about it? You said earlier that you were afraid for the world of what would happen if he got his hands on it. Why? What would happen?"

"You said you didn't want to hear it!"

"Well, I want to hear it now!"

She tore her gaze away from me, looked down, and suddenly started to move away from me, farther along the Finger. I followed her, holding up the gem, waving it angrily. "Tell me, Sharee! This isn't making a good deal of sense to me! If there's an abundance of these, then you shouldn't care about this single one! You wouldn't have had to steal it from him in the first place!"

"You need it to enter the mountain!" she said, speaking with what sounded like desperation. Except I couldn't tell whether that desperation resulted from the specific circumstances of our being out in the middle of the sea with drowning as a distinct possibility, or if she was foraging for whatever explanation seemed reasonable without dallying with the truth.

"How? How does it get us into the mountain? And how will getting into the mountain have any sort of impact on the world?"

"We don't have time for this—!"

"We're making the time, Sharee!" I informed her, doing my best to make myself heard over the surging water. The sun was starting to vanish behind thick cloud cover. That was all we needed: Huge gusts of wind to come blasting through, stirring things up even more and making traction upon the already slippery rock even more treacherous. *"Because it was one thing when Beliquose wanted both our skins! But now you're asking me to put my neck on the line for you when there's another way out, and I don't do that! Ever! I put my neck on the line for me, and even then I avoid it whenever I can! Beliquose says he'll let me go!"*

"He's lying!"

"Perhaps! But I don't know that you're any more truthful! But one thing I do know: If he has you and the gem, he has no reason to

harass me further! It's bad enough that I let myself get in this far!"

She looked appalled. *"You'd turn me over to him just to save your own miserable hide!"*

"Of course! Where the hell have **you** *been?"*

And because things simply were not remotely frantic enough at that moment, that was when Beliquose chose to bellow, "YOU'RE RUNNING OUT OF TIME, POE! IF YOU MAKE ME COME OUT AND GET YOU, MY GENEROUS OFFER WILL NO LONGER BE AVAILABLE TO YOU! AND IN CASE YOU THINK I JEST . . ."

I never heard the *twang* of the bow, but the arrow sliced past my arm just as I turned to face in Beliquose's direction. It went right past, and Sharee threw herself to one side to get out of its way. Unfortunately, she moved so quickly and with such vehemence that she threw herself right off the Middle Finger.

Another woman would have let out a shriek of alarm. Not Sharee. Her arms pinwheeled a moment and she tumbled off, but not once did she cry out. I froze in my spot, wrestling with the notion that if she died, my problems were over, versus . . . well, versus nothing, actually. If she died, my problems were over. But my brain desperately sought some rationalization to rescue her, some reason that it would be to my advantage. None readily volunteered itself, although I did find it intriguing in an analytical sort of way that I was actually trying to find some cause to come to her aid. I wondered what it said about me.

Sharee, meantime, wisely wasn't staking her continued existence to my generosity of spirit. With a Herculean display of strength, while in midair, she twisted herself about and her hand snaked out toward the rocks. She caught herself, bent into a "V" shape, the toes of her boots barely finding purchase on the rocky face of the Finger. She clung there, pulling herself together, but unable to gain sufficient leverage to haul herself to safety. She looked up at me accusingly.

"Oh, hell," I muttered, and started toward her, reaching out to pull her up.

Another arrow sailed past, between us, driving me several steps back. I pivoted, overbalancing slightly but then regaining it quickly. A lifetime of favoring one leg enables one to learn quick adaptation. I looked furiously in Beliquose's direction.

"IT'S YOUR LAST CHANCE, POE!" he called out. I saw that a bowman next to him, probably his best archer, had a longbow ready with another arrow.

I didn't like Sharee. But I liked being targeted even less, and Beliquose's manner had long gone past simple annoyance.

There was one thing of which I was certain: Something was special about this gem. Maybe it was what Sharee had claimed, maybe it was something else. The only thing that wasn't a "maybe" was that I had it and they didn't, and they wanted it.

I stuck my arm out to the side, holding the gem high, and held it straight out over the crashing surf of the ocean. *It's not my last chance, you great sack of entrails! It's yours!* I shouted, and even though he likely couldn't understand a word I was saying, the gesture and intent was all too clear. If his archer shot me, or shot at me, I was going to drop the gem into the surf. Simple as that. And with the way the tides were surging about, unless he was part fish, there was no way he was ever going to find it.

A moment stretched into eternity then, and I met his gaze straight on and he knew me then as an enemy with whom no reasoning could be made. He touched the archer on the shoulder, and the bowman lowered his weapon

Quickly I crouched and grabbed Sharee by the wrist. Waves leaped up at that moment, dousing my head, soaking me so thoroughly that I almost lost my grip upon her. But by chance—good or bad chance, I leave to you to decide—I managed to keep a hold on her and haul her up alongside me. She did not thank me. No great surprise there.

"Now back up," I said. "Slowly."

"Run."

I looked at her in confusion, feeling a by-now-familiar swell of frustration. "Why the hell can't I give you so much as one directive without—"

"Apropos, look at the water!"

I did as she bade and instantly saw the problem. The tide had swept up with terrifying swiftness. The water was lapping at our feet and within minutes would be upon us, trying to pull us in. The waves were coming up higher and higher.

I heard a howl of anguished fury. It was Bicce, the hellhound of Beliquose's, venting her frustration over the situation from a distance. Beliquose was holding her steady, keeping a firm hand upon her shoulder.

And then, as it turned out, the hand wasn't firm enough, for Bicce suddenly tore free of his grasp. "BAD BICCE, BAD!" shouted Beliquose and grabbed for her, but she vaulted out of his reach and sprinted toward us. She apparently didn't give a damn whether I took the gem and dropped it in the ocean or shoved it up my ass. She was still smarting from our previous encounter and was looking to even the score by tearing me to shreds. I could see as she bounded closer to us that the left side of her face was covered with a makeshift patch. She'd lost an eye, thanks to me. Certainly that had endeared me to her no end.

Abruptly Sharee's suggestion didn't seem to be such a terrible one at that.

"Run!" I echoed, and suddenly we were fleeing along the Middle Finger, Bicce in pursuit and closing the gap. The difficulty of what we were endeavoring was nearly overwhelming. We had to maintain our balance, navigate the rocks which were terribly wet, and every so often we would stagger to a halt and just try to hold our positions as massive waves slammed down upon us. In those instances we would drop to the ground and hold on, allowing the waves to wash over us. Within seconds we were utterly sodden, and naturally when you're being pursued by a slavering harridan of a creature, that's precisely the time that you want to be weighed down by sopping clothes.

Clouds had wholly covered the skies, the world darkening around us. Returning was no longer an option; sections of the Finger had already been completely submerged. Every passing moment, as we ran for our lives, I fancied that I could feel Bicce upon me, bearing me down to the rocks, knocking us both under and sending us to a mutual watery grave.

I chanced a look behind us, hoping that she was at least forty, fifty feet behind.

She was five feet away.

I froze in my tracks, whirled to face her, grabbing for my sword which was strapped to my back. But my movements felt leaden; it was as if I were sleepwalking. Sharee cried out a warning, which was pretty damned useless, because I was looking right *at* the creature, for pity's sake. Far, far in the distance, Beliquose was madly waving his arms, probably commanding Bicce to come back, but even his extraordinary voice couldn't carry the distance.

Bicce let out one hell of a roar, which sounded as if it originated from somewhere around her ankles. If the purpose of that blood-curdling war cry was to paralyze an opponent with fear, I can assure you that it worked. I stood there, utterly frozen, and Bicce leaped through the air at me, covering the distance with ease, and I could almost feel her teeth sinking into me.

That was when the wave hit her.

One moment she was in midair, and then she was gone, the gargantuan wave caressing her like a monstrous lover's hand. It enveloped her so completely that I didn't even see her go in. I just heard her startled yelp, and the splash of her body going into the water was lost in the surging of the water.

The waves leaped up again, crashing against the rocks, and I looked from one side to the other, and as the gods bear witness to my words, I tell you that there were faces in the water. They were bizarre mixtures of seaweed and brine and dark, swollen crests of water, and part of me was convinced that I had to be imagining it. It was not as if the faces were hanging there and staring at me. They were visible to me only for an eyeblink, if that. There and gone again, leaving my mind's eye wondering if the impression that it had received upon seeing the infuriated sea around us was simply an imagining conjured by my own franticness, or whether there was something or somethings actually there, sizing me up for who-knew-what?

I had no idea whether Sharee saw it as well. All I knew was that she was pulling at my sleeve, and I followed her, desperately using my staff to maintain my balance. The rise in the Finger was just ahead, and although our position would still be precarious, it was marginally better than where we were.

Then something knocked me off my feet.

I barely managed to hold on to my staff, my sword never having left my scabbard since Bicce had been brushed away by the whims of the sea before I could wield the weapon. I had not heard anything, and the pain hadn't registered yet. All there was was the impact, and at first I thought it was another wave, or a stone of some sort, and then I was flat on the ground and that was when the pain began to hit. I twisted myself around, trying to see what had happened. The sight that met my eyes forced impulses of crying in terror or laughing in disbelief to war within me, and ultimately the crying won out, although there was a choked sob or two of incredulity.

The shaft of an arrow was quivering out of my ass. To be specific, it was lodged securely in my right buttock.

Another arrow flew then, and a third and fourth. Beliquose's attempts to advance were frustrated by the crashing seas, but his archers were endeavoring to take some final vengeance upon us. Or perhaps they hoped that, if they managed to immobilize us, they could wait until the tides and ferocity of the seas subsided and then come after us on foot.

I suppose I would have been within my rights to chuck the gem into the water at that point. But I assessed the situation with surprising calm, all things considered. At the moment, I had a gem in my hand and an arrow in my backside. If I tossed the gem, then all I would have was an arrow in my backside. Hardly seemed worth the sacrifice somehow, considering the arrow was a constant while the more promising variable wouldn't do anyone any good—particularly me—if it was at the bottom of the briny.

The wind was taking most of the arrows before they could draw within range, it seemed to me. So my little onboard visitor had just been fortunate enough to beat the odds. Yes, somehow that was my luck in microcosm.

And that was when I heard Sharee cry out, her shout lifting over the waves. I had forgotten about her for a moment, caught up in my own pain and misery, and saw that Sharee had likewise taken an arrow. She, however, had been spared the indignity that had been visited upon me. In her case, she now had an arrow projecting from her upper left thigh.

She was down on one knee, the water cascading about her with such intensity that I thought sure it was going to take her as it had Bicce. But she managed to hold her position with remarkably bull-headed determination, and bracing herself she broke off the arrow just above where it entered her leg. That one outcry I had heard from her had been the only one. Obviously she wasn't going to let another burst of pain take charge of her.

And then she was on her feet, and so was I, limping after her as fast as my staff would take me. The roaring of the sea was thunderous. I felt as if there had never been a time when I had known dryness or quiet or safety. It was like the damned thing was alive, trying to torture us and torment us right into the arms of madness so that we would throw ourselves into the waves of our own volition just to escape the situation.

Yet escape it we did. For the rise was just in front of us, and we clambered up it as quickly as we could. It was a high rise, but a steady incline rather than anything sharp, so it was extremely manageable. It was as if someone had lifted his middle finger in a slow, steady elevation which was easily accessible for us. More arrows came, but either they fell short or the wind easily knocked them away from us. I resisted the temptation to turn around and stick out my tongue in derision at Beliquose. After all, there was no telling when or if we would meet again, and I certainly did not need him saying, "Ah yes, Poe, the fellow whose trespasses I could have forgiven in their entirety . . .

except for the tongue thing. Yes, for that, you must surely die."

The seas continued to rage, but the height gave us some measure of safety. The stony surface we trod at that point was barely wet save for some sea spray, indicating that this section never went beneath the seas' surface and was not subject to the pulls and thrusts of the tides.

"Gods, have we made it?" I muttered, gritting my teeth. The pain in my backside was throbbing and radiating from the point of entry. The prospect of never being able to sit again was not a pleasant one.

"Not yet," she said. Then she stopped, saw the arrow in my buttocks, saw the blood that was tricking down my backside probably at about the same time that I saw the blood welling from her own wound. "Wait," she said.

"No, you wait!" I shot back in alarm, but it was too late as she took firm hold of the arrow and snapped it off just under the point, as she had done with herself.

"We'll save the rest of it for later," she told me.

Obviously I was less than enthused. "Well that's certainly a reason to go on living," I told her. But she ignored me. Sometimes I think some of the happiest times of my life were those times Sharee was ignoring me.

We staggered, we lurched, and several times one or the other of us almost went into the still-challenging waters. Fortunately there was no time at which both of us started to go in simultaneously, because each of us was the only thing keeping the other from going in and possibly—considering the intensity of the tides— going under.

The roaring in my ears was so persistent and so intense that it took me some moments, or even perhaps minutes, to realize that the noise was subsiding. It was as if one half of my brain was saying to the other, *Excuse me, have you noticed this bit over here?*

But Sharee most certainly noticed it, and she stopped and turned to face me. Her cloak was so sopping that the weight of it might well have dragged her into the seas if she had not watched her step. Not that my own cloak was in much better shape, but at least I had my walking staff to lean upon for some extra bracing. Sharee was on her own. I never thought I'd consider lameness to be an advantage. In truth, I never had to worry about my legs getting worn out. I only had one leg to exhaust, and if I was leaning on my walking staff, well, that never got tired.

Sharee reached out a hand to me. There was nothing romantic in the gesture or demeanor. Her expression could not have been more "all business" than it was. I couldn't tell whether she felt sorry for me, or really wanted me around for some reason. Well, either way would have been suspicious for me.

Nevertheless, I took her hand. I was surprised at the strength in it. I suppose I shouldn't have been. She had, after all, displayed considerable physical prowess when she had slammed me down in the cave and had her way with me all that time ago. But I had partly ascribed that to the bewitching aspects of the ring itself. Apparently that was not the case. Sharee was simply stronger than she looked.

We made the rest of the way in silence. The waves were still fierce, but they were no longer vaulting into near geysers, although there was a consistent spray upon us. The massing clouds parted and streaks of light filtered through in dazzling array. I remembered how my mother had used to say that when light came down from on high in that sort of focused manner, it meant that the eyes of the gods were upon us, gazing down with interest upon our doings and no doubt finding great amusement in our antics. One would have wished they might have found a nice puppet show or something instead of choosing to indulge their tastes for merriment in inflicting hardship upon us. But go argue with gods.

At first we moved quickly, but then we started to slow down, the stress and strain of what we had endured taking its toll upon us. Eventually we came to a formation in the rocks that I can only describe as a sort of elevated crest, where the formation extended outward an additional few feet. Comfortable it certainly was not, but the marginal addition of space was enough for our purposes and we sank to the ground, hungry, tired, thirsty, and aching.

"Lie flat," Sharee said with authority, her first words spoken to me in several hours. The sun was moving on its course, orbiting our little world which—as everyone knew—was the center of the universe. I was too exhausted and in too much pain to argue with her, and did as she said.

She clambered around me, undid my breeches, and started to slide them down to expose my bare backside. "I'm warning you," I said weakly, "I don't think my performance is going to be up to its usual standards."

"Don't flatter yourself. Your performance wasn't that great on your best day."

I was going to argue the point, but I chose to let the remark pass. Considering where she was at that moment, and the position I was in, it seemed the politic move.

I couldn't exactly see what she was up to, but I assumed she was studying the wound carefully. She pulled on gloves then and placed her hands delicately on my posterior in what can only be described as the least sensual manner that any woman has ever touched me in that area. "The point doesn't appear to be barbed, fortunately," she said. "So take comfort in small favors. Now, I'm going to do this as gently as I can. On the count of three. Count with me—one . . ."

Well, naturally she yanked it out on two. And even more naturally, she wasn't gentle. I took it like a man . . . a man who tends to shriek loudly when confronted with pain. Fortunately, I was not embarrassed by my lack of fortitude. I had long gotten over any blushes for that failing in my personality. Indeed, there were so many failings in my personality that intolerance for pain seemed one of the more minor ones.

She then proceeded to dress the wound, and I have to admit that in that instance her ministrations were indeed cautious and even tender. "It could have been worse," she said.

"How?"

"You could have turned around just before the arrow hit you."

"Ah." I shuddered, envisioning the arrow quivering in the depths of my groin. "Well . . . that's one of the advantages of being a coward, I suppose. You're far more likely to be struck in the backside."

"You're not a coward, Apropos," she said suddenly and with such certainty that she was almost ferocious in her conviction. "There's many things you are . . . but that's not one of them."

"I'll thank you not to tell me my mind," I replied. "And what would you say I am, if not that?"

"Confused," she said.

"Confused? I don't understand."

"And thus is my point proven."

I blinked at the bizarre turn the conversation had taken, and then mentally shrugged.

Once she was done, attention was turned to the remains of the arrow that was in her leg. I would like to tell you that I was as zealously fierce in yanking clear the arrow in her as she was in my circumstance. But I wasn't. There is very little I will not stoop to if it will benefit me, but the bottom line was that—at that moment— Sharee was simply a helpless female, and I could not bring myself to take joy or cruel mirth from that situation, no matter how much I would have liked to.

I tore away some of the cloth of her leggings from around the area of penetration, and then as gently as I could, worked the arrowhead out. As near as I could tell, the arrow was lodged in a muscle, and I was concerned that if I just ripped it out, I might do serious damage to her and impair her ability to ever walk normally again. That was the other thing going through my head, you see. Whatever animus I might have for Sharee—the woman had, after all, completely disrupted my rather comfortable existence—I knew all too well what it was like to go through life hampered in the simple act of walking. I would not have wished that condition on anyone, including my worst enemy.

All right, *maybe* my worst enemy. And his lieutenants. And underlings. And immediate family. But no one else. All right, perhaps cousins, but only if they were utter cretins in their own right.

Sharee, to her credit—and unlike me—did not cry out even as the point of the arrow came clear. I tossed it into the sea and studied her injury. I didn't like it at all. The area around it was red and inflamed. I had seen wounds from arrows before. This looked far nastier. And I suddenly had the feeling, particularly judging from the dull ache radiating from my buttocks, that mine probably looked much the same.

As I dressed her wound, I said slowly, "Sharee . . . is it possible that there was something on the ends of those arrows beyond just simple points?"

"You mean poison" was her blunt response. Obviously the same thing had occurred to her when she saw the damage that had been done to me.

"Yes."

Slowly she nodded.

"Wonderful," I said.

Sharee forced herself up to a seated position, and then reached around and opened her carry sack. She began to extract small bottles and vials and lay them out in front of her, studying them thoughtfully. Then she selected a couple of them, unstoppered an empty one, and began mixing small drams of several of the liquids.

"What the hell are you doing?" I asked after watching this odd procedure for several minutes. "Preparing some sort of magic brew? I thought you said your magiks were depleted for some unknown reason."

"This is not magic. This is good, old-fashioned potioning." She put down another vial, picked up a third, and added a bit of the contents of that one. "If there was a poison on the arrow, this antitoxin I'm preparing may help."

"Don't you need to know what sort of poison was used in order to produce such a solution?"

"Generally, yes. What I'm making here is a sort of all-purpose brew. Because it's so broad in its nature, it's not as effective as something specific to a particular poison would be. But it will have to do. Ideally it will last us until we can find a healer who can do more for us than my poor skills will allow."

"From where I'm sitting, your skills don't look too poor to me."

Something akin to a smile passed across her face. "From where you're sitting, you can barely sit."

"True," and I actually gave a short laugh.

Considering we were perched atop rocks in the middle of the sea, with waves surging about us, an unknown destination ahead of us and certain doom behind us, it was a surprisingly genuine moment of warmth. "What is it about you, Sharee? What is it that causes the time I spend with you to be involved mostly in running away while people are trying to kill us . . ."

"When you're not raping me, you mean?" Her eyes were hard then, and I found to my annoyance I could not meet her gaze.

"We've been over that," I said. "I see no reason to belabor it at this point."

"No. No, you wouldn't." She sounded almost disappointed in me, and for a moment my temper flared at the thought of her sitting in judgment on me yet again. But I found I was too tired to get myself worked up about it.

She finished her crafting of the potion, poured off half into a bottle for me and handed it to me. I paused, looked at it, passed it under my nose. It smelled vile. I looked to Sharee and she was simply sitting there, staring at me. "Ladies first," I said.

"Meaning you suspect I might have poisoned it, and you want to see me drink it first." I nodded. She looked at me pityingly. "Apropos . . . if I wanted to poison you . . . I would give you something harmless and let the cargo the arrow bore do the work for me."

That was certainly an unassailable observation. With that depressing truth at the forefront of my mind, I downed the concoction. She followed a heartbeat later, and then we sat there a moment and stared at each other, each of us likely thinking the same thing: *I wonder if it worked.*

"Come," she said abruptly, and stood. "Let's be off."

"The sun hasn't much farther to go in its path," I pointed out. "We have a place here to rest. Perhaps we should do so. . . ."

"Tides ebb and flow, Apropos," she reminded me. "I would not be one to assume that Beliquose wouldn't endeavor to follow us should the waters recede. Nor do I think he will let nightfall daunt him. Are you interested in going to sleep and never waking up again?"

"If we keep moving," I pointed out, "and there is poison in our systems, the movement may hasten its work."

She blinked, and then her mouth thinned in annoyance. "Yes. Yes, that's true," she admitted. "It seems we may be doomed and damned either way, Apropos."

"A status with which I am unfortunately quite familiar." I thought a moment and then said grudgingly, "Best if we keep moving, I suppose. If I am to die, I'd rather not give that bastard the satisfaction of it being under his sword." She nodded and, as we started to walk once more, I said, "Sharee . . . generally the fate of my corpse is of small consequence to me, but I'd sooner not give that buffoon the satisfaction of mutilating it. So in the unfortunate event that I should die before you . . . push my body into the sea, would you?"

"That won't be a problem, Apropos. It's all that I can do to restrain myself from pushing you into the sea while you're still alive."

Unsurprisingly, I took little comfort in that.

We kept the conversation to a minimum as we continued on our hard path. The rocky surface of the Middle Finger was not conducive to comfort. In addition to the notions of being dry and warm seeming to belong to another lifetime, soon I couldn't recall a time where my legs did not ache thanks to the unyielding nature of the surface upon which we trod. There still seemed to be no sign of land, and soon the sun had set. There was a half-moon up,

which provided us at least with some light by which we could see
our path, but the area to either side of the Finger was dark and
black. Save for the slapping of the waves against the rocks, the
silence was unmitigated. I felt as if we were the only two creatures
alive on the planet. Indeed . . . what if we were? What if, as we
were making this insane crossing, massive wars had erupted at
home, and every man, woman, and child had been slain in a final
orgy of annihilation? Or if a plague had broken out and even now
the bodies were being piled twenty high, with the last of the victims coughing up blood even as they piled more corpses onto the
stacks. If Beliquose and his followers had been overwhelmed by
the waves, dragged into the depths of the sea . . .

Sharee and I might be the only man and woman alive on the
face of the planet.

"Idiocy!" I said out of nowhere. Sharee was a dim form just in
front of me, the darkness making it difficult to make out details.
She paused a moment and I think she turned in my direction; it
was hard to tell.

"What is?"

"Nothing. Nothing," I said impatiently. Both our voices
sounded strained, hoarse whispers of how we normally came
across.

We kept moving, for moving had become an end unto itself.
The steady *tap-tap* of my staff echoed in the silence. I had no idea
whether the antitoxin that Sharee had given us was doing anything
productive. All I knew was that I was getting more and more tired
with each passing step. I wondered if I collapsed whether Sharee
would keep going without me. I then wondered if Sharee collapsed, whether I'd go on without her. Part of me said yes. Most of
me did. But a small part of me said no, and that annoyed me no
end. If I was developing an annoying strain of compassion, I might
as well count myself among the dead right then and there, for that
would surely be the death of me as it was for every other altruistic
fool, and that list included my former best friend.

I realized I couldn't remember walking anymore. I was just making the motion automatically. Overwhelming fatigue caused my joints to become slowed, and I felt as if I could barely move. That was when I further realized that I'd stopped walking altogether. My body had simply ceased locomotion, and the message was only just then getting to my brain.

I began to waver, to topple, and I heard Sharee's voice cry out, *"Apropos!"* from ahead of me, and at that moment I not only didn't care whether I stood or not, but whether I lived or died. I'd been pushed to endurance and beyond, and I was done. The Finger was narrow where we happened to be at that moment, and with a low moan I toppled off the side and fell, the world spinning away from me, knowing that the icy fingers of the sea would reach up for me and pull me down, and also knowing that I just didn't give a damn anymore.

And I hit ground.

I lay there for a moment, stunned, wondering if somehow the entirety of the sea had turned to ice. "Apropos?" came Sharee's voice from above, and I understood her confusion, for my vertical departure had been absent a splash.

"I . . . believe so, yes," I said slowly. I reached around, spreading my fingers, grasping what I now realized was ground beneath me. It seeped through my fingers, tiny granules. "Sand. I'm . . . lying on sand."

An instant later Sharee was by my side, looking around in wonderment. "We made it. . . ."

"We made it?" I couldn't quite believe it. I used my staff to push myself to standing, and then I squinted.

Sure enough. It had not been evident while standing on the elevated rock of the Finger, but from this new point of view we saw that we were standing on what appeared to be a vast plain. It was hard to tell, for the moon had ducked behind clouds and now seemed to have no inclination to reemerge. But it was land, definitely land.

I let out a sob of relief, and Sharee did as well. She actually sagged against me and for a moment, just a moment, we embraced, two warhorses coming through a difficult campaign. Then, just as quickly, the moment was gone, and Sharee straightened up.

"Let's go," she said briskly. "We have to keep moving. Beliquose may be behind us, and for all we know, gaining. But with any luck, the worst is over."

Well, you know about me and my luck.

Chapter 7

The Tragic Waste

I'm sure you remember—going on the assumption that you're not mentally deficient in some manner—how I said earlier that I could scarce remember what it was like to be dry as we clung desperately to our lives during our crossing on the Middle Finger. Well, in very short order as we embarked upon our trek across the Tragic Waste, I quickly forgot what it was like to have moisture in the vicinity.

It was not until daylight that we were fully able to discern just what it was that lay ahead of us. The ground had been shifting and unpleasant to walk upon, and once we had light available to us, we could readily see why.

Now, as it happened, I didn't actually see the sun rise. We had been moving under the night sky for what seemed an eternity, and I had not had a proper night's sleep in possibly days. At one point I sat down to rest, over Sharee's protests. I have to admit, the woman may have been incredibly irritating, but her stamina was simply staggering. I had trained with some remarkably sturdy knights in my time, and any of them would have been hard pressed to keep up with her. Her assertions that we had to keep moving became reduced to little more than an annoying buzz, as I was unable to focus on her at all. The next thing I knew, the sun was on my face and I was slumped sideways, coming to startled wakefulness. The first thing to greet my eyes was Sharee, seated a short distance away in a cross-legged position. Her hood was up and her head was slumped forward, her breathing slow and steady. I was almost relieved to see that she was sleeping. It gave me some hope that she was actually mortal.

I sat up slowly, stretching out my body as best I could, feeling the creaking in the joints. Then I looked around. And around.

The Tragic Waste was a desert of the first magnitude. It stretched on and on, to the horizon and farther, and there was nothing there. I mean nothing. Just sand, blowing across the plains in leisurely manner. No grass. No trees. Not the slightest shrub. No hint of animal life of any kind. Just sand. Sand in small, mountainous ridges in one direction, or sand that was unyielding and flat in another. Sand that I could already taste between my lips, sand that I had to squint against to prevent it from getting in my eyes.

Sand and nothingness in all directions, save for the very, very far distance, so far that it could have been the end of the world. And in that distance, there was what appeared to be a mountain range, but it looked as inhospitable as the rest of the place.

I looked behind us and saw that there was no sign of our tracks. The blowing sands had completely covered them. It was as if we had not been there at all.

Now, if one were of a rational frame of mind, this might have been good news. Bicce's status was uncertain; if the bitch had managed to survive being washed into the sea, then she could probably track us through the pits of Hell. But if she had been removed from the equation, then Beliquose—were he still of a mind to pursue us—would be limited to more conventional means of tracking, in which case we might well have given him the slip.

But none of that went through my mind at that moment. Instead, nothing went through my mind.

I could never have anticipated the effect the Tragic Waste had upon me. In retrospect, however, I suppose I should have seen it coming.

All my life I had been surrounded by something. A forest, much of the time . . . the Elderwoods, where I grew up, learning forest craft and the tricks of staying alive. Or I had resided in a castle, safe and secure within four great stone walls. I had traveled, yes, but usually through forest paths, or valleys, or glades.

I had never seen anything like this. Never. The emptiness, the . . . the nothing. Even now as I write of it, separated by the passage of time and experience, I feel a chill fist closing about the base of my spine. Back then, when I was first struck by my new surroundings, the impact was catastrophic.

My mind was so locked down that I didn't even realize at first that something was happening. I went blank, blacked out, the world suddenly becoming a great white haze. From what seemed a great distance I heard Sharee calling my name. I looked up at her, tried to focus upon her. My chest was thumping in agony, and I realized that I'd stopped breathing. I forced myself to draw a deep breath through my nose and then out through my mouth. The air was hot and raw and hurt going in and coming out.

I was shivering violently, as if I was having a great chill despite the heat. At first I thought that the rapid transition from wet to dry had made me ill, but I quickly realized this wasn't the case. The trembling wasn't just physical; it was in my head. I was shaking not from cold, but from fear. That was it. Pure, stinking fear in my nose, in my throat, in my mind, just paralyzing me.

"Stand up, Apropos," Sharee said sternly. I shook my head so violently it might have tumbled off my shoulders, and again—this time with even more vehemence—she said, *"Stand up!"*

I did so, but with great reluctance, balancing myself with my

staff. But my right leg was questionable under the best of circumstances, and now my left leg was giving way as well. I trembled so
violently that it nearly collapsed beneath me, sending me to the
ground. "What the hell is wrong with you?" demanded Sharee.

She was standing directly in front of me, looking me full in the
face. I looked past her shoulder at the endless vista of nothingness
in front of us, to the side of us, behind us. I had never felt so
naked and vulnerable, and this time I did fall. I hit the ground
hard, dropping to my knees, shaking my head furiously as if I
could make the entire desert go away through simple denial of its
existence.

Sharee crouched in front of me, grabbed my face, and turned it
to look up at her. Her exasperation and impatience with me was
evident, but then she saw something of the sheer, stark terror that
was in my eyes, and instead of becoming angrier, or even just
leaving me to fend for myself—as, I must admit, I might have
done—her face softened, and she almost looked sympathetic.
"Apropos . . . what's wrong?"

My jaw twitched furiously as I fought to bring it under control
so I could get the words out. "The . . . the desert . . . en . . . ensorcelled somehow . . . making me . . . with fear . . . filled with . . ."

Amazingly, she was actually able to discern what I was trying to
say from my half-witted rantings. "It's not the desert," she said
firmly. "There's nothing mystical about the desert. It's just a desert.
This is coming from within you. Look around, Apropos. It's just
sand and a few dunes and some plains. Nothing here to be afraid
of."

"It's the nothing. That's what it is. Nothing . . ."

"What?" Her eyebrows knit in confusion. She was gently
pulling me to my feet. Her hand rested on my shoulder, and
although it didn't make me calmer, it did prevent me from becoming even more panicked than I was. "Just . . . walk with me,
Apropos. One step at a time. Place the staff. Pull yourself forward." Her voice was slightly singsong, as if she were dealing with
a child. At that moment, though, I was hardly in condition to take

offense at being condescended to. I did what she said, endeavoring simply to walk with as much concentration as a toddler might exhibit. "Now . . ." she continued, "how is 'nothing' so upsetting to you?"

I knew perfectly well what she was doing. She was trying to divert me from my concerns with distracting chitchat. My fundamentally perverse nature almost prompted me to ignore her obvious maneuvers, but instead I focused on what she was saying . . . mostly because I was trying to understand it myself. "There's . . . there's so much . . . nothing . . . so much . . . it's . . ."

"It's not like at home, is it," she acknowledged. "With the forest, and the trees . . ."

"Danger . . . danger everywhere." The quaking in my knees was causing a similar disruptive sound in my voice. It was amazing that she could understand anything I was saying. "We're out here . . . in the open . . . exposed. . . ."

"If it's danger you're worried about, consider this: Back home, danger can hide in the trees, behind brush, inside a cave, waiting to spring out at you. Here," and she made a sweeping gesture, "nothing can surprise you. You can see it coming from miles away."

"And when it comes," I said darkly, "there's no place to hide from it. And . . . and it's more than that. Much more. It's . . ."

"It's what?" she urged.

Everything I was feeling, everything I was trying to express, warred for dominance in my mind, and the truth of it was out of my mouth before I'd even realized what it was going to be.

"This . . . this is Death's Domain," I said.

I know. It sounds absurd, coming from one such as me. So trite, so overblown a sentiment. And yet, at that moment, I truly felt Death to be an actual entity, stalking the cruel sands, seeking out anyone who had been so foolish as to wander into his arena. I even kept glancing over my shoulder in fear of the notion that he was standing directly behind me.

She looked at me strangely. "What?"

I stopped, turned to face her. It was getting harder for me to breathe again, and it took all my will to get the words out. "This . . . is not a place of life. This is a place for . . . for the loss of life. The absence of life. You can die in the forest, in the sea . . . but there are living creatures there as well. Here . . . there's nothing. Nothing. This is where Death resides. Here he has dominion . . . and we trespass here. We . . . will die here." My voice choked, and I felt weak and helpless. "We are going . . . to die. Death will take us because nothing is supposed to live here. Nothing—"

"All right, all right, I get it," said Sharee with sudden impatience. "Nothing is supposed to live here, you've made that clear. Death's Domain. Maybe you're right." She shrugged indifferently. "Maybe . . . you are. Maybe this is Death's stronghold, and we're not long for it."

I couldn't believe her tone of voice. "Don't you care?" I managed to ask.

"No."

"You don't care if you die."

"No."

"Nonsense," I retorted. My fear was giving way to annoyance. "You're just saying that. Everyone fears Death."

"That's everyone's problem, then. But it's not mine."

Walking was not an easy task, even if I hadn't been trembling. The sands kept shifting beneath us, and the lack of a regular surface was extremely hard on the bottoms of our feet.

"I don't believe you," I said flatly.

"Fine." She shrugged beneath her cloak. "Don't believe me."

"You're telling me that you don't care if you live or die."

"I didn't say that," she replied. She was shorter than I, but she navigated the sands with such assurance that it was a struggle just to keep up with her so that I could hear what she was saying. "If given the choice of living or dying, I'll opt for the former. But I have no fear of the latter."

"But that's suicidal," I protested. "If you have no fear of dying, then you won't hesitate to wander into life-threatening situations because you won't be deterred by the jeopardy of it."

"There's a fine line between refusal to be deterred and rank stupidity," retorted Sharee. "Obviously one shouldn't be such a fool as to walk blithely into traps because of a limited understanding of one's mortality. Although if such creatures do exist, better that they make short work of themselves at a young age so they do not live to create more of their kind. But the truth is that the fear of death can get you killed."

"How?" What she was saying made no sense to me. "And would you please slow down your infernal gallop?"

She slowed just a little, but not much. "Fear of Death can cause deadly hesitations, terminal doubts," she said. "The scream of a great beast, and the threat of death that accompanies it, is designed to freeze prey in its place for the second or two the predator needs to reach its target. Or look at yourself. What possible good could come from being so afraid of death that you stand trembling in a desert? Fearing death can overwhelm your common sense, can make it impossible for your fundamental survival instinct to function at all. And what good have you done yourself then, eh? For that matter, what is so terrifying about death?"

"Are you about to romanticize it?" I asked sarcastically. "The pain of that final moment of—"

"Pain?" and she whirled to face me, and there was anger in her eyes that bespoke something truly frightening. "Dying is not painful, Apropos. Living is where the pain is. The moments leading up to death, they can be as excruciating as our fellow creatures can devise. Every moment of life is replete with pain, and yet you would cling with all the force and energy and desperation that you can muster to the agonizing privilege we call life. But death, which is the cessation of pain and suffering . . . death, which is the merest blowing out of a candle . . . that you would fear down to your very soul. It's a lousy way to live, Apropos. A lousy way to live."

I had been taken aback by the vehemence of her response, but then I pulled myself together and said simply, "It's gotten me this far."

"No. *I've* gotten you this far," and she pointed behind me. "Look."

I turned and gasped. I couldn't believe the amount of distance that we had covered. The shifting sands were well on their way to covering our tracks, as I knew they invariably would. Even so, I could easily discern that we had come quite a ways. Not that we were all that much closer to anything of use . . . but at least we were farther away from where we had been.

"Not bad, eh?" Sharee asked with a smirk. "And there were you, shaking with such dismay that you couldn't move from the spot. If it weren't for me, you'd still be trembling and yammering about Death's Domain. For gods' sake, Apropos," and she smacked me on the upper arm. It hurt. "You're a knight," she continued. "You may have come by the title in the oddest way that any knight ever did, but a knight you are. Down deep within you, you must have some strength of character. Stand up! Be tall! Be proud!"

We stood there, we two, as the sands migrated around us. She with that challenging look on her face, and me feeling weary and nervous despite all her high-sounding words. "Once," I said finally, "back in the days I resided near the Elderwoods . . . a great storm came through. A great, powerful wind. Tacit and I were out in the forest at the time, seeking passing merchants to prey upon. You remember Tacit. Master of woodcraft. Eyes like a hawk, ears like a rabbit, attuned to nature. Tacit sensed the storm on its way moments before it arrived. We took refuge in a cave, and I remember watching from just within the cave's mouth. I couldn't have been more than ten at the time, but it was the most frightening sight of my young life. The sheer ferocity of the wind was . . . well, it was awe-inspiring. And in the course of it, I saw weeds bending in the wind, whipping about, but staying rooted in their spots. Meantime the wind, howling, screaming like a thousand angry souls, hammered against mighty, powerful oaks. Some of the trees held up for as long as they could, and then snapped over, crashing to the ground with a noise that I can still hear.

"When the storm passed, I walked about the woods and marveled at the fallen oaks. That such majestic things could be toppled by . . . by air. By nothing. It was mind-boggling. And as for the weeds . . . they were still there. Every one. And they were already standing back up as if nothing had happened. Because they knew which way the winds blew, Sharee, and they bent with the prevailing breeze. They lived, while the oaks died. There's something to be learned from that."

"You would truly rather be a weed than an oak?" I had never heard her sound quite so pitying.

"I wouldn't rather be one, but it certainly presents a lesson on living."

"If you learn anything in your life, Apropos," she replied, "it's that there's a world of difference between living and not dying. That's all you're doing at the moment: Not dying. But only when you discard your fear of dying can you truly call yourself one of the living."

I shook my head. "You simply do not understand."

"Yes. Yes, I do. The problem is that you don't."

I sighed. "I knew you would say that."

We continued to walk until close to noon, when the intensity of the sun simply became too much for us. Traveling in the desert during the day is never the best of ideas, but we had done so in order to try and put as much distance between ourselves and the possibly pursuing Beliquose as possible.

I still had the gem on me. I was surprised that Sharee had not tried to take it off me, and could only conclude that she was simply waiting for a moment when rescue or salvation was in sight. In that way we wouldn't have an ongoing grab-back-and-forth of the jewel, which might be diverting but was a waste of time and energy.

Upon ceasing our forward trek, we pitched camp as best we

could considering we were in the middle of nowhere in inhospitable terrain. Despite Sharee's efforts, my terror for our surroundings—or lack of surroundings, as the case may be—was still as palpable as before. I dealt with it by keeping the hood of my cloak pulled low over my eyes, and my gaze raptly upon the ground. The expanse was still solidly there in my imagination, but at least that wasn't enough to prevent me from moving forward.

Obviously our greatest concern was the rationing of water. We had food as well, but we could afford to be minimal in its distribution, for the human body can survive far longer on no food than no water. I took but a mouthful of water from one of the skins, swirled it in my mouth and then swallowed it. Sharee did likewise.

I looked far into the distance ahead of us, in a direction that appeared to be southeast. The mountain range looked no closer to us than it had before. The air was shimmering in the heat; I'd never seen the like. Suddenly struck by a thought, I asked, "Those mountains . . . are they the ones the gem came from?"

"Maybe."

Gods, the woman could be absolutely infuriating at times. Well, at all times, really. I was tempted to curse her out in frustration at her manner, but I withheld my invective. First, it was too damned hot to become so worked up, and second, it was never a wise move to hurl invective at someone who was a magic user. Which immediately prompted a thought that I voiced as we lay there, huddled beneath our cloaks to keep the pounding heat from searing us. "Do you feel as if your magiks are reaching their potency again?" I asked. "Because we could really use a rainstorm about now."

But she shook her head and there even seemed to be a hint of despair. Nothing. She had nothing.

I nodded and looked off to the mountains once more. "'Maybe,'" I echoed her nonanswer about the mountains, with a tone of undisguised disgust. "What is it about you weavers that you so treasure and covet secrets?"

"We don't covet them," she retorted. "We hoard them. Your

type covets them. And believe me, if your kind knew what our secrets were . . . you wouldn't want them."

For a long time, then, we simply sat there, conserving our energy, eating minimally and waiting for the sun to set. The entire time I kept worrying about Beliquose and his people catching up with us. I told myself that they had to rest as well, and would be no more inclined to traverse the Tragic Waste under the pounding sun than we were. I even tried to convince myself that Beliquose might have turned back, given us up for lost, assuming that the fierce seas would have put an end to us. But I kept having the feeling that I was just kidding myself. That any moment we would catch sight of him upon the plains behind us, bearing down upon us at high speed, and us with nowhere to hide, nowhere to hide. . . .

It was not a mindset conducive to relaxation.

I dozed off every now and again. Restful it most certainly was not. Every time I would approach any sort of deep sleep, I would find myself back in Ba'da'boom with the shadows coming for me, or traversing the Finger with the oceans crashing around me, or Bicce leaping upon me while my tavern burned around my ears.

I woke up, startled and sweating, to realize that the sun had nearly gone down. I glanced a short distance away to see Sharee, curled up and snoring softly. I felt a surge of envy and anger. How could she possibly be sleeping so soundly?

Gods, the fire, the shadows, the flight across the Finger . . . how brief a period had that all occurred within? Days, weeks ago, I was happy and comfortable, and in no time at all my entire life had unraveled . . . all because of that woman, lying there sleeping with such serenity that one would have thought her an utter innocent. Instead of slumbering comfortably in my bed back at Bugger Hall, I was flat on my back in a damned desert, trying not to let my newly discovered fear of wide-open spaces paralyze me into uselessness.

That was when I realized she was watching me through slitted eyes. "You're awake," she said rather unnecessarily, and her voice was hoarse and fractured from thirst. Without a word I handed her one of the water skins. She shook her head. "I can wait."

"No, you can't," and my voice didn't sound much better than hers. "You'll be no good to me if you collapse."

"Your sympathy is gratifying," she said with no humor in her voice, but she took the skin anyway and drank down the slightest of droughts.

We stared at each other for a moment, and then I asked something that had been preying upon my mind. "Why didn't you leave me?"

She tilted her head slightly. "Leave you? What do you mean?"

"When I was . . ." I searched for a judicious word. "Disoriented," I finally said. I kept my focus upon her, trying to limit my awareness of the vast expanse that surrounded us, lest I dissolve into paroxysms of anxiety again.

"You mean when you were lying there and no good to me?"

I winced at the word choice since it was obviously my own from moments before. She seemed rather pleased with herself, that she had thrown that back at me. But I wasn't about to back down at that point. "Yes. That's right," I said with as much candor as I could muster. "I was no good to you, no good to myself. Why didn't you just walk away, leave me behind? You've no love for me, certainly. Indeed, you hate me for what happened with the ring. I should think that you could have just taken the opportunity to go on your way . . . or even slip a dagger between my ribs in revenge."

"Weavers don't have all that much interest in revenge, as a rule," she said.

"Not much interest? You try to blow me out of existence with a lightning bolt."

"Well . . . I never thought much of that rule," Sharee admitted.

That actually seemed to be slightly akin to a joke, but she wasn't smiling. "We deal in forces of nature," she continued. "Nature has a tendency to notice things and react accordingly. Foul actions beget foul consequences, Apropos. Your punishment will come."

"What, this isn't it?" I asked, indicating the desolation around me. "My tavern gone, I'm back to having nothing in the world, on the run from ruthless barbaric lunatics. That's not enough punishment for what happened?"

"That's up to nature to decide."

"Weaver's riddles," I snorted in disgust, taking a small drink of water for myself. My lips were parched and cracked; they barely seemed to notice the moisture upon them, as if they'd lost the capacity to absorb it. "You didn't answer my question. Why burden yourself with me?"

"Because," she said brightly, "I'm the hero of this story. You're my sidekick. Or have you forgotten?"

"Ohhhh no," I told her.

"Oh, yes. A sidekick is always required in such endeavors, in order to make the hero look as heroic as possible. To provide a contrast. You're a contrast to my heroism."

"And you are a contrast to sanity. I am no one's 'sidekick,' and I will be the central figure in my own heroics . . . such as they are," I finished with a marked lack of enthusiasm.

She shrugged. "Would you have left me behind?"

"In a heartbeat."

"You lie, Sir Knight."

"Don't call me that. And I never lie."

That caused her to burst out laughing. Despite the constraints of her parched throat, nevertheless it was as musical as the other time I'd heard her make that noise. It was also somewhat more annoying. "I never do," I repeated defensively.

"You?"

"Yes."

"Never lie."

"That's right."

"Apropos," and she shook her head, "how can you say that with a straight face?"

"I never lie," I said again, and then added quietly, "I just have a different definition of truth, that's all."

"That definition being," she said, "whatever enables you to survive from moment to moment."

"I am not going to dignify that comment with a response," I said archly, and with that I planted my staff firmly and got myself to standing. I hopped slightly before I achieved my balance, as I usually do whenever I first arise. I had become painfully aware in my life that the act of walking is really just a form of controlled falling. You push off with one foot, start to topple, and your opposite foot prevents the fall while balancing you for the next step. Since my right leg was not up to the challenge of hindering a fall, it was left to my staff to make up the difference, and it sometimes took me a few moments to position myself.

Sharee, still on the ground, watched me. Then she said, "Back on the Finger, when the seas almost claimed me, you hauled me out. You didn't leave me when you could have. Why not?"

"Because you got me into this," I told her. "And if I'm going to suffer, I was going to make damned sure that you were there right beside me sharing in every moment of joy. That's why."

She didn't look like she believed me. I didn't especially care. Instead I looked ahead to the mountains, so far off into the distance. "Are we actually walking toward anything, or just away from something else?"

"There are cities," she said, "beyond that mountain range." There was something in her voice approaching genuine excitement. "You wouldn't believe it, Apropos. Cities like none that you have ever seen. Cities dedicated to art, to the sciences. Cities filled with wonders such as you cannot possibly conceive. People of peace, people of learning. And there are cities filled with bazaars as well, crammed with peddlers hawking wares of such exotic nature that it staggers the imagination. Delicacies as you have never known. Tell me, Apropos . . . have you ever heard of . . . chocolate?"

I rolled the word about in my mouth. "Chaw-ko-lit?" She nodded. "No. Should I have?"

"It's a sweet. Small, brown, and round . . ."

"Sounds like shit."

She shook her head vehemently. She seemed like the little girl I could only imagine that she once must have been, back before she grew up to become my own personal tormentor. "No. It's amazing. I have no idea where they get it from, but you will see . . . you will see. . . ."

"See with what? Obtain it with what?" I patted myself down. "We do not exactly have money in abundance. Some coins, yes, but we've no reason to assume that such currency would be accepted where we were going." My voice hardened. "Tell me this time, and save your talk of secrets: Will we acquire riches in passing through the mountains? Is that where the true cache of gems came from? You lampoon me for what you call lack of veracity, but are less than forthcoming yourself. Well?"

"Yes, all right? Yes," she said so impatiently that I naturally had no idea whether she was telling the truth or not. "Is that all you care about, Apropos? Riches?"

"And survival, yes. That more or less covers it."

She made an annoyed sound of dismissal and started walking. I fell into step behind her.

We walked.

And we walked.

Always I cast brief glances behind me, certain our pursuers would be there. Always I had to fight my fear of the vast emptiness. I literally had to concentrate every waking minute lest my resolve falter.

And still we walked.

Night into day, and we huddled under our cloaks, and back into night. On and on, and there was just no end to the Tragic Waste.

And the mountains . . .

. . . came . . .

. . . no . . .

. . . closer.

Miles we walked, and stumbled, and staggered, and dragged our carcasses with their dwindling reserves, and still the mountains and the cities which supposedly lay on the far side of them remained not only out of reach, but the exact same distance as they had the day before, and the day before that, and the day before that. Insane as it sounded, I felt as if someone were hauling the mountains away from us. That they were actually just a monstrous joke, a towering apparition that we would never arrive at.

It might have been the fifth day, or perhaps the sixth. That was the day that the water ran out. The food supplies were wearing thin as well, but it was the end of the water that I knew would spell the end of us as well. The notion that Death was spying upon us had returned with full force to my fevered mind. I could swear I felt his hot breath down the back of my neck. When I slept it was with his flaming eyes blazing into my brain. When I awoke it was with full awareness that he was calmly waiting for that final moment of collapse. Time was entirely on his side. He did not have to do any work, fight any duels, engage us in a battle of wits or contest of physical strength. He needed but wait. He did not have to come to us; we were, step after agonizing step, coming to him.

And to make matters worse, the wounds that we had sustained from the arrows were flaring up. It may well have been that the antitoxins which Sharee had prepared for us had saved us from immediate death . . . but there was still some sort of infection now lurking within us, eating away at what few shreds of resolve and determination we might have left. Simply put, my ass hurt like hell. I wasn't sitting all that much, so that wasn't the problem. However, there was a constant burning sensation that had at first been localized to my backside, but had been radiating outward over the past few days. It had reached a point where every movement of my hips was agonizing.

Sharee wasn't in much better shape. The limp she had developed was even more pronounced than mine. But she said nothing. She didn't even acknowledge that there was a problem. Every so often I would see her dealing with the pain in her own way, taking in deep breaths and letting them out slowly, her eyes almost closed. It was

as if she was trying to wish away the pain, or at the very least iso-
late it to some other part of her brain where she could then ignore
it. But sometimes the pain would be too much, and I would hear
her gasp if she came down too hard on her leg. Then she would
compose herself and draw that inscrutable air about her once
again.

But she couldn't fool me. She was dying.

We both were.

The sun rose on whatever the hell day it was, and we just sat
there, staring at each other bleakly. There were no japes, no jibes at
one another, no philosophical discussions. Just the looks of two
people who were wondering which one was going to get to watch
the other die before succumbing himself or herself. My tongue felt
swollen to three times its normal size. My lips were so brittle that
they would have been bleeding, had I had enough moisture in my
body to allow blood to flow. The ache from the wound I'd taken in
my backside had consumed the entirety of my body from the waist
down; I strongly suspected that I was no longer capable of any sort
of locomotion, and didn't have the energy to test my theory. My
eyes were dry and aching. Even my hair hurt. I think we both
understood that we had gone as far as we were going to go, and the
mountains were no closer. Yes, that more or less confirmed my
original guess; they were a cruel joke. Much like my life.

"I saw faces," I croaked out while the sun reached its zenith. She
looked at me curiously, having no idea what I was talking about.
For that matter, I had no idea why I was telling her. I simply felt
like I wanted to say something. "In the waves. When they were
crashing around us. I thought . . . faces. Watching us."

She spoke, and at first I didn't understand what she said because
the voice coming out of her mouth didn't sound like anything
human. I shook my head, indicating that I hadn't comprehended.
She repeated herself, and this time I barely made it out.

"Gods?" I asked. "Did you say—?"

I have no idea what the voice of someone from beyond the

grave would sound like, but it probably would have borne a strong resemblance to what I was hearing emerging from her tortured face just then. "Gods," she said in a hoarse whisper. "Water gods. Might have been . . ."

"Why?" I demanded. Perhaps *demanded* is too strong a term, for there were corpses with more energy than I possessed at that moment. "Why . . . ?"

She made a movement that I think might have been a shrug, except she didn't have the strength to fully accomplish it. "The gods . . . might have taken . . . notice of you. . . ."

"Wonderful," I said with a grunt. "Noticed by the gods. Now I know . . . why I'm so completely fucked. . . ."

She actually smiled at that, even though that simple gesture seemed to be painful to her. And those were the last words that passed between us there in the Tragic Waste. We did not move a muscle for the rest of the day, and as night approached I tried to stand. It took a massive effort of will, and even though I exerted every ounce of strength left to me, I only got halfway to standing before collapsing face first into the sand.

I wanted to sob in frustration, I wanted to pound the sand in fury as it worked its way between my broken and bleeding lips. I had strength for neither. I felt a pain in my chest and thought I was having a heart attack, and then realized it was the gem pushing against me, a silent reminder of the utter futility of dreaming of riches.

Now that Death had come for me, it seemed almost anticlimactic. *What an utterly stupid way to die,* I thought. There was one thing I knew, though, and that was that I didn't want to expire facedown in the sand. It may seem absurd to spend one's last dregs of strength in the simple act of turning over, but that's what I did. My mind went blank with the exertion, and then I was on my back and staring up at the night sky. The stars were absolutely, perfectly bright against the blackness above, and a full moon was staring down at us like one great Cyclopean eye.

I thought of all the people whom I had known. All the people who were better or more heroic or more noble than I. And the fact that I had managed to outlive them all . . . except for Entipy and her family, whom I still thought about every now and again when I was really of a mind to put myself in a foul mood. I wondered if they ever thought about me, and tried to decide whether I would be happier if they did or didn't, and realized shortly thereafter that I might well have lost the capacity for being happy long ago.

I wondered if the stars were more of those gods looking down upon me. I hoped that they had derived sufficient amusement for one day, watching a cripple's dying moments.

"I hope you all die," I growled to them, and then I spiraled away into darkness.

BOOK TWO

The Conqueror Worm Turns

Chapter 1

Strange Awakening

I woke up dead.

Not only dead . . . but in Hell.

I had always been somewhat sketchy on what the afterlife—were there actually such a thing—would be like for one such as I. From all accounts and all my imaginings, I figured it would be one of two things. Either I would be surrounded by great, burning masses that were endlessly immolating souls in torment . . . or else I would find myself trapped within my own mind as a helpless bystander, condemned to watching me live out my life over and over again and powerless to do anything to change any of it. When idle speculation prompted me to dwell on these two options, I would find myself drawn invariably to the former, since the latter was just too hideous to contemplate.

It appeared that I had been granted my wish, because the smell of burning was so overpowering that I thought I was going to vomit. I felt my gorge rising . . .

. . . and then came to a surprising realization. In order to feel a desire to vomit, one actually had to have something resembling food in one's stomach. Such was the case here. Something was surging in my innards, and from the taste leaping into my mouth—even befouled as it was—it was some sort of mutton. And wine. I'd eaten recently, eaten rather heartily. This awareness brought me up so short that the nausea went away due to lack of attention.

Nevertheless, there was still that overwhelming burning smell pervading the air. Surely I was in some sort of hellish afterlife . . . ? Moreover, I could hear distant screaming. The voices of men, women, and even children, crying out over some sort of horrible misfortune that had befallen them. They sounded very far away, and their wailing blended into one single lamentation that would have struck me to the heart, were I of sound enough mind at that moment to comprehend what was going on. I was almost afraid to open my eyes, because once I did, I would know one way or the other. Perhaps I could have just lain there forever. Perhaps I was supposed to. Perhaps that was my true condemnation: to simply reside in hell with my eyes closed, afraid of opening them lest matters deteriorate even further than they already had. This, in turn, made me dwell on the fact that every time I had believed things couldn't get worse, they promptly had done so with almost gleeful enthusiasm.

Unable to tolerate the indecision any longer, I slowly opened my eyes.

I was on my back, just as I had last remembered myself being. My arms and legs were splayed, and I was staring up at the night sky. Except . . .

. . . the stars had shifted.

I'm no astronomer, understand, no stargazer, but even I comprehend the shifting of those sparkling orbs as the seasons passed. And not only that . . . but they were just barely visible against a sky that was moving from darkness to day once more. It was not a standard transition from night to day, however. Instead it was as if a great, black shadow had covered the sun. As if evil were having the audacity to make an assault on the purity of light.

I recalled tales that were supposedly told by men in far northern climes, of how the sun was pursued by a great wolf, and that when the End of All Days arrived, the wolf would catch and devour the sun. For an instant I wondered if they had in fact been correct, and that somehow I had been salvaged from death just so I could witness the end of existence. Or maybe I had indeed died, and death had simply been nothingness (for I certainly didn't remember anything of the event) only to be recalled from oblivion specifically to see the world meet its termination. Why such a thing would transpire, I hadn't the faintest idea.

All of these musings about the world's end came to a halt, however, when I realized that the light from the sun was, in fact, increasing. The premature and unnatural nighttime was being chased back into its proper place by the power of the sun. I squinted against the intensity of the rays as the sun resumed its proper place in the sky, and finally turned my face to one side.

What greeted my eyes was no less astounding than the sight that I had beheld in the sky.

There was a city burning less than a mile away. It seemed that, once upon a time, it had been filled with proud structures. Towers protruded above a mighty wall that surrounded it for protection . . . but clearly the protection had been insufficient. Great portals which had guarded the main entrance had been smashed down, and through the newly created gap I could see the buildings in flames. I caught brief glimpses of people running back and forth. It was easy to tell who the conquered were: They were the ones who were ablaze as well, sometimes rolling to smother the flames, or else wildly beating at themselves to try and extinguish the fire. There were other shadows as well, swaggering men raising swords over their heads and shouting triumphant battle cries. But those battle cries kept being drowned out by suffering and lamentations. At that moment one of the burning towers toppled over out of sight behind the wall, and there came a swell in the howls and cries, presumably by people upon whom the structure had fallen.

The unnatural night continued to give way to the proper day, and the sight of so much death and destruction, and a deep revulsion for the kind of barbaric mind that would inflict so much torment upon the helpless, prompted me to turn my head in the other direction. I was still flat upon my back, but at least I didn't have to keep looking at the horrific sight of that obviously conquered city.

What I saw looking away from it was no less bemusing.

My staff was lying a couple of feet away. It was exactly as I remembered it . . . except for one difference. There was a series of notches in the lower half. They were small, and not deep enough to cause any sort of weakening of the wood, but they were most definitely there. At least a half dozen, maybe more. It was not the staff, however, that really captured my attention. No, it was the man lying just beyond that.

I had known my share of powerfully built individuals in my time. King Meander, the mad wandering monarch who might or might not have slain my mother. Sir Coreolis and Sir Granitz of the court of King Runcible had been rather formidable physically. Even my one-time fellow squire, Mace Morningstar, had been a daunting fellow. And then there was my most recent acquaintance, Lord Beliquose, wide as an oak and twice as thick. But they paled in comparison to the monster who was lying there now. A mountain of a man, all beard and hair upon arms so massively muscled that he could have picked me up and thrown me halfway back to Isteria without any strain. I thought he was wearing an extremely furry shirt before I realized that he was bare-chested. His mouth was drawn back in a rictus of frozen hatred, exposing teeth that were sharpened to a point, and there was blood still bubbling out from between his lips, indicating that his death—for dead he most definitely was—was a very recent occurrence.

Of the greatest interest to me, under the circumstances, was that my sword was buried deep within his chest.

"What in hell—?" I whispered, and discovered that my voice was normal, bereft of the increasing raspiness that had befallen it in my increasingly parched state. I wondered if my exclamation of surprise was geographically accurate, but I was starting to think that it wasn't the case. I didn't know what death felt like, but somehow I couldn't help but suspect that it didn't feel identical to being alive. And that was how I felt: very much alive, if utterly befuddled.

Slowly I staggered to my feet, and then I looked down at myself. Not only was I not wearing what I'd been before, but it was clothes that I had never seen before. I was clothed in a leather tunic of bloodred, with black leggings of similar material. My tunic was trimmed with green, scaled edging around the shoulders and collar that might have been snake skin, although I couldn't be sure. There was a thick leather band across my chest, attached presumably to a scabbard across my back. I had black bands that reached from my wrist to my elbow; otherwise my arms were bare. And for that matter, I hardly recognized my arms. There was marked muscle definition where there had been none before, and when I experimentally poked my flexed biceps and triceps, I was astounded to discover that they were iron hard. I was no Heracles, but neither was I what I had been. As for the armbands, I couldn't help but notice an odd array of scratches in them. They were uniform in number and pattern: Four and four, separated from each other by a fairly small distance. They were predominantly on the left armband.

I coughed several times, and my eyes stung from the smoke and ash that was drifting through the air. Very tentatively I made my way over to the gargantuan corpse that was wearing my sword through its chest and looked at it cautiously. I glanced around to see if there might be the body of another combatant around, because all I could think of was that someone else had grabbed my sword and used it to cut this brute down. But there was no one else. The ground was not sandy, like the desert, but instead thick and gravely, so it was easy to see the nature of the

battle that had occurred there. There was the tread of the behemoth, the oversize footprints unmistakable. There was only one
other set of prints, maneuvering about on the treacherous
ground. A set of prints with a firmly planted left foot, and a right
foot treading very lightly as if it had some sort of infirmity. Very
gingerly, disbelievingly, I placed my own foot inside the print. It
fit exactly.

My footprints and mine alone. The conclusion to be drawn was
inescapable. I'd killed him. We had fought, and I had killed him. It
was incomprehensible. How could I possibly have allowed myself
to be drawn into a battle with someone who could likely slay me
with his breath alone? It was far more typical of me to talk my way
out of such a confrontation. And once having been pulled in . . .
how could I have killed him? I was more muscled than I had been,
true, but there was simply no way that I could have slain the creature before he cut me to shreds.

Struck by a horrible thought, I glanced behind me to see if my
body was lying there and I was simply a shade that had arisen from
a newly made corpse. But no, there was just me. Well . . . me and
my new dead friend.

That was when I felt the ground rumbling beneath my feet in a
manner that I knew all too well. There were horseman drawing
near, thundering toward me. At first I had no idea where they were
coming from, for even though there was now full sunlight, the sun
was being obscured by the increasingly thick clouds of smoke that
were billowing everywhere. It served to disorient me even further. I
wanted to run, but I had no idea which way to go.

Taking two quick steps, I grabbed my sword by the hilt and
yanked it out of the great oaf's chest. It did not emerge without
effort; the damned thing had really been wedged in there. The
body jolted a little when I did it, and for a moment I thought he
was coming back to life so that he could break me in half in a
cursed fit of postmortem vengeance. But no, he just continued to
lie there, an eventual feast for whatever scavengers and vermin
might be crawling about the area.

The smoke was drifting thicker and faster as I wiped the blood from my sword on his leggings. It was hard for me to tell from which direction the hoofbeats were coming as they echoed from all around. My mind was racing with desperation and confusion. Where was this place? How had I come to be there? Where had I gotten these clothes, and who was this beast that I had apparently slain? Where was Sharee? I had been dying in the midst of the Tragic Waste. Was all this some sort of demented dream, some final last-gasp hallucination before death? Or, despite all appearances to the contrary, was I indeed in the afterlife?

I had always prided myself on knowing exactly where I was and what I was about. As I've noted earlier, it had been my mind (and, admittedly, a helping of occasional luck) that had enabled me to survive as long as I had. If I was in a state of mental disarray or confusion, then that greatly reduced the chances of my living out the day . . . presuming the day didn't suddenly vanish behind another great shadow upon the sun.

I thought perhaps that I was dreaming. That matters would escalate in insanity, and then I would awaken . . . although whether it would be back dying in the Tragic Waste or blissfully back on my cot in Bugger Hall, I couldn't guess. Unfortunately I can tell you with a certainty—as I scribe these memoirs with my aged hand—that it was not a dream. A nightmare perhaps, in tone and spirit, but a fully waking one. My predicament was genuine, and all that occurred thereafter truly did transpire, for good or ill . . . mostly ill.

I picked a direction at random, started to walk in it . . . and came up short. From out of the smoke came horsemen, riding three abreast, and the horses they were astride were huge, fearsome beasts. I had once had the acquaintance of a glorious bit of horseflesh known as Titan. These reminded me of him, only slightly larger. They were uniformly black, foam flecking their mouths, and their eyes were as intense and wild as those of their masters.

The men were attired in clothing not dissimilar from mine own.

The only difference was that they wore furs about them in orna-
mentation, with the animals' heads still attached, staring out life-
lessly and with expressions of perturbation at the world. Also they
sported some sort of wild war paint upon their faces, in varying
shades of blue. Some seemed smeared on in a random manner,
while others were in intricate designs.

Reasoning that they might well be friends of the fallen individual, it was probably in my best interests to try and be elsewhere,
even though I doubted I could cover any serious distance before
they were upon me. Suddenly, from overhead, there was a screech
such as I had never heard.

I looked up and there was a small creature that was quite
singular in all my experience. Its facial features were birdlike,
with a long beak and pale blue feathers adorning its head. But
the rest of its body looked more akin to a dragon. The smooth
skin was a paler blue than the crest of feathers. Its wingspread
couldn't have been more than a yard, tip to tip, and its tail was as
long as its own body and snapped through the air as it descended
toward me. The horsemen were approaching swiftly, but the
creature was coming in even faster. I threw up my arms to defend
myself, certain that the creature was going to clamp its beak
around my throat and begin tearing itself a meal as quickly as it
could.

Instead, to my utter shock, the creature nestled on my
upraised left forearm, its claws wrapping themselves delicately
but firmly around my armband. The creature was behaving like a
falcon or hunting hawk. Slowly I lowered my arm and stared in
astonishment into the creature's face. I even bobbed my arm up
and down experimentally; the creature didn't seem off put.
Instead it was busy readjusting itself slightly on its perch, its
eight taloned toes clinging securely, and I realized what the
source of the odd nicks in the armband were. For additional
security, it wrapped its tail around my wrist, and then turned and
peered at me with its birdlike eyes. It appeared slightly confused,
as if there was some brief question as to who I was. Obviously

the creature wasn't all that perturbed by it, though, for after a moment or two it lowered its head on its long neck, tucked its head under, and drew its wings around itself in the easily recognizable posture of sleeping.

The horsemen were almost upon me. There was no escape. After having been positive that I was about to die in the middle of nowhere, instead I was about to die on the edge of a place that might have been somewhere, except I would never know where it was or how I got there. The foremost of the horsemen vaulted off his steed before the animal had even come to a halt. He was wearing a massive horned helmet which he removed as he strode forward, revealing a glistening bald pate. His face bore the same blue makeup which, upon closer inspection, appeared to be some sort of dark blue clay. It might have been my imagination, but it appeared as if the paint was decorated into the face of a human skull. That, as far as I was concerned, did not bode well. He stopped at the body of the fallen brute, staring at the gaping wound in the fellow's chest, then looked to me with fierce, dark eyes.

I drew myself up, cleared my throat, and said the first thing that came to my mind:

"A black-skinned fellow did it."

The skull-faced man stared at me, then back at his fellows. For all I knew they didn't even speak my language, but I persisted because I didn't see any other way out. "He was . . . a very large black man," I said. "And he had . . . several large black friends. They surrounded this man and assaulted him, and then took his valuables and ran away . . . because . . . because they were . . . black-skinned . . . and that's what such people do. . . ."

The farthest back of the horsemen urged his steed forward several steps, and upon closer inspection, even though he had blue clay upon his face, I realized that his lips were thick, his nose wide, and his skin under the clay was dark as coal.

". . . at least, so I'm told," I finished weakly.

Then the coal-black fellow's mouth split in a wide, white-toothed grin that was a very stark contrast to the color of his skin, and let out a loud, bellowing laugh. The man with the skull face joined in an instant later, and then all three of them were hooting with raucous amusement. The creature on my arm cast an annoyed glance from under its wing and then with a slight huffing sound endeavored to return to its restful state.

"Most amusing, Peacelord!" bellowed Skullface, and then to my astonishment he went to one knee, bowing his head. The other two men remained on their horses, but likewise bent their heads in deference to me. They remained that way, obviously waiting for me to give them leave to return to some other posture.

"As you were," I said hopefully.

That must have been what they were waiting to hear, for Skullface stood then and approached me, stopping several feet short and thereby maintaining what I could only think was a respectful distance. "You startled us, Peacelord. We were not expecting you to emerge from your tent."

"You weren't?" I asked, resisting the momentary impulse to look behind my shoulder to see just whom they might be addressing. The term "peacelord" was completely meaningless to me, but it obviously meant something to them. Even more obviously, I was the one who apparently bore the title, and if that was what was keeping me alive, then I was going to hold on to it with all the zeal I could muster.

"Of course not," said Skullface. "It would be foolish to risk our leader needlessly. But apparently the sneering challenges of this one," and he shoved a toe disdainfully into the behemoth's side, "were too much for the Peacelord to endure. Is that not right, Peacelord?"

"So it would seem," I said guardedly.

The black-skinned man on horseback said, "With all respect, Peacelord . . . I beg of you, do not allow the taunts of such a one to draw you into such situations. He is not worth it, even if he was the chieftain of the city."

"Imagine," said the Skullfaced one, shaking his head in disbelief, "endeavoring to forestall a good, old-fashioned rout by challenging you to a one-on-one battle in order to settle it. What was there to settle? The city was ours. There was nothing to be gained. Nothing at all."

"Yes, well," I said slowly, trying to choose each word as if it might be my last . . . since, for all I knew, it might be. "Some people . . . take foolish chances."

"Foolish in going up against you, Peacelord. Still . . . I wish that you had given us some warning," he said. "You simply disappeared from your tent. With the combination of your vanishing and . . . that . . . that strange darkness," and he shuddered as if speaking of something deplorable. "Well, Peacelord, the men were in a bit of a state. They could barely concentrate on the pillaging."

"Oh, well . . . that's tragic. Can't have that." I was trying to maintain a casual air on the outside, but inside my mind was racing. There seemed to be only two possibilities. Either these bruisers had me confused with someone else . . . or else I had somehow become this . . . this person. This "Peacelord," whatever that was. Perhaps . . . at the moment of death back in the Tragic Waste, my mind had somehow been transferred into the body of this person. But no, no that made no sense, for my staff and sword were right here beside me. I was definitely me. The question was, Who was I?

"Fortunately, Mordant was able to lead us right to you. Such a clever beast," said the black man. Realizing that he was referring to the creature on my arm, I just nodded. "How did you arrange to meet the chieftain here, Peacelord?" he continued.

I didn't have the faintest idea. But before I could say anything, I heard an agonized female shriek. For a heartbeat I thought it was Sharee, and then I saw a woman approaching out of the smoke. She was not a young woman, but still a handsome one. Her blond hair was streaked with soot from the burning city, as was her face, except tears were cutting through the ash upon her cheeks. I had no idea how she got as close as she did before being detected. Perhaps she had been in hiding nearby, waiting for the outcome of the battle. Considering that she was clearly distraught over the nonliving status of the man upon the ground, I decided that my surmise was accurate.

But Skullface clearly hadn't made that intuitive leap. Angrily he called out, "Where did she come from?" Instantly the black man and the third fellow were in front of the woman, their swords drawn. I could scarce believe the size and obvious weight of the blades. It was like they were wielding two teenagers. Still on horseback, they stepped into her path, crisscrossing the blades in front of her so that she could approach no further.

"Bastards!" she howled. "It takes two of you, with swords that could cleave a horse in twain, to halt the progress of one woman?!"

That was the moment that I decided to start pressing my new role, even though I didn't particularly understand it. "Let her pass!" I called in as arrogant a tone as I could muster (which, truthfully, wasn't all that hard). The swordsmen cast a glance at me as if to ascertain whether I was sure of what I was doing, and then they obediently urged their horses to step aside. They dismounted as the woman slowly approached the unmoving body, her hands fluttering to her lips, a desire to scream and sob clearly at war with a compulsion to hold herself together as much as possible in our presence. As a result her chin was trembling, but no sound emerged.

"Your lord husband, I take it," I inquired. She did not respond immediately, instead simply coming to a halt a couple feet away from him, as if afraid that death was a contagion and would leap from his corpse to her, annihilating her as well. "He believed the city was a loss and brought you here with him, not wanting to leave you to the mercy of "—I glanced at the men—"pillagers. So he hid you nearby, told you he'd be back for you once he had killed me. . . ." It was all guesswork, but it seemed reasonable.

She looked upon me as if only just then realizing that I was standing there. Her face twisted into a rictus of hatred then, and she shrieked, *Vladamore was a hundred times the leader, the warrior, the man that you'll ever be!*

I felt as if I was living out some demented dream. The only thing I could think to do was keep going along with it, hoping that either I would wake up soon, or else that somewhere along the way the entire business would start to make some sort of sense. All I knew at the moment was there was no need to upset the woman even more than she already was. Her city was sacked and her husband dead. I didn't see much point in thumbing my nose at her just to further annoy her. "I know that is how you will remember him, madam," I said quite formally.

"And what of me?" she demanded. "How shall I be remembered? As simply another one of your victims, you monstrous bastard?"

"Hold your tongue, woman," shot back Skullface, "lest I remove your tongue and hand it to you so that you can hold it literally." She silenced herself, but she was still smoldering as Skullface turned to me and inquired solicitously, "And what is to be done with this woman, Peacelord?"

"Yes, Peacelord," said the black. "Do you wish her killed? Do you wish to ravage her yourself, and then kill her? It is entirely your decision, Peacelord. We will carry out your desires."

Her face turned even more ashen than the ash that was already upon it, and for the second time that day, I felt a wave of nausea coming up from within. I managed to suppress it once more as my mind raced furiously. Whoever I was . . . was that what I was? A rapist and casual murderer? Is that what I had become? But how was it possible?

Before I could determine the answers to any of those questions, however, I needed to deal with the situation at hand. And certainly just standing by and letting the woman be killed was no way to deal with it. With my voice as firm and steady as I could make it, I said, "Let her go."

The men looked at me with the same amount of incredulity that I was probably feeling about the entire affair. "Let her go, Peacelord?" asked the black.

"Yes."

They exchanged glances, and as if in unspoken agreement, it was Skullface who voiced the query that all of them had. "We will of course obey you with our dying breaths, Peacelord. But I believe we have some . . . curiosity . . . as to why you would simply release the woman?"

"Because . . ." And I smiled as slyly as I could. "It is not what anyone expects."

Blank looks.

"Did you expect it?" I asked.

There was a collective shaking of heads to that, and I paced a bit as would a teacher lecturing students. "That, gentlemen, is precisely the point," I said. "One must always keep one's enemy off balance. The last thing that anyone would expect of your Peacelord is mercy. And so mercy is what I shall now extend. Let her go, I say," and I ratcheted up the firmness in my voice. Clearly still not understanding, but nevertheless acting out of obedience, the black and the other stepped aside, releasing their hold upon her.

I walked toward her slowly, my hands at either side so I did not appear in the least bit a threat. "Go," I said to her. "Go . . . and tell others of my merciful ways."

Her mouth moved at first with no sound emerging. Then, with a voice soaked in disbelief and contempt, she said, "*Merciful?* **You?** Last night my daughters were taken, my beautiful daughters . . . and your lieutenants raped and killed them while you stood there and laughed! *Merciful! You bastard! I'll die before I accept your mercy!*"

And before my shocked mind could fully process what she had just said, she spat at me. The glob sailed across the air and smacked me full on the face, the wet spittle running down my cheek, and 'ere I could make any sort of reaction, she came at me with her fingers curled like claws.

Skullface turned to intercept her before she'd gotten two paces. His sword was already a blur even as I cried out, *"No! She's harmless!"* and the sword sliced clean through her. I had never seen anything like it. From one side of her waist to the other, just right through, slowing down only marginally as it cut through sinew, bone, and muscle, and emerging on the other side. She didn't realize what had occurred at first, and then her legs buckled at the knees and she twisted toward the corpse of her husband. The motion caused her torso to topple clean off, and it thudded to the ground a short distance from the outstretched hand of her spouse. The full horror of what had happened to her had apparently not yet filtered through to her brain, and she flopped about horribly, single-mindedly trying to reach him, unaware that she was bereft of legs or even hips. Her fingers barely brushed the fingertips of her dead husband as blood and guts spilled out from both halves of her upon the ash-stained ground, and then there was an awful rattle from her throat, and she was gone.

"The nerve of the ungrateful bitch," growled Skullface as he wiped clean his broadsword on a cloth and then sheathed it. He looked to me, and my teeth and lips were clamped as tightly closed as I could make them. A grin split his face then, made all the more horrible by the blue death's-head mask painted upon his face. "I understand now, Peacelord. You intended for her to make others believe you were capable of mercy . . . so that, when they face us, they will quickly surrender in anticipation of their lives being spared. When actually—"

"When actually," took up the black, apparently 'comprehending' as well, "we will annihilate them once they have given up! Was that the plan, Peacelord?"

I managed a nod.

Immediately there was raucous laughter as they now "knew" what I had been plotting. "My deepest apologies, Peacelord, for cutting the woman down and aborting the plan," said Skullface when they had recovered. "But I am sworn to protect you from both physical harm and, even more, shows of disrespect. After what she did, she could not be permitted to live. You do agree, do you not, Peacelord?"

I nodded once more, then raised a finger to indicate that I

would be right back. I walked a short distance away and found some ragged bushes, possibly the former hiding place of the dead woman whose name I had never even learned. Once behind the bushes, I shook loose the creature perched upon my arm, the one they'd called Mordant. Mordant looked somewhat annoyed with me as he lifted clear of my arm and flapped a short distance away. And then I finally succumbed to the roiling of my innards and unleashed what was within. My guts spasmed until I felt I had surely vomited up not only the contents of my stomach, but possibly the stomach itself. I was bent over, my breath coming in ragged gasps, and it was only then that I noticed the dagger strapped to my left calf.

I did not hesitate. I yanked out the dagger and held it over my breast. Right then and there, there was nothing that I desired more than to take my life. For either I was already dead and in hell, in which case my actions were really irrelevant to the proceedings. Or else I was alive and had become—through no fault of my own— the sort of monster that I had spent my life fearing.

It has been said that suicide is the coward's way out. Well, I can tell you with assurance that such is not the case, for I am an inveterate coward, and I couldn't do it. The knife was poised, ready to be plunged into my heart . . . provided I still had one, considering the number of times I had been accused of being heartless . . . but I simply could not bring myself to complete the act. I've no idea how long I remained like that before, defeated by my own weakness, I slid the dagger back into its scabbard on my leg. I then made my way back to the men, who looked at me questioningly.

"Call of nature," I said simply, not being able to bring myself to look upon the bisected woman who had stained the ground dark with her life's blood. I should have given the order to bury her, or . . . or something. But I couldn't think of anything to do. All I wanted was to leave that appalling place as quickly as possible.

Mordant flew around me, but I made no effort to raise my arm, which felt as weak and useless as the rest of me, so he circled one more time and then headed off in some damned direction.

"We'd best be heading back, Peacelord," said Skullface. "Nothing more is to be gained here. The city is fallen and sacked, its leaders dead. You have successfully overseen another campaign. There is no reason not to break down camp and return home. Certainly," and he laughed knowingly, "your lady misses you."

"My lady," I echoed.

"Yes, Peacelord. We passed Entipy on the way, but she would not come with us. She only comes when you call."

I was leaning on my staff, trying to make sense of the world. I was so cloaked in ash and soot that I felt as if I could sit and soak in water for a full day and still not wash the grime of the place from me. Nevertheless I heard what he had just said, and it made absolutely no sense to me. "En . . . tipy?" I asked.

"Yes, Peacelord," the black spoke up. "She awaits your summons."

They all looked at me expectantly, and so—still not understanding, but feeling as if I should do *something*—I cupped my hands to my mouth and called, *"Entipy!"*

At first there was no response, and realistically I had no idea why there should be one. The only Entipy I knew of was miles away back in Isteria . . . unless . . .

A horrible thought occurred to me. What if . . . what if I was, in fact, back in Isteria somehow? And I had ransacked it with some sort of army at my command, and now Entipy was my slave? I didn't know which was a more hideous notion. That I had conquered my former homeland, or that I had been so insane that I had actually gone out of my way to hook back up with the demented little princess.

But all my questions dissolved when I heard an answering whinny, and a few moments later a magnificent white horse with a mane of hair that was almost flaming red galloped up to me and stood there, awaiting my pleasure. She wore a gorgeous, ornate saddle with lions and dragons etched within it. "Good Entipy," said Skullface approvingly.

I'd named my horse Entipy. No doubt so that I could finally

control her and mount her without guilt whenever I wished. Well, whatever the hell had happened to me, clearly I had not lost my sense of the ironic. I slipped my left foot into the stirrup and then hauled myself up and over, swinging my useless right leg into place. Gods, from that vantage point she was an even more glorious piece of horseflesh than I'd thought. I could sense the muscles and power beneath me. I wanted to snap the reins, start her galloping, and ride away from this insanity as hard and quickly as I humanly could. I wondered if there was a way that I could leave these brutes behind, even leave the memories behind. But I had every reason to assume that they would easily be able to overtake me, and once they did . . . then what? What pretext could I possibly come up with to explain my turning and bolting?

None. None at all.

For better or worse—and it was most definitely leaning toward worse—I had to play this insanity out. I had to determine just why all this had occurred, and where I was and for that matter, who I was. Where was home, and who was this "lady" to whom they'd referred?

As we set off, I afforded a final glance behind myself at the two corpses lying on the ground, forlorn and tragic, and I swore right then and there that—whatever had happened while I was not in my right mind—no more lives would be lost now that I had regained control of myself.

How little I knew.

Chapter 2

The Woad Home

*W*e proceeded at a brisk trot, and I learned a few things along the way. The first was the names of my "companions." The Skullfaced monster, the one who had casually split the woman in two with no more thought or effort than if he'd been chopping wood for a fire, went by the name of Boar Tooth. Somehow I had a feeling that wasn't his birth name. Boar Tooth, as near as I could tell, served as my right-hand man. I immediately resolved to spend time trying to determine the best way to cut off my right hand. The black riding alongside him sported the daunting name of Salaahaahkim, although Boar Tooth tended to refer to him simply as "Slake." And since he answered to it, I took that to be his accepted name of battle. He hailed from a land called Uhfrika, and was a rather convivial sort when he wasn't laughing over the misfortune of others. And the third fellow, the one who seemed to have nothing to say about anything, was simply referred to as That Guy since no one had ever learned his name and he'd never bothered to introduce himself. He'd just shown up one day, joined up, and had proven himself to be a formidable fighter who followed orders without question. He seemed to care about nothing except doing as he was told, ravaging and pillaging as it was convenient, and otherwise just waiting around for the next order. It was unknown whether his tongue was cut out or he knew no language or if he was just bone stupid, and no one much seemed to care since it had no impact whatsoever on his performance.

The second thing I learned was something rather significant about myself.

We were riding along, the burning city already fading into the background. We had made our way over toward what appeared to be a main road of sorts, and were pounding down it when I chanced to reach up and scratch an itch on the side of my face. I was astounded to discover that there was blue clay under my fingernails. As quickly as I could find convenient, I signaled a stop when we passed what appeared to be a well. My men looked at me questioningly. "I want to water the horses," I said.

"Peacelord," Boar Tooth said reasonably, "the animals are not in need of—"

"Entipy is. I can tell." *Keep it light, keep it light,* my inner voice warned me, and it always seemed to have more intelligence than I in these matters. *These men are stone-cold killers, and if they think that you are no longer of use to them, they might serve you up as they did that unfortunate women. So keep it light.* Doing my best to sound as casual about the matter as possible, I added, "And we wouldn't want the other horses to get jealous of Entipy's special treatment, would we?"

This caused some brief laughter among the men, which I reasoned was better than a cry of "Kill him!" Moments later That Guy was pulling water up in a bucket that was hanging conveniently on a rope, and I took the bucket from him in order to bring it over to Entipy.

Except that wasn't the real reason I'd ordered the stop.

I stared into the water and saw my reflection.

I looked at least a year older than I remembered myself. Whether that was because of the actual passage of time, or because of emotional draining that had occurred as a result of my apparent change in vocation—going from tavern and inn owner to slaughtering overseer of death and destruction—I had no way of knowing. Either way, it was difficult for me to tell just how much time had passed because my face was covered with the same blue makeup as they were sporting. Parts of it reached all the way across my face, while others came only part way. Most curious of all, there was what appeared to be a sort of demented smile etched in blue in the middle of my forehead.

"Peacelord?" The curious prodding came from Boar Tooth, and I looked up at him and was glad that my face was painted, because I was sure that I was pale beneath the makeup. "Is something wrong?"

"Wrong?" I echoed.

"Yes." Boar Tooth smiled. He'd had that exact same smile on his face when he'd cut down the hysterical widow several hours earlier. "You look as if you've never seen woad before."

"Woad."

Slake was walking over toward us, and there was concern on his face. "Woad, Peacelord." He took a bit of the blue makeup between his fingers and rubbed them together. "This. This is woad. Peacelord, are you quite all right?"

"Perhaps he sustained some sort of blow to the head in his battle with the chieftain," Boar Tooth suggested, sharing Slake's look of worry. "Peacelord . . . were you injured in any way during that fight?"

My reflex was to say no, but I immediately caught myself. Instead I slowly lowered the bucket and then fought to "remember" what had transpired. As if speaking from very far away, I said slowly, "In dodging one of his blows . . . I think I fell backward . . . struck my head. Difficult to be sure . . ."

Boar Tooth nodded as if this confirmed his worst suspicions. "We'd best have a healer take a look at him when we get back," said Boar Tooth to Slake, as if I were not even there. "If he was injured in some way, we have to know. . . ."

"No healer will be necessary. I'm quite sure I'm all right," I said in a conciliatory tone. "I trust, however, that you will be understanding of me if I seem a bit, well . . . slow every now and again. Given time, I will undoubtedly be up to my old self."

"Of course, Peacelord!" said Boar Tooth, and Slake echoed his agreement. That Guy just watched the proceedings while bringing the bucket over to his own mount to drink.

"Wuin," I suddenly said.

"Yes, Peacelord?"

"That is where home is."

"Well, of course, Peacelord," Slake said. "Wuin, which was once an assortment of tribal colonies, now all under your rule. And now you are expanding your rule beyond the borders of Wuin. You will be the greatest Peacelord in the history of Wuin."

"You . . . remember that, do you not, Peacelord?" asked Boar Tooth cautiously.

"Of course," I said, and then forced a smile. "I just like hearing about it, that is all." *Good. Keep it light. Keep it light.*

As we mounted up once more, my mind raced back to the words of the Visionary. The one who had spoken of a road to ruin . . . except it appeared that such was not the case at all. It had indeed been woad, not road, and it was with this bizarre blue face make-up that I was wearing which was bringing me to Wuin . . . or back to Wuin, as the case may be.

The creature called Mordant continued to track us overhead, although occasionally he flew on far ahead, only to return to us at random times. At one point he swooped down and dropped a dead rodent in my lap. Clearly it was intended as an offering of some sort, a desire to share his food. I tossed it back up to Mordant, who snatched the tidbit in midair and gobbled it, before emitting a squawk and flying off once more, his tail twisting in the air.

As we rode, we passed men along the way. My men. They, like

we, were returning from the city that was in flames (a city which, I learned, had been known as Jaifa). They were loaded down with loot, and they were laughing and singing my praises, and were all the more overjoyed when I arrived in their midst. Eventually, as the sun went down and the shadows lengthened, we made camp and pockets of returning men joined us. There was plenty to eat, for much food had been stolen from Jaifa, and there were women, gods yes, there were women, who had been taken by the men to be used as they saw fit. Most of them were bound at the hands, and some walked free, but they all had a downcast and frightened look to them. Many of them were horribly, horribly young, and they cast apprehensive glances in my direction every so often. I couldn't determine whether they were hoping I would intercede, or were afraid that I might take my pleasure of one or more of them. Well, the former was not really an option, and as for the latter . . . despite what Sharee might have believed, I was not a brutalizer of women and had no intention of taking up that occupation. Still, I felt terribly guilty about my helplessness. How incredibly tragic that I was apparently the commander of these troops—which had swelled to over a hundred in our encampment—and yet I was powerless to remedy these women's plight. I dared not do anything, take any action, that would be drastically different from that which I had done before. I dared not arouse suspicions, and if the choice was giving precedence to the predicament of these women versus mine own, I knew who I was going to vote for.

There was much singing and rough laughter throughout the night, and many of the songs were about my exploits. I had been the subject of ballads and chants before, although invariably I was the butt of jokes or the target of scorn within them. Not this night. Every song, every chorus of every song, focused on some new great deed that I had performed. The Peacelord did this, the Peacelord did that, the Peacelord did some other damned thing. And all of the accomplishments of which they sang were uniformly brutal. I overcame some town, or overthrew some monarch, or slaughtered enemies right and left with a sword as unstoppable as a typhoon and the strength of a hundred demons spat from hell. I knew that the subjects of these songs tend to be exaggerated out of all proportion to their accomplishments, but I had to admit, if I'd been accomplishing even a fraction of what I was hearing about, I'd done far more than I'd ever expected to do in my life.

But all of it, all of it was destruction. No songs about creating anything. About building a city, or sparing people out of compassion, or inspiring great deeds and achievements not having to do with war. It was all bloodshed and slaughter, chaos and misery inflicted throughout the land of Wuin, all from me. I truly had no idea what I had become, but it sickened me.

As we sat around a campfire, our bellies filled with freshly cooked meat, I tried to turn my attention away from the piteous female cries in the near distance. Mordant had returned and curled up around my leg. Meantime Slake, seated a few feet away, was strumming a lyre. He hummed a few notes. Then he called out, "A newly written chant, Peacelord. Find favor in it, if it pleases you to do so." And he sang out . . .

Sing ho, sing ho, for Apropos, he'll conquer and he'll slaughter.
Sing ho, sing ho, for Apropos, and lock away your daughter.
He cuts a path of death and blood throughout our land of Wuin.
The chieftains do not have a clue of any plans he's brewin'.
Sing ho, sing ho, for Apropos, with hair so fiery red.
Sing ho, sing ho, for Apropos, don't cross him or you're dead.
The foolish Vladamore he thought to challenge our great leader,
Who knew that Vladamore would be so copious a bleeder?
His widow sought, through foul means, to kill him! What a laugh!
His sword cut through and now she is a woman and a half!
Sing ho, sing ho, for Apropos, the greatest of the great!
Sing ho, sing ho, for Apropos. Surrender! Ah, too late!

Up until that moment, I had held out hope that I wasn't known for who I was. After all, they'd just addressed me as "Peacelord." Obviously, however, my hopes were in vain. If my real name was in a song, then the identity of the Peacelord of Wuin was widely known in all the territories. But I didn't betray my thoughts. Instead, as Slake bowed his head slightly, clearly waiting for approval, I nodded in acknowledgment and then joined the others who applauded in raucous approbation. Then I pointed out, "Well constructed, Slake, but not entirely accurate. Boar Tooth slew the woman, not me."

Boar Tooth, seated just to the side of Slake, shook his head and shrugged. "It is of no consequence, Peacelord. The song works far better focusing on your deeds. Introducing me that late into the lyric . . . it serves no purpose. The joy of the kill was sufficient for me; let the songs be about others."

The joy of the kill. The woman's face, the sight of her dead next to her husband, haunted me long into what I anticipated would be a sleepless night, and those words followed me as well.

Boar Tooth offered to have a tent pitched for me, but I demurred, instead saying that I preferred to sleep under the stars this night. This got a rousing ovation from the men, who saw in that decision the common touch of their beloved Peacelord. As for me, I simply chose to be out in the open because if someone was coming for me with a sword, I wanted to be able to see them in enough time to do something about it.

I lay there for a while, Mordant curled up at my feet, staring up at the sky. I stared at the constellations, those great mind games in the sky, and wondered what it was about humanity that required that we see a pattern in all things. There were the stars, random bits of light caused by the eyes of gods, or souls of heroes who watched over us, or souls of villains who looked in frustration upon those whom they failed to annihilate, all of it depending upon what one's individual philosophy was. And stargazers enjoyed looking to the skies and drawing imaginary lines to connect them, desperately speculating that the stars actually formed pictures. Pattern-seeking, as I said.

Yet I looked upon my life and saw no pattern at all. Once again, I found myself dwelling on the notion of gods and their ostensible plans for us. Why was it that people could not accept the notion that things happened for no good reason to people who didn't deserve it? That there was no pattern? Just random events strung together until the inevitable conclusion that awaited us all?

I felt myself drifting, wondering if sleep would indeed claim me. There were patches of raucous laughter, stories of great deeds told, but all of the noise began to blur together in a haze. I floated in that eerie realm that was just in the twilight place between wakefulness and sleep, and then realized that Mordant was no longer at my feet. Instead the strange birdlike reptilian creature had placed itself directly in front of my face, and was staring at me with those slitted eyes. I saw my face reflected in them. "What do *you* want?" I heard myself say.

"What do *you* want?" returned Mordant. His voice was thin and reedy and had an air of dripping sarcasm and infinite superiority.

It took a few moments for my fatigued mind to process what had just occurred. "You . . . you spoke," I said. "You can speak."

I sounded rather stupid to myself. Obviously I sounded the same way to Mordant, because he snorted and little puffs of smoke came from the edges of his beak. "Brilliant observation. Now, how about telling me something I don't know? Like what you've done to yourself. Why you've changed."

I sat up slowly, feeling that the world was lurching in a strange haze around me. "Changed? I . . . don't know what you're talking ab—"

"I saw you vomiting up an entire day's worth of food behind the bush," Mordant reminded me. He had turned his head sideways and was staring at me in a most cockeyed manner. "And then you tried to take your own life, except you lacked the spirit to finish the job. All because Boar Tooth sliced that woman down. Back in the day, you would simply have laughed. And your aura's different."

"My . . . aura." This time I really didn't have any idea what he was talking about. My mind was still trying to wrap itself around the notion that this . . . this winged thing had struck up a conversation with me.

He gave out an annoyed squawk. "Yes, your aura. Everyone has a different aura that comes from a sort of bodily energy. You didn't know that?"

"No, but then I didn't know that you talked, either, so there's apparently a lot of which I am unaware." I leaned closer in toward him. "Do you always talk?"

"No, humans always talk. Even when they've nothing to say. Actually, especially when they've nothing to say. At times like those, they substitute volume for sense." He glanced around a moment, apparently tracking something small flying through the air. Then his beak speared out and snagged what I saw at the last moment was some sort of insect. He chomped down on it and munched it. "Now, me . . . I only talk when it seems as if it'll be of value. Tell me, do you have the faintest idea what's going on?"

I shook my head forlornly.

"Didn't think so," said Mordant. He tapped the ground thoughtfully with one of his curved talons, making a loud clicking noise as he did so. "Guess I'll have to do the thinking for both of us then."

"Hey!" I said in protest, starting to feel a bit ill-used by this insect-eating little monster. "I've been doing fine handling my own thinking until now."

"Uh-huh. What's your consort's name?"

I stared at him.

"Where exactly, geographically, are you?" he continued, relentless. He was drumming his talons harder on the ground, little sprays of dirt bouncing up from where his claws hit. "How many men do you have at your command? How long have you been Peacelord of Wuin?"

The blankness of my expression obviously didn't impress him very much.

"Right. Excellent," he said sarcastically. "You're doing bleeding wonderfully on your own then, aren't you. You know, I hooked up with you because you seemed a rather interesting individual, and also because forces for destruction tend to leave a lot of nice pickings around for creatures like me. But now, I don't know. Something's happened to you, and I'm not sure what it is, and I know you don't know. . . ."

"Yes, yes, you've made very clear how little I know," I said, my patience wearing thin. "But I can tell you one thing with certainty: You're starting to annoy the hell out of me."

"Well, the hell in you is the problem, isn't it."

I looked blankly at him, which seemed to be the only expression I was capable of having anymore. Every bone in my body felt achy, as if I was being weighted down by my own carcass. The world was starting to thicken around me. I could have been a swimmer who was sinking beneath the waves, drawing his final breaths of air and knowing that it wasn't going to last him very long.

And Mordant was looking away from me, actually studying his talons like a casual human examining his fingernails before delivering some final, parting shot. "But you've made it clear. You don't need my help. That's fine. That's perfectly fine. I won't open my mouth again. You can just take care of everything, while I sit by and watch this entire life of conquest you've built collapse around your ears."

"Yes, well you just do that," I said, but my voice sounded within my own head as if there was the rushing of the wind accompanying it. I was slumping over to one side, and the next thing I knew my head was hitting the ground as I became overwhelmed with the desire to go back to sleep . . .

. . . presuming that I had ever woken up to begin with.

I awoke just before dawn, just as the sun's rays were beginning to filter over the horizon. I propped myself up on my elbows, and the first thing I saw was Mordant lying there, by my feet just as I'd initially recalled. "You!" I whispered as I shoved at him with my foot. "Wake up! I'm not done talking to you yet!"

Mordant opened one lazy eye and raised his head, looking rather put off that I had rousted him from his slumber.

"What did you mean, the hell in me? What hell? How is it *in* me?" I demanded. "If you want me to admit I could use your help, fine, I admit it! There! Happy?"

Mordant opened his mouth, and I thought he was about to speak, but all he did was widen his beak in a powerful yawn and then start to rest his head back upon his talons, which were neatly crisscrossed over each other upon the ground. I shoved at him again and his head snapped up once more. This time he really looked irritated. But I was too incensed to care.

"You want me to beg? Is that it? You want me to beg for your help? Do—"

"Peacelord?"

For a moment my heart jumped as I thought that Mordant had spoken. But then I realized it was Slake's voice. I sat fully up and turned at the waist to see that Slake was seated on the ground nearby, rubbing the sleep from his eyes and looking at me most oddly. "Peacelord, are you . . . talking to Mordant?"

"Yes," I said guardedly.

"But . . . Peacelord . . . Mordant is a drabit. Drabits don't talk . . . as a rule."

"I know that. Of course I know that," I said quickly. "But . . . sometimes . . . when I'm trying to think things through, I talk to whatever's near, however incapable of speech it may be. Just to . . . say things out loud, see how they sound."

"Oh," said Slake, clearly not understanding but also not wanting to make his confusion so evident. "Well . . . as you wish, Peacelord. Shall I rouse the troops? It's still early, but . . ."

I looked at the sea of snoring men, and considered the notion of waking them from their slumber prematurely, thus certainly annoying every one of them.

"I hardly think that's necessary," I said quickly. "Go back to sleep, Slake. I . . . wish to be alone with my thoughts."

"As you desire, Peacelord," he said uncertainly, and he settled back down to sleep . . . although before he did so, he cast one final, wary look in my direction.

Mordant, in the meantime, smoothed his feathers and settled himself back down at my feet. As softly as I could—so softly that I was reasonably sure Slake wouldn't hear me—I muttered,

"You're going to leave me wondering if I dreamt it all, aren't you?"

The drabit (for such was his species called, apparently) looked at me with a sideways glance that told me absolutely nothing, and then settled back down.

"This is just getting better and better," I muttered and went back to sleep.

The rest of the trip went uneventfully. Mordant did not open his mouth again, although every so often I fancied that the looks he was giving me were filled with the same judgmental contempt that he'd displayed when he'd vocalized. By that point I was so utterly confused that I truly had no clue whether he'd spoken or I'd dreamt the whole thing. Which, if he was capable of speech, was exactly what he was hoping would happen.

I kept mostly to myself on the sojourn back to wherever the hell we had come from. This was not all that difficult; I simply told Boar Tooth that I wished to be alone to contemplate future excursions against our potential enemies. No one questioned me. That was one of the advantages of being a supreme ruler, or whatever my status might be. It also benefited me greatly in that I didn't have to spend all the time worrying that someone would say something to me that put me in a difficult position . . . namely having to admit that I didn't recall something that was common knowledge to everyone around me.

I knew enough about how these things worked, you see, to know the main reason for the downfall of people in my position. And that reason was weakness of any sort, be it real or perceived. I had awoken from what might have been some sort of lengthy, even mystical coma, to find that I was in exactly the situation in life that I had always sought to avoid: a target. There is no greater target than someone in power, because there are always those without it who want it, and perceive that the quickest way to obtain it is to kill you.

My main candidate for that philosophy was Boar Tooth, who seemed deferential enough, but I didn't trust him for a moment.

Not that any of the others were more trustworthy. The only person I trusted implicitly within a ten-mile radius was myself, and considering I knew how duplicitous I could be, that left me feeling rather friendless. Oh, I might have had a friend in the drabit, except I was beginning to suspect that he was indeed just a dumb animal who had briefly occupied an odd place in my waking dreams.

Nothing caused decay in one's power base faster than one's followers believing that one was incompetent to lead. I dared not leave myself exposed in that manner . . . not in the company of beasts so brutal that they could cut down a grieving widow and think nothing of it. If a hysterical woman elicited no mercy or pity from them, a confused and crippled warmonger was hardly in a better position.

Well into the third day of travel, I saw people running toward us. At first I thought they might be people fleeing more of my army, but then I saw that they were calling my name and cheering us as if we were conquering heroes. I realized then that they were greeting us, welcoming us for the purpose of escorting us back to my stronghold. That was how I knew we were getting fairly close to it. Boar Tooth, astride his own horse, rode in close to me and grinned. "It will be good to be home, Peacelord. This has been a profitable and exciting campaign, but every so often it's good to rest and replenish the spirit in familiar haunts, eh?"

"Well said, Boar Tooth," I said, and then mentally added the words, *you murdering swine,* while keeping a smile fixed upon my face.

They were all about us, and not just men. Women were looking up at us, laughing and singing my name, and children as well. Children were smiling, skipping and dancing around us, and I wanted to scream, *We're murderers! Murderers, ravagers, brutes! We fall upon helpless cities and annihilate them as if we have some sort of right to do so, while the gods sit by and welcome their tortured souls because they couldn't bother to help them in life! How can you acclaim us? How can you cavort about and treat us as if we are heroes when we are, in fact, bullies and barbarians of the worst kind!*

Naturally they didn't respond, since they couldn't hear me. But Mordant circled around once and then landed on my outstretched arm, staring at me coolly. I wished I knew what was going on through that birdlike head of his. Was he just staring at me in brainless anticipation of his next meal? Or was he somehow intuiting what was in my heart and mind, and feeling either sympathy or—more likely—pity for me?

"Go find something to eat," I told him and shook him loose, as children bounded about me and threw dried flowers upon me.

Just over a rise I saw our destination, and I had to admit that even I was impressed.

There was a small brace of mountains ahead of us, and literally built into one of them was a fortress. Towers stretched tall and proud toward the sun, flags fluttering from the uppermost spires. Rather than a wall having been built around it, the fortress—as near as I could tell—instead sat within a wide, flat crevasse, surrounded by a headwall that was a natural extension of the mountain's ridges. Although naturally I couldn't see it from where we were positioned, I had a feeling that the opposite side of the mountains were utterly sheer and incapable of being climbed by anything human. If there had been snowfall there of any size, the place would have been ripe for avalanche. But here in the fairly barren wastelands of Wuin, I strongly suspected that excessive snowfall was not a major consideration. In short, the placed looked . . .

"Unassailable," I said softly. A child pawed at my leg, begging me to favor him with a look. I pushed him away and kept my horse riding forward, resolutely ignoring the pleadings of others to speak kind words to them. The thought of innocent children worshipping the evil that I represented was repellent to me. I had just spent three days listening to songs and poems about all the barbaric, brutal activities that had been undertaken in my name. I didn't feel worthy of worship.

Boar Tooth overheard my muttered comment, and he laughed loudly. "As the song goes, Lamalos thought much the same thing, did he not?"

"Lamalos." The name meant nothing, but I hazarded a guess. "The previous . . . resident."

Again Boar Tooth laughed. "The previous, until you dispatched him in his sleep! Haw! The look of stupidity on his face, frozen forever on his decapitated skull!"

"In his sleep. Yes, that was . . . that was very clever of me." I was relieved that I had had almost nothing for breakfast that morning, for it might very well have made a return engagement.

"What a day of glory that was, when you captured Dreadnaught fortress. Although," and he lowered his voice in a conspiratorial fashion, "there are some who still mutter that the Lady Kate was the instigator and developer of the great plan. The songs credit you, of course, but still . . . you should have a chat with the Lady to make certain—"

I fired him a look that instantly silenced him. "Are you tendering advice to me, Boar Tooth, as to how I should conduct myself with my consort? You overstep yourself."

What I could see of Boar Tooth's face beneath the woad flushed significantly. *You're angering a man who cut a helpless woman in half! Are you insane?!* That fairly reasonable reaction passed through my head as the jeopardy of potentially antagonizing Boar Tooth presented itself, but the barbarian simply bowed his head slightly and said, "Forgive me, Peacelord. I overstepped myself. It shall not happen again."

"See that it doesn't," I said, impressing myself with how brazen I was being.

A cloudless sky hung over us, and the air was so warm as to border on oppressive as we approached the stronghold known as Dreadnaught. I wondered how it was that I had managed to overcome this place. Indeed, even more than the method, I couldn't comprehend the motivation. What in the world had possessed me to embark upon such a mission of conquest, even if I was not in my right mind? And if I wasn't in my right mind . . .

. . . then whose mind was I in?

The way down from the plateau we were on was steep, but the

horses handled the descent with surefooted confidence. All around me were warriors, my warriors, laughing and chatting and bellowing about triumphs they had achieved in my name, while thumping their chests with their massive fists. In some cases women clambered up onto the horses with them, insinuating their bodies against them and half hanging out of what little clothes they were wearing. I did not get the impression these were overjoyed spouses greeting their returning mates, but rather former conquests who were trying to please random masters. Trailing behind our entourage were captives, tied at the wrists, young women for the most part who looked frightened and haunted. They saw what they perceived as their likely future, and they huddled together, pulling back reflexively and slowing down the entourage. That Guy, who was overseeing the captives, pulled a whip from the side of his saddle and cracked it with expertise near them. They cried out, cowered, and That Guy pointed angrily that they should fall into pace with the group. They did so immediately and meekly.

At that moment I wanted nothing more than to order them all to be released. But if I did that, I'd likely be signing my own death warrant, and as much as my heart went out to them, I valued my own skin over theirs. So I, the Supreme Ruler of the group, said nothing out of fear.

Once we descended from the plateau, the road leading up to Dreadnaught was fairly clear, except for the fact that it was lined with welcomers and well-wishers. Little bits of gaily colored cloth were thrown in our path, and names of various warriors were called out from people who were either family members, lovers, or simply fans of assorted individuals. One would have thought that we were conquering heroes instead of beasts and brutes.

And yet . . .

. . . and yet . . .

I felt myself smiling.

I didn't realize it at first because, truth to tell, I don't smile all that much. I allow myself a knowing smirk every now and then, or a wry upturn of the lips in observing life's foibles. But for the most part I disdained full-blown displays of genuine joy, since I disliked such overt exhibitions of sentiment and because, well . . . I was almost never that happy. So a full-out grin upon my mien would find itself on quite virgin territory.

But that's precisely what I was doing. A broad grin upon the face of Apropos the Peacelord, greeting the revelers and well-wishers and celebrants. They clustered around Entipy (the horse, not the princess) and all they wanted to do was just get close enough to touch her, or me, or both of us.

I remembered being a squire back in the keeping of King Runcible, and I would witness the homecoming of knights who had been out and about fighting some damned war or another. This would be the sort of welcome they would receive, and jealousy had always stirred in my guts over it. I myself had never been the recipient of such mass accolades. The closest I'd come was when I'd received my knighthood, and that was done in the court of King Runcible rather than outside where the peasantry could participate. And besides, that one brief moment of acceptance had quickly been transformed into a nightmare, so that hardly seemed to count.

In this case, though, the nightmare had been everything leading up to this point. The slaughter, the songs of my beastly deeds, that surreal twilight-waking discussion with Mordant. But if that was nightmare, this was the joyful wakening to acclaim and adulation. I had to admit, there was something to be said for it.

The hand of worship has most seductive fingers, and they were beginning, ever so slightly, to wrap themselves about me.

The joyous caravan approached the wall of rock that surrounded the stronghold, and I wondered how in the world we were supposed to pass. I had been supposing that, upon closer inspection, there would be some sort of narrow canyon or fissure through which we would traverse. But there was nothing at all, not a damned thing. I almost leaned over and inquired of Slake how we were supposed to make our entrance, but fortunately caught myself at the last moment.

And then I heard what sounded like a massive scraping, and grinding, and for a moment I thought that the ground beneath my feet was beginning to quake. That was when I saw it, and I could scarce believe it. An entire section of the wall was sliding upward. As we drew closer still, I saw that the whole thing was being accomplished through a system of gears and pulleys so complicated that I could scarcely comprehend it. Yet so efficient was it that, despite the massive heft of the stone, it was being raised with ease by about half a dozen men whom I could see pulling taut chains on the far side. They made fast the chains then, and the processional passed under the rocky gateway.

I had some momentary trepidation about doing so. If the links broke or in some other way the moorings were released, that thing would come slamming down and there wouldn't be enough left of me to pour over into a small urn. But no one else seemed the least bit concerned, and I figured that it would hardly do for their nominal leader to be faint of heart about something as simple as entering through the front door. So I scraped together what I laughingly referred to as my resolve and tried to look as relaxed and nonchalant as possible as we passed under what had to be several thousand pounds of certain death.

Once the last of us were through, the main gate was lowered slowly back into place, sealing the rest of the world out . . . and, unfortunately, sealing me in. "Unfortunate" because I was a great advocate of leaving myself a route out of town that could be taken as quickly as possible should matters head precipitously south. That was not an option here in Dreadnaught, although I found myself wondering just how in the world I had managed to conquer the previous occupants. What, had I somehow mastered the power of flight and soared over the walls as easily as the drabit? I might have ridden Mordant had he been some sort of full-sized flying beast, but the drabit wasn't large enough to carry a baby much less a full-grown adult. So what in the world had I done?

The stronghold itself was nothing spectacular. Oh, the strategic positioning of it was unparalleled, and the construction was solid enough, I suppose. But the design of the place was not only uninspired, but positively dreary. There was no elegance, no grace, no majesty to it as there had been in the domicile of King Runcible. There were no intricate carvings in the walls, not much in the way of statuary to speak of. And what there was, was hideous. Grotesque dragons, and twisted gargoyles, and in one corner was, if I wasn't mistaken, a Gorgon. The place reeked of dark doings and foulness and unpleasantries behind the walls. It didn't strike me as quite as depraved as the domicile of the dreaded Warlord Shank—he with his furniture made from bones of his victims. But it certainly approached that level of perversity in its own way.

The procession drew to a halt outside the main archway that led into the castle, and at first I couldn't quite determine why. But then I saw a woman emerging through the archway, the entirety of her attention fixed on me.

It may sound overstated to say that she nearly took my breath away, but I assure you, that was no exaggeration. She was quite simply the most beautiful woman I had ever seen.

She was dressed in silks of the purest white, with cleavage cut low enough to be seductive but not so low as to be slattern. The gown clung to her, giving a healthy idea of the bounties of her body, with its generous hips and full breasts, and legs that seemed to end somewhere around her collarbone. Her hair was a waterfall of blonde cascading around her shapely shoulders, and her skin was quite pale, but with vibrant spots of red on her cheeks as if she were literally a blushing bride. Her eyes were blue and wide and luminous and full of . . . well, full of me, for clearly to her the rest of the world had dissolved away into irrelevance, and only I mattered.

In short, she was my kind of female.

I climbed down from Entipy (and how I delight in saying that, even now, I cannot begin to tell you) and, with my walking staff firmly in hand, made my way over to her with as much confidence and polish as my lame leg would allow. She took my hand in hers, held it to her cheek, and said loudly, addressing the crowd as much as she was me, "Welcome home, my conquering beloved."

Well, this set off a hullabaloo as you can only imagine, with cheers and shouts and "Huzzahs!" ringing off the walls of the stronghold and filling the air with joy and celebration.

She put her arm around mine and led me toward the main hall of the stronghold itself. From within the aroma of a bounteous feast being prepared wafted out to me, and my nostrils flared with delight. There was beef, and poultry, and fresh-baked bread, and other scents that I could not even begin to identify. It had been an eternity since a banquet such as that had been presented me, and after all that I had been through, I felt as if I deserved it.

It was at that instant, for no reason I can relate, that I realized I hadn't given Sharee, or her fate, a moment's thought in days. But as quickly as that occurred to me, it passed. And for just an instant I wanted to glance behind me and see how the female prisoners, bound together and frightened over what was to become of them, were reacting to the welcoming festivities. But I did not. It wasn't because I was afraid to. It was because, at that moment, I didn't care one way or the other.

And thus did those same seductive fingers of the hand of worship increase their hold on me ever so slightly more.

Chapter 3

Bathing the Family Jewels

*T*he interior of the stronghold was no more impressive than the exterior. It was immensely drafty, and many of the rooms seemed functional at best. But there were also copious decorations and riches spread about casually . . . so casually, in fact, that the place seemed to be furnished in Early Chaotic. Statues, busts, tapestries, trinkets, and the like were simply tossed about with neither rhyme nor reason. I could scarce comprehend it. If anyone had given any thought to the layout or adornment of the place, that thought had apparently been limited to "Let's put things anywhere we want." I nearly banged my leg against an elaborately festooned chair which was sitting out in the middle of a hallway, near no table or any other furniture.

The members of my escort party were peeling off in different directions, most of them in the company of attractive young women. The Lady Kate was pulling me firmly by the arm and guiding me in one particular direction, which was fortunate, for if

I'd been left to my own devices I would likely have wandered the place helplessly until doomsday. Her voice was low and throaty as she spoke, and tinged with excitement. Truly she was a vibrant and delicious creature. And intelligent; I could see that in her eyes. That made me nervous, of course. Much of the harm that had befallen me in my life had been at the hands of extremely intelligent women, and part of me had almost been hoping that the Lady Kate would be a mere step or two above dunce. Still, I had to admit that for the occasional tumble, I would take an empty-headed creature every time. But for someone who was ostensibly supposed to be of aid to me and serve by my side—or, preferably, just behind me—a woman with a few brains in her head could be a handy enough thing to have around. Just so long as she wasn't so intelligent as to think about finding ways to cheat me or rob me or make my life a living hell, which is what had happened to me in previous encounters dating back to the very first woman I'd ever been with.

The sounds of laughter and celebration trailed off, and I asked hopefully, "Aren't we going to be eating first? It smells delicious. . . ."

"Eat?" she asked in that throaty voice of hers, as if I had suggested that we climb to the uppermost tower, flap our arms, and leap off in hopes of achieving flight. "Beloved, we must get you cleaned up first. You have the stink of battle and the road upon you. How can you possibly go before your court in such a manner?" Before I could agree, or disagree, or even get a word out, she continued, "I saw your caravan approaching and took the liberty of having a bath drawn for you. I trust I did correctly?"

I liked the sound of that. "You did correctly, Lady Kate."

She stopped, took both my hands in hers, and smiled seductively. "Call me by the name."

"What?" I suddenly felt nervous.

"The name. The name you always use when it's just the two of us."

My mouth had gone suddenly quite dry. Now I am not an especially romantic or, gods knew, cuddly individual. I was having trouble imagining that, short of becoming a stark raving lunatic, I had ever concocted any sort of elaborate term of endearment for her, or anyone. So, taking a stab at it, I thought of the blandest appellation I could come up with. "You did correctly, my love."

A grin split her face, which seemed to light up from the smile, and she threw herself against me and kissed me heatedly. Understand, it was just a kiss, but the passion that burned within her lips was a thing alive. If I had been made of wood, I would have been ashes within seconds. Although, as chance would have it, thanks to the ardor of her lips against mine, there was one part of me that indeed seemed transformed into wood.

She didn't appear to notice as she smiled seductively and turned away, continuing to pull my hand. I walked after her, albeit it with even more pronounced difficulty than I usually had.

Her enthusiasm, her pure joy in my presence, was palpable. She could not contain herself, practically bounding along in front of me. It was, in its way, charming, albeit slightly exhausting.

"I was so concerned while you were away, Apropos," she chattered away. "Every day, not an hour went by that you were not foremost in my thoughts. Your absence seemed interminable. But I never doubted you would return, not for a moment. No one can best you or conquer you, beloved. You are invincible."

"Yes, well . . . Lamalos thought the same thing about himself," I ventured. "So I should have a care lest I make that same mistake."

But she shook her head dismissively as she pulled me down another corridor, and then up a short flight of stairs. I was starting to wonder if she was just taking me in circles in order to either impress or confuse me. "You would never make such a mistake, Apropos. You are far more audacious than Lamalos ever was. That's how you were able to conquer him; because he never suspected the audacity of our plan."

"Yes, yes, the sheer audacity of it," I echoed.

She brought me through a door, and immediately I could feel warmth radiating from within. There was an exceedingly large tub awaiting me, and the steam was rising up from it. Enormous towels were draped over a table nearby. There was no one else in the room. The sun was filtering through the single window that was set into the ceiling overhead.

"Your bath awaits you, my Peacelord," she said, with a bow. She was moving toward another door on the far side of the room, never taking her eyes off me. "Your servants shall be along shortly to aid you in your bathing, to scrub your back and such."

"That would be fine," I told her, and she shut the large wooden door behind her.

There is nothing like a waiting tub to make every muscle in your body ache in anticipation of it. It seemed to me that I had been riding nearly forever. There was not an inch of me that was not covered with dirt or saddlesores, and although I still had no idea how I had come to this situation, I knew one thing beyond question: I was going to soak in that tub possibly forever.

There was one thing I could not wait to attend to, however. The woad had completely caked over after all the time wearing it, and much of it had already cracked away and fallen off. But some of it remained, and I could only imagine how ghastly it looked. I took one of the towels, wet it thoroughly, and cleansed my face. It took a few minutes, but soon all the blue clay was gone. Looking in a mirror that was lying on the table, I saw the roots of my beard were blue. Probably the simplest thing to do would be to have the facial hair shaved.

I stripped off the rest of my filthy clothing and left it on a pile in the floor, and then stepped into the hot bath. And "hot" it most definitely was. It was with great delicacy that I eased myself in, allowing myself to become used to the high temperature of the water. The water came halfway up my rib cage, and feeling lazy but secure, I reached up and scratched my chest.

That's when I felt it. Felt it before I saw it.

At first I thought it was some sort of hardened lump beneath my skin, and for a panicked moment I thought I had a tumor which could have indicated the onset of the Plague, or perhaps the

Rot, or some other disease that I wasn't even familiar with. *Wonderful! Wonderful! Just your luck, that you have everything, and now you're dying!*

But then my fingers began to explore the clearly defined edges of it, pushing apart the chest hair to investigate it more closely. The hard edged lump was situated in the middle of my chest, several inches south of my collarbone. But the angle of my head prevented me from seeing it clearly. A moment later, however, I came to a further realization.

The lump wasn't skin. It was some other substance altogether.

Half out of the tub, I grabbed the hand mirror off the table and held it up so that it would reflect my chest. I gaped at it, barely able to comprehend what I was seeing.

It was the gem. The gem that glittered like fire. The gem that I kept stealing off Sharee after she had stolen it from Beliquose. The gem that I had kept in my single-minded possession even as I was dying in the midst of the Tragic Waste.

The gem that was lodged in my chest.

It was impossible. It was just impossible. There was no way in heaven or hell that the gem could just . . . just insert itself into my body. I pulled at it, figuring that somehow it had simply been ornamented upon me with some sort of adhesive. I was wrong. I pulled and yanked and a string of profanities escaped my lips as I realized the damned thing was attached. *Attached.* It had actually fused with my body somehow, my skin grafting itself around the edges of the gem and bonding with it. I could no more rip the thing off my chest than I could pull off one of my arms or pluck out an eye.

Obviously this was no natural phenomenon. This was some sort of sorcery, magiks of the blackest kind. I remembered how Sharee had told me that something was causing magiks to drain away, siphoning the source of sorcery in our world. Well, whatever was doing it, it obviously hadn't affected whoever or whatever had done this to me.

Even though I knew it wasn't going anywhere, I pulled and

pulled at it, and still couldn't even come close to getting it off me. It seemed no more inclined to release its hold upon me than it had been before.

Something was stirring at the window overhead. I looked up.

Mordant was there. He seemed to be chuckling.

"Get out of here!" I bellowed.

The drabit stared down at me, cocked his head for a moment, and then flapped his wings and took off. From outside the door, I heard the Lady Kate's voice float to me, "Beloved . . . who are you shouting at? Is there someone in there with you?"

I tried to compose myself, to fight down the panic that was surging through me at the discovery of dark sorcery perpetrated upon my body. "No. No, my love, there's no one in here," I called, trying to make my voice sound not too strangled.

The door opened. Kate was standing in the doorframe, wrapped in a single towel.

"Well, well," she purred. "We should do something about that, then."

She dropped the towel while she was still halfway across the room. She had the sort of body that should be unclothed as often as possible.

My mind was a tangle of knots, and I had no idea in which direction to send it. Certainly she was alluring enough, but the discovery of this hunk of valuable rock in my chest was disconcerting, to put it mildly. And . . . what if this was a recent development? What if she hadn't seen it before? What would her reaction be?

As it turned out, she was obviously aware of my curious attachment, for as she climbed into the tub with me she looked at it lovingly, and even traced the edges of it with her finger.

"You said the servants would be coming in to help me," I said, my throat suddenly feeling as if there was an excess of blood in it.

"And am I not your humble servant?" she said teasingly. She glided through the water to me, placed her arms about my shoulders and then wrapped her legs around my hips. I barely knew what was happening, but my body was far, far ahead of my mind, already operating on instinct. And the instinct was good and true, and she gasped in my ear as I entered her. "Your servant," she whispered, grinding against me, her fingers raking my back in her craving, and I surrendered to the moment.

"Oh, gods, Kate," I moaned, and she sank her teeth into my throat. And if she'd been a vampire at that moment, I would gladly have given myself over to her, but no, she was just kissing the skin passionately, and then to my chin and my mouth, and she was everywhere, her copious breasts mashing against my chest, the water splashing wildly out of the tub as we thudded against the sides. And all my exhaustion and all my pain was forgotten, washed away in the water and the heat of the single best bath I have ever had.

Afterward, I felt as if I was floating as I leaned back, using Kate as my cushion in the tub. Her back was against the edge, her legs open and encircling me as I leaned back against her and sighed a greater sigh of contentment than I had ever known. I had reached a point where not only did I not know how I had gotten to where I was, but I didn't care in the least.

If nothing else, it was nice to know that a woman could be attracted to me if she wasn't looking to rob me, wasn't psychotic, or wasn't under the influence of a magic ring.

Then a thought struck me as to how to elicit information without tipping the fact that I had no recollection of it myself. Nuzzling the back of my head between her breasts, I said, "Tell me about my conquest of this castle." But I said it in a very lazy, tired voice rather than one of genuine query.

She paused and then laughed lightly. "Don't you remember?"

"Of course I do. But I wanted to hear you tell it. You make it sound so . . ." and I sighed once more, ". . . heroic."

"Would you like me to sing the song of it?"

There's a song? What, is there a song about everything I've done? But of course, being the Peacelord, I would have known that, and so instead I shrugged and said, "If you'd prefer. Either way, I love hearing your voice." That much, at least, was true.

　She cleared her throat, hummed a few notes to ascertain which notes to start with, and then she sang:

Oh, Apropos, the lord of peace, looked upon the Dreadnaught keep.
"It shall be mine!" quoth Apropos, with hair of fire and thoughts so
　　deep.
"Yes, I shall capture Dreadnaught and the benefits I'll gladly reap!"
Claimed Apropos, the lord of peace, upon one starry night.

Now many thought that Dreadnaught was impregnable at best,
For Lamalos had built it strong and put it to the test.
"I have a cunning plan that Lamalos has never guessed!"
Claimed Apropos, the lord of peace, upon one starry night.

He summoned all his men to him, and said, "Bring me your wealth.
"I shall employ it all, you see, and with my guile and stealth
"By next week we'll have Dreadnaught and be drinking to my
　　health!"
Claimed Apropos, the lord of peace, upon one starry night.

Then all the riches he acquired, he piled into wagons,
Adorned with gold and jewels, trinkets, shields from hides of dragons,
And meats and sweetmeats, fruits and more, and wine in fifty
　　flagons,
Did Apropos, the lord of peace, upon one starry night.

The wagons rolled up to the gates, one old man at the helm.
"These offerings are sent as gifts to the great lord of this realm!"
"Who sent them?" asked the guards. "Our lord asks; we would
　　tell 'im."
"From Apropos," the old man said, upon one starry night.

The wagons rolled into the keep, and Lamalos took it all,
The food, the riches, all of it, secured inside his hall,

He kept the wagons, too, and that's what led him to his fall
From Apropos, the lord of peace, upon one starry night.

For in each wagon was secured, beneath a bottom faked,
A warrior of Apropos, with face in blue woad caked,
And they emerged when all was still, and not one victim waked,
By Apropos, the lord of peace, upon one starry night.

For Apropos was there as well, he led his soldiers in,
They slew their opposition with a minimum of din,
And Apropos slew Lamalos, so fast it was a sin,
By Apropos, the lord of peace, upon one starry night.

The residents of Dreadnaught woke next morning, to their shock,
The heads of Lamalos and crew were mounted on a block,
And Apropos called, "Listen, friends, I swear it is no crock,
"I'm Apropos, the lord of peace, and on one starry night,

"I took this stronghold, now it's mine, but with you I am sharing,
"The riches sent to Lamalos, to show you that I'm caring."
The people cheered his name then and commended, too, the daring,
Of Apropos, the lord of peace, upon one starry night.

She smiled at me when she'd finished, and even bobbed her
head slightly like a shy singer having just performed for a large
audience. Remembering belatedly, I quickly applauded, and her
grin was wide and genuine. "Very nicely done, my lady," I said
approvingly. And, frankly, it had sounded pretty good.

So that was how I'd managed to take the place. Well-done, me.
Obviously any sort of frontal assault was hopelessly doomed. So
instead I had conceived a scheme wherein those I intended to conquer actually brought us straight into their own midst, all
unknowing, while my men and I hid within concealed compart-
ments in the wagons. Yes, indeed, a most excellent notion. Most
excellent.

Kate reached her arms around and began lathering my chest. I wondered whether Kate had been the consort of Lamalos before I'd taken the place, but then I remembered that supposedly she had helped me develop the plan. So she must have been with me before the taking of Dreadnaught. I wondered where I'd met her, and what her own background was. But in this matter I couldn't really think of a way to inquire without it seeming odd.

And I realized that, when it came down to it . . . what did it matter? The past was really of little consequence. It was only the here and now that was important. She was there with me, in the tub, the lovemaking had been exquisite, the future looked rather rosy.

Except . . .

. . . well . . . I was still a conquering murderer.

But as I relaxed once more against her, I pondered whether it was really all a matter of point of view. After all, I had never considered King Runcible to be any sort of barbaric brute. Yet had I done anything, really, that he hadn't done? He secured his position as King of Isteria by conquering those who would have stood against him. I had done no more than that. Certainly Runcible's conscience was clear, and he was generally considered to be a great king and a great man . . . at least by those who did not know the dark underbelly of his court the way I did. Why should it be that I held myself to a higher standard than he did, or anybody did?

"Oh!" Kate said suddenly. "Have you heard the news? A band of rebel assassins has been captured!"

She sounded so chipper about it that I actually smiled at that . . . until the full impact of what she'd just said hit me, at which point I turned around and stared at her in shock. "Rebel assassins?"

"Yes. That's right."

"*Assassins?* As in, they're out to kill me?"

"Well, of course," said Kate, matter-of-factly. She seemed amused that I was at all concerned or thought it even slightly odd. "Apropos . . . you're a Peacelord. You're the first Peacelord in the history of Wuin. Naturally there are people who are going to want to kill you."

"Naturally," I said, trying to keep my voice from cracking. Suddenly the water, even though it was still warm, felt considerably colder. Risking the revelation of my ignorance, I said, "Remind me, my love . . . whence came the term of *Peacelord?*"

"Why, from you. Have you forgotten? Your reasoning was that there are so many warlords about, or have been in the history of the world. So when someone hears that a particular warlord is on the rampage, there is a lack of gravity about that. But a Peacelord, well . . . no one has ever heard of such a thing. It makes an impression. Even strikes fear into the heart of the listener. After all, a warlord has to announce his warlike presence through a title intended to stab fear into the hearts of those who hear it. A warlord is saying, 'Look at me! I am a great, fearsome thing!' Now a Peacelord, on the other hand, is so confident in his ability to take whatever he wants, that he need not apply intimidating titles to himself. He speaks softly . . . but carries a great sword. Thus is a Peacelord a more frightening appellation, for the truth is that anyone who faces a Peacelord knows that, in fact, they are in opposition to someone who is interested in anything but peace." Her brow wrinkled in concern. "Is any of this sounding familiar?"

"Yes, yes, all of it," I said quickly, and then turned in the bath and kissed her. "Once again, my love, I just enjoy hearing you say it. So . . . where were these rebel assassins found?"

"They had set up camp on the Cartesian Plains," she replied. "But forces loyal to you, my dearest heart, tracked them down and rounded them up. The current plan is that they are to be brought forward during the banquet to have your judgment rendered upon them."

"Oh. I see. That's the plan, is it?" I was having a difficult time keeping the quavering out of my voice. Understand, I'd grown accustomed to the concept of people trying to kill me. Sooner or later, it seemed, just about everyone I met wanted to kill me. Just one of the many joys of being me. But the concept that a group of people would band together specifically to plot my annihilation . . . that was a bit much for me to handle. And yet, I didn't know which I found the more disturbing: the concept that they were planning my death, or that I was now being expected to pronounce death upon them.

Only a handful of times in my life had I slain, and in every instance, it was either by accident or in mortal combat. Never had I simply looked someone in the eye and said, "Your life is forfeit," and then made it come to pass. I strongly suspected I didn't have the stomach for it, even though my demise was their priority.

I thought quickly and said, "Perhaps . . . perhaps it would be wiser of me to spare them." I cast a quick, hopeful glance at her. She did not exactly seem taken with the notion.

"Why in the world would you want to do such a thing?" she inquired.

Opting to fall back on that which had worked reasonably well with my henchmen, I said in as canny a tone as I could muster, "Because . . . that would be the last thing they'd expect!"

She pushed me away with a splash and gaped at me. So many emotions seemed to be at war in her face: anger, confusion, worry, disappointment, all lobbying for dominance. "If that's what really interests you, Apropos—doing the unexpected—you could try cutting your head off with an ax. That would certainly catch everyone off guard. But I've no idea why you would want to."

"Kate . . ."

But she was hauling herself out of the water. Her naked body looked as good going as it did coming. Water dripped off her as she reached for a towel and wrapped it around herself. "Kate," I started again, but she waved me off, indicating with a gesture that she just wanted silence. I bristled slightly at the preemptory manner that she was displaying, but chose not to say anything about it.

The silence remained for a long moment, and then she turned to face me with her arms crisscrossed in front of her. "You remember what you told me just before you left for your latest campaign?" For an instant I panicked, because I thought we were about to engage in trivia questions about things we'd said and done, and I knew I would lose a significant enough percentage of them to be suspicious to her. But she continued, apparently having intended for the query to be rhetorical. "You said, 'I worship you, Kate. I worship your mind, and your body, and the ground upon which you walk. I am your devoted worshiper, your supplicant.' And I took you at your word. And I worship you in return, Apropos . . . and because I do, I don't wish to see you hurt or fall from grace. You have potential, my love . . . tremendous potential. But not if you are seen as weak and indecisive." She was clenching and unclenching her hands nervously as she strode toward me. "These people, these rebels . . . they sought to hurt you because they are jealous of you. Jealous . . . and afraid."

"And because they are afraid, they wanted to kill me?" I asked. I had risen from the tub by that point as well, and wrapped a towel around my middle since—thanks to the combination of my recent lovemaking and the cooling of the water—I was looking embarrassingly unimpressive at that moment. "Is that it?"

"Yes, that is exactly right."

"Well," and I shook my head, picking up another towel and starting to rub dry my hair with it, "if they aren't afraid of me, wouldn't it follow that they then would not want to kill me?"

"If they're not afraid of you," said Kate patiently, "then they will want to kill you because they perceive you as an easy target."

"So . . . either way, we're talking about my condemning people?" This was hardly a conclusion that I was particularly enthused about.

Kate was pacing back and forth, but never removing her gaze from me, as if she were truly seeing me for the first time. She shook out her hair, catlike, fine water droplets spraying all over the floor. "Yes, Apropos, either way, that's what is going to happen. You are a conqueror. Conquerors kill people in order to gain power, and kill people in order to keep power. If you wanted to do something other than that, you could have gone into the clergy where you could content yourself to officiate at holy wars. That way you wouldn't have to do any killing yourself, but instead simply sanctify those who did the killing in the name of their respective gods."

"And that makes killing acceptable?" I asked. "If it's being done in the name of a god?"

"Of course," said Kate matter-of-factly. "When it comes to the affairs of gods, any death is acceptable."

I stared up at the lone window in the room. Mordant was no longer flying around outside it. I found myself hoping that an archer had mistaken him for a possible meal and put an arrow through him. "Thank you, my love, for clarifying that for me," I said, trying to keep the bitterness out of my voice and failing utterly.

She drew close to me then and rested a hand on my shoulder. Her touch was warm and vibrant, and I shivered slightly from the sheer electricity of it. With greater concern in her tone for my welfare than I'd heard from any woman since before my mother died, she asked, "What happened to you out there? Something's happened, I'm sure of it. Because when you left here, you were so confident, so proud. And now you seem so . . . so . . ."

"So what? Say it." I held my breath, uncertain of what she was going to say.

She took my face in her hands and said, "So sad."

I looked into her eyes, and a small smile came surprisingly naturally to me. "If I am sad," I told her, "it is because I have been away from you for as long as I have. That tends to affect the way I see the world."

She sighed at the sweet-sounding nature of my words. Kate was a head shorter than I, but she stood slightly on her toes, tilted her face up toward mine, and kissed me tenderly. "I understand," she said.

"You do?"

"Yes. You have been killing and killing and killing, and you associate that with your work. And you're loathe to bring your work home with you because you'd rather be concentrating on me."

This, of course, was not remotely it, but I wasn't about to correct her point of view since it so nicely dovetailed with my own trepidation. So instead I simply brushed a few stray strands of hair from her face and said with a laugh, "Well, you've certainly got me figured out."

"I thought as much," she said happily. "Here, turn around." I did as she told me, and a moment later felt a towel briskly and efficiently drying off my back. "I sympathize, dear heart. I really do."

"Excellent."

"So this evening, at the banquet, we will not dwell on such matters as death and destruction."

My shoulders visibly sagged in relief upon her saying that. "I'm most pleased to hear you say that."

"We'll dance, we'll sing, we'll eat sumptuous meats, we'll condemn the rebels to death, we'll have dessert." She put her arms around me from behind and rocked back and forth like a ship at sea. "It will be a joyous night all around."

"Oh . . . huzzah," I said with a marked lack of enthusiasm.

Chapter 4

Hate Cuisine

*T*he Lady Kate was certainly right about the joyousness of the festivities, I'll give her that much.

When we walked into the main hall, I was almost knocked over by the intensity of the volume within. Musicians were playing a variety of instruments, dancers were gyrating about with such wild abandon that I think they had only the vaguest sense of the rhythms involved. I was attired in a doublet of dark crimson, with a skull-shaped pendant hanging around my throat. A short, black ceremonial cape hung off my right shoulder. Kate was dressed in a silken gown of purest ivory, with gold trim upon the bodice. She did not seem to walk across the room so much as float.

I noticed Boar Tooth over in one corner, a woman on each arm, laughing and chewing on a bone of some sort of meat. And over in another corner Slake was wildly dancing with a lightly clad female. He was flinging his arms about so crazily that I thought for sure he was going to smack someone in the face. And in the farthest, farthest corner of the room, away from everyone else, sat That Guy. He had his sword out and was calmly sharpening the edges with a whetstone. That image chilled me although I had no idea why.

The room had been as cold as any other in the stronghold, but the spinning and dancing and celebrating bodies of at least two hundred revelers had gone a far way toward warming the place up.

Not only that, but the great hall had been decorated in early- and middle-period Apropos. There were paintings and tapestries hanging upon the wall, and busts of me mounted on pedestals. All of them depicted me in various scenes of conquest, standing upon piles of casualties or going sword to sword with a dozen men at one time. The expressions on busts were serenely smug in their sculpting, which gave them the closest resemblance to me, but the visual displays . . . in all of them, I could scarce identify my own face. I mean, it was mine, but my expression was twisted in a dark and fearsome look of loathing for everyone that opposed me.

Most striking of all was a window inset into the far wall, about a foot or so from the ceiling. I had heard about such things, but never seen the like.

It was made of stained glass, an object so rare that only the best alchemists and metallurgists were able to craft something so complex. I had heard about such artistic wonders, but never before actually seen one with my own eyes. And the object of art that it constituted was the most stunning thing of all.

It was me. Or at least a depiction of me, seated upon a horse, holding my sword in one hand and my staff in the other. This, of course, left me no hands to grip the reins, and in real life I would have fallen off the dumb beast in no time at all. But this was art, a depiction not of the Apropos that was, but instead the idealized Peacelord Apropos conveyed through the genius of the artisans that had created it.

And that face, likewise, had the obvious tint of blackness upon it. Staring into that face so close to my own, and yet so different, I could no longer repress a shudder that ran the length of my spine.

And yet, in a way, I did recognize it. It was the face of how I saw
the world. The face of anger and contempt that I held for a civi-
lization so depraved, so without moral bearings, that it would have
me in it. Me, Apropos of Nothing, born of a mother who was
raped by knights purporting to be defenders of a code of chivalry. I
had always thought that if I permitted that face to be seen, if I
wore it on the outside, all who beheld it would run from it in
revulsion. Instead apparently I had sported that grim and frightening visage for the better part of a year, and had garnered only followers, wealth, fame, and gratification of all kinds. It made no
sense to me at all. I fancied myself a cynic, someone who knew the
true way of things while others lived in their pleasant fantasy
world. Instead it was beginning to seem as if I was the one who
knew nothing at all . . . and I couldn't say I was all that enthused
about the lessons I was learning.

Scattered all over was loot taken from our various excursions.
Outrageously fancy clothing was being sported in jaunty fashion
by the celebrants, tossed together and upon their bodies in the
haphazard manner that signifies stolen goods being flaunted by
those who stole them.

It sickened me.

I stared at one woman gallivanting about with her man, and she
was wearing a gleaming tiara and furred cape, both of which were
too big for her. I wondered about the woman who had previously
owned them. Was she alive? Had the dancing woman's conquering
hero cut the previous owner to pieces and pulled them off her still-
steaming body? How many lost lives, how many dashed hopes,
were being celebrated this evening?

I had never made any pretensions to being heroic, or caring
about the concerns of anyone save myself. But seeing this orgy of
joy being celebrated by people who had no right to celebrate
beyond the fact that they were the biggest bullies in the valley—
and the notion that it was I who had made it all possible—made
me feel creepily uncomfortable in my own skin.

So naturally I did what anyone in a situation that leaves them with a foul moral taste in their mouth tends to do. I proceeded to rationalize it. Make it livable for me.

The fact was that I knew nothing about any of the peoples that we had conquered. Perhaps . . . perhaps they were deserving of it. Perhaps they were rich and indolent, and were perfect examples of everything that was wrong with humanity. It could very well be that these people, my followers, my legions . . . it could have been that they were, in fact, more entitled to enjoy these pleasant trinkets. Perhaps it was their hard work which had placed the previous owners of these objects in positions of wealth and power, and in stepping in as the first "Peacelord" of Wuin—indeed, of anywhere, most likely—I was making the balance more even. And maybe . . .

. . . just maybe . . .

. . . the gods wanted me to do it.

For what I think was the first time in my life, I suddenly understood just why it was that people embraced gods. It was definitely an attractive notion, this whole business of operating as a result of the will of beings before whom I was helpless. I also reminded myself of the entire business of the Visionary. There was absolutely no point in denying it at this juncture: He had foreseen the future. My future. Unlike Soothsayers that I had encountered who had spoken in broad prophecies that could be interpreted a variety of ways, the Visionary who had come to Bugger Hall had spoken plainly and true. Granted, his visions had been somewhat truncated thanks to his demise . . .

. . . and, of course, there was no reason to think that this life I had undertaken was part of that already-determined destiny . . .

Quit while you're ahead, my ever-wise inner voice suggested, and I saw the prudence of that advice. As long as I didn't overthink the matter, I could take solace in the twin notions that I had simply acted in accordance with the whims of the divine and fate, and that I might actually be making the world a better place while doing it. Those beliefs would be more than enough to get me through the evening without dissolving into tears or having fits of uncontrolled screaming.

Kate had wanted to wait and make a proper entrance, announced by some jackass with a booming voice who lived for stopping the proceedings dead while bellowing the name of every new arrival. But I turned my nose up at the thought. "These are my people, and I am one of them. I'll not stand on ceremony," I informed her as archly as I possibly could. And with that, I strode out into the throng, leaving Kate to catch up as best she could.

I was spotted within moments, of course, and cheers started that increased in waves, building to an earsplitting crescendo. Well-wishers converged on me, much as they had when I'd first arrived at the stronghold. Somehow That Guy made it through the crowds to get to my side. I'd no clue how he'd managed it, considering he was nowhere near me when I'd first arrived. The man moved like a specter. Perhaps it resulted from all the energy he saved by not talking.

But I was in no danger. Everyone around me was my friend, after all, and why shouldn't they be? Was I not responsible for this bounty that they were all enjoying? All hail to me, Apropos the Peacelord, master of all he surveyed. I wondered for a moment just how many cities I had actually ransacked. And was there any purpose or plan to my rampage aside from simple destruction? It did not seem as if I was endeavoring at all to string cities together into a unified state over which I could rule, and which could defend itself against foreign attackers. Instead I seemed satisfied to destroy all that I saw.

Kate was by my side once more as we moved through the crowd, smiling and shaking hands and nodding to all well-wishers. We were making our way toward what was obviously the places of honor: huge, ornate chairs, with plush red cushions that reminded me of nothing so much as the thrones upon which King Runcible and Queen Bea had sat. Carvings of exotic beasts ran the length of the chairs' edges, and the feet were genuine clawed feet.

I thought of all the rulers I had encountered in my time. Of Warlord Shank and his grand hall of depravity; of King Meander, the Keepless King who wandered from realm to realm as he sought surcease from memories that would never grant him peace; of King Runcible, of course. And now . . . here was my place of power, my seat of authority. As I slowly walked up to the great chair, I mused upon the notion that most lowborn creatures such as myself never had the opportunity to set their eyes upon even one ruler. And here I had not only encountered more than my share, but I had risen to a degree of rulership myself. That was one hell of an accomplishment, even if I couldn't remember how in the world I had done it.

And here was another thing: There were several steps leading up to the throne. I couldn't help but notice as I climbed them that I did so relatively easily. It is, of course, little cause for remark or celebration just for climbing a flight of stairs. That is, unless one has a lame leg, in which case even the simplest of such endeavors can prove a challenge. Not in this instance, though. I walked up the steps with such brisk efficiency that it was only upon reaching the chair that I realized I had done so with no effort at all. My right leg was not as strong as my left . . . but it was far more than the useless appendage it had been until that point. I cast my mind back to my bath and realized that even then, there had been more strength in the leg. I hadn't perceived it because it seemed such a natural thing that I had taken no more notice of the proper functioning of my right leg than I would have of my left leg, or my arms.

I stood in front of the chair, paused dramatically, and then turned to face the others. Kate was in front of her own chair, but she was waiting for me to sit. Her hands were gently folded one upon the other, and she had a pleasant, almost beatific look upon her face. People started calling her name as well, and she basked in the adulation with a smile of pure joy fixed in place, soaking up the attention as if she were a sponge.

Spreading wide my arms, I called out, "My good friends! It is a pleasure to be back among you!"

Oh, the huzzahs that went up at that point, the cheers and the exaltation that were being given me. I was their Peacelord. In their eyes I could do no wrong. I gestured for quiet and they immediately obeyed. "I will be taking my time before my next excursions," I continued. "I shall meet with my lieutenants, decide which cities are the most ripe for conquest, and attend to them in their own good time. In the meantime," and I raised my voice, "may the joy that is Dreadnaught never be diminished!"

Well, this got even greater cheers, and they were shouting my name and stamping the floor repeatedly with their feet, doing so with such vehemence that for a moment I thought they were going to jar loose the stained-glass window and send it crashing to the ground in a thousand stained-glass shards.

I turned to the Lady Kate then, took her extended hand, drew her to me, and kissed her firmly on the lips. The warmth of her flooded over me, and the crowd was certainly as enamored of the moment as I was, for they let loose a deafening howl of approval.

"All for you, my love," she whispered, "all for you."

We took our seats then to oversee the revels. Food was brought to us in abundance, and I sank my teeth into it with relish and gusto. There is nothing like thinking that you are about to die in a gods-forsaken desert to make your first good meal taste all the sweeter. I had never been more glad to be alive.

At one point a plate with small round, brown balls was placed before me. Naturally I regarded them with some suspicion, as I think anyone would have been wont to do. At the "Try it! Try it!" urging of my consort, I picked up one of the balls in a most cautious manner with my fingertips. Even at that point I was concerned that this was a nauseating practical joke, and I was holding a small wad of excrement between my fingers, but the smell that wafted from it quickly set that notion aside. The scent was exquisite, sweetness mixed with an aroma promising an energetic burst of taste that bordered on the sensual. I bit off a piece carefully, allowed it to slide down my tongue, and could scarcely believe it. I realized that this had to be the "chocolate" that Sharee had made reference to. Gods, it was practically a taste that was worth dying for. I rolled it around, smacked my lips together, and marveled at the things that humanity could produce when it put its mind to it.

And so it went, an evening of frolic and hilarity, right up to the point where Boar Tooth approached me. I noticed that he, too, had washed the woad from his face, and I was depressed to see that he looked even more vicious without it than with it. He bowed low without taking his eyes off me, and then bowed again to the Lady Kate. Revelers noticed that he had come toward me, and the merrymaking dimmed in volume just a little, enough so that Boar Tooth could be heard.

"You have been informed of our newest prisoners, I trust, Peacelord?" inquired Boar Tooth.

By that point, I have to say, I was feeling pretty damned relaxed, considering the amount of ale and mead that I had imbibed as the evening progressed. I had not gotten that stinking drunk since the days I drowned my sorrows as a put-upon squire in King Runcible's castle, sneaking down to the hidden wine cellar and availing myself of its contents. Here, no sneaking around was involved. Everything we had was at my disposal, and I was all too willing to dispose of it. Moral conundrums, struggles of con-science, are battles best fought at sea . . . in my case, upon the sea of blissfuly alcoholic haze. Well, I was certainly out to sea on this occasion, with my three sheets billowing solidly to the wind. I still had a generally sound idea of who and where I was, but I wasn't capable of much beyond that. Even the simple act of locomotion might have proven a challenge. Fortunately enough I wasn't endeavoring to go anywhere, although I was slumping quite a bit in my chair. I was resting my chin on one hand, except my chin was developing the annoying habit of slipping off the support. As a consequence I kept nearly punching myself in the face. I had to focus very carefully on what Boar Tooth was saying, because if I let my attention wander for even a moment, then his words would have gone floating past me, and I would have cheerfully waved as they passed. "Newest prisoners?" I asked, overenunciating each word so that I was comprehensible to him, and to me.

Kate reached over and touched the top of my hand. "The rebels, my Peacelord," she reminded me in a soft voice.

Immediately I perked up, and spoke in a voice that was considerably louder than it needed to be. "Of course! The rebels! Wanted to kill me! Those bastards!"

"Yes, indeed, Peacelord," Boar Tooth concurred, bowing once more.

"Kill me! Me! Me! Me! Me!" I paused, my brow furrowing, and I stared blearily at Boar Tooth. "Was I warming up to sing just then?"

He looked at me with open amusement. I wondered why he was tilting his head at such an odd angle, and then realized in some distant sector of my brain that he was doing it in order to maintain eye contact with me, since my head was similarly slumped over. "Peacelord . . . if you prefer . . . this can be attended to when you are less . . . how shall I put it . . . ?"

"Drunk?" I asked. This candor on my part caused ripples of laughter throughout the great hall. I waggled a finger scoldingly at Boar Tooth and admonished him by saying, "I'll have you know I'm not nearly as think as you drunk I am."

"That's comforting to know, Peacelord."

"My dear," suggested Kate, leaning toward me, "perhaps it would be better to wait for another—"

"*Nonsense!*" If any noise from the crowd had been drowning out my voice up until that point, that was certainly not the case after my little outburst. I had the full attention of everyone in the place. "My good friends!" I called out, once again struggling not to slur my words. "Who wishes to see the rebels attended to, eh?"

Well, naturally cries of support and multiple "huzzahs!" rang out, and that was all the incentive that was needed. Boar Tooth gestured toward That Guy, who sheathed his sword and exited the great hall. There was a good deal of buzzing going on among the people, excited whispers and speculation as to whether I was just going to have the rebels executed right then and there, or make them suffer the agony of condemnation and subsequent waiting for their demise.

As for me, it was as if I had stepped completely out of my body and was observing myself from a very great distance. A warm haze had descended upon me. The persona of Apropos, barbarian Peacelord had taken hold, as if I was playing a part in some great pantomime rather than doing anything that had any bearing upon reality. There was a faint warning in the back of my head that I was going to regret the actions I was taking once sobriety returned, but it couldn't begin to penetrate the buzzing in my skull that urged me to enforce the rule of law. To show any other would-be murderers who might be watching what would happen if they even considered going up against the Peacelord of Wuin.

There was a creaking and groaning of wheels then, and the doors to the hall swung open to reveal a large cart being hauled in by two bulky slaves dressed in loincloths, with perspiration slicking their upper bodies. Some of the women were murmuring in appreciation, and even Kate seemed interested. I was too far gone to care at that point. Indeed, so much of it was a blur that to a degree I'm only guessing now, as I write of those events of days gone by, about the specific order of things and what exactly was going through my mind, since the definitive details are lost to an alcoholic cloud . . . or at least they were until I had cause to sober up quickly.

A cage had been built atop the cart, and inside it were what appeared to be about eight or nine prisoners. Whatever they'd been wearing when they first arrived at Dreadnaught was long gone, replaced with tattered rags that barely maintained their modesty. They did not look particularly rebellious. Their reactions varied from man to man: Some appeared defiant, looking with a sneer at the crowds who were shouting imprecations. Others looked scared, and one of the older men was swaying back and forth with his eyes closed, his mouth in almost constant motion. Obviously he was praying. I had no idea if anyone was listening. There were several more in the middle of the group, but I couldn't make them out.

Then again, considering how soused I was, it was amazing that I was able to see the cart.

The cart, which creaked along on two large wheels, was brought to about twenty feet away from me, before it came to a halt. The slaves stepped away and Boar Tooth swaggered up to the cart. He was saying something, but I couldn't make it out at first because the roaring and chanting of the crowd ("Death! Death! Death!" Uninspired, but effective) was drowning out any one single voice.

It was Kate who silenced them. She rose to her feet, the motion commanding instant attention, and her outstretched hand instantly quieted the mob. "Thank you, my dear. Well handled," I said, and she bobbed her head in appreciation of the compliment. She sat, and once more I had to focus all my attention on just being able to string coherent syllables together. "Boar Tooth . . . do they have a defense they wish to give? A spokesman, perhaps?"

"Do they need one, my love?" inquired Kate. "They conspired to kill you. What possible defense could be given for that?"

The room was starting to swirl around me, and I marveled over the fact that there were now three Kates where there had only been the one before. I was going to have one hell of a lot of fun once I got the trio back to the bedchamber. The Kates began to spin in circular fashion, and I did my best to keep my eye on them. As a result, I appeared to be bobbing my head with enthusiasm.

"The Peacelord agrees!" called Boar Tooth, playing to the crowd.

And Slake was there, stalking the perimeter of the clearing, playing off Boar Tooth perfectly as he said, "Are they condemned, then?"

I nodded, the reason being that I was trying to stay awake.

"They are condemned!" Boar Tooth bellowed, and a roar went up from the crowd then that was so deafening, it punched through the cloud of confusion upon me ever so slightly. I rubbed my eyes, trying to focus on the sequence of events, to remember where I was, and who was seated at my side, and who these poor wretches in the cart were. I had a vague recollection that they were a threat to me, but the specifics were beyond my ability to recall.

"Bring out the first one for execution!" called Slake. The slaves, now acting as muscled prisoner escorts, moved toward the cage and unlocked it. The rebels within began to cower back as they saw That Guy stepping forward, pulling his sword from its sheathe. He whipped it through the air with frightening speed, swinging it this way and that to please and delight the crowd with his unquestioned ability to murder an unarmed opponent who was being held in place.

Boar Tooth laughed loudly as he looked at the rebels shrinking back to the far end of the cage, and he called out, "We seem to have a dearth of volunteers! I guess we'll have to pick someone to start!" The crowd joined in, their raucous chortling filling the hall and providing the only impetus to my staying awake.

And then a female voice cut loud and clear above the crowd, full of anger and strength and defiance, and it called out, *"I'll go first, you pack of bastards!"*

The brave cry had a twofold effect. The first was to briefly surprise the crowd into silence. And the second was to shock me straight into sobriety, or at least a very close approximation thereof. Don't let anyone tell you that a drunken man must wait a certain number of hours before he is fit to think for himself. It is entirely possible to be kicked directly out of your stupor if the reason is sufficient. And in this instance it most definitely was.

For stepping forward out of the cluster of rebels, her shoulders squared, her head held high, was Sharee. Her hair was longer and stringier than I remembered, and there was a shining purple bruise below her right eye, the origins of which I couldn't even begin to guess. But it was her, and she looked right past her intended executioner, straight at me, with such hatred and loathing as I had never thought possible.

"Do your worst, Apropos," she sniffed. "You always do anyway."

Chapter 5

Bye Low, Cell High

*T*he full weight of what was about to happen thudded upon my shoulders as I watched Sharee take several steps toward me and stop half a dozen paces away from That Guy. One of the slaves was now running forward with thick cloths which he was placing on the floor. Naturally. Her headless (or possibly bisected) body was about to flop to the ground, and blood was always hell to get out of flagging.

People were crowding in to get a better view, and Slake called as if he were the master of ceremonies at a circus, "Please be aware: There will be blood and gore flying! Any of you in the first three rows, you are very likely going to get wet!" This was all that was required to prompt the crowd to back away once more to a safer, and drier, distance.

Sharee had not taken her gaze from me, even though her death was standing several feet away and preparing to swing his sword. Everything that Kate had said to me about needing to be firm, about sending the right message, and letting everyone know the dangers of defying me . . . those were all fresh in my mind. But how in hell was I supposed to just stand there and watch Sharee be cut down in front of me?

Easily. By keeping your big mouth shut. She's done nothing but cause you heartache and pain, and now she was scheming to kill you? You owe her nothing! Nothing!

And that was right enough, of course. I did owe her nothing. There was no earthly reason to stick my neck out so that hers would be spared. If it weren't for her, I would still be taking it easy back at Bugger Hall, and none of this would have happened. She had shoved her nose in my business and turned my life on its ass. If her life was forfeit as a result, that was of no consequence to me.

Except . . .

. . . she might have answers. Answers to the puzzle of how I had come to be here. Answers that, if I did not obtain them, would haunt me to my dying day. She had, after all, been right there dying with me in the Tragic Waste. Whatever happened to me must have, somehow, impacted upon her.

Before I even had the notion fully formed in my head, I was on my feet and calling out, *"Wait!"*

Sharee's expression never wavered, the contempt for me still writ large upon it. That Guy looked quite puzzled, however, for he had been pulling back his sword and preparing to let fly. My pronouncement certainly startled everyone else into silence as well.

"Peacelord, with all respect," Boar Tooth said cautiously, taking several steps toward me, "what, precisely, are we to wait for? They have been condemned. That should be the end of it, should it not?"

You'd think so, wouldn't you. My mind raced. Kate stared at me with open bewilderment, obviously wondering what in the world could possibly have possessed me? Well, I was wondering the same thing, except about a different circumstance that only Sharee might be able to shed light upon.

I spoke without knowing where I was going with it, which is

always a risky endeavor. But I could not appear hesitant. Befuddling, arbitrary, yes, these were permissible. But, as noted earlier, hesitation will get a leader killed, every time—either by the enemy, or by his own people.

"This . . . would be an abomination against the gods!" I declared.

I don't think anyone could have looked more surprised than the Lady Kate, who stared at me as if I'd lost my mind. No one else looked any more certain of my sanity, though. "It would?" she asked. "How do you know it would?"

"How do you know it wouldn't?" I responded.

Her mouth opened as if she had some sort of answer to that, but then she closed it again and just sat there and stared at me expectantly.

"Do not think to dispute me on this, for I know these things!" I said, addressing the comments to her but encompassing the entirety of the assemblage as I did so. "You cannot possibly think that I would have accomplished all that I have—obtained all riches, all this greatness in the name of the residents of Dreadnaught—if the gods were not on my side? And because I am so favored, I have a certain . . . awareness, if you will . . . of what will be pleasing to the gods, both above and below."

"That . . . makes sense, Peacelord," said Boar Tooth, scratching the underside of his chin thoughtfully, "although I've never heard you express it that way."

I drew myself up. I was not favoring my right leg at all by that point. Not only that, but I felt a faint burning in my chest from the area where the gem was embedded. It was not painful, however; instead it actually felt invigorating, as if new strength was surging through me. I felt as if I was literally radiating charisma. I wasn't simply trying to come up with some sort of cover story. I was instead barking divine words of wisdom. In short . . . I was starting to believe my own fabrications. "Are you under the impression, Boar Tooth," I demanded, brimming with confidence, arrogance, and a dollop of threat, "that I am obligated in some way to share with you every thought of mine?"

"No, Peacelord!" he said immediately. I fired a glance at the others of my followers, and they promptly shook their heads in response. I noticed from the corner of my eye that only the Lady Kate wasn't responding in the negative. She was just watching me like the proverbial hawk.

Nevertheless, satisfied with Boar Tooth's acknowledgment, I pointed angrily at the prisoners. I endeavored not to make eye contact with Sharee, whose baleful glare hadn't lost any of its venom.

"This," I continued, "is a time of celebration and festivities. It is not a time for bloodshed, even if it be the blood of such as *these*," and I put as much contempt into the word *these* as I could. "As much joy as it would give those of us assembled here to see these bastards die, that pleasure must wait until tomorrow, lest blood spilled at a time of celebration place a curse upon all of us here."

There was a collective gasp of fear from the assemblage, and then they jumped as one when a loud, earsplitting shriek pierced the air. It was Mordant, curled around the massive chandelier hanging overhead. He let out a second scream as if to further punctuate what I'd just said, and his head bobbed up and down. It was, of course, the simple reflexive gesture of a dumb animal, but it nevertheless apparently carried weight with the onlookers.

"So trust me, my friends," I called out. "The prisoners have been condemned by me. They will die. But it shall be done on the morrow, while they have a final night to stew in their cells, listening to our merrymaking while knowing that the sands of time are running out on their pathetic existence . . . ses . . . existences . . . lives! On their pathetic lives!"

Well, as you can imagine, there were more huzzahs and more cheers. Men were pounding their fists upon the tables or their feet on the floor with such enthusiasm that I thought for a moment the place was going to come crashing down around our ears. The slaves shoved Sharee back into the cage, slammed shut and locked it, and proceeded to wheel them out once more. And not once, in all that time, did Sharee look away from me. I could practically feel the air crackling with her hatred for me.

Gods, what did the woman want from me?

And I realized . . . that I was going to have to ask her.

It was some time later, the revelries having gone long into the night, before I finally returned to my bedchamber. The Lady Kate accompanied me, but she did not look pleased. Also at my side was the drabit, having nestled on my arm once more. Despite her obvious discomfort with the situation, Kate gamely endeavored to make small talk. "The people were most impressed with Mordant this evening. Particularly his well-timed reinforcement of what you were saying."

My imagination told me that Mordant understood every word she'd just said, but I couldn't be sure. "Why so impressed?" I asked.

"Why, Peacelord . . . drabits are extremely rare creatures. There are some who say they are familiars of the gods themselves. When one such beast becomes as attached to you as Mordant has become, that naturally has an impact on your followers. And when you speak of the will of the gods and Mordant chooses that moment to chime in, well . . ." And she shrugged as if that more or less said everything that needed to be said. Which, perhaps, it did. I couldn't help but notice, however, that she had called me "Peacelord" rather than "my love." I wasn't sure what that entailed, but I didn't think it indicated anything good.

The moment the door to our chamber was closed behind us, Kate turned to me and her demeanor seemed to change completely, becoming far more intense and focused and frankly impatient with me. Her arms folded, she said simply, "Why?"

"Why what? Why did I delay their execution?" She didn't nod. She didn't have to. We both knew that was what was on her mind. "You heard my reasons."

"I heard reasons," she corrected. "I just . . . Apropos, I am not sure that they were true reasons."

I shrugged off the cape and turned to face her. "Are you imply-ing," I asked coldly, "that I have lied? That I have been less than candid in some way?"

"I'm not saying that, no. In fact, I'm not saying it's your fault at all." She drew a deep breath as if summoning strength for a great task and then she told me, "I saw the way that one rebel was looking at you. I recognized her from her description. She's the one called Sharee. There are some who say," and she lowered her voice as if in fear that somehow we were being overhead, "that she is a Weaver. That she possesses magical powers of some sort."

"No!" I said, trying to look as shocked as I could. I found interesting that such rumors existed, particularly considering that Sharee was relatively powerless. At least, so she'd told me those many months ago. I couldn't know for sure if the situation remained the same . . . although I suspected that, were her weatherweaving powers in full force, she would never have been captured so easily, or even at all. "A weaver, you say? One of those creatures who can perceive the threads of mystical energy that exist in nature and 'weave' them together into spells and such?"

"Yes. And it is my concern that perhaps, somehow . . . she has cast some sort of spell upon you."

I made sure to be properly taken aback. "Impossible! Impossible, I say!" Then I walked over to her and took her hands in mine, fix-ing a look of as much love and adoration as I could muster upon myself. "Why . . . how could any spell that such a being might cast possibly compare to the spell that you have placed upon me with your enchanting personality and beauty?"

She actually smiled at that and looked down, her face flushing slightly. "I know it sounds foolish. There have been no weavers in these parts for . . . well . . . it's ridiculous to think on it. Still," and then she returned her gaze to me and there was that same obvious concern. "The way she looked at you, and you upon her . . . as if you recognized her somehow . . ."

For a moment I considered dismissing the concern out of hand. But my experience with women—as calamitous as it had generally been—had taught me one thing at least. It was far preferable to come up with an alternate explanation for a woman's worries than just claim that they were baseless . . . especially when there was, in fact, good reason for them that you simply didn't want the woman to know about.

"You know . . . I felt that way as well," I said slowly. I released her hands and draped my own behind my back, pacing thoughtfully. "It was as if I did, indeed, know her in some way. And I think I may have sorted out just how such a circumstance would be."

"Pray tell!" Kate seemed enthused, genuinely interested, as if the secrets of the universe were about to be laid out for her. She threw herself across our spacious four-poster bed, propping her chin upon her hands and watching me with rapt attention.

I paced the room like a brilliant mystery solver unraveling a conundrum. "It is said by some that all of us live multiple lives. That the existence we experience now is merely one of many, and with each passing through this plane of existence we acquire more and more knowledge. Eventually those who become knowledgeable enough sit at the right hands of the gods themselves."

"I've heard such things!" she said excitedly. "Go on!"

"It is further said that, as we live each life, we tend to encounter the same people. The bodies change, but their spirits, their essence, remain consistent. That is why there are times when you meet someone and you take an instant dislike to them. It is because, in a previous life, they did you some great disservice."

"And likewise the reverse!" Kate declared. She was practically bouncing up and down on the bed. "When one is experiencing love at first sight, one is meeting a previous lover!"

I pointed at her triumphantly and said, "Yes! Exactly! The way that I felt about you when we first met!"

That brought her up short, and I instantly sensed I had made a mistake. Tilting her head in confusion, she said, "When we first met on one of your earliest raids, you beat me and then kept me bound hand and foot for three days."

My mind froze, and the only thing I could think of to say was "At the time, it was the only way I was capable of expressing the immediate affection I felt for you."

"Oh." To my astonishment, the explanation actually seemed to satisfy her. Then, as if solving a great enigma, she declared, "So . . . you are saying that you encountered that Sharee person before! That you 'recognized' her in some way."

"Precisely," I said, relieved that we'd glossed past a potentially disastrous detour. "I recognized her as an enemy from a past life."

"Not a lover?" She said it teasingly, but I could tell there was serious concern in her voice.

I shook my head. "No, of course not. You saw the hatred she bore for me; chances are she recognized some of that same carry-over resentment. Mayhap in a previous existence, we battled and I slew her, and she knew in me her past destroyer. And I likewise knew her as someone who had caused me some measure of grief."

Kate bounced up to her knees like a joyous child. "Well, then! The best thing that you can do is send her on to the next life! And better luck next time, I say! Hopefully one of the lessons she will learn is not to cross swords with the mighty Apropos!"

"We can only hope," I said approvingly.

"Be strong, my Peacelord," said Kate, "for together, you and I . . . we can remake this world into our vision, and not all the rebels or plotters or schemers can stop us!"

She reached over for me then and yanked me onto the bed. The eagerness and aggressiveness of the Lady Kate, for a moment, gave me uncomfortable recollections of the time when the ring had had its way with me—along with, it seemed, just about every female in Isteria with a pulse. But then I reminded myself that those encounters were long past, and I gave in to the passion of the moment as clothes flew everywhere. The room was lit by a small candelabra which got knocked off its table in our gymnastics, and the light was instantly snuffed out. In the darkness I disappeared into her.

An hour later, as the darkness continued and the gentle snoring of the Lady Kate assured me that she was dead to the world, I tossed on some vestments with only the filtering rays of moonlight as my guide.

Suddenly I heard a faint *tchk* sound in the darkness, and froze. A skittering, a sound like talons clacking on a stony surface . . . and then I realized. I had totally forgotten about Mordant. Obviously he had taken up a perch somewhere in the upper rafters of the room during our horizontal festivities. Now that they were over and I seemed preparing to go out and about, he wanted to be a part of whatever I was doing. On the one hand it was touching. On the other, if he let out a single one of his ear-splitting caws, it would awaken not only Kate but everyone in the vicinity.

I put a cautioning finger to my lips. Mordant stared down at me, extending his neck and cocking his head, and I was struck for the first time by the golden glow that suffused his eyes. I thought of how the presence of drabits had been described to me, and wondered whether or not there was indeed something to be said for it. Then I walked carefully toward the door, my lame leg feeling strong enough by that point that I no longer required the staff to lean on. That was fortunate, else the tap-tapping of the staff upon the floor might also have roused Kate.

I made it to the door and opened it carefully, and that was when I heard the sudden rushing of wings. Since I was awake, I knew it for what it was, but it was not enough to cause Kate to stir. I stood half out in the hallway and extended my arm, and Mordant landed on the outstretched forearm.

It was all I could do to stifle a scream.

I had neglected to don my armbands, and as a result Mordant set down upon my unprotected forearm and casually wrapped his talons around my bare flesh. I clamped my teeth down into my lower lip so hard that I could taste blood in my mouth. Mordant was aware that something was bothering me, but apparently didn't have the slightest clue what specifically that might be. So he casually readjusted his perch, causing new bolts of pain to shoot through me. Exerting every ounce of self-control I possessed, I gripped the door firmly and eased it closed so that we were out in the corridor.

I clamped my free hand over my mouth to stifle an agonized scream as I shook Mordant loose of my arm. The startled drabit hovered in the air for a moment, beating his wings furiously since he'd been caught unaware, and then landed on the ground. He looked up at me in a faintly accusatory manner, and I dropped to my knees and pointed to my arm. Miraculously, he apparently hadn't broken the skin, but it still hurt. *"Happy?"* I whispered.

He stared at me. He didn't seem especially happy; he didn't seem especially anything at all, really. He was, after all, just a dumb animal. *Or is he?* I wondered. I brought my face closer to his and said, "Can you talk?"

He cocked his head once more and said nothing. I could only be grateful that no one was walking past at that moment, lest the Peacelord of Wuin find himself locked away in whatever happy place they kept madmen in these parts.

"Look," I pressed on, undeterred, "I can probably find the dungeons on my own. It's not that difficult; you just find stairways and keep going down. But it'd be easier if I had a guide, and Boar Tooth and Slake claimed you were exceedingly clever. The girl. The one I condemned to death, her and the others. Can you bring me to her? Can you?"

Still he made no reply. It was impossible for me to determine just what he might be thinking. Or he might not be thinking about anything except when he was going to be eating next, because he was just a stupid winged creature with no more comprehension of what I was saying than an onion might have.

Then, abruptly, he took flight. He soared down the hallway, moving in extraordinary silence, and for an instant I thought he was going to be off on his way, searching for rodents who might be skittering around the stronghold to provide him with a late night tasty treat. But then, at the far end of the corridor, he stopped, clinging to some overhead molding, turned and stared at me. His intent was unmistakable; he wanted me to follow.

I obliged him.

We encountered a few straggling revelers along the way, but I doubted they would remember much since every one of them, to the man, was blindingly intoxicated. A couple of them recognized me, barely, and certainly none of them would even remember the encounter.

I couldn't help but feel a bit foolish as I followed Mordant down one corridor into another, down a flight of stairs, up another corridor. The chances were that the stupid creature had, in fact, no idea what I was looking for, and was just playing some sort of odd game of follow the leader. But just as I was reaching the point where I was going to give up and go back to bed, Mordant stopped at a heavy door and tapped it with an outstretched talon. There was a heavy lock upon it, but I saw that a large key was hanging on a hook a short distance away. I took the key off the hook, inserted it into the lock, and turned. It was not done without effort, but moments later I was rewarded with a loud *clak,* and the unlocked door swung open.

I was immediately hit with the distinctive aroma that can only come from a dungeon. The stench of people crowded together in a confined area, of excrement and sweat and hopelessness. My instinct was to slam the door shut, lock it, hang the key up, and forget I'd ever found the place. But I pushed past my intuitive response—never a good move, really—and stepped through. There was a stairway heading straight down, studded by softly burning torches along the way mounted upon the wall. I turned in Mordant's direction to see if he wished to accompany me, but there was no sign of him. Obviously he'd decided he had better things to do than root around in a dungeon. In point of fact, so did I, but here I was going to go and do it anyway. How comforting to know that a mute beast had more intelligence than I.

Then again, he'd also known where the dungeon was. Either he'd understood my words or, at the very least, my intent. Considering the vast number of people I'd encountered who never understood anything I desired in my life, he might not only have been smarter than I, but smarter than a sizable percentage of humanity.

I swung the door shut behind me, locked it lest I be followed by some inquisitive soul, and made my way down. I'd been carrying a small bundle under my arm, which I now set down just inside the door, and then turned to study the descent. Despite the nominal illumination, I squinted since it was difficult for me to see. My hand ran along the cold stone wall for additional support, and about thirty steps later I stepped off onto a floor thick with dust and possibly slime. It had hardly been warm in the stronghold before, but the farther I descended into the pit, the colder it became. If not for the minimal warmth generated by the torches, I might well have lost all sensation in my fingers and toes.

"Who goes?" came a voice from the darkness ahead.

Well, there was no way to avoid being recognized at that point. I removed one of the torches from the wall and held it close enough to my face to provide recognition. Sure enough, a startled gasp came from the darkness ahead. "Peacelord! What brings you here?"

"Rumors have reached my ears," I said readily, having prepared myself for possibly encountering a gaoler, "that the plots against me go beyond the prisoners we presently have. I wish to speak to the woman. Guide me to her."

The gaoler stepped forward. It was probably a good thing that he had drawn the duty that he had, for he really was a repellent creature to look upon. Deathly pale, teeth rotting away in his head, a face covered with warts, his eyes set in a perpetual squint. Although as far as the standards set by women who fancied gaolers, he might actually have been considered quite the catch. "She has the evil eye, that one," said the gaoler ominously. He certainly seemed the authority on the matter, considering his right eye appeared to be somewhat lifeless and just rolled around a bit in its socket without actually focusing on anything. He wore a uniform that bore a startling resemblance to a potato sack. But he was also obviously the man for the job when it came to handling prisoners, because he was an imposing figure even though he was partly hunched over. And he had massive arms that were so long, I was surprised they didn't drag behind him on the ground.

"I'll risk it," I told him.

There was a sharp intake of breath. "The Peacelord knows no fear." He shambled back toward the darkness, gesturing once to indicate that I should follow him. That went without saying, of course, since I was hardly going to head backward away from the cells, but I made no comment on that. It really didn't matter to me if the man had the I.Q. of porridge, as long as he got me to where I needed to be.

We went past several doors, and then he stopped in front of one, looking it up and down as if to affirm for himself that he was in the right place. Then he reached for a large ring of keys dangling from his belt and began, very slowly and with slightly trembling hands, to sort through them. They all looked identical to me, but obviously he knew his business as he fixed his one good eye upon each key before allowing it to slide down the ring and go on to the next one. Finally he selected one and stepped forward toward the door, but before he inserted it I stepped forward and rested a hand on his arm. In a low voice I said to him, "Leave me the key for this cell and then go on about your business. I'll want to attend to this one . . . *personally.*"

His breath hissed out. "*Personally,* Peacelord?" A leer lit up his foul face. Gods only knew what precisely went through his mind at the word, but obviously he was thinking of something specific, probably involving molestation, rape, or other cheery pastimes.

"Yes, that's right. And . . ." I glanced right and left. "I may be bringing in some people of my own to handle her privately . . . when I'm done, you understand. If you catch my drift."

"I think I do, Peacelord," said the gaoler, and he winked his one good eye, which was rather disconcerting because it made the other eye appear to bulge out a bit. "You're saying that if I should happen to look back on her cell and it's empty, I shouldn't be too surprised."

We shared a fine chortle over that, and then the gaoler removed the ring from the key, handed it to me, and lumbered off into the darkness. I didn't trust my vision, however, but instead waited until his shuffling echoed off into the distance. Then with a quick move I turned the key in the lock and swung open the door, holding the torch in front of me for two reasons: to illuminate the cell, and to ward off Sharee in the event she was lying in wait and lunged at me in an effort to escape.

I need not have been concerned. Sharee was seated on the floor of the far end of the cell. There was a sliver of a window space at the top of the wall which provided air and—during the day—a small shaft of light. Otherwise the room was absolutely empty; not so much as a stick of furniture. Not that even a full bedroom set could have done much to bring any joy or style to the dank chamber.

She didn't realize it was me at first, for the sudden light from the torch blinded eyes that had grown accustomed to darkness. "Sharee," I whispered.

She leaned forward, looking surprised for a moment, but then her face settled back into the contempt that I had seen back in the Great Hall. "Oh. It's you."

"Sharee . . . I know what you're thinking," I began.

"Really," she interrupted. "If so, then you'll know better than to turn your back on me. This is all your fault."

"*My* fault?" I was taken aback for a moment with pure annoyance, closing the door behind me as I stepped in. This way we had a modicum of privacy at least, with the door acting as a barrier to sound. I was reasonably sure that the gaoler was far enough away from us to provide us privacy, but one could never be too careful. "Is it my fault that you decided to try and kill me?"

"It's your fault because of the oath I violated."

I stared at her. "What?"

"My weaver's oath. The one I swore . . ."

"Ohhhhh." Then I knew what she was referring to. "When you saved my life, that time that King Meander was ready to have me executed because he believed I was a spy among his troops. And you—"

"I, his faithful weather manipulator, swore a weaver's oath that you were known to me; that I was your lover," she said sourly, voicing that last word with as much distaste as she could muster. "I told you—"

"I remember what you told me. You said that when a weaver lies under that oath such actions have long-term harsh consequences for all who benefit in the short term."

"That's right." She made a grand gesture around her. "And I'm living proof of that. This is fate's retribution, all because I was foolish enough to save your lousy life."

"As I recall," I said hotly, "I saved your life first. And I've saved your life since then. So far I'd say we're pretty even."

"*Pretty even?*" She hauled herself to her feet. "I'm stuck in a dungeon awaiting execution, and you're a warmonger with fools who worship you and with the power of hundreds of swords behind you! In what way is this even?"

We had gone completely off track. Sharee had that effect on me, able to divert me from the relevant topic just by dint of her incredibly annoying personality. I took a deep breath to compose myself rather than let myself get pulled further into anger and vituperation, and then I said with as much calm as I could muster, "I don't want to execute you, all right? I need you to listen to me."

"Listen to you? *Listen to you?*" She raised her voice despite all my gesticulation that she should quiet herself. "When I collapsed out in the Tragic Waste, I thought I was done! Finished! The next thing I knew I awoke in a tent to discover that I'd been found by a nomadic tribe of herdsmen who called themselves the Sand Eaters!"

"Well, they were certainly in the right place for it," I ventured.

"Shut up!" She leaned forward, her eyes blazing. "A quieter, more peaceful people you could never hope to meet! They took me in, cleaned me up, shared their meager supply of water. They even had a healer who was able to cure me of the final infections from Beliquose's arrow. And do you know the only thing I asked them about? You! I asked them why they hadn't rescued you as well! And when they said they'd only found me there, I begged them to go back and look for you, and they did and discovered nothing! No sign of you! You abandoned me in the desert!"

"I didn't—!"

She was shaking her head, seemingly directing her anger and loathing at herself. She was now on her feet, pacing, gesticulating wildly as if this was all bubbling out of her after having been pent up for who-knew-how-long. "And even then, I was too stupid to realize what had happened! I thought you'd wandered off in a haze or been kidnapped! Despite all you'd done to me, I was foolish enough to think that there were lengths to which you would not go, cruelties that you would stop short of! More fool I!"

"Sharee, for gods' sake—!"

Her voice was in a singsong pattern, up and down. "And so I kept looking for you! For months! Wherever the Sand Eaters went on their journeys, so, too, did I look for you! Never giving up hope! And then the poor bastards had the misfortune to be in the wrong place at the wrong time!" She pivoted and stabbed a finger at me. "The city of Mishpuh'cha! Does it sound at all familiar to you, Apropos?" I shook my head, tried to speak, but she kept right on going. "Well, why should it? All the cities you've destroyed, the lives you laid waste to. Why should one be more recognizable than the rest? It was a free and open city, was Mishpuh'cha, and the Sand Eaters were restocking supplies at the exact time invading hordes descended upon them! Slavering bastards with great swords in their hands and cruelty in their blood, and they annihilated all the Mishpuh'chas! Well, not all of them, no. Some they kept in order to amuse themselves, or to have their new prisoners serve their every whim. I was one of the few who managed to escape their heartless endeavors . . . but not before learning to my dismay just who it was who commanded them, and in whose name their atrocities were committed." Her hand swung with surprising speed, taking me across the face before I could get out of the way. "*You, Apropos!* The 'Peacelord.' Apropos, the destroyer, Apropos the monster! Have you been enjoying it? Does it give you pleasure?"

"Sharee—"

She was getting louder and louder, and slapping at my chest. "*Is this some sort of perverse payback for all the wrongs, real or imagined, that you think were done to you?* **You sick, twisted, perverted—!**"

I smacked her. Hard.

It took her across the face and knocked her clean off her feet. She landed on the ground with a *thud,* and I was atop her in an instant, clamping my hand over her mouth. Instantly she sunk her teeth into the base of my palm.

"*Shut up!*" I hissed, gritting my teeth against the pain. "*And stop biting me! You idiot, you're going to get us both killed! I need you to shut up and listen to me, because histrionics aren't going to help, and neither is screaming at me! Arrhhhh—!*" Unable to take the pain anymore, I shoved her away from me and quickly shoved the wounded hand against my tunic.

"Why should I care if I get you killed? You're going to kill me," she said defiantly, rubbing her face where the redness from my strike throbbed. "And how would I get you killed?"

"Because if the gaoler hears you berating me, and I let you rant and rant to your bloody heart's content, word could start circulating that I'm weak-kneed. And that's a very good way to get cut off at those selfsame knees." I risked looking at my hand where she'd bitten me. I fully expected to see that she'd drawn blood, but apparently I'd been lucky. There were faint impressions from her teeth, but no bleeding. "Besides," I added, "when someone is hysterical, that's what you're supposed to do. Slap them."

"I wasn't hysterical. I was furious." Her eyes narrowed. "You're trying to tell me something. What new deceits are going through that villainous brain of yours?"

"No deceits . . . well, that's not true." She started to say, "A-ha," but I interrupted her. "I do have deceits in mind, but they are purely to benefit you."

Sharee leaned back and snorted contemptuously. "That I'd like to see."

"I need you to listen to me."

I suppose the urgency in my voice was sufficient to capture her attention or interest, at least for a few moments. "All right," she said neutrally. "I'm listening."

"You're right. I don't remember Mishpuh'cha."

"I knew it. Bastard."

"Or," I continued, "any other town or city, village or the peoples therein. I don't remember any of it."

She stared at me for a long moment, and then she shook her head. "This is the most pathetic—"

I gripped her by the shoulders, perhaps a bit too hard, because she winced and tried to pull away. I eased up a bit but still didn't let her pull clear of me. "Sharee . . . one minute I was dying in the desert . . . and the next thing I knew I was standing outside a burning city, and there was this dead man with my sword sticking out of him. Everyone's calling me 'Peacelord,' they've all sworn fealty to me, and I couldn't name a single one of them if you put a sword to my throat."

"I'm willing to test that claim if you are," she said. She didn't look impressed by what I was saying.

"You have to believe me," I told her with rising urgency. "It's all a blank. All of it. I have no idea how I got there, or how I came into this situation. It's as if I've woken up in the midst of some great nightmare."

"You didn't seem to be too nightmarish when you drunkenly condemned myself and my fellows to death."

"Is it . . ." I licked my lips, which felt suddenly very dry. "Is it possible . . . the gem had something to do with it?"

"The gem?" She looked at me strangely. "You still have it? Where is it?"

I was about to tell her . . . and then I remembered exactly who I was talking to. Bare minutes ago she had been speaking very loudly and aggressively about killing me. It would be sheer folly to tell her that her precious gem was affixed to my chest. The next thing I knew, someone might be trying to cut it out of there with a dagger, and they'd likely be none-too-delicate about it.

So I settled for saying, "It's safe," and then, anxious to turn the conversation away from the gem, I continued, "And once I get you out of here, you will be, too. At least as safe as your own wits and ingenuity can make you."

Sharee stared at me in bewilderment. "What are you talking about? 'Out of here?' I don't—"

"I have no intention of executing you," I told her. "Listen . . . here's what's going to happen. I'm going to take you out of here with me. The gaoler is already expecting to find this cell empty, and in that regard I do not intend to disappoint him. Once I get you upstairs, you'll switch into a simple but effective disguise; a cloak with a hood that I left in a bundle at the top of the stairs. You sneak out with your appearance thus concealed. Most of the stronghold is sound asleep, so you should not be challenged—"

"Am I to be on my own, then?" she asked with a trace of sarcasm. "The brave Apropos not to be by my side?"

"I'm taking enough of a chance as it is," I told her sharply. "I'm giving you a chance at freedom. The major problem is getting past the front gate, that massive thing of stone. Frankly, I'm not sure how in the world you'll manage it. But if you're ingenious enough, which I believe you to be, then you should be able to find a way out. From there you can go back to the Cartesian Plains or wherever you—"

"And what of the others?" demanded Sharee.

At first I had no idea what she was talking about, so alien to reality was the notion that she was suggesting. But then I understood. "The others? You mean your fellow assassins?"

"My fellow warriors against a dark and frightening presence . . . namely you," she corrected me, and I couldn't believe the poison in her gaze. I couldn't believe it because here I was taking these mammoth risks, and all she was doing was glaring at me because in her mind I wasn't doing enough.

I got to my feet. I know that she noticed the alacrity with which I did so, but I did nothing to let on that I knew she had seen it. "Sharee . . . the risk I am assuming by arranging for your freedom is horrific enough. One missing rebel can be—"

"What, tracked down? That is what you were going to say, is it not?"

I reached up and rubbed the bridge of my nose between my fingers, trying to ward off a headache I sensed thundering toward me. In the meantime Sharee continued, "You wish to make the hunted prey out of me, isn't that it? I appear to have escaped, and the next thing I know, your men are in hot pursuit and it's all a great day of sport."

"No, it's nothing at all like that!"

"That's how it seems to me!"

I waved my arms about like a headless bird. "Believe it or not, Sharee, not all the world is automatically the way that you perceive it! I am trying to set you free!"

"Why?"

"Because—!"

Her scorn did not diminish one iota. "Because why?"

Because this is all my fault and I'm sorry I did what I did to you when I had that ring on me and because I care about what happens to you.

I couldn't believe those thoughts crossed my mind. They were horrific admissions for me to make, even to myself. And naturally I would be damned if I said as much to her. There'd be no point to it. She would just laugh in my face, or accuse me of lying, or start whacking at my chest again.

I must have had a truly ludicrous expression, because Sharee was staring at me as if I had suddenly turned into a drooling imbecile. It took me a moment to focus on her as she said with annoyance, "Well?"

And I said the first thing that came into my mind. "Because you're not expecting me to." I figured it had worked one time, not worked the second time, so I'd see how it fared this time around.

She laughed low in her throat. "So out of sheer perversity, is what you're saying? I'd believe that of you." But before I could congratulate myself on having pulled it off, she backed away from me, her arms folded resolutely across her chest. "Just the same, I'll stay put here, thank you."

I couldn't believe it. I wanted to knock her unconscious, sling her over my shoulder, and haul her out of the cell just because I couldn't stand to see her standing there defying me with such casual haughtiness. The fingers of my free hand (the other still holding the torch) curled into a fist and trembled in frustration. "Damn it, Sharee! What the hell do you want from me? I'm trying to save your life!"

"Save the lives of the others. I'll not wander free while they die for the same crime which we conspired upon together."

*"I **can't**! Don't ask more of me than I'm able to give!"*

And in that infuriatingly arch tone that she was so adept at producing, she replied, "That's when people are at their best, Apropos. That's when they become greater than they are. When they try to give more than they can give . . . and succeed."

In total frustration I slammed my hand against the walls of the cell. "I am sick of this! I am sick to death of being lectured by you! You're the one who's stuck in here, not me! *You're* the one who conspired to murder me! You still haven't given me a solid explanation for that one."

She approached me and I actually backed away, keeping the torch between us. She didn't appear to notice it, and we went in a small circle as she advanced. "An explanation is required? Look at what you've become! You've not only turned into everything that I was afraid you would, but into everything *you* were afraid you would!"

And then something she had said in passing came back to me, and things began to click together in my head. I pointed at her and said, "You once commented that you thought I had potential for great evil . . . and if I achieved that potential, you'd stop me. Is that why you wanted to know where the gem was? Because you think it has some sort of power that can be used against me?"

Her jaw set, she said disdainfully, "I don't have to tell you anything."

"No. No, you don't," I concurred. "And I don't have to let you go. But I tried. And you wouldn't have it. So my conscience is clear."

"Is it?"

"Yes! And the notion that after tomorrow I won't ever have to listen to your lectures or your condemnations or your arrogance . . . it brings me more joy than I can possibly express." I backed toward the door, still maintaining the torch between us. I didn't actually think she was going to try and make a break for it. I doubted she would have given me the satisfaction of thwarting an escape attempt. "We've taken turns getting each other out of life-threatening situations, Sharee. But you've landed yourself into this one now, and if you don't want my help—"

"I don't need your help."

"Says the condemned woman. Oh, but I forgot," I sneered. "You're not afraid of dying."

"No. I'm not," she said coolly. But as she said that—as she was faced with my exit from the room that would seal her fate—I saw, ever so slightly, a flicker of apprehension in her eyes. It could just have been my imagination, of course. Or it might have been that she had just put up the bravest front I had ever seen. It might have been that, like me, she had become a consummate actor as a means of surviving in our little world of brutality, one day at a time.

I paused at the door, and then, on impulse, I held it wide for her. "It's your last chance, Sharee."

But she just shook her head and replied, "No, Apropos. It's yours."

I walked out, slammed the door behind me and twisted the key in the lock, making sure that the bolt slammed home. And I wasn't sure, but as the lock clicked shut, I could have sworn that I had heard a very brief, choked sob. However, I was more than happy to chalk that off to my imagination . . . because it was so much simpler that way.

Chapter 6

Gallows Humor

*R*arely is there anything as festive for a people as an execution. If there's one thing that brings citizens together in large number, it's the government-mandated slaying of someone other than they themselves.

Monarchs know this. That is why the more canny ones try to arrange for as many executions as possible. Supposedly this is to serve as a warning to criminals near and far that their activities will not be tolerated. But the truth is that citizens are starved for entertainment. Bored citizens become rebellious citizens. So giving them something to watch, such as executions, allows them to redirect those gloriously hostile impulses that all humans possess toward something other than the monarchy itself. It doesn't matter if the economy is deteriorating, or if the streets are lined with horse manure, or if the nation is in a state of war that is draining both their resources and the lives of their young men. As long as the people are distracted by entertainment, they can forgive just about anything.

Obviously, in my new incarnation as Peacelord, I was quite aware of this, for at some point in the past months I had had a gallows erected in one of the larger courtyards. I realized bleakly that that might be one of the uses to which I put prisoners when I took them from their various cities. As I had endeavored to justify my actions in other endeavors, so now did I try to find some sort of rational reason for such brutality. Unfortunately, nothing came to mind. But after a few blasts of some very potent ale, I found myself caring significantly less about it. I did not, however, allow myself to become as drunk as I had been the night before. I wanted my head clear. I wasn't sure why. That perverse aspect of my nature, I suppose, to which Sharee had alluded. I didn't want Sharee to think for a moment that I was unable to withstand, sober, the sight of her dancing on air.

I wondered why the opinion of an annoying little weaver that I was about to have slain should have been of any consequence to me. I had no reason to want to please her. She had been more trouble than she was worth from the very beginning. A niggling conscience when none was asked for, a constant reminder of my infinite shortcomings . . . as if I needed someone to present a perpetual catalog of them.

And the fact that I was so clueless in the matter began to anger me. As I dressed to head down to the courtyard, dark thoughts flittered across my mind like shadowy sparrows and then began to build nests there. Kate, the picture of excited joy, was bustling about the chamber, studying in the mirror the ivory gown she was wearing. She chattered endlessly about what a great day it was going to be and how pleased she was that I had not let the little enchantress sway me in any way. The Lady Kate was oblivious, of course. Oblivious to my mood and the fearsome notions that wrestled for control of my mind, oblivious to the fact that I had sneaked down to the dungeon just the previous night. Once I would have found such mindless prattle annoying. Now it seemed a pleasant diversion from the remorseless demands for introspection that Sharee insisted on foisting upon me.

Damn the girl, I thought. Damn her for refusing my generosity. Damn her for sitting in judgment on me. *Me!* The constantly bustling Kate had moved away from the full-length mirror, and I stepped in and studied myself in it. I was dressed entirely in black leathers this day, with a black half-cape over the shoulder. My beard, which I had decided not to shave off, was neatly trimmed to a point, and I was pleased to see that my signature smirk was firmly in place upon my lips. Any sympathies I might have had for Sharee were dissolving like parchment in water. She had brought this business on herself, I reasoned. I was simply doing what obviously I had been destined to do.

Yes . . . destiny. I was starting to become a big believer in that. Destiny, I realized, was not what you predicted you would become, and then you tried to live up to it. Instead, destiny was that which you achieved, and then you looked upon your accomplishment and decided that it was always intended to be yours by divine right.

In the back of my mind, some of the old fears remained. Sharee seemed to have an inordinate amount of lives and luck, and part of me was concerned that somehow she would manage to get out of her present predicament. If that was the case—if she did escape—she would never rest until she had her revenge upon me. Why, I must have been insane ever to even consider allowing her to escape. I had deluded myself at the time into thinking that Sharee, on her own, would pose no threat. That she required her cronies and coconspirators to present a danger to me. But upon reflection, I realized that it was she and only she who was the real danger. She would never rest, never stop plotting to get me.

Why?

Jealousy. Had to be. She saw where I was in life, how I had outgrown her. She knew that I possessed the jewel that she craved. Oh, she cloaked her motivations well enough in high-flown words and criticisms of me, but it was all tripe. She wanted to tear me down because she could not stand to see how far I had risen.

Sharee wasn't great or wise or clever or mysterious. She was just a petty, jealous little thing, and now she was going to meet the fate that all her kind met.

"It saddens me, in a way," I said, unexpectedly (even to myself) finishing the train of thought out loud.

Kate, who had been adjusting a tiara in her hair, stopped and looked at me quizzically. "What does, my love?" she asked.

"Having to execute Sharee."

She froze at that and then lowered her hands, even though the tiara was still lopsided. "You're not . . . thinking of—?"

"Sparing her?" I shook my head vigorously as I strapped on my sword. "Of course not."

She breathed a visible sigh of relief. "That's fortunate. Because she does present a great peril to you, you know. If you value nothing else, you must value your safety and dispose of her."

"I know all that," I said, securing the sword. "It's just that she is clearly so galled over seeing all the success that has come to me. The sight of it makes her suffer with jealousy. Once she dies, her suffering will cease."

"No, my love," Kate assured me, coming over to me and draping herself upon my shoulder. "Her suffering will have just started as she burns in the afterlife for scheming to bring about your demise. The gods have fiendish plans for her, I'm sure."

"The gods have fiendish plans for everyone, my dear." I laughed. "We should not take too much rejoicing in them, for who knows what awaits us and whether our fates will be even more dire than the weaver's."

"They won't be," said Kate with confidence.

With that, she extended an elbow to me, and I took it as suavely as I was able. And together we headed down to the courtyard to watch the execution of the extremely and excessively annoying Sharee.

The courtyard was absolutely packed with apparently everyone who resided within the walls of Dreadnaught. Vendors were sell-ing anything they could to a crowd that was anxious to acquire their wares. The most popular item was a tunic that was illustrated on the front with the silhouette of a hanged man. Little boys were running around with executioner's hoods on their heads, pursuing shrieking girls while waving their little nooses at them. Small strips of steak were being offered on spikes of wood—"Steak on a Stake," it was called. In one corner of the area, a puppet show was being presented. I could see that I was clearly the hero of the piece as a puppet (which wasn't a bad likeness of me at all) was seen whacking away with a diminutive paddle at another puppet. Children and adults alike were watching it and clapped their hands with delight.

Naturally as Kate and I made our appearance, a roar of approval went up. And I have to say, if a day has to be your last, then one couldn't have asked for a nicer one. There was not a cloud in the sky, which in turn was the purest blue I had ever seen. We made our way across the courtyard, and I caught a glimpse of the executioner stepping up onto the gallows in response to our arrival. I tossed off a salute to him, and he returned it, which got yet another cheer. Like me, he was also dressed in black, but he wore no leggings—simply a tunic that came to about mid thigh, and large buccaneer boots, plus the traditional mask. The garment was sleeveless as well, enabling us to assess the awesome musculature of the man. He was solid muscle and sinew; obviously in addition to hangings, he excelled in putting people on the block as well. He could have swung an ax with enough force to drive it halfway to the center of the planet. At this time he bore no ax; however he did have a dagger shoved through his belt, its razor-sharp blade gleaming almost blindingly. It was a common enough instrument for a hangman to carry. Sometimes those being hanged had the remarkable lack of sportsmanship to not die. Particularly if they were not heavy enough, the noose would not break their necks, and then they would just dangle there, their feet flopping about in the air. That could be amusing for the first minute or two, but sooner or later people would tire of—or even become uncomfortable with—their gyrations. So the executioner would pull out his knife and either stab them to the heart or slit their throats for them. All part of the job.

"What do you predict for your customers, Lord Executioner!" I called to him in the traditional manner.

And he, in turn, called back the equally traditional response: "I predict they will be well hung, milord!" This exchange, of course, caused yet another raucous outcry of delirious mirth.

Kate, for her part, was utterly taken with waving and blowing kisses to the enthusiastic crowd. Her feet kicked up little puffs of dirt as she all but skipped across the courtyard, although she continued to hang upon my elbow. I, the royal escort.

I was being treated like royalty; that's what it really came down to. For the briefest of moments I flinched at that notion. After all, had I not seen firsthand the terrible shallowness that came with such an office? The hollow ideals of those below? The secrets, the scheming, even the madness that seemed with astonishing regularity to inflict those of royal lineage. Did I really want to be someone in that vein?

Then I drank in the cheers and approbation, the huzzahs and the undying adoration of those around me, and I thought, *Hell yes.* Just because all those whom I had met in positions of power didn't deserve those positions, did not mean that I was therefore undeserving as well. I was, in fact, more deserving, for all of those other rulers and monarchs and warlords and such . . . they had been born with nobility or title or, at the bare minimum, two good legs. I had been Apropos of Nothing . . . and now, at least here in the stronghold of Dreadnaught, I was Apropos, Peacelord, overseer of Wuin and the most formidable entity around. No one was going to take that away from me . . . no one.

Especially Sharee.

We had been given a private viewing box not far from the gallows. Boar Tooth and Slake were already there waiting for us, and bowed deeply upon our arrival. "Superb morning for it, wouldn't you say, Peacelord?" asked Boar Tooth jovially. I noticed his eyes were slightly red; obviously he'd been celebrating even harder than I'd credited him.

"Superb indeed, Boar Tooth," I responded readily. I thought vaguely about how I'd had some sort of initial revulsion to something that he'd done with a woman . . . a sobbing woman, I seemed to recall. But the reason for her upset was beginning to elude me, and I was left with the growing conviction that Boar Tooth had done exactly the right thing when it was required. Beyond that I did not know or care to think.

We took our seats and Slake, ever the showman, took several paces out so that he could raise his arms and silence the crowd with a gesture. He paused a moment and then, bellowing, he shouted, *"Do you want to see some hangings?"*

"Yes!" thundered the crowd in response. No, Slake wasn't going to have to work hard at all to get this bunch completely into the moment. They were dying for some dying.

As we sat in the observer's box, Kate reached over and excitedly grabbed my hand. Her face was alight with the thrill of what she was witnessing. It was a look that bordered on the orgasmic. I made a mental note to have my way with her once we returned to the privacy of our chambers. Indeed, I suspected that it wouldn't take much urging on my part. She kept casting sidelong glances at me, and at one point I noticed her licking her lips ever so slightly. Oh, yes. Yes, she was going to be a very willing partner when we were alone once more.

"Peacelord!" called Slake, his teeth gleaming starkly white in the sun against his black skin. "Shall we bring out the prisoners?"

I turned to the Lady Kate and grinned mischievously. "What say you, my lady?"

"Bring them out!" called Kate, and here came another roar. My ears were starting to hurt from the collective "huzzahing" that was pounding at us in wave upon wave of sound.

A great door opened at the far end of the courtyard, and, one by one, the prisoners were prodded out into the sun by armed guards. The condemned blinked furiously against the glare of the morning sun. They would have brought their hands up to shield their eyes, but each of them had their hands tied behind their backs with thick ropes.

Sharee was in the lead.

Naturally.

The crowd had hotly anticipated their arrival and was ready for them. Overripe fruit and vegetables hurtled through the air. The guards wisely hung back a bit to give the crowd a clear shot at the prisoners. Most of the missiles did not strike their targets, but as a result of the sheer volume of foodstuffs being thrown, some did indeed manage to hit home. They "splutched" against the prisoners with that singularly disgusting noise that only fruit can make, and the prisoners flinched or tried to fall back. The guards, however, had spears with them, and didn't have to get in the trajectory of the missiles to be able to prod the prisoners back into line.

Only Sharee did not flinch. She did not even acknowledge her tormentors, which naturally angered them all the more. In short order she was the central target of their ire, and they let fly at her with everything they had. The shabby clothes she was wearing quickly became multicolored rags, and still she gave no sign that she was even aware of what was happening. She didn't look at me, or them, or anything; it seemed as if she was entirely withdrawn into her own consciousness. I reasoned that it was possible she wasn't even aware of where she was. That she had taken herself "out" of the moment, as it were. All things considered, that might have been the wisest course for her, for certainly things were going to get much worse before they got better. Actually, they weren't going to get better at all . . . at least, not for her.

"Dead men walking!" shouted Slake to the joy of the crowd. Boar Tooth stood nearby, his arms folded, and he was grinning broadly as he took in the pulse-pounding excitement from all around. It was heady stuff, this.

Sharee arrived at the base of the steps and glanced up at the executioner with no change in her expression. The executioner's own face, of course, remained concealed beneath the mask. Dramatically—a bit melodramatically, I thought—he pointed at Sharee and gestured for her to step up to the gallows. Eight nooses hung in a row on a long pole, and under each of them was a support onto which the condemned were supposed to step. The plan was for the executioner to bring them up, one by one, to their individual platforms, place the noose around their necks, tighten them, and then—again, one by one—kick the supports out from under them and leave them dangling.

I noticed that several of my soldiers were taking bets as to how many would die instantly, and how many would dance on air for a bit before expiring. Considering her petite stature, apparently the smart money was on Sharee to last so long that the mercy of the executioner's knife would be required.

The executioner put a hand on her arm, but Sharee pulled away from him fiercely. This gesture of defiance brought raucous laughter from the crowd as Sharee took several steps away from the executioner. "I can find my way without you putting your paws upon me!" she snapped at him.

"Whoooooooaaaaa," called the crowd mockingly. They did not seem particularly inclined to give Sharee high marks for bravery. It just wasn't that kind of lynch mob.

For his part, the Executioner simply bowed as if to a great lady and gestured for her to proceed him. Sharee took several steps . . .

. . . and paused.

"What's she doing?" asked Kate with obvious impatience.

Sharee was bending over slightly. It seemed she was coiling herself up somehow, as if she was undergoing some sort of stomach cramps. Despite his all-covering hood, it was clear that the executioner was likewise befuddled over just what Sharee was up to. "Are you ill, miss?" inquired the hangman in a surprisingly solicitous tone.

And suddenly Sharee leaped straight up. Her arms moved so

quickly that it was a blur. Down and under herself, under her leaping feet and up, and abruptly Sharee's hands were in front of her.
They were still tied together, but there was about a foot of rope
between them that was now slack. She had literally vaulted over
her own bound hands.

It caught the executioner completely flat-footed. Reflexively he
started toward her, since all he was seeing at that point was a prisoner who was trying to make some last-ditch show of bravado
with a hopeless escape attempt. He must have expected that Sharee
would back up, would try to run.

She did the opposite: She lunged toward him. Once again
unprepared, the executioner's great arms swung out and tried to
grasp her, but Sharee was too quick. She swept down and in,
brought her wrists up in one smooth motion, and the length of
rope between them hit the edge of the executioner's knife blade
protruding from his belt. The blade effortlessly parted the rope,
and just like that, Sharee's hands were free.

The entire thing had transpired in less than five seconds, and then
Sharee reached up, grabbed the executioner's mask, and twisted it
around. The eyeholes now in the back of his head, the executioner
was effectively blind. Although it was only for a moment, a moment
was all Sharee needed as she pivoted and shoved as hard as she
could. The executioner stumbled back and off the gallows and hit
the ground some feet below with a mighty thud.

Pandemonium had now broken out among the crowd, who
thought the thing was simply the greatest show they had ever seen.
Everyone was screaming and shouting at once, and it was so loud
that the captain of the guards barked orders that none of his men
could quite make out, and the guards turned in his direction so
they could hear him properly.

Sharee didn't wait for them to sort things out. Instead she
charged forward and vaulted off the gallows. She landed squarely
on the shoulders of one of the spear wielders whose back was
unfortunately to the gallows at that moment. Quickly she bore
him to the ground as the other guards, realizing that she had taken

the initiative, charged upon her as one and succeeded only in getting in each other's way.

I was on my feet, watching the display and not quite believing what I was witnessing. I looked to Kate then and asked in wonderment, "I've managed to terrorize all of Wuin with *these* idiots at my command . . . ?"

And that was when Kate, rooted to the spot by fear, let out a shriek as her eyes practically leaped from their sockets. *"Look out!"* she screamed

In the brief instant that I had glanced away from Sharee, she had grabbed up the spear of the fallen guard, taken two quick steps forward, and with a smooth and effortless grace had thrown the spear as hard and as straight as she humanly could, screaming, *"This day you die!"*

It hurtled straight at me.

Her aim was flawless.

Had I not been the target, I might well have felt some degree of admiration for her newly revealed skill with a spear. But I had absolutely no time to marvel at her proficiency. In fact, I did not even have time to let out a panicked and startled scream as the spear flew through the air and slammed into my gut with a noise not at all dissimilar from the sounds of the rotting fruit that had struck Sharee and her cohorts.

The spear didn't go completely through; Sharee didn't have quite that much arm strength. But the damage was more than enough as it hit my stomach with sufficient force to lift me clean off my feet and send me crashing into my chair.

"She's killed him! She's killed him!" Kate kept screaming, and it would have been difficult to find anyone there—including me— who would have disagreed with her.

I lay there, stunned, clutching at the still-quivering spear, not quite able to comprehend what had just happened. The world seemed to be spiraling around me. Kate's screeches blended in with the horrified howling of the crowd. The entire execution had

devolved into a hurricane of insanity, and I was the calm eye of the
storm as I lay there and waited for my life to pass before my eyes as
my blood fountained from my gut wound. I hoped, in a surprisingly detached manner, that it would play better the second time
around than it had the first.

No visions were forthcoming. Then again, I'd also heard that
gut wounds could require several days to finish their grisly work.
Just my luck, I thought bleakly. *I finally prove Sharee definitively
wrong about something—namely her belief that this would be the day
I die—and it turns out to involve inordinate amounts of pain
attached to the act of death.*

My hands were gripped around the spear where it entered my
stomach. And as there were wails and lamentations and cries of
"Get a healer!" and *"Too late! Too late!"* and, of course, *"Kill the
bitch!".* . . as all that was happening . . .

I noticed something.

Something very, very odd.

There was no blood. No blood leaking from the wound, no
blood pooling upon the ground beneath me. I noticed no blood at
all.

What I did notice was a distinct and rather painful burning
from the gemstone embedded in my chest. At first I gave it no
thought, far more interested in trying to determine just why my
hands were not thick with red liquid and spilling innards. But then
it slowly began to dawn on me that there might be a
connection . . . and it could be a connection that suggested staggeringly profound possibilities.

"Hold on, my darling! My love! Hold on! Endure the pain!" Kate
was sobbing.

"I . . . don't feel any pain," I said with slow realization.

Kate didn't comprehend. *"He's dying! He feels nothing below his
neck! The final paralysis has seized him!"*

With growing impatience I shoved Kate back with such a surprising show of strength that she, who was bent over me and very
likely believing that she was ministering to my final needs, was

utterly dumbfounded. Slake and Boar Tooth had been heading in my direction, although it was pitifully little, pitifully late. What good was there in protecting a target after the arrow (or spear in this case) had landed true?

And one by one, the members of the hysterical mob fell into complete, astounded silence as I hauled myself to my feet, the spear still solidly affixed to my stomach. I wasn't sure which was more surprising to them: that I wasn't bleeding, or that I was standing at all. All I knew was that, by the time I was fully upright again, every single eye in the place was upon me and no one was saying a word. I glanced in Sharee's direction. She had a guard on either side of her, fiercely gripping her arms, and one behind her, with a knife to her throat clearly ready to carve her a new mouth directly under her jaw. But they too were frozen in place, and even Sharee looked stunned. That look of astonishment on her face was worth everything, up to and including the spear in my stomach.

And I realized that what I had said to Kate was absolutely correct. Not only was I not seeing any blood . . . I was feeling no pain. None. The only sensation I was experiencing was the burning of the jewel on my chest, and even that wasn't painful. It actually felt . . . empowering somehow.

Every bit of medical training I'd ever undergone (mostly for learning how to survive while wounded on a battlefield) told me, in no uncertain terms, that the one thing you never do is simply yank out a spear to the gut. If it wasn't bleeding profusely before, the geyser would come the instant you tried to pull it out, and you would likely take half your innards with you. But I was feeling a bizarre sense of exhilaration, of confidence. Opting to defy all logic and common sense, I gripped the spear with both hands and pulled as hard as I could.

At that moment there was an earsplitting screech.

For an insane instant I thought it was me . . . that I had become so disconnected from myself that I was screaming without even being aware of it. But then I realized with great amusement that the noise had originated from Mordant. The drabit had come swooping down from the upper spires of the stronghold to land atop the gallows themselves, bobbing his head and unleashing that bizarre birdlike caw from the depths of his throat.

And there I stood, with the cries of Mordant echoing across the courtyard, and the spear now in my hands. The point had come away from my body completely devoid of any blood or gore.

I pulled away the section of my tunic where the spear had pierced to reveal my belly.

It was clean. Absolutely clean. No sign of the spear's penetration at all.

I had to know. I had to see. I looked up at Mordant, and, as if knowing what I intended to do, he nodded his head and there was that same bizarre glow in his eyes.

I tossed down the spear, pulled out my dagger from its sheathe, and drew it across my bare arm in full view of the stunned assemblage. There were gasps and shrieks of horror, but these came more from reflex than anything else, for even the dullest of those observing was already figuring it out.

I watched the skin part beneath the blade, and for a heartbeat I thought that I had made a horrible mistake. But as quickly as the skin came apart, it closed back up again. There was no blood. There was no pain.

There was no mistake.

"I can't be killed," I whispered, and then more loudly, I shouted, *"I can't be killed!"*

"It's . . . not possible. . . ." It was Boar Tooth who had spoken, and he was approaching with a look of total disbelief. Slake looked equally as flabbergasted. "Such a thing . . . is not possible. . . ."

"Possible? *Possible?*" With a quick and easy movement that would have been impossible for one whose leg had been as lame as mine once had been, I vaulted over the edge of our private booth and strode out into the middle of the courtyard. Sharee wasn't even struggling in the grasp of the guards; she was instead watching with as much astonishment as anyone else there. Clearly she had not expected this. How could she? No one had.

A wave of almost demented euphoria had seized me.

There is no greater priority for human beings than the instinct for survival. Everything we do, *everything,* stems from that. We eat to survive. We flee danger to survive. We sleep so that we can rest our bodies for the hard work of continued survival. We have carnal knowledge of one another in order to propagate the species so that the species will survive. And I liked to think that my survival instinct was not only as highly developed as anyone else's, but more so. I had spent my entire adult life, it seemed to me, coming up with ways and means to avoid getting myself killed.

Yet now, gloriously, miraculously, that consideration had been lifted from me. How could I not be giddy with joy? And giddy I was; I could not stop laughing. My laughter echoed through the courtyard, and probably through every hallway in the stronghold. Even Mordant took up the sound, making a bizarre noise from his throat that sounded somewhat like a chortle.

"Back off, gentlemen!" I called loudly . . . much more loudly than I had to, really, considering I was standing no more than two feet away. "She cannot harm me anymore!" The guards automatically obeyed my orders, partly out of training, and partly because I think they were so stunned by my transformation that they couldn't wait to distance themselves from me. I could not have cared less. Beings who are incapable of being vanquished did not have to worry themselves over what lesser creatures thought. Sharee was rooted to the spot, staring at me wide-eyed, and I leaned in close to her and whispered with a demented grin upon my face, "This is why you wanted the gem, isn't it. The true reason. You knew that it had this power, and you wanted it for yourself. But you couldn't unlock its functions. I succeeded, Sharee, where you failed. Carry that knowledge with you, Weaver. Carry it for a good, long time."

I stepped away from her, then. Still no one had said a word, stunned as they were by the supernatural drama they were witnessing.

I spoke to them with utter confidence. The notion that they

might turn on me or run from me in fright never even occurred to me, and it was very likely that charismatic confidence I exuded that kept them in their places.

"My good and dear friends!" I cried out to them, arms spread wide. My voice echoed throughout the area. And unlike other times where I had spoken without the slightest idea of what I was going to say, here I knew precisely the sentiments to express. "This . . . is a great day! A joyous day! A miraculous day! You, my loyal followers, have rewarded me with your devotion! With your good will! With your support! But now we see that the gods themselves have chosen to reward me as well! They have bestowed upon me the greatest gift that they can bestow! They have looked down upon your leader, and made me the ultimate source of power in all of Wuin! And do you know in whose behalf I shall wield that power?"

There was a bare moment of hesitation, and then it was the Lady Kate who cried out, *"Us!"*

"Do you know who will benefit from that power?"

And more people took up the cry. *"Us!"*

"Whose coffers will become filled to the overflowing?!"

"Us!" cried out everyone within the sound of my voice. Grammatically speaking, it was an inept response—"ours" would have been preferable—but I decided not to point that out.

I picked up the spear that Sharee had hurled at me, and defiantly I snapped it over my knee. It was a waste of a perfectly good spear, but from a dramatic point of view it was most effective as another roar of approval went up. I discarded the broken weapon, and then yanked my sword from its scabbard and held it high. I looked Sharee straight in the eyes and lunged forward with the sword, and she flinched back, certain that I was about to run her through. Instead a wolfish smile spread across my lips. Never had I felt so empowered in all the time I'd known Sharee. Indeed, in all my life. It was a grand and glorious feeling.

I took a step back and pointed the sword first at Sharee, and then at the other prisoners. *"Release them!"* I shouted. *"Release them and let them go!"*

The mood of the crowd changed instantly. There were protests, shouts of *"No! No! Kill them! They must die! No mercy!"* One would have thought that I was the most unpopular lord of any realm that existed in all the world.

Did I concern myself over the turn in the crowd's response? I most certainly did not. I didn't have to. What was the worst they could do to me? Kill me? That factor was no longer part of the equation of my life.

I spoke over their shouts, which was not difficult, for I so had them in my spell that all I had to do was open my mouth and instantly they quieted enough so that I could make myself heard. *"It has nothing to do with mercy, my people!* Rather, it is to make their punishment all the more stinging! They can do me no harm! They know that now! The entire intent of their crimes no longer has purpose! They will be escorted out of Dreadnaught, sent on their way! And when they return to the Cartesian Plains, and others of their ilk ask them how they escaped, they will have no choice! They will have to tell them that the Peacelord of Wuin cannot be destroyed!

"Imagine the word spreading, my people! Imagine the terror that will induce in every village we visit, in every city we sack! Let it be known far and wide that the forces of Dreadnaught Stronghold cannot be stopped! I, your Peacelord, cannot be stopped!" The crowd had turned back to my side once again, the roaring and shouting, building and building to a massive swell of support. And why not? They had actually borne witness to a genuine miracle. How often in a lifetime did such a thing occur?

And even my lieutenants were now caught up in the spirit of the moment as Boar Tooth shouted, "We are the chosen of the gods!"

"The chosen! The chosen!" echoed the crowd.

Slake was striding about the courtyard, slamming his hands together, and the crowd was beginning to imitate him. The applause was literally thunderous. "The gods are on our side!" he cried out.

"Our side! Our side!"

Every humiliation I had ever suffered, every piece of dirt I had ever been forced to swallow in my life, spun away from me as a new tapestry with my boots crushing any who stood in my way came into being. I felt as if I were a hundred feet tall. I wasn't even bothering to look at Sharee. I was finally rid of her. Even though I was leaving her alive, I had killed the demon of being crippled by her constant disapproval. I was beyond her disapproval, far above it, as far as those glittering stars were above me. Now, finally, my entire life made sense.

"If I have to," I shouted triumphantly, "I can do anything! I am strong!"

"Strong!" shouted the crowd in response.

"I am invincible!"

"Invincible!"

"I am Apropos!!"

"Apropos! Apropos! Apropos!"

Again and again they shouted my name, and with each outcry I felt as if new strength was being pumped into my veins. I had never been more powerful, more alive. And I had never been more certain that I was going to be able to achieve everything that I had ever wanted. There was nothing I could not do, no goal I could not accomplish.

There was no longer a question of "if" or "how." The only thing up for discussion was timetable, and I intended to waste no time at all.

I finally did bother to glance in Sharee's direction as she and her cronies were being led out of the courtyard. You would have thought that she carried within her at least some dregs of gratitude for my generously sparing her life. No. No, not at all. Instead the last I saw of her, she was looking over her shoulder at me and she did not seem afraid or angry or jealous. She seemed . . .

She seemed to pity me.

I gave it no more thought and set off to conquer the world.

BOOK THREE
Pas De Dieu

Chapter 1

The War of Art

*W*hat makes a decent man decent?

What causes people to behave in a moral manner as opposed to an immoral manner? What dictates good and generous behavior over that which would be considered less so? Is it something that is ingrained in each person's fundamental makeup? Is it inculcated into different people by their parents or their upbringing? Are some people simply born with demons perched upon their shoulders, while others attend to the counseling of heavenly beings?

In short: Why do we do the things we do?

I do not pretend to be a philosopher, or to have easy answers, or any sort of answers, to the many questions that have plagued us throughout the years. But I will put forward to you my theory as it applies to people in general, and you will then comprehend how it in turn applies to me specifically.

I believe that what makes good and decent people good and decent stems directly from fear of punishment. That without that fear, the baser instincts which sit at the root of mankind's collective family tree will invariably seize hold.

The fear can take a variety of forms. The most likely of people to "behave" themselves are those who are excessively concerned about whatever punishments might await them once they pass from this mortal coil. They believe that the gods have nothing better to do than watch their every foible, every mistake, every display of human weakness, and add it to a sort of cosmic tote board upon which they will add all the pluses and minuses of an individual's existence and then pass ultimate judgment. That ultimate judgment will then determine if one spends the afterlife cavorting with celestial beings or writhing in torment. So afraid are these poor souls of whatever nasty business a harsh judgment might inflict upon them, that they spend their lives never wavering from the path of righteousness lest they suffer for it subsequently.

There are others who concern themselves about more mundane punishments. To be caught and penalized for crimes committed against neighbors or spouses or humanity in general. The punishments could be brutal. Thieves might lose their hands. Rapists might lose their . . . weaponry, or at least so went the law in certain kingdoms that I knew about. And murderers or those committing sufficiently high crimes could lose their lives altogether . . . although, frankly, if I were the punished rapist, I doubt I'd have all that much interest in living anymore anyway. And so, in order to avoid such earthbound penalties, these individuals likewise make certain not to spend a dishonest day in their lives.

I know, I know . . . it sounds grotesquely boring.

Then there are those who care not a fig for what happens to them in the afterlife, either because they do not think such a thing exists, or because they have the sort of swaggering confidence that allows them to declare, "Let me be sent to Perdition! Inside of six months I'll be running the place!" As for what mortal law might do with them should they be called to account for their actions, the response is simple: "Catch me if you can."

I had always walked a gray area myself between evil and . . . less than evil. I had been skeptical, to say the least, over the prospect of any sort of afterlife infliction of chastisement. On the other hand, I did not quite possess the bravado to openly challenge the law to come after me. Oh, I had my moments of theft, certainly. But it was not my life's work, and I was always judicious enough in my endeavors that I was reasonably certain I would not be apprehended. My thieving activities had been small and unambitious enough to avoid any serious attention from knights or other enforcers of the law . . . which was how I liked it, of course. Generally, though, I preferred to think that my behavior was tempered by my own self-interest . . . that self-interest consisting of my being interested in keeping myself in one piece. What moments of conscience I might seemingly display, or those instances of my acting in accordance with a higher calling, were all easily ascribable to self-interest mixed with a healthy fear of doing something that would get me killed.

When that concern was removed from consideration . . .

Well . . . there's no gentle way to say it.

I went berserk.

Much of what occurred over the subsequent weeks was, and is, a blur to me. I do not know whether this is because it all happened so fast that I could barely keep track of it, or whether I find it so repulsive in retrospect that I wish to forget it ever happened. But happen it did, and there is no way to continue this narrative without dealing with it in as straightforward a manner as I can muster.

That day when I discovered that I was literally invincible, it was as if I stepped outside of my body entirely. Over the next weeks, as lieutenants came to me with new plans and strategies for new campaigns, my mind became bifurcated. I felt I was on the outside looking in, admiring in an abstract manner everything that was happening. I was amazed at the efficiency with which my organization was run, and the zeal with which I pursued my new endeavors.

The question is whether the responsibilities for the sins that followed should be laid at my door or not. It was unquestionably I who did the deeds. My mouth cried *"Attack!"* My eyes blazed with the fire of the truly demented and power hungry, my sword arm swung down and around and slew mine enemies. It was all me . . . or at least an aspect of me. An aspect that had been unleashed like a ravening dog long chained that had finally slipped its collar.

I wish I could tell you that I was torn in some sort of inner struggle, that there was some part of me crying, "Enough! Hold enow!" There wasn't, however. In retrospect . . . I wish there had been. I'm not saying that matters would have turned out differently. In truth, they probably wouldn't have. But at least it might provide some additional, interesting shadings to the study of the mind, or minds, behind the great path of slaughter that my forces carved across the land.

What I'm saying, really, is that I do not know even to this day whether to be proud of what happened . . . or ashamed . . . or neutral. Neutral would seem the easiest. To say, "I was not in my right mind, I accept no responsibility." Or, even better, "I received poor advice by power-hungry underlings; they have been disposed of. Sorry for the inconvenience." That last is a very popular angle to take, particularly among kings. I, however, choose not to take that tack. Instead I tell you, as I have sworn to do, the simple and unvarnished truth: I don't know how to feel about it. I wish I did, but I do not. Both Sharee and, later, the mentor I eventually met in Chinpan, said the same thing: The first step to true wisdom is the acknowledgment of how little you know. If that is all it takes, then I may be well on my way to being the wisest man in all the world.

The simplest thing would be for me to back away from it entirely, to repudiate it utterly. But I cannot do that. Because what happened stemmed from me. From my anger, my frustration, my darkness and rage. From all the times that I had seen people who had power over me and resented them for it. From all the times that I had seen people overflowing with more wealth than they knew what to do with, and I found myself wondering, "Why them? Why not me? Why do I, who started with nothing, continue to have nothing, while they who started with so much just get more and more?"

The realization that I was invincible—that I could laugh off whatever wounds weapons might inflict upon me—unshackled not only my inhibitions, but every negative or hostile thought I had ever had in my life. And believe me when I say . . . that is a goodly share of hostility.

In short order I had assembled my top men, and we studied the maps of the area with the intention of rewriting them in my image. Although I had made a great show of parading my power, I had in fact been confining my raids and attacks to those targets which I was reasonably sure would be vulnerable to us. I had never endeavored to attack anyone larger than our own forces. In short, I had acted as a bully, focusing on those who could not effectively strike back.

As a result, this left a sizable number of larger cities as rich in possibilities.

It didn't take long for us to zero in on the likeliest and most enticing of potential conquests. Due south of the Cartesian Plains was a vast area of steppes . . . semiarid, grass-covered plains, lightly wooded. For some time the area had been subject to intense battles and rivalries between assorted tribes—some thirty-nine of them—and had been beset by civil war. However, about fifty years ago a confluence of events combined with hard work by a handful of aggressive peacemakers had finally brought a cease-fire to the area. It took a good deal of maneuvering and compromise, but ultimately the steppes had been divvied up and a loose confederation of tribes had been formed, known collectively as the Thirty-Nine Steppes. Working sometimes independently and sometimes together, they had created an impressive array of mighty cities scattered throughout the Thirty-Nine Steppes. They were grand and proud achievements, and the tribesmen were fierce and dedicated fighters who would unhesitatingly have laid down their lives to protect all that they had accomplished.

Well, if self-sacrifice was their intention, then the Peacelord of Wuin was more than happy to accommodate them.

Freed from guilt, freed from fear from death, freed from conscience, I led my troops into a full-bore attack upon the Thirty-Nine Steppes.

For days I worked with my lieutenants, planning troop movements, ensuring supply lines, determining the best way to proceed. And somewhere during the planning stage, I underwent a most curious mental process.

I forgot who I was.

I don't mean to say I had amnesia. I did not find myself staring into the mirror blankly and asking the identity of the individual looking back at me. No, I never lost sight of the fact that I was Apropos. I knew at all times that I was the Peacelord of Wuin, a mighty conqueror who swept away all those who opposed him as casually as one might swat away a worrisome fly.

What slowly became affected was my knowledge of where I had come from. Actually, not my knowledge so much as my awareness. It seemed to me on some level that I had always been Apropos, Peacelord of Wuin. I knew in a sort of abstract way who and what I had been before that time. But it began to dim to unimportance, and as time passed, I remembered my previous life as if it had happened to someone else. As if it were the faraway recollections one has of things one has done in childhood, viewed through a pleasant haze of nostalgia. Or perhaps my activities in days gone by did not happen to me at all, but instead to a distant relative of Apropos, whom I didn't really hold in very high esteem. In either case, it wasn't terribly relevant to the Apropos that existed in Wuin.

Apropos of Nothing had been filled with doubts, fears, duplicity, and anger. Apropos of Wuin brimmed with confidence, feared nothing, and said exactly what was on his mind since he was not the least concerned that anyone would gainsay him. All the two creatures had in common, aside from their given name, was the anger. But although the anger simply informed the decisions made by Apropos of Nothing, Apropos of Wuin was fueled by it. He nurtured it, embraced it like a lover, and savored every last black drop of it.

And in my divided mind, I couldn't help but feel that I was working toward a time when all the aspects of my consciousness would be united. For I still could not remember the events that had transformed me into the Peacelord that I was, and I felt a vast emptiness over the fact that this was so. The churning need to conquer was only part of what was driving me; there was also the belief, although whence it came I could not tell you, that at some point I would be rewarded by becoming a whole being. That the two aspects of Apropos the Peacelord—before awareness and after—would become united into one unstoppable whole. Whatever invincibility had been handed me already was merely a foretaste of what was to come, as soon as I accomplished . . .

Well, that was the question, and one to which I had no ready answer.

This, then, was the mindset I possessed when I launched my strike against the Thirty-Nine Steppes.

This was, of course, not the first campaign I had ever wagered, although it was of necessity the most sweeping. However, it was destined to be different from any previous endeavor of my time as Peacelord, because I made it very clear to my men that I intended to be in the forefront of each and every battle. This had evidently not been my practice in earlier times. I had been perfectly happy to plan every step of every operation, but I had always positioned myself behind the front lines of any battle. I had displayed no desire to risk myself. Surprisingly, my men understood. I say surprisingly because more often than not, hardened warriors only respected those leaders who genuinely led. Leaders who would sit at the head of an army, brandish a sword and yell "Charge!" But for the most part, I had let my men do the actual fighting while I remained within my tent and plotted.

Occasionally, though, I had joined them directly in our battles for conquest . . . whenever the plan called for night maneuvers. Then, with my face smeared in woad, I would be in the midst of the fray, lending a hand or a sword. The explanation seemed self-evident: At night I was a much harder target.

But all such trepidation was tossed aside once it became clear that worrying about being injured or killed was a thing of the past. I wondered for a time why my imperviousness had only just now been revealed. The conclusion came quickly: I had never allowed myself to get into such a directly dangerous enough situation that I was at physical risk. Even on the night maneuvers upon which I had occasionally joined, I was not only cautious, but I had maintained a phalanx of guards around me for protection. I was valued for my cunning and ruthlessness, not my sword arm.

Well, that was about to change. I had spent years of running from confrontations while silently envying those who had the physical prowess to stand up to any challenge. I did not have to run anymore. I did not have to envy others; now I could destroy any who opposed me, and take everything and anything that was of value to them. Their lives, their mates, their homes and wealth . . . all, all was mine to do with as I desired.

Power, it seems, tends to corrupt. And as for absolute power, well . . . even more so, I'd say.

Thoughts of Sharee vanished from my mind shortly after she and her associates vanished from the city. I had reached a point where I no longer thought of the past, and the past was something to which Sharee very much belonged. No, my thoughts were only of the present and the future, both of which seemed filled with vast, even infinite promise.

It was a dark and dreary day when we embarked on the war against the Thirty-Nine Steppes. Indeed, Boar Tooth even recommended that we wait for a less inclement day to depart Dreadnaught.

I wouldn't hear of it. I found that I preferred the overcast skies, even felt invigorated by them. "No, Boar Tooth!" I bellowed. "Prepare the troops! This very day the plains of Wuin will tremble beneath the thundering hooves of our advance!"

In point of fact, we didn't have all that many horses. But we had enough to present a fairly impressive mounted presence, and enough foot soldiers to inflict even more damage.

As I'd predicted, we thundered out of Dreadnaught, out across the plains, bearing west and then south toward the Thirty-Nine Steppes. Our advance was methodical and organized, and took many days, but never once in all that time was there any flagging of confidence in our eventual triumph.

I'll never forget that first battle.

The Steppes did not have individual names, but simply numeric designations. The founders of the Thirty-Nine Steppes deemed that the best way to maintain their fragile nation as a unified whole. Individual names tended to breed excessive nationalism which could spill over into more foolish pride-based conflicts, and so the Steppes were simply referred to as Steppe One, Steppe Two, and so on. It was my intention to be as murderously methodical as possible; I guided our troops unerringly to Steppe Thirty-Nine, deciding that we would whittle them down in reverse order.

However, the defenders of Steppe Thirty-Nine caught wind of our advance. No surprise there; we made little effort to conceal our approach and our intentions. As we drew toward Steppe Thirty-Nine, we saw a rather formidable army upon the horizon. They were lined up, shoulder to shoulder, some on horseback, most not. But they had swords in their hands and no fear on their faces. There was about a mile of territory between the two armies. Most of the ground was rather dried out, cracked, and brown, albeit with a few shrubs here and there that served to break up the monotony.

We drew up and I muttered to Slake and Boar Tooth, "Brave bastards, I'll give them that."

"Foolish bastards, I'd say," sniffed Boar Tooth, glancing around. "Rather dreary place to make one's home, much less fight to keep it."

Slowly the army of Steppe Thirty-Nine parted, to allow several riders to pass through. They rode in a quick trot toward us and I watched them come, my face deliberately impassive.

"I believe, Peacelord, they wish to parlay," commented Slake.

"Well, then," I said, "let us not disappoint them." I snapped my reins, and Entipy galloped forward, with Slake, Boar Tooth, and That Guy riding hard behind me.

The wind was in my face, the nearness of battle making my blood run hot with anticipation. The closer we drew toward our opponents, the more anxious I was to get on with it already. The Apropos of old might have enjoyed discussion, banter, and conversation. The new Apropos cared only to know when and from where his next battle was going to come, and now that it appeared imminent, every second that dragged by seemed an eternity.

We reined up within thirty feet of one another. I stared at the chieftain of the Thirty-Ninth Steppe. He was not a behemoth, but neither was he tiny, and his bare arms seemed sinewy and powerful. He wore a plumed leather helmet and leather armor so thick that it could turn away all but the most powerful of blows.

It didn't concern me. Nothing did but the impending fight.

There was a screech from overhead and I looked up. Mordant swept down from the sky, and I extended my gauntleted arm. Mordant, his wings beating the air and his tail sweeping gracefully through it, landed squarely on my arm. Entipy and our horses were quite used to Mordant, but the opposing horses were not. They whinnied fearfully and tried to back away as Mordant eyed them with what appeared to be either amusement or contempt, or possibly some of both.

"They don't seem to like my pet," I said as I swung one leg over and hopped to the ground. If you had told me, back when I was a humble, crippled squire, that I would someday be able to expertly dismount with no care as to the limits of my right leg, I would have thought you mad. By this point, though, it was so routine a maneuver for me that I barely noticed it.

The man whom I took to be the opposing chieftain likewise dismounted. Carefully removing his gloves . . . a tradition to indicate that he carried no weapons in them . . . he then stepped toward me with an extended hand. His face was swarthy, his hair black and bristling. "I am Suliman," he said in a deep and faintly annoyed voice, as if I had forced him to awaken at some ungodly hour. "Sometimes called Suliman the Magnificent. Leader of Steppe Thirty-Nine. And you are the Peacelord of whom we've heard tell?"

I nodded gravely. "And if you've heard of me, then you know that it would be wisest for you to lay down your weapons and surrender to me, unconditionally and immediately."

"And if I do not?" Suliman inquired. He was contemptuous in his look and attitude. I felt the ire within me growing exponentially, a black haze descending upon me, further inflaming my senses. "If I do not do this thing, what do you plan to do? Conquer all the Thirty-Nine Steppes in one great orgy of violence? Do you seriously believe you can overrun all the Steppes at once?"

"No," I said, not giving the slightest indication of anything unusual. Poor fool did not have the faintest idea what he was facing. Truthfully, I wasn't entirely sure of what he was facing, either, but I at least was in a position not to feel threatened by it. "No," I continued with a smirk, "I'm not so ambitious as to endeavor to take on the entirety of the Steppes in one grand orgy of violence. Rather, I was thinking of attacking a dozen at a time and achieving my goal that way."

Suliman gave a knowing nod. "So you would embark on a twelve Steppe program, then. A canny choice . . . but foolishness. As much foolishness," and he looked me up and down, his contempt oozing from every pore, "as your not even bothering to wear armor. You wear the woad of battle, but are not dressed for it."

"Armor is too damned hot," I said dismissively.

He shook his head and actually looked sorry for me. "You cannot possibly triumph."

"I do not know the meaning of the word *cannot*."

"It means, 'incapable of' or 'beyond one's ability,'" Slake said helpfully.

I fired him a glance. "I knew that."

"Well, then why . . ." Then his voice trailed off and he looked a bit chagrined. "My apologies, Peacelord."

I grunted acknowledgment and turned back to Suliman, who conveyed the attitude of one who was perfectly willing to wait all day. "Have you come to discuss terms for surrender?" I asked him.

He regarded me with cold disdain. "Of course not. It is simply traditional that heads of armies meet prior to a battle, in hopes that it can be averted in some—"

Enough of this.

The voice was in my mind, in my soul, and when it spoke with grim clarity, I did not hesitate for a second. I yanked my sword from its scabbard with such speed that by the time it registered upon Suliman what was happening, it was too late. My blade whipped down and around and sliced across Suliman's shoulder, right where the leather armor was missing in order to allow freedom of movement. There was a horrific "splutch" noise, and my blade hacked clean through, severing his arm. Blood fountained from the gaping wound as his right arm thudded to the ground. Suliman's face went deathly pale from shock as his life's blood gushed from the remains of the stump, and reflexively he tried to reach for his sword . . . with the arm that was missing. It was rather comical to watch, really, if one doesn't mind truly morbid humor.

"You'll have to pardon me," I told him as he sagged to his knees. "I've never been much of a traditionalist."

There was a howl of fury from Suliman's lieutenants. They had dismounted when their leader had, so they were on foot when they yanked out their swords and charged me. Boar Tooth, Slake, and That Guy prepared to meet them, but I shouted, "No! They're mine!" And I strode forward, arms out to either side, making no effort to bring my sword around to defend myself.

Their swords cut through me, hacked through my chest, and one actually cleaved my skull. My wounds closed over so fast that it was as if no damage had been done at all. One of them tried to decapitate me. I distantly felt a thud as the blade went in one side and out the other, and then there were faintly disgusting, moist sounds as my throat reknit itself even as the blade passed. It had taken merely a second for the blade to slice through my throat, but half a second for the throat to heal even as that happened. They might as well have been hacking away at water for all the damage they were managing to inflict.

They stepped back, stunned and horrified at what they were seeing, and then it was my turn. With a bloodcurdling shriek I came at them, swinging my sword. They stumbled back, crying out in confusion and terror. Had they been facing an ordinary— dare I say, human—foe, they would have been undaunted. But they knew in opposing me that they had encountered something far beyond their comprehension.

My blade scored several times, bloodying them badly, although I stopped short of any fatal wounds. My lieutenants noticed this, and started to advance, with Boar Tooth saying loudly, "We'll finish them for you, Peacelord!"

I whirled and brandished my blade, stopping them in their tracks. "You will do no such thing!" I said sharply as the wounded men bolted for their horses, stopping only to drag the maimed Suliman along with them. He was moaning and murmuring some woman's name; I think he had no idea where he was. They threw him unceremoniously across the back of his charger and, moments later, were riding away at full gallop. And I shouted after them, *"Tell your people they have one chance to surrender! One! Or I'll do them as I did your leader!"* I was quite sure they heard me.

Lying on the ground, looking rather pathetic, was Suliman's arm. Once I would have flinched at such a grisly trophy. Instead I simply picked it up and, without even having to call him, I heard Mordant's familiar, triumphant cry. I held the arm up and the drabit swept down, its mouth opening wider than I'd have thought possible. He snapped up the rare treat, snagging it by the wrist and arcing upward even though the arm itself was longer than he. He carried it some yards away, then went to the ground with it and proceeded to strip it of meat with delicate precision.

"Do you expect them to surrender, Peacelord?" inquired Boar

Tooth, choosing to look pointedly away from where Mordant was having his feast.

My eyes no doubt glittering with excitement, I said, "I hope they don't."

They didn't.

I later learned that they flatly didn't believe Suliman's lieutenants when they spoke of what they'd witnessed upon trying to attack me. They thought the "fabricated" stories were designed to cover the fundamental ineptness of Suliman's honor guard. And Suliman himself had lost too much blood and was too far gone into shock to be able to verify what they were saying. So the angry soldiers of Steppe Thirty-Nine put the frustrated lieutenants to the sword themselves, placed their maimed leader into safekeeping, got themselves stoked to a howling paroxysm of rage, and charged across the plains at us.

My men met the charge, and I was in the forefront. And this time, I did not hold back. I met the attack on foot, for although I was impervious to death, the powerful mare I rode was not, and I had no desire to lose her to the swords or spears of the enemy if it was not necessary.

I also made sure that I was ahead of my troops by a good fifty paces, so that the men of Steppe Thirty-Nine would immediately converge upon me, thinking me overeager and therefore easy pickings. They did not converge, however. Instead their archers were at the forefront. I have to credit them: It is not an easy thing to fire arrows while in motion, but that is precisely what they did. Apparently thinking to teach me and, by extension, my troops a quick lesson, they opened fire upon me and within seconds turned me into a pincushion.

I stopped. And stood there.

The Thirty Niners stopped. My own men stopped. An instant in time froze as I simply stood and stared down at the arrows which protruded from me every which way. And then, very calmly and deliberately, I proceeded to pull them out of my body one at a time, causing no bleeding, leaving no holes.

Within seconds I was standing there with a fistful of arrows, and the Thirty-Niners were flinching back in confusion and horror. Perhaps they were regretting having slain Suliman's lieutenants at that moment, who obviously had known what they were talking about. I raised the arrows over my head, screamed defiance, threw them upon the ground, and that was all that was required to trigger the full-blown charge of my men. The Thirty-Niners tried to rally themselves, to reignite their battle-passion, but they had been thoroughly disconcerted by what they had just witnessed, and for a heartbeat a sense of hopelessness infested itself in their bones. That was all that was required for my men to overrun them. The archers of the Thirty-Niners tried to inflict damage, but even they—the most self-controlled of our opposition—were so thrown off by what they had just witnessed that many of their shots either went wide or lodged harmlessly in the upraised shields of my men.

My men were everywhere, stampeding over the opposition, and I was in the thick of it. My sword flashed to the left and right, hacking and skewering my opponents all about me, and my blood sang the song of death . . . which, if you must know, goes something like this. . . .

Death death death death death death death la la la la death. . . .

The plains became soaked with red and gore, staggeringly little of it from my own men, and in short order the opposition was in full retreat. We came after them, hounded them across the plains of the Thirty-Ninth Steppe. We took down as many of the strong ones as we could get our swords upon, and the weaker ones we captured with the intention of turning them into slaves and pack mules. Because they were weaker, naturally they wouldn't last as long as the stronger ones might have. But they would be easier to control, and once they wore out, we could dispose of them and bring in new ones.

With the main defending army routed, the cities of the Thirty-Ninth Steppe were ours for the taking.

We took them.

There was some minimal opposition, but the Thirty-Niners

had been counting on the main body of their army to stop us. They had been wrong to do so, and now they were paying the price.

My men pounded through the largest city, actively enjoying all the activities normally engaged in by successful invading armies. I had sent Boar Tooth, Slake, and That Guy off to enjoy themselves, feeling utterly confident in my imperviousness that I didn't need them near me to protect my safety. Nor did they hesitate to take me up on my offer, since they had seen all too well that I was quite capable of taking care of myself.

It was a well-built city, with gleaming towers providing sharp contrast to small houses built low to the ground. I realized that most of the towers were places of worship. Obviously the Thirty-Niners were a deeply devout people who had provided minimal comforts for themselves in favor of focusing their energies on temples and shrines to their gods. Well, a fat lot of good it had done them.

Nearby I heard shrieking, and screaming, and people crying out in supplication, begging either their assailants to leave them be, or their gods to deliver them from harm. I could tell that both sets of prayers were being met with disdain.

I looked at the fires which were billowing forth from the towers, smoke blackening the air, and listened to the juxtaposition of screams against raucous laughter, and I thought, *This is not war. War is a barbaric undertaking, the slaughter of innocent creatures. No, this . . . this is a work of art. We are not simple invaders. We are . . . artists.*

My pulse was pounding in my head, urging me forward. My skin itched; I could barely stand still. I wanted to join in the revelry. More than that, I wanted to make my own artistic statement. But I wasn't sure where to go or what to do first. It wasn't out of a sense of conscience; such things had been long lost to me. I just didn't know which way to turn or in what indulgence I should engage.

"You keep away from here!"

My head whipped around and I saw, standing in the doorway of one small domicile, an angry young boy waving a small knife. He couldn't have been more than ten years old, but this day he had no doubt witnessed enough death and slaughter to last him the rest of his life. He also had only one arm, his right; I could see the stub of his left waving around under his tunic. A bizarre birth defect, no doubt. Not that I cared.

No, what I cared about was the toothsome wench who appeared at the door next to him in great alarm. "Get in here!" she fairly snarled at the boy, and then she looked up and saw that I was staring at her. Oh, yes, quite a dainty morsel she was. No doubt she was the boy's older sister, and what a difference ten years or so made. Lissome and slender, but with exceptionally rounded hips and a face that was not classic beauty, but certainly attractive enough from what I could see of it, considering her black hair was falling in her face. She yanked the boy into the house and slammed the door.

The Lady Kate was miles away, and I was feeling peckish for a little treat.

In the cold light of years later, it seems incomprehensible. I should have identified with the young boy, thinking of my own infirmity, thinking of how fiercely at that age I would have offered hopeless defense against barbaric intruders who might have intended to do harm to a beloved female family member such as my mother. There is no way that thoughts such as *How dare he* or *Who does he think he is* or *I'll show the little pissant* or *She's certainly attractive enough for an entertaining diversion* should have gone through my mind, except in the darkest and most loathsome recesses which would normally have never seen the light of day.

However, as I think should be clear by this point, there was nothing normal about my time as Peacelord of Wuin.

With several quick steps I was to the door, and I kicked it furiously. The door shook but held, and I heard an alarmed screech from inside and a cry of *"Why did you attract his notice?!"* and then a second kick and a third, and the door flew open with the cracking of the makeshift lock.

The room I entered was a simple one, with a few sticks of furniture and a fire burning in the hearth. The young woman shrieked and shrank back to the farthest corner of the room, as if she might elude my notice.

The boy, however, did not shrink, or even hesitate. He ran to the hearth and grabbed a burning tinder from it, gripping it firmly by one end that by chance had not caught fire yet. But the end he was now waving toward me was burning right enough. He interposed himself between me and the girl, his face set in defiance, and wielding his makeshift torch he yelled, "You keep away from my sister!"

"You drew me here, boy, with your foolish bravado. So you've none to blame but yourself. Now run, boy," I said harshly. "Run . . . lest I tie you to a chair and make you watch." The girl was whimpering, paralyzed with fear, offering no help whatsoever.

He said nothing, merely set himself and waited, whipping the torch back and forth to create what he no doubt thought was an impervious fire wall that would force me back. Obviously, however, he had no idea with whom he was dealing or what my capabilities were.

I strode forward, uncaring of whatever threat he might attempt against me, and with a shout of *"I warned you!"* the brave-but-foolish lad lunged at me with the flaming limb. I made no effort whatsoever to get out of its way, looking forward to the expression on the boy's face when he saw the futility of his actions.

The torch slammed just under my rib cage, and the moment it came in contact with my skin, I let out a shriek. I fell back, howling, and there was the nauseating stench of burning meat which I immediately realized was me.

I tripped over a chair and went down, clutching at my agonized side, and the boy leaped upon me, trying to shove the torch into my face. It was the merest luck that a desperate sweep of my arm knocked the burning limb aside, for my mind was overwhelmed with the pain radiating from where he'd damned near incinerated me.

It's gone! It's gone! The power is gone! shrieked my terrified mind, and then both of the boy's knees were upon my chest while my previously smug and confident demeanor lay in tatters at this horrific discovery. Before I realized what was happening, the boy had yanked his knife from his belt and he plunged it into my chest. It was not a dead center thrust, but was still accurate enough and deep enough to puncture a lung.

I felt nothing. No pain, nor even discomfort. Pulling my scattered wits together, I slammed the base of my hand up and caught the boy squarely in the forehead, knocking him off me. Staggering to my feet, I looked down at the knife which was still sticking out of me. I yanked it out, turned it over and over. No blood. I felt where it had gone into me, and the wound had already healed. I was still invincible . . .

. . . except that there was agony emanating from where the torch had been shoved against me. And now the boy had scrambled back to standing, and he had picked up the limb from where it had fallen and was waving it about once again. His sister had not moved from the spot.

If I had simply waited there, time would have been on my side. For his was not a proper torch, and in another minute or two the flame would have consumed the entirety of the limb and he would no longer be able to hold it. They would both be helpless before me then.

But my taste for the opportunity had faded. I was totally befuddled by what had just happened, could not begin to comprehend it, and had no desire to stand around until I did manage to sort it out. With a grim snarl of "To hell with both of you!" I backed out of there, leaving them to whatever fate was in store for them.

I staggered a short distance away and then rolled up my tunic to examine the damage. There, right where he had jammed the torch, the skin was blackened and blistered. I had been severely burned, and just the sight of it was nearly enough to make me faint. The pain was already so intense that I could barely move my entire torso. Gingerly I dropped the tunic back down to cover it, and then started to make my way back to our base camp.

I passed many of my soldiers going about their business, and each of them greeted me and bowed to me and hailed my name and my greatness. To each one I smiled and waved, and tried not to let the agony I was feeling detract from the festive mood. Under no circumstance could I let anyone know what had happened to me. They had gained so much confidence from the notion that I was impervious to all harm that to let them know otherwise might have dealt a lethal blow to their conviction that we were, as a group, invincible.

By the time I reached my base camp, however, I was feeling better. Reexamining the wound, I discovered it was already healing. And by the morning, I found not even the slightest hint of any damage having been done to my body.

But still, the experience had been somewhat daunting for me, and left me wondering if there was anything else to which I was vulnerable. At the very least, it served as a warning that I'd best steer clear of any assault which involved flaming arrows.

A small one-armed boy had issued a daunting rebuke to the indestructible Peacelord. Then again, even the greatest of artists, I reasoned, had to deal with critics.

Chapter 2

The Ice Man Cometh Again

*A*nd so we continued our assault across the Thirty-Nine Steppes.

The degree of resistance we encountered varied depending upon where we went. Some of the tribes were made of sterner stuff than others. Some of the tribes joined forces in their endeavor to stop us. They tried to overwhelm us. They tried to ambush us. They tried to outthink us, to outmaneuver us. They tried catapults, they tried lances, they tried poisons. In short, they tried everything they could conceive of in order to try and slow us down.

And they did manage that much. They slowed us down.

But they did not stop us.

Our march across the Thirty-Nine Steppes continued, Steppe by Steppe, inch by inch. The tribes even endeavored to hire free-lance swords to go up against us, but more often than not the free-lancers wound up joining our side.

What we further discovered as we advanced were the cracks in the unity of the Thirty-Nine Steppes. Ancient hostilities and long-forgotten enmities between tribes started to surface as different tribes began to blame one another for the misfortunes that had befallen them. My favorites were those who accused others of acting in an impious manner that had brought the wrath of the gods down upon them, as personified by my troops and I. Honestly, if all the remaining tribes had banded together against the common enemy . . . well, I do not know if they could have stopped us, but it would have made our task all the harder. But they were so busy arguing with one another over whose fault it was or what to do, that they made themselves that much more vulnerable.

The bizarre incident with the flames hurting me faded into distant memory as my imperviousness to harm continued unabated . . . although, as noted earlier, I opted to steer clear of not only flaming arrows, but boiling oil, having no idea just how much imperviousness I held to anything having to do with extremes of heat.

And whatever interests I might have had in ravishing helpless females quickly faded when, one day, the entourage of the Lady Kate showed up at one of our base camps. The Lady came to me in my tent, her face wild with excitement, telling me that she was no longer able to simply sit still at Dreadnaught stronghold and hear intermittent reports of my triumphs. She wanted to be there to witness them with her own eyes.

I had to admit, she was a stunning sight to behold. She looked even younger and more vibrant than when I'd departed, and tales of my exploits made her so sexually charged that she could barely sit still as she listened to them. Thereafter I divided my time between carnage and slaughter, and entertaining the increasingly enthusiastic and, frankly, insatiable Lady Kate. Feared in battle, adored in bed, life simply did not get better than that.

And yet . . . it was about to. . . .

I had been lazing about in my tent the evening that we had conquered the Twentieth Steppe, the Lady Kate snuggled at my side.

Mordant was seated on his perch nearby, his wings drawn about him, sleeping. Boar Tooth had sought audience with me, and Kate urged me to refuse him entry, for she had other ideas about how to spend the evening than in, as she termed them, "Yet another dreary strategy meeting." When I tried to emphasize to her the necessity of such things, she would say dismissively, "You need no strategy. You are the Peacelord. You are the greatest warrior in all the history of Wuin. None can stand against you."

"All true, my love, all true," I had assured her. "But just because I make these things appear effortless does not mean they come without effort. If my lieutenants feel the need to talk with me, I must attend to those concerns."

And so it was that Boar Tooth came before me and imparted news that placed an entirely new slant upon our campaign.

At first I laughed scoffingly when Boar Tooth told me that several of the remaining tribes had banded together under the single leadership of an outsider. "They actually agreed upon a leader?" I asked. "That fractious bunch? I find that rather hard to believe."

"Well . . . apparently, he's a king of some renown."

"A king?" It was the Lady Kate who laughed mockingly. "A king who comes wandering into the middle of a war? Ridiculous. Kings tend to their own kingdoms unless directly threatened, and they certainly don't take up with—"

"*Quiet!*" The order had burst from me with such vehemence that Kate was shocked into silence. Indeed, the sharpness of the tone I had taken with my lady love surprised everyone in the room. Even Mordant was startled from his slumber and looked at me quizzically. But I could not have cared less at that moment, for pieces of suspicion were starting to click together in my mind. On my feet I slowly approached Boar Tooth and said, hardly daring to hope, "This so-called king . . . would his name be . . . Meander?"

Boar Tooth blinked in surprise. "Why . . . yes! Yes, Peacelord, it is! How did you know?"

"Apropos the Peacelord knows all!" Kate proclaimed. "Beloved by the gods, he is—"

"*Will you for the gods' sake shut up, woman!*" I snapped in exasperation.

Kate was taken aback, but meekly she said, "Yes, my love."

My mind was racing. I could scarcely believe my good fortune. Boar Tooth looked at me uncomprehendingly and said, "This man is known to you, Peacelord?"

"Ohhhh, he is most very well known to me," I said intently. "He is known to me as the murderer of my mother."

Kate gasped upon hearing that, and Boar Tooth's face darkened. "Then he is a dead man."

"Yes. Very much so," I replied. "But he's my dead man."

Had King Meander actually been the one who killed my mother? I didn't know for sure. If I was looking for a confession, then I was never going to get it because Meander himself didn't know.

But I was in a state of mind where there was no room for "maybe" or shades of right and wrong. The business with Meander the Keepless King was a dangling thread in my life, and I now intended to tie that thread off for good.

It did not take long to amass the troops and prepare them for the assault on Steppe Nineteen. Word had spread throughout the camp that there would likely be greater opposition awaiting us there than at any of the previous Steppes, but that was of no consequence to the men at all. For they were convinced that the gods were on our side, as made clear by their having favored me with the gift of invincibility. I had once been told that wars are won in the mind before they are won in the battlefield, and if that was the case, then all that was going to be required from this point on was mopping up. The men would loudly sing my praises until all hours of the night, sharpening their weapons, girding themselves for battle. As for me, I cheerfully serviced the Lady Kate in my tent. While she moved under me, purring and scratching at me in her enthusiasm, my mind was already vaulting ahead to the confrontation with Meander and the settling of some very old scores.

Was he responsible for my mother's death? At that point, the truth of it no longer mattered to me. Or at least, it mattered less than the notion that I wanted someone to pay.

I learned that Meander and his Journeymen had supposedly assembled in the capital city of Steppe Nineteen. It was a city with a variety of names, but many referred to simply as the Golden City, supposedly a favorite of the gods. That was perfectly fine to me. Let Meander and the residents of Steppe Nineteen make their stand there, convinced that they would be protected because of the "sacredness" of the city. I would be more than happy to disabuse them of any notions that their faith afforded them safekeeping in any way.

My men had been part of the campaign for close to six months. There had been some discussion of returning to Dreadnaught for a time, to rest and recuperate. We had sacked so many cities, acquired so much in the way of loot and slaves that it seemed we had crossed over the border from raiders to dabblers in wretched excess. I might indeed have attended to their concerns, but hearing of Meander's presence fired me onward. Assembling my troops, I informed them that the Golden City would be our last stop for a while. Our supply lines were admittedly stretched a bit thin, and the troops were looking somewhat haggard . . . if for no other reason than that they had been constantly pillaging, plundering, and debauching nonstop for half a year. That would take a toll on just about anyone.

So with the promise that this would conclude the first stage of the initiative, we set out for the Golden City. We were nearly a thousand strong, and utterly confident in our ability to overwhelm whatever enemy might face us. I had suggested to the Lady Kate that it might be advisable that she return to Dreadnaught, but she would not hear of it. She wanted to see the sacking of the Golden City with her own eyes, and so was carried along on a litter hauled by four slaves. Her entire manner was one of barely controlled excitement, and her constant queries of

"Are we there yet?" seriously began to get on my nerves by the third day of travel.

We anticipated resistance. That was why we sent out advance scouts as we wended our way toward Steppe Nineteen. On the sixth day of travel I called a halt as I saw our scouts returning, but the report they presented to me and my lieutenants was nothing short of befuddling.

"No troops? Are you sure?" I asked skeptically. Boar Tooth and Slake likewise looked extremely doubtful of what our scouts were telling us. That Guy just sharpened his sword, as he usually did.

But they were adamant. They told us flatly that the road to the Golden City seemed completely clear. There were no troops anywhere along the way to oppose us.

"It's a trick," growled Boar Tooth a short time later when we conferenced in my tent.

I was laid out with my head resting comfortably in the Lady Kate's lap as she fed me dates. Outside I heard the customary songs of my greatness being sung. I realized I had heard them all before, and resolved to have some new ones written.

"It has to be a trick. An ambush," continued Boar Tooth.

"What ambush?" Slake demanded. "How? Where? The scouts claim they had a clear view of the territory all the way to the walls of the Golden City. It's not as if there's a good deal of vegetation behind which they can hide."

Boar Tooth had been pacing furiously, but now he turned to Slake and said, "What are you suggesting?"

Slake shrugged. "Perhaps they realize that their cause is hopeless."

"Nonsense!"

The Lady Kate spoke up, pausing with a date dangling over my mouth. "Why is it nonsense? Is it not true that their cause is hopeless? Nothing can stand against the Peacelord! We all know that! Perhaps they do as well."

"Or perhaps," I said slowly, "our scouts have been corrupted by Meander. That would be consistent with the manner in which he operates. He uses bribes and generosity to sway opposing soldiers over to his side."

But Slake and Boar Tooth, although they had been in disagreement over what to make of the reports, were adamant that this could not be so. "We swear on our lives, Peacelord," Boar Tooth said firmly, "that these men are unimpeachable."

I sat up, scratching my chin thoughtfully. "It is indeed your lives that are being sworn upon, gentlemen, since it is already quite evident that mine is not at risk." I had continued to tell no one of the odd incident with the fire. If I did indeed have a vulnerability, which seemed to be the case, informing anyone of it—even those I ostensibly trusted—would be pure foolishness. As far as they knew, I continued to be impervious to all harm, and that was the way I wanted it. "Well, we shall know soon enough, I suppose. We march for the Golden City . . . on the morrow!"

Well, it rained on the morrow. And the morrow after that.

We sat there in our camp, bored out of our minds, but I refused to command an attack in such foul weather. It would provide far too many variables. If we were marching into new territory against an enemy of unknown size, we certainly didn't need to add to our woes by battling in inclement conditions. For a time I wondered if Sharee was involved somehow . . . whether she was manipulating the weather patterns to slow me down. But finally I dismissed the notion. The simple fact was that sometimes it rained. That was all. It needed no weatherweaver to cause it to happen; nature was sufficient to attend to it.

The sun broke on the third day upon a ground covered with muck and mire. The weather was humid, zealously preserving the moisture so the terrain wasn't drying as thoroughly as it would have been. But the men were becoming impatient, and I admit I was also getting tired of sitting about. So we set off shortly after breakfast, with a song in our hearts and murder on our minds.

We were in sight of the city before noon. In the distance I saw a small mountain range, including one that seemed to tower above all the others, so high that snow actually dusted the upper reaches of it. I inquired as to the name of it from one of the captured guides, who was reluctant to talk at first until Boar Tooth threatened to loosen his tongue permanently, at which point the guide said, "That is Mount Aerie. It is said to be the home of various flying creatures who prefer to make their homes at high altitudes." At that time I had Mordant perched upon my arm, and the guide looked nervously at the drabit as he spoke. "Some say that beasts such as those," and he pointed apprehensively at Mordant, as if afraid the drabit might snap his finger off, "originate from Mount Aerie."

"He's not a beast," I said sharply, "or at least, not in comparison to some of the human monsters who walk upon two legs that I've met in my time." Mordant seemed to appreciate this and made an odd "cooing" sound in the back of his throat. The guide wisely chose not to press the matter.

The Golden City was now less than two miles off, and new scouts went out this time to see what the situation was. We were on the main road leading to the city, and called a halt as we awaited the appraisal from the scouts. From where I was sitting, though, it appeared that our first reports had been absolutely correct. There was no sign whatever of any organized resistance. What, did they plan simply to sit there and welcome us into their city so that we could bring it down around their ears without a fight? Considering we had initially heard so much about their endeavors to stand against us, I had to admit to myself that I was feeling somewhat disappointed over the apparent ease with which we would achieve our victory.

Not much later the scouts returned, riding hard all the way, and there were looks of both incredulity and concern on their faces . . . the former because of what they had witnessed, and the latter out of fear that they would not be believed. Considering what they told us, I could easily understand their worries.

The men had been milling around, but many drew close as the scouts prepared to make their reports. We were standing in about three inches of mud, so none of us was in an especially good mood. We ringed them, our faces already painted in the battle designs of woad, and we looked fierce and eager for battle. So the woad exaggerated the expressions of wonder upon our faces when the scouts gave their reluctant report.

"The gates to the city are wide open," said one of them.

This caused exchanged looks of confusion among my men. "Wide open?" said Slake skeptically. "You mean . . . they are not even barred against us? They do not offer the most minimal of defense?"

"That," said the other reluctant scout, "is not the least of it, or even the most insane." He took a deep breath then, with the air of a man who is about to hurl himself off a very high cliff, knowing that a large array of pointed rocks awaited him at the bottom. "We saw a man who, by all descriptions, was likely King Meander. But . . . but he has gone mad."

"Mad?!" There was now confused babbling from all around. The scouts had no idea which way to look first or whose question to answer. As for me, I simply stood there, taking it in, almost not daring to believe while all the time suspecting the next words I was going to hear.

It was the Lady Kate who took charge. Stepping forward, she said firmly, "How now? 'Mad' in what way?"

"He . . ." The scout gulped, looked to the other for assurance that what he was about to say was not the height of insanity, and then told us, "He has climbed to the top of one of the parapets . . . and he is strumming a lute and singing bawdy songs. And he appears to be the only one there; the rest of the city, for all the activity we were able to perceive, was empty."

Well, that was enough to get everyone talking at once, each man shouting to be heard while Kate tried to calm them and answer their fears. Some were shouting that it was ill-fortune to battle a madman, for such creatures were often the beloved of the gods and had divine backing. And many others were crying out that it was a trick, an ambush. That Meander was expecting us to come riding in, confident in our victory, only to find ourselves under attack, and that the last thing we should do is give him what he wants and go barreling into the city to certain doom.

And then I could not contain myself anymore. I began to laugh, louder and louder with each passing second. My men looked perplexed, as if concerned that whatever insanity might have grabbed hold of Meander had now gone to work upon me as well.

"Peacelord?" inquired Boar Tooth nervously, for now all attention was upon me and my demented cackling. And Kate, equally apprehensive, said, "My love . . . ?"

"It's a trick!" I finally managed to get out once I'd gotten enough breath back to speak. "But not a trick concealing an ambush. It's a bluff! A colossal bluff!"

Kate came forward, resting with obvious concern a hand upon my shoulder. "My sweet . . . my beloved Peacelord . . . are you *quite* certain?" And the men did not look any too pleased, either, not exactly eager to throw themselves into a situation that seemed to defy every known law of combat tactics.

But I never doubted it for a second. "It's a desperation ploy," I said with what I hoped would be enough confidence to inspire the men to believe me. "Obviously what happened was that Meander was unable to keep his volatile collection of sellswords and gangs in order. Nor was he able to inspire confidence in the hearts of the men of Steppe Nineteen. Knowing that we were coming, knowing that their defeat was assured, all have fled."

"Fled?" asked Kate. She did not appear entirely convinced. "But then why . . . ?"

"Why would Meander stay behind? Take this crazed chance? Because," I said, slowly circling the men and chuckling as if explaining the most simple avenue of warfare instead of one which was highly unorthodox. "Because he is just egotistical enough, or brash enough . . . or insane enough, if you will . . . to think that he can save this city single-handedly. And the bluff might have worked were I not familiar with it."

"Bluff?" They seemed more puzzled than ever.

Slake and Boar Tooth were standing next to each other, so I

stepped in between them and draped an arm over either shoulder. "King Meander," I explained, "has a very selective memory. Apparently he recalls a time, some years ago, when a desperate young squire—left with the impossible task of defending a fort populated only by a king, a princess, and a jester—hit upon a desperate scheme that caused an entire army to become frozen by its own uncertainty." When they persisted in staring at me blankly, I let out an exasperated sigh and said, "This is *my gambit* he's instituting. I did this very thing! I convinced a king, known for his wiles, to do exactly what Meander is doing now . . . except at that time, it was Meander himself who headed up the invading army! And his army became so convinced that it was a trap that they turned around and left . . . rather than charge a completely empty fortress! Cold steel works its wonders on man's spirit, but nothing paralyzes people more than cold, stinking fear. And that's what he's trying to do now . . . to us!"

"But . . . he must know you wouldn't fall for such a trick, considering it's your own scheme!" the Lady Kate pointed out.

I released my hold around Slake and Boar Tooth's shoulders and walked around back to her. Shaking my head, I said, "Remember, I told you his memory is selective. He very likely does not associate the trickery foisted upon him by a lone squire, whose name he probably doesn't even recall, with an invader backed up by an army five hundred score strong! We have him, I tell you! In fact," and I was struck by a thought, "there may well be helpless citizens in the city, hiding in their homes, praying that this folly is successful because their own army was unwilling to face up to the odds and be cut down! This will be the easiest attack in our history!"

All around me now there was nodding and smiling and laughter as my men realized not only the foolishness of their own concerns, but were also beginning to envision the absurdity of a king perched upon a parapet, hoping to scare off invaders by singing ludicrous tunes. Soon the entire army was rocking with laughter, and then one of them started chanting repeatedly, "Peacelord! Peacelord!" Others took up the cry and soon the dreary day was filled with soldiers cheering me. Never had I felt so exhilarated, so alive.

By this point, with the plundering of cities in the previous Steppes, we had amassed a considerable number of horses. Over half my men were mounted, giving us a considerable complement of horsed warriors. It was they who took the lead now, with me at the head, of course, firmly astride Entipy and anxious for retribution and further glory. We pounded down the highway leading to the Golden City, howling battle cries, not the slightest bit hesitant in our purpose or our belief that we were going to win.

We drew within sight of the Golden City. It was an impressive sight, I'll admit, with elaborately curved and crafted towers, beautifully painted in shades of blue and brown, that seemed capable of touching the sky. As was not unusual for most larger cities, mighty walls ringed it to afford it protection . . . not that it would do any good against us. As we got closer, I could see him, perched right where the scouts had said. My blood boiled with fury, pounded behind my eyes and I could already see in my mind's eye my sword gutting the bastard. Oh, but first . . . first, perhaps, I would tie him up and let a half a dozen harlots attack him. Rake his face, his bare chest, any part of him they chose with the fingernails they routinely kept so sharp. In short, give him just a taste of the suffering that my mother had undergone under his less-then-tender ministrations.

The road was still thick with mud, Entipy's hooves chewing it up and sending it flying to either side. I was relieved, frankly, that we were not going to have to fight a major battle on foot; slogging through gobs of mud to hack away at an enemy was never my idea of a fun time. But carving up a helpless foe . . . yes, that would be most enjoyable.

Less than a mile now remained between us and our target. I could see him up there, and he tossed off a jolly wave. He was much as I'd remembered him. The solid gray hair, the thick gray-and-black beard, the face with a craggy, weatherbeaten look. From that distance I couldn't make out those old, tortured eyes, or the four scratches upon his face which I believed had been left by my mother when he had tried to commit brutal acts upon her. I held no delicate beliefs about the woman whose loins had spat me out into the world. She was a whore; she plied her trade with her body. But there were some things that a right and decent whore simply did not do, and when she had refused to submit to Meander's desires to do them, he had slain her. He . . . or at the very least, one of his men, and since he was their leader, that made him responsible enough as far as I was concerned.

Closer and closer still, and I could almost feel the sudden shock that would greet my arm when I drove my sword through his face . . . or perhaps his gut. Yes, that would be preferable. It would take him several days to die from a wound to the stomach, and during that time, he could be . . . played with.

And while all this was going through my mind—as I was in the forefront of the charge—Mordant suddenly angled down, and he was screeching at me. I afforded him barely a glance at first, and then I saw that he seemed agitated somehow. But I was in full gallop at the moment; I didn't have the time to devote any attention or energy to the concerns of a pet.

And that was when Entipy let out a sudden, alarmed shriek, jerked suddenly, and with no warning beyond that, toppled over.

I barely had time to throw my sword clear, out of reflex, as Entipy went down. I hurled myself clear of the saddle and hit the ground, coming up in a roll and covered with mud and dirt. I looked around desperately, saw my sword sticking up out of the ground, and lunged for it.

It was incredibly fortunate that I had been as far ahead of my men as I had been, because had they been close behind me when I'd toppled, they'd have run over me before they were able to stop themselves. As it was they reined up, but barely in time, and a number of the mounted soldiers crashed into one another, their beasts whinnying in alarm and my men crying out as their legs were mashed between the sweating, heavy bodies of their beasts.

I yanked my sword out of the muddy ground, and my feet

almost went out from under me. Had my right leg still been lame, I would not have been able to stand at all, but fortunately it had become as powerful as my left. I righted myself before I fell and looked at Entipy. Beneath my woad, my face went deathly pale.

A still quivering spear was sticking out from the base of her throat, right at the jugular groove. Poor Entipy was done for, flopping about like a beached fish, her blood mixing with the dirt and mud beneath her. Her eyes looked at me with what seemed open accusation even as her body was rocked with spasms.

Seeing a creature called Entipy die so brutally had more impact on me than ever I could have expected. I screamed out in rage, spun to face Meander, whom I held responsible, blinded by my fury to the slow-in-coming realization that he could not possibly have been responsible for the missile which had cut down my horse.

And suddenly they were everywhere. The ground to either side of us literally seemed to come alive, and at first I thought that somehow a weaver of gargantuan power had actually ensorcelled the very ground against us. But then I saw flashes of black and silver, the colors of Meander's Journeymen, and howls of challenge as we were beset on either side. And above it all, the mocking laughter of Meander.

Then I understood, but too late to pull my men out.

I could see them in my mind's eye the previous days now. They had no magiks at their disposal, but they must have been able to tell that rainstorms were moving in. They had used the knowledge of the incoming rains to plot their strategy. They had offered no initial resistance, waiting for the storms, and when they had arrived, there had been Meander's men with shovels, picks, whatever digging implements they could find, burrowing channels into the muddy, rain-soaked ground on either side of the highway. Row upon row of them, enough to conceal who-knew-how-many hundreds of them, and then rolling about in the muck and mire to cover themselves in it. And then they had lain there in hiding, camouflaged, displaying infinite patience, waiting for us to come riding right in between them so that they could outflank us.

It had been no bluff. Meander had taken my strategy and not simply copied it, but improved upon it. And in my arrogance and overconfidence, I had led my men right into the trap which had snapped its strangle hold upon us.

I heard my men crying out, I heard Meander's laughter, louder and louder. I heard the dying cries of my horse, my startled and frightened men calling my name as they suddenly found themselves in the midst of an ambush, and—although I had not been present for it—I heard the death rattle of my mother.

Darkness and black fury surged within me, and a burning in my chest that liked to cremate me where I stood. And then I screamed, a howl of agony and fury combined that might be vomited up by a hundred voices of the damned, crying out in unison as they are consigned to the depths for eternal punishment.

And a black cloud of madness descended upon me, filling me within and without. It was like nothing I could ever recall experiencing . . . like nothing that anyone had ever witnessed, including me, for I saw none of it. My mind simply went away, darkness fell upon me as the heat radiating from my chest consumed me, and the world spiraled away.

Chapter 3

Hallow Pursuits

*R*ETREAT! RETREAT!"

You would have thought that it was my voice crying out that ignoble order, but it was not. No, it was a voice that I had not heard for some time, but recognized all too quickly. And it was a voice that, because of its sheer volume, was enough to jolt me from the walking coma that had fallen upon me.

My awareness of my surroundings returned to me by degrees.

First and foremost was the burning in my chest. It had begun to subside from the depths of intensity to which it had plunged me earlier. Then I thought that I was blind, only to realize that there was a sort of black haze and fog upon me that was generated, not by lack of light (although the cloudiness overhead blocked all but the most determined of the sun's rays) but by something from within my mind. A "brain fog," as it were. But the haze was starting to lift, and then not far from me, I saw an arm on the ground.

There was a head beside it, and then another arm . . . but as near as I could tell, from a different person. And then more body parts, strewn all about. Not just a few . . . dozens. No, more than that . . . as my eyes adjusted, as the fog upon me cleared, I saw dozens upon dozens, hundreds even. The ground was as thick with blood and gore as it was with mud, and I looked upon my sword and saw that there was barely an inch of clean steel upon it. It was covered up to the hilt in blood as well, so wet that it was still dripping from the blade. I was experiencing the sort of slow return from "blackout" that I had known back in Jaifa, except this time I remembered everything that had led up to the experience, and knew precisely who and where I was after it. Which meant, obviously, that I had not "vanished" into myself for anywhere near as long as before, or as deeply.

But the body count was nevertheless significantly higher . . . had I been able to even begin to determine where the bodies started.

Then sound returned to me, and I heard the clanging of swords and the victorious howls of my men. I knew it was my men because they were shouting out my name. It was not in panic or fear or anger, however, but instead in triumph.

Although there was fighting going on all around me, none was near me. As I surveyed the area, I realized that even if they wanted to get near me physically, they would have had serious difficulty doing so. The damage around me was far greater than my initial impression had led me to believe. Taking a very quick, and very literal, head count, the remains of three score and more soldiers were strewn around me in a vast circle. Looking down, I saw that my own clothing was tattered, cut to ribbons by swords and spears that had obviously pierced my body, but had done me no damage. There was blood on me, I realized, a lot of it . . . but it was all spatters from the men, or their remains, around me.

I saw soldiers being cut down, soldiers on the run, and for the most part it was the enemy. Beyond my immediate sphere, the field was littered with bodies, and again the vast majority of it were the men who had been waiting in hiding to ambush us.

"RETREAT!" I heard yet again, that familiar voice recapturing my attention. I looked in the direction whence it had come, and then I saw him, surrounded by four of his men, all on horseback. It was the great Lord Beliquose, he who had laid waste to my inn and, in conjunction with Sharee, had wound up sending me into this insane land of blood, mud, and death. He was dressed much as I remembered him from all those months ago, but he was wearing a cape of black and silver that indicated alliance with Meander and his men. The troops who were within range of Beliquose's voice—which really meant just about everyone in the vicinity—endeavored to distance themselves from the field of battle.

"Beliquose!" I howled in fury. *"I'm not done with you!"* I pointed my sword at him, continuing to shout challenges and imprecations. I had no idea whether he heard me or not. He was riding too fast.

I wanted to pursue him immediately, but it was impossible. I had no horse. The poor creature named Entipy was a ruined carcass, and I could only stare down at her with a tremendous feeling of loss and anger. Meander would pay, and Beliquose would pay. They would all pay. There was no reason at this point to let a single individual who had ever done me harm or disservice remain unaccounted for. I would take every last one of them down, displaying as much pity and remorse in the process as any of them had ever shown me. Beliquose wanted the gem? I would show it to him, then . . . show it bound to me, giving me power undreamt of by any mortal man, right before I shoved my sword into him and gutted him.

Boar Tooth came running up to me, his mouth a lopsided grin, the woad on his face smeared with sweat and blood, his hair in wild disarray. I had never seen a man look more alive than I had Boar Tooth. His breathing was ragged, and he was clearly exhausted, but also alight with the sort of passion that only massive bloodletting can bring . . . especially when the blood being spilt is one's opponents. "Glory, Peacelord! Glory to us all!" he cried out, waving his sword high in the air. And then, with more reverence than I would have thought it possible to display, he said, "You . . . are a god among men."

It took me a minute or so of judicious questioning to determine what precisely had happened, but it really wasn't all that difficult. Boar Tooth was one of those people who tended to recite triumphs at length, even if they were only moments old, because he loved to dwell on gory accomplishments.

You must understand that there are far more things involved in the winning of battles beyond force of arms. First is planning. In this instance, there was no denying that Meander had outthought and outmaneuvered me. Had that been the deciding factor in the battle, our cause would have been hopeless, for we had been caught completely flatfooted. As a result, the implicit confidence and esteem which my troops held for me was sorely threatened with dissolution.

But that confidence, that belief that one will emerge triumphant, is another one of the primary forces necessary in winning a battle. No army which believes that it will lose can possibly win. Triumph never emerges as a pleasant surprise or accidental byproduct. One wins because one cannot envision losing; it is simply not an option.

Caught in the carefully crafted trap of my opponents, surrounded and outflanked, I had lain into my attackers with a single-handed effort that was not only unlike any they had ever seen, but had no peer in all of known modern warfare. Supposedly the far Northern people have warriors on whom berserker rages have been known to fall. Such, apparently, had been the case with me. I had torn into any and all who approached me with unmatched, even unbelievable, ferocity. They were already calling me "Apropos the Vicious," "Apropos the Unmatched." Fueled by my righteous wrath, I had been an unstoppable juggernaut. Again and again my enemies had scored direct hits upon me, and they had not slowed me in the least. There had been tales of my invincibility, yes, but the great joy of such tales is that any rational and reasonable individual concludes that they are merely fables and wartime exaggerations. As a result, I have an endless advantage of surprise, for none can fully prepare themselves to face an opponent who cannot be stopped.

I had heard tell, although I had never seen one such, of weather creations called wind spinners which would descend from nowhere, with no warning, and lay waste to anything in their path. Such a creature was I in the face of any who opposed me. Like a butcher faced with a herd of cattle, I carved through them, body parts flying everywhere, blood fountaining like a geyser. One would almost feel some morsels of pity for the pathetic creatures who tried to stand in my way.

It had been the obvious intention of our opponents to bear me to the ground, cut me down, utterly defeat me within seconds in the full view of my men. That would have been a most disheartening set of circumstances, to put it mildly. Instead the plan backfired completely. For what my men saw instead was a single-handed display of imperishability. No matter how many descended upon me, it was not near enough; there were, in fact, not enough in the world to bring me down. My sword had been a blur of metal, unstoppable, hacking right and left with abandon and none to oppose me. At one point I grabbed the sword out of the severed limb of one of my victims and started swinging both blades. There were screams and shouts and lamentations galore, and cries of *"He is but one man!"* It made no difference. It was more as if I were a thousand men in the body of one.

I only wished I'd been there to see it.

Boar Tooth bowed to me, and I clapped him on the shoulder and said tightly, "Take the city. But remember: Meander is mine. And find Beliquose . . . the one with the grand voice that will shatter your eardrums. He, too, is mine." Once more he bowed, and then shouted orders to reorganize the troops for the final assault.

Our opponents were in disarray, on the run. Their strategy having fallen apart, they belatedly endeavored to close the great gate against us. It was too late. A squad of my men got in just as the gate slammed shut. But they were invigorated by the heat of battle,

and it was only the work of moments for them to cut through the
guardsmen at the gate and reopen the portal. My army flooded
inside. A handful of reserve troops stood in their way, but not for
long.

And I stayed behind. As my men rushed past me, many of them
stopped and bowed, or made odd gestures which I quickly realized
were signs of respect in their varied religions. Hands to heart and
then palm up, or crossed in front of the face, or both hands open
and down . . . a seeming endless variety, depending upon which
entity of the sky they worshipped.

I bobbed my head in acknowledgment of them all, but I was
barely paying them any mind. Instead I found that I was just staring . . . staring . . . at the carnage that I had left in my wake. One
would have thought that my musings would have been upon the
capture of Meander, or of Beliquose, or perhaps even entertaining
the notion of heading into the city and engaging in some mayhem.
But no. No, I just stood there and stared at the corpses.

All dead. At my hand. All dead.

And I found myself wondering what it had been like for them.

Were they scared?

Did they plead and beg?

Did they meet their deaths bravely? Did they even know they
were going to meet their deaths? At what point in the battle did
they realize that they didn't have a chance against me? Did they
realize it and then try to run, but I came after them? Or did they
battle on obliviously, thinking that there would be some last
minute miracle that would enable them to triumph against that
which seemed, on the face of it, unstoppable? And if they did
think they could defeat me . . . how did they propose to do so?
They must have seen sword after sword plunge into me without
slowing me. Did they think that theirs would be the one to finish
the job? Or perhaps . . . perhaps they called upon their god to provide them with strength or purity of spirit or the heart and luck of
a hero to accomplish the deed when others had fallen.

I picked up a head at random . . . but then I recognized it

instantly. Meander had had a second-in-command named Grimmoir. A decent enough fellow, so I recalled. Well, now he was dead, at my hand. My blade had sliced through his neck cleanly, so at least I had dealt him a quick death. Unless . . . the head was the last thing that I had cleaved from his body. I couldn't be sure; there were so many bodies it was impossible to distinguish who belonged to what.

His eyes were open. There was no life in them, of course, but I tried to figure whether there had been fear in them at the last. No . . . no, they just looked a bit puzzled. Yes, I wasn't imagining it. His eyes, his entire final expression, was one of puzzlement. Had he been looking into the next life and been surprised at what he had seen? Or was it something more earthbound, such as surprise that I had survived the attack or bewilderment as to why a perfectly executed plan had failed to garner its intended result.

"Peacelord . . ."

There was a soft voice from behind me, and I turned to see one of my soldiers. I didn't even know his name. He was an innocuous-looking fellow, and he was clutching a sword urgently with both hands. The sword was clean and unbloodied. He had no beard to speak of. A beardless boy with a sword untouched by mayhem.

"Yes," I said tonelessly.

"The Lady Kate wishes to hear from your own lips the events of this day. She is most anxious to see you." He couldn't help but grin, and even colored slightly. "She . . . asked me to emphasize the 'most anxious' part."

"Thank you." I stared at him a moment, my head cocked. "How old are you?"

"Thirteen summers, Peacelord."

"Thirteen summers. Hunh. New recruit?" His head bobbed up and down in response. "Had a chance for any fighting yet?" This time he shook his head as vehemently as he had nodded it before. "What's your name?"

"Gavin, Peacelord."

"Gavin. Hunh." I paused. "Fighting is a dangerous game, Gavin. You're a bit young for this business, aren't you?"

"When my time comes, I will fight with the strength of a hundred, Peacelord, for I will emulate you!" he said with a fervency that chilled me. "I would have fought in this battle . . . had there been anything left for me. I was toward the back."

"I see. And . . . what will you do now, that you've delivered your message."

"Well . . ." He smiled shyly and pointed at the city. "I was hoping to . . . well, I've never ravished and pillaged before, Peacelord. It sounds ever so exciting."

"It can be. Well," I said brusquely, "go to. Go to."

"Yes, Peacelord. Peacelord," he said as I started to leave. I turned and waited expectantly. And he said, with that same shyness, "Can I . . . worship you? They said you are a god on earth."

"Do as you will," I said, suddenly feeling quite tired. "Oh . . . and Gavin . . ."

"Yes, Peacelord?" he said eagerly, clearly waiting to hang on my every word.

"I will not tell you what to do. I will simply say that it's been my experience that no good ever comes from inflicting cruelty upon women."

He stared at me blankly. "Ravishing is cruelty?" he said, dumbfounded. Clearly the notion had never occurred to him. "But . . . it is a right of conquest. How can it also be a cruelty?"

"I just . . . think it is. There are some, I admit, who would disagree with me. But . . ." I shrugged. "There's my opinion, for what it's worth."

He stood there for a moment, looking as if he didn't know what to do, and then he quickly bowed. "Thank you, Peacelord," he said, and then scampered off toward the city.

As for me, I took one last, sad look at the fallen Entipy, and then turned away and started back along the main highway. Along the way I passed others heading for the city to indulge in the same excesses as young Gavin intended to pursue. The bowing and scraping and religious gestures continued without letup. I was beginning to find it quite tiresome.

I found the Lady Kate a half mile down the road. A makeshift tent had been pitched, and she dragged me in there and began to do the sorts of things that normally would have enflamed my senses. But to her surprise, and to some degree mine as well, I pushed her away from me. She flopped down onto some pillows, her dress already in disarray, falling down at the shoulders, her hair wildly askew, and she looked up at me with confusion in her eyes. "Have I . . . displeased you, my love?"

"Look at me!" I said, my arms outstretched. "My clothes are in tatters! I'm covered with the blood of my victims—!"

I stopped, and realized that I had never said that word aloud before in regards to my activities. *Victims.* I had always known that those who suffered at my hands were my victims, but still . . . saying it out loud . . . it disconcerted me for a moment, and I had no real clue as to why. It was as if, having undergone the release of such unadulterated black fury in slaughtering so many men, it had drained me slightly of my resolve, and it was going to take me some time to get back that ferocity that had served me so well.

But that was all right. I had time. I had plenty of time, all the time in the world . . . did I not?

Instantly contrite over having caused my foul mood, the Lady Kate fetched basins and towels with which to clean me of the grit and grime of war. She did not make any further attempts that evening—for evening it had become—of a sexual nature, but instead simply tended to me. Mordant, upon his perch, watched the proceedings with what appeared to be very little interest.

Some hours later Slake came to fetch me. I had been resting, but sat up with my cloak draped around my bare shoulders. The Lady Kate, naked beneath the blanket upon the makeshift bed, looked so alluring that it was a physical effort for Slake to look elsewhere rather than directly at her, lest he be accused of harboring inappropriate thoughts. He was covered with sweat and dried blood, and various valuable-looking trinkets now adorned the front of his armor. He had been busy. "Peacelord," he said formally, "I am told by reliable sources that we have captured the Keepless King."

I instantly shook off any last remains of fatigue. "Are you sure? Are you quite certain that it is he?"

"Yes, absolutely, Peacelord," Slake said firmly. "He attempted a last stand outside some sort of elaborate temple. Perhaps he thought the gods would be his last-minute savior." He laughed disdainfully at the notion. "He did not realize that the gods walk upon this very world and battle on behalf of our army."

"I'm not a god, Slake," I said, suddenly feeling tired once more.

"But . . . Peacelord . . ." He appeared most befuddled by my protesting any claim to divinity. "Your fighting prowess . . ."

"A gift, Slake. Nothing more. If the Lady Kate presents you with a vase as a gift, that does not make you the Lady Kate."

"I should hope not," said Kate, sounding rather amused at the notion.

"But . . . Peacelord . . ."

He looked uncomfortable, and I said impatiently, "Out with it."

"Well . . . Peacelord . . . a number of the temples in the Golden City have already been converted over to shrines in honor of you. Men kneel, bow, and scrape before them. You are being worshipped by any number of your soldiers. They . . . but seek your approval, Peacelord."

The entire matter had devolved into a conversation which I had no desire to pursue. Rather than do so, I stood, reaching for clean clothes and dressing quickly. "What of Beliquose?" I demanded. "I have scores to settle with that one as well."

"He has not yet been found, Peacelord. We have, however, captured some of his band . . . including the most bizarre creature I have ever encountered. . . ." Mordant promptly cawed in what could have been interpreted as annoyance, and Slake amended the statement with a mocking bow to the drabit. "*One* of the most bizarre creatures I have ever encountered . . . second, of course, to

Mordant." He might have been imitating Slake, or he might have just been sarcastic, but Mordant bobbed his head in response.

But Slake's comments had naturally caught my interest, so much so that I ceased dressing and walked quickly toward Slake. Stopping just short of him, I said with urgency, "This 'creature' . . . is it female in its aspect? But covered with hair? And missing an eye?"

Slake could not have looked more amazed. "That . . . is absolutely correct, Peacelord! However did you know?"

I smiled grimly. "I've had dealings with her before. Her name is Bicce. She's Beliquose's hound. She could prove quite valuable . . . or, at the very least, provide some serious amusement value." Then I nodded, as much to myself as to Slake. "We will go at once to the Golden City. I want to see her with my own eyes."

Kate seemed surprised by the pronouncement, but Slake was clearly pleased by the decision. "That is as it should be, Peacelord. On the evening of your greatest triumph yet, it is not meet that you should be here in this makeshift shelter. There are many excellent residences within the Golden City. I shall make ready a horse for you. . . ."

"And for me," Kate said firmly. She had risen and was standing next to me, running her hand up and down my arm. "Where my lord goes, so go I as well." She looked up at me with unbridled adoration. As she did, I felt as if something small and dark was crawling around within me, for she saw me as some great divine being, and I knew that it was not true. . . .

Or maybe it is, and you just don't want to admit to it, suggested my inner voice, which didn't go very far toward settling my mind on the matter.

I had to admit that the city was a rather impressive affair. In addition to the massive outer wall that served as the city's primary line of defense, there were inner walls which divided different sections of the city from one another. The most prominent was a jagged wall that separated what was popularly known as the lower city, east of the wall, from the upper city which was to the west. The lower city, through which I was in the process of passing, was the more crowded and heavily commercial section . . . when it was fully functioning. There was not a good deal of commerce going on at that point, however. Instead many of the stores had already been pillaged and looted. Carpets and tapestries were strewn about in one place, necklaces in another, prayer garments in yet another. There was raucous laughter, some of it floating from shadows, and at other points clearly being produced from revelers in the streets who wore my colors and sang my praises. As had been the case all evening, they would bow if they saw me, or offer me prayers or sacrifices.

I rode through the narrow streets, tall and proud upon a horse that I had borrowed from one of my men (who had, naturally, given it to me with all praise offered in the highest). It was not remotely as majestic and powerful as Entipy had been, but I made do. The horse's hooves clip-clopped steadily on the street's raised paving. Kate rode nearby, on horseback rather than a litter, her legs arranged daintily to one side. She looked the ideal picture of sophistication and elegance. Slake and half a dozen other men were serving as our escorts, lining up in front, beside, and behind us. The security was largely to protect Kate and provide a show of force, naturally. It wasn't as if I needed to be concerned about my continued health.

There was a general aroma of burning in the area as fires were breaking out in different sections of the city. I briskly informed several of my people to scatter throughout and put a stop to such activities at once. From a safety point of view, it would have been sheer madness considering that we were actually taking up residence there, for however brief a time. We certainly didn't need our temporary residence burning down around our ears.

I have no idea what prompted me to react to one particular scream out of all the ones that I was hearing. Perhaps it was the proximity, occurring just down the street from where we were. Or perhaps, if one is so inclined, one can think that I was divinely inspired. Whatever the reason, I suddenly veered my horse off the twisting road and darted down the side street from which the cry had originated. This caused a burst of confusion from our escort, but by the time they reacted I was already halfway down the street, leaving them to catch up as best they could.

The scene I came upon drew me up short. Two of my men were holding a struggling young girl steady, while a third was stepping up to her with a knife at her throat, clearly ready to send her blood cascading down the front of her clothes. Not for a moment, though, did I think this was simple murder. No, I knew it to be retribution the moment I arrived upon the scene. For lying upon the ground, moaning, with a small, dainty dagger protruding from between his ribs, was Gavin. He was staring up at the sky and looked extremely puzzled that such a thing had come to pass.

"*Stop!*" My voice thundered through the narrow alley, and at first the soldiers were about to ignore my direct order until they realized who was issuing it. The knife-wielder dropped the weapon as if it had suddenly transformed into a scorpion and stepped back, raising his hands into the air in utter compliance with my command. The others likewise froze in their places, although they continued to hold the girl so that she could not bolt. Kate reined up behind me, but I didn't give her a glance. Instead my attention was on the bizarre scene before me . . . except that it was not so bizarre, for I had already intuited much of what had happened before a single question had been asked.

I looked to the moaning form of Gavin upon the ground. "You tried to ravish her, did you not?" I asked without preamble.

The most he could manage was a weak nod.

"After I warned you?"

The boy took a deep breath and let it out unsteadily. "I . . . thought it was what you wanted, Peacelord."

I could scarce credit my ears. I urged my steed a few steps closer so that he could clearly see the look of pure astonishment upon my face. "You thought . . . *what?* Are you mad? Did I not say to you, in our common language and with sufficient volume to reach your ears, that no good came from treating a woman with cruelty? And look what happened!"

"I . . ." He gulped deeply. "I thought . . . you were testing me. Challenging me."

I moaned loudly and put my hand to my face, shaking my head in disbelief.

And apparently in an endeavor to justify his actions, he cried out, "Gods move in mysterious ways!" Then he groaned, clutching at his side. I could see from the angle and positioning that the wound wasn't going to be fatal . . . and certainly the volume and energy in his voice was enough to confirm that.

As for me, I was strongly considering riding my horse over his head for that last remark.

Apparently thinking he was helping the boy's cause, the knife-wielder and would-be executioner stepped forward, each dropping to one knee to show proper respect. "Peacelord . . . I saw the entire thing. The boy was simply attempting to have his way with his captive. She did not cooperate. She had the dagger hidden in her hair, and I was passing by when I saw her plunge it into him as he tried to shove her to the ground."

"The nerve of her," I said dryly. Apparently it was a bit too dryly, because there were concurring nods from my men, and even—as I saw out of the corner of my eye—the Lady Kate.

The entire business left a bad taste in my mouth, and I saw no reason to chew it alone. I gave the impression of deeply pondering what had happened, but really I had made up my mind in the briefest of instants. "Release her," I said firmly. And when I saw their hesitation, I repeated—effortlessly sounding as angry as I already felt—"*Release her!*"

They did not comprehend, but there was no requirement for them to do so. They pulled their hands away from her, leaving her standing there by herself and looking rather suspicious. Clearly she wanted to bolt, but figured that any such action would be met with immediate, and lethal, consequences.

Gods . . . she was so young. She was only just in the bloom of young womanhood, perhaps by the merest of months. And Gavin a bare-faced boy, not even shaving. Children molesting children. What in all the hells was the world coming to?

"Do you know who I am?" I demanded. When she shook her head, I said, "I am the one saving your life. Go."

She stayed where she was.

"Is everyone in this city insane? I said go!" I bellowed, and this time she went. She turned and sprinted away down the alley and was gone in a heartbeat.

And still they didn't comprehend. "Did you . . . wish us to engage in a hunt, Peacelord?" one of them asked tentatively.

"No. I just wanted to let her go."

From the ground, still obviously afraid to remove the knife lest a flow of his blood spurt forth, Gavin called, "But . . . but Peacelord . . . I did nothing that many others are not already doing! Why . . . why did you spare her punishment for her assault upon me?"

I smiled wanly and replied, "You said it yourself: I move in mysterious ways. And in my mysterious way . . . I feel you deserve punishment."

"But . . . but . . ." Clearly desperate to understand, he cried out, "But . . . Peacelord . . . you have ravished women, have you not?! Taken advantage of them?"

I paled slightly, but I doubt it was evident in the evening light. "If I have or have not, what of it?"

"Well . . . if you did . . . then did you deserve punishment?"

And one of the soldiers, his face twisted in fury, stepped quickly over and kicked Gavin in the ribs right where he'd been stabbed. The boy let out a shriek and curled up into a ball, sobbing. *"How dare you? How dare you question the god on earth!"* bellowed my man, and he drew back his foot with the clear intent of delivering another message.

"That's enough," I said brusquely, freezing him in his place. I glowered at all of them, then pointed at Gavin and told them, "Get him attended to." I snapped the reins briskly, turned the

horse around and continued on our way to the upper city. The rest of my entourage followed a short distance behind, clearly not understanding why I had done what I had done. It was rather liberating not to give a damn about what they were thinking.

In the midst of chaos and carnage, one of the fanciest houses had been readied for our arrival. Obviously word had been sent on ahead. They had done a superb job readying it for us. Illumination was provided by hundreds of candles, suffusing the place in an almost romantic glow. There were ten rooms in the place, and the Lady Kate and I chose the largest bedroom for our own. We didn't intend to stay there indefinitely; Dreadnaught stronghold beckoned to us. But the Lady Kate had pointed out that, all too often, we simply stormed through cities, burned and pillaged, and then continued on our way while leaving flaming ruins behind. It seemed reasonable that, considering the majesty of the Golden City, we use it as our temporary base while we attended to the enemies who had dared to challenge us and had—however temporarily—caused us inconvenience. Not to mention the fact that they'd killed my horse.

Servants were already in place, tending to our every need. There were still screams mixed with raucous laughter in the distance, but it seemed mostly concentrated in the lower half of the city which was still separated by the jagged wall. And although there was a good deal of looting going on in the upper city as well, a squadron of men had already fanned out in a one-block radius to make certain that there would be no accidental pillaging of our temporary domicile. As the dirt from the road and the ashes from the air were wiped from our sweating bodies, updates were brought to me with regularity over the status of our incursion. There were pockets of resistance, but my men were able to root them out with ruthless efficiency.

I stretched out upon the bed, which was surprisingly soft, and stared up at the ceiling, resting my head upon my hands. Lady Kate, as exhausted as I was by the day's activities, curled up next to me and rested her head upon my shoulders. And to my mild

PETER DAVID

annoyance, I heard Gavin's voice echoing within me. *Did you deserve punishment?* he had demanded.

I felt something dark creeping about within my soul, something from which I found myself recoiling even as I mentally embraced it at the same time. Did I deserve punishment? I murmured, "What do you think *this* is?"

"Mmmm?" purred the Lady Kate, half asleep.

"Nothing, my dear," I told her, and let my mind slip away into the darkness.

I had been angry any number of times in my life, but it was hard for me to recall a time that I had been angrier than I was at that moment. If I'd had a sword in my hand, I might well have been moved to manslaughter.

I was standing in the main courtyard in the back of the mansion, facing my lieutenants who looked, to the man, rather contrite. It might have been a sunny day, but the sky above was still thick with smoke from the fires that had been raging during the night. Even though they were by and large extinguished, the soot and blackness still hung there. It was beginning to make my throat somewhat scratchy, which did nothing to improve my mood. Mordant was perched upon my extended arm, and I was seriously toying with the notion of shouting, "Mordant, rip their faces off!" just to see if he would. As it was, my ire was reflected in the drabit's own disposition, because he was making loud hissing noises at Boar Tooth, Slake, and That Guy that clearly had them rather concerned for their continued health. They had every reason to be.

"Refresh my memory," I said coldly. "Was there not an individual with a voice remarkably like mine—and who, in fact, resembled me greatly—who issued an order that stated Meander was to be mine and mine alone?"

"Yes, Peacelord," Boar Tooth began, but—"

I didn't wait for him to finish, instead stepping toward him and making casually sure that Mordant was practically thrust into his face. "And now you gentlemen are here to tell me that he has been captured . . . but is in no condition to be brought before me. Do you know what that suggests to me, gentlemen? It suggests that he is dead . . . and if that is the case, then I promise you," and my voice rose with barely contained fury, *"that he shall not be predeceasing one or more of you by very long!"*

"He is not dead, Peacelord!" Slake cried out, looking the most apprehensive of the three. Boar Tooth didn't look much happier. Only That Guy seemed unperturbed, which was about typical for him. "By the gods on high—by you—I swear, he is not dead! He is simply . . . indisposed . . ."

"And what the hell is that supposed to mean?"

"Peacelord," Boar Tooth spoke up gamely, trying to sound as placating as possible. "By all accounts, the Keepless King fought with the strength of ten lions when he was cornered. Our men were at a sore disadvantage, for they were mindful of your orders to take him alive, whereas he was under no similar constraints when it came to fighting back. The truth is—"

"The truth is," Slake spoke up when Boar Tooth hesitated, "that Meander might well have gotten away if our men had not taken . . . stronger measures."

"How strong? Is he going to die?"

"In his own time, Peacelord, but that time will not be hastened by any acts of ours," Boar Tooth assured me. "He is gravely wounded, but our best healers are with him now, and they assure me he will recover. It will, however, take a while."

The Lady Kate was seated nearby, idly skimming through parchments that had been left by the previous owners of the mansion that we had taken over. I had no idea who those occupants were, or what had been done with them, nor did I care particularly. Without glancing up from the parchments, she suggested in an offhand manner, "Why not simply kill him on his sickbed and have done with it? You intend to dispose of him anyway. Why wait?"

It made a certain amount of sense. I turned back to my men and said, "Is he conscious?"

"Not at this time, Peacelord," Boar Tooth said with regret. "As his healing progresses, though, that will certainly change—"

I didn't bother to listen to the rest of his words, instead saying impatiently, "What is the point in slaying an unconscious man? All he will do is go on to the next life without knowing who it was who ended this one. It lessens the joy of vengeance. Besides, I want to get him to beg for his life, as my mother very likely did for hers before he slew her. No . . . we will wait until he comes out of his unconscious state. See to it," I warned them, "that he is thoroughly bound so that he cannot possibly escape. I will not tolerate any mishaps with this." They bobbed their heads eagerly, sensing that they might well have just narrowly escaped a most unfortunate fate. With no reason to dwell upon the condition of Meander, I continued, "And Beliquose? What of him? I owe that bastard a debt that I intend to repay in full."

"A mixed bag of news in that regard, Peacelord," admitted Boar Tooth. "Beliquose had the luck of the devil. He managed to elude capture . . ."

"With that voice?" I said incredulously. "You should have been able to track him down from a mile away! How could he have escaped?"

"As near as we can determine," said Boar Tooth, "he slew one of our own men, donned his uniform and slipped away thus disguised. He also came close to freeing several of his band whom we had captured. There was a battle . . . and most of those who were our prisoners were killed endeavoring to escape."

My fury bubbling over, I slammed my hand against a nearby decorative pillar. Kate looked up with momentary concern, but then returned to her reading. "Damn them! My enemies benefit from fortune at every turn! One postpones his reckoning through injury, the other through conniving!" Mordant let out a sympathetic screech and looked hopefully at my lieutenants as if to say, *Can I eat them now?* I wondered briefly if Mordant would be able to track down Beliquose, but I couldn't quite see how. My assumption was that Mordant tracked by scent, and there was no way for him to distinguish Beliquose's spoor from any other. "What of Bicce? She has not gotten away as well, has she? Or been killed? From what I'm hearing, any act of incompetence is possible."

But Slake said, "No, Peacelord. She is still in our grasp."

"Bring her here. Now."

For response, Slake turned to That Guy and nodded. That Guy immediately exited the courtyard, and returned moments later hauling the one and only Bicce. I recognized her instantly, of course; how could I not? Some of her fur was singed, and she had a few more bruises, but it was most definitely her. Her clothes were in tatters, but since she was so hirsute, there was never any question of defiled modesty. Thick cords were wrapped around her upper torso, and she was partly hunched over like the animal that she was. Her nostrils flared before she was within twenty feet of me. Oh, she recognized me, all right, and didn't look especially happy to see me. I could hardly blame her.

"Well well well," I said as That Guy hauled Bicce before me.

"On your knees before the Peacelord," Slake snarled at her, and when she did not comply, he came in behind her and slammed the backs of her knees with the flat of his sword blade. Bicce let out a yelp and sank to her knees, but she didn't even bother to afford Slake a glance. Instead she never took the baleful glare of her one good eye from me. She wasn't even struggling against her bonds anymore, which surprised me somewhat. Given the nature of the creature that she was, I would have thought that she would be rolling about on the floor in fits of struggle to free herself, rather than just gazing upon me.

"Pathetic, wretched creature," I said. "Pity that it's not capable of . . ."

"Master."

I was dumbfounded to hear the word come from her throat. I had just assumed that she was more dumb beast than anything remotely human. I looked up at my men and demanded, "Why didn't you tell me she could speak?"

"I . . . we had no idea, Peacelord." Slake was almost stammer-

PETER DAVID

ing. "We thought it mute. Inarticulate. It has said nothing before now. . . ."

"She." Her voice was low and gravely, and was virtually a snarl with every breath, but she was perfectly understandable. She was looking poisonously at Slake, clearly irked at being referred to with such a neutral form of speech as "It."

Slake looked to me for guidance, and I simply shrugged. Mirroring the gesture, he amended, "She has said nothing before now. . . ."

"Yet now she does. Interesting." My hands draped behind my back, I walked slowly around her, keeping my gaze as focused upon her as hers was upon me. "She says 'Master.' Are you asking me the whereabouts of your master, Bicce?"

Confusion passed through her face. "Master is here," she said.

My lieutenants immediately started to reach for their swords, to "protect" me from Beliquose who—according to Bicce—was near. But I was having a glimmer of a notion, and seeking clarification, I asked, "Beliquose is here?"

She shook her head vehemently. "*You* are here. *Master* is here."

And now it was the Lady Kate who followed me into the land of comprehension. "She's saying," Kate said as she put down the scrolls, now utterly caught up in the moment, "that you are her master now."

Bicce nodded vehemently.

But Slake was instantly shaking his head. He walked quickly around her, pointing at her with irately trembling finger as if she were something unclean. "Don't believe it, Peacelord. It . . . *she* . . . is a wretched creature and perfectly capable of some sort of trick. Do not unbind her. Slay her. She was beloved by Beliquose. Her death will hurt him."

"Beliquose left me," Bicce growled with unmistakable resentment. "You capture. Am yours now by right of capture. You new master."

I considered this announcement for a long moment. Mordant squawked at her, and she bared her teeth with such feral abandon that it actually caused Mordant obvious discomfort, and he slunk back against me. I found that, to some degree, amusing. It was entertaining to see the normally boisterous Mordant disconcerted for once.

"Do you wish to make your new master happy, Bicce?" I asked. "Would you like to be well attended to, and fed and pampered, and treated much better than that brute Beliquose ever did?"

She didn't seem to have the slightest idea what I was talking about. She frowned at me, and said again, "You new master." The message was obvious. Such things as how she was treated were of no consequence to her. She was treated the way her master—whoever that was—chose to treat her, and for her life didn't really extend beyond that. Speaking to her about perks of decent and caring ownership meant as much to her as describing the palette of colors in a rainbow meant to someone blind from birth.

So I jumped directly to the matter that was of most concern to me. "Can you lead me to Beliquose?" I asked.

And without hesitation, she said, "Yes." She turned and looked off to the west. "There."

"Will you take me? Will you help me hunt down your former master?"

"Yes."

I turned to one of the servants. "Prepare a horse for me at once."

"*Peacelord, no!*" Both Slake and Boar Tooth were crying out in unison and indignation. Boar Tooth overshouted Slake, continuing, "There is no need for you to—"

"Risk myself?" I looked at him disdainfully as the servant scrambled away to do my bidding. "Is that what you were going to say? Are you forgetting, Boar Tooth, to whom you are speaking? What could Beliquose do to me?"

"At least bring a regiment with you. We can assemble—"

"—a squad of men who will be eager to take on Beliquose himself. I see no point in that. Besides, gentlemen . . . you saw the remains of the ambush they attempted upon me. Do you seriously think that, desperate and on the run, Beliquose poses some sort of physical threat to me? If I bring a squad of men, that will just present Beliquose with numerous vulnerable targets." I shook my head. "No, thank you. I will, however, bring That Guy to hold Bicce's leash, for I do not entirely trust her."

"As well you should not, my love," said the Lady Kate. "Creatures such as this are never dependable." Gods, she looked gorgeous. For a heartbeat I considered tossing aside the entire thing and instead hauling her away to bed, so enticing was she. It was as if the war and subsequent discord had brought out the best in her.

"I share your concerns." I turned back to Bicce. "Do you hear that, hound? You are on probation with me. You will lead us, with That Guy," and I pointed to the malevolent, silent swordsman, "as your keeper. If you lead us astray, if you endeavor to betray us . . . if there ever comes a time when we think that you are acting on behalf of Beliquose instead of serving my interests . . . That Guy will cut you down where you stand. Is that clear?"

"Clear," she said immediately.

"With any luck," I said, slapping my hands and rubbing them together briskly, "Meander will have recovered by the time I return, and we can make a considerable show of disposing of him as well." I strode over to Kate, took her in my arms, and kissed her firmly. "I shall return to you," I said with as much of the devil-may-care attitude in my voice as I could muster, "before my side of the bed has completely cooled. And I will bring the head of an enemy with me."

"For me?"

"Yes. To celebrate."

She sighed sadly. "And here I didn't get you anything."

Chapter 4

Ifs, Ands, and Buttes

*Y*ou do realize, it's intended to be a trap."

I was speaking to Mordant, who was crouched upon a rock nearby. He was watching me with that combination of curiosity and vague disdain that I had come to know all too well. A distance away, That Guy had brought Bicce over to a watering hole where she was eagerly lapping up liquid refreshment, while That Guy filled the water skins. He never took his eyes off her. I was beginning to think that the reason That Guy never spoke was because he wanted to be able to consistently concentrate on everything around him.

We had been traveling for several days, and Bicce had never slowed in the least. Having sworn fealty to me, she loped on ahead as far as the makeshift leash we had her upon would allow her. Every so often she would stop and sniff the ground or the air, occasionally even moving in slow circles before satisfying herself in the direction that she was going.

But I had my suspicions nonetheless. I had not voiced them to any of my followers, because I had no wish to make them apprehensive. Nor did I want to say anything in Bicce's presence and therefore arouse her suspicions. To Mordant, however, in the privacy of the moment, I could say whatever I wished.

Mordant stared at me patiently, and I wondered—not for the first time, of course—just how much he was comprehending. I had gone behind the rock to answer the call of nature; invincibility had not relieved me of the necessity of attending to such mundane functions. And as I went about my business, I muttered to Mordant, "Hounds such as Bicce do not simply turn against their masters. She may have surprised me with her ability to speak, but there are certain things that I believe are inviolable, and a hound's loyalty is one of them. Besides, I saw how she interacted with Beliquose. She would do anything for him. She adores him to such a degree that it wouldn't surprise me if she bears love for him . . . or as much love as such a semi-human creature can lay claim to."

Mordant actually seemed interested in what I was saying, tilting his head slightly. His eyes were utterly unblinking as he appeared to hang on my every word.

Even though we were not in danger of being overheard, I lowered my voice even more. "What I think more likely is this: I think she's operating on Beliquose's instructions. She allowed herself to be captured and is functioning, as she always has, in his interests. This suggests one of two possibilities: She's leading us toward him, or in the totally opposite direction from him. However, I don't think it's the latter. We're trailing *someone.* I've seen enough signs, the markings that men on horseback invariably leave behind, to be sure of that. Of course, we could be trailing someone *other* than Beliquose. And if it turns out that Bicce has been less than honest with us, we simply kill her and are none the worse for our time. But I suspect," I said slowly, "that she is in fact bringing us to him. Which means . . . he has something planned. And you know what?" I grinned broadly. "I don't care."

And I didn't.

My invincibility had totally liberated me from any concerns as to how I would proceed in whatever circumstances were thrust upon me. No longer was I second-guessing my opponents. No longer was I feeling as if I was engaged in a battle of wits with the world. I was more than content for the world to come at me with everything it had to offer, confident that—aside from my little difficulty with fire—I would be able to handle it. And I didn't think that Beliquose was planning an inferno to greet me.

Not where he was headed . . . for it was Mount Aerie that loomed before us.

Barely a day's ride ahead of us was the impressive mountain. It was not all that long ago that Sharee and I had been staggering across the Tragic Waste with the mountains coming no closer to us no matter how much we struggled. Such was not the case here. Mount Aerie grew closer and closer, and the closer it came, the more daunting it appeared.

There was a range of mountains around it, but Mount Aerie was unmistakable. It was the largest, with peaks so high and swathed in such clouds and mist that I would almost have been given to speculate that gods were sitting atop it, looking down and wondering whether any humans would be so vain as to think they could approach the skylords. In the upper reaches I saw the whitecaps that indicated snow sat upon them, which made me wonder just how cold it was up there. Impervious as I was to harm, I couldn't help but wonder whether frigid weather would prove daunting to me. After all, if extremes of heat had been a problem, it was possible that opposite extremes could also give me difficulties.

But I was not about to back off the chase now . . . even if it was, as I thought it might be, an attempted ambush.

Bicce and That Guy were well-matched. She rarely spoke, and he never did. That was fine as far as I was concerned. I wasn't interested in chitchat; I wanted to find my man, put paid to him, and ride back to the Golden City so that I could take some well-deserved rest. Every so often I even regretted having embarked on this newest, maddest adventure. When you got down to it, what was Beliquose, really? Yes, he'd cost me Bugger Hall. Considering, though, everything that I had garnered in exchange, I couldn't help but think that in the end I had gotten the better part of the bargain.

Still . . . he had allied himself with Meander. And one of his men had shot me in the buttocks with an arrow, back at a time when such wounds were far more than a mere inconvenience. Yes, on further consideration, this endeavor was time well spent.

We passed several buttes that were not part of the mountain range which contained Mount Aerie, and I wondered if Beliquose was hiding in one of them. But Bicce passed them by without hesitation. She seemed quite confident in where she was going, and if this was indeed a trap, then naturally she had every reason to be self-assured.

It was midmorning of the fourth day of our pursuit when Bicce guided us into a canyon leading up to some foothills. Mount Aerie loomed, and as we rode our horses up through the canyon, I was quickly becoming aware that we were not going to be able to take the animals much farther.

Suddenly I chided myself as an idiot. We were in a canyon, for the love of the gods, with towering walls on either side. A canyon was an ideal place for an ambuscade that provided no danger for the attackers whatsoever. All they needed to do was position themselves anywhere above us and send a mass of carefully prepared rocks down upon our unprotected heads. It didn't matter how invulnerable I was. If I was immobilized beneath a ton of rubble, I would lie there until the end of time . . . or until I starved to death, which would come much sooner. I hadn't tested that aspect of my endurance, but as far as I knew, I required food to survive just like anyone else. And I wasn't willing to risk being buried alive to test whether that was true or not.

"Stop!" I called, and That Guy immediately reined up. He

yanked sharply on the rope, bringing Bicce to a halt as well. She turned and looked at us. Her expression was carefully neutral. I had no idea what was going through her feral little mind.

I scanned the upper reaches of the valley as best I could. I saw nothing. That, of course, didn't necessarily mean anything. Mordant was perched upon my arm, and I turned to him. Whether the creature truly spoke, whether it comprehended spoken language, all that was uncertain . . . but there was one thing that was indisputable. The little drabit understood intent and need. "Listen to me, Mordant. I need you to be my eyes in the sky. Fly up there and see whether the valley ahead of us is clear of traps."

He paused a moment, seeming to consider the words, and then with no thrust from me, he leaped skyward, flapping his wings several times for added lift before catching easy currents through the valley. He soared higher, higher, and I watched him go. Then I looked to Bicce. If she was concerned with any sort of ambush being discovered, she certainly was doing a masterful job of hiding it, particularly considering that she would have been buried alive with us. But instead of seeming perturbed, she was busy licking her fur to clean herself. I hoped she didn't start licking her own privates. I didn't need to see that. That Guy, for his part, seemed content to sit upon his horse and await further development. He certainly had a calm approach to life. I envied him a bit.

Some minutes passed, and then a screech heralded the arrival of Mordant. As heartless as it sounded, the fact that he was returning at all was a good sign. If there were archers hidden above and they recognized him as belonging to me, they might well have taken a chance of putting an arrow in him so as to head off any possibility of their presence being tipped. I extended my arm and he landed upon it obediently.

"Well?" I said, knowing that the chances of Mordant promptly launching into a full and articulate report were fairly slim. I was counting on my ability, really, to interpret his mood.

If that was what I was using to guide me, then I had to assume by his relaxed demeanor that there was no danger ahead. I reasoned that if there was, he would be squawking or jumping about or endeavoring in some way to warn me. Either that or I was putting the safety of myself and one of my lieutenants in the hands— well, wings—of a dumb animal who hadn't a clue what I wanted to know and instead had just coincidentally gone in search of a midmorning snack.

For a moment the old Apropos reared his head and suggested in no uncertain terms that this was sheer folly, I was risking my life for no damned good reason, and we should turn tail and run while the opportunity was still available to us. I could not, however, bring myself to do it. Call it hubris if you will, overconfidence if you desire. Even pride, an attribute which was a luxury that I had never afforded myself before. In some small measure, though, I had begun to believe what everyone else had been saying about me. I knew perfectly well I wasn't a god . . . but I was about as damned close as anyone was ever going to see in this world, and demigods simply didn't run away from suspicions.

"Let's go," I said briskly, and so we did.

Farther into the valley we went, and then into a ravine, and the horses' footing was becoming more and more unsure. I knew we'd pushed the creatures as far as we dared. A fall was nearly inevitable if we kept going on them, and a horse with a broken limb meant a dead animal and a slow ride back with two of us on one beast. If both horses injured themselves, well . . . it was going to be a hell of a long walk back to the Golden City.

"We go on foot from here," I called to That Guy. Naturally he didn't argue. Convenient soldier, he.

We dismounted and tied the horses' reins off onto a natural outcropping of rock. Bicce seemed most anxious to keep going. *Probably eager to rendezvous with her true master and see the intended trap snap upon us,* I thought. My walking staff had been strapped to the horse's side. I no longer had the limp that it had once compensated for, but along the grounds that we would be traversing, it might well be a help now even for a man with two strong legs. Plus it remained a formidable weapon in its own right. So I removed it from its holder and, gripping it firmly, set out.

And so we climbed.

And climbed.

Morning became afternoon as we made our slow way up. At one point Bicce let out a cry, and I thought, *This is a signal! This is it!* But then a great predator, a snarling dusky mountain cat, unleashed a roar of challenge and leaped toward us. Bicce shrunk back, for as fearsome as she was, she was dwarfed by the creature bounding toward us. That Guy, however, did not hesitate. He had his sword out and swinging while the beast was still in midair, and an instant later the creature's body landed on the ground ten paces to my right, while his head rolled to a halt twenty paces to my left.

Bicce was whimpering in confusion. She was unable to right herself, for her hands were still bound. That Guy reached down, took her under the crook of her elbow, and drew her to her feet with what appeared to be surprising gentleness.

And to my utter astonishment, he spoke the first words I'd ever heard him say, addressed to a creature whom I once would have thought incapable of understanding them.

"You're safe," he said. His voice was astoundingly soft and gentle. It sounded more the voice of a poet or a singer of romantic ballads than a warrior. Perhaps that was the reason he preferred to keep his silence. Remain speechless and be seen as darkly threatening. Speak and risk contemptuous laughter. Silence was obviously preferable.

She looked at him wonderingly. That Guy's face remained impassive as she stared at him with unmistakable gratitude in her eyes.

"Good" was all she said, but it seemed to me that she was feeling something more than simple gratitude . . . and perhaps was even concerned or afraid that she was doing so. Mordant, meantime, did not bother to offer thanks, but instead nestled atop the creature's severed head and proceeded to pluck out his eyeballs for a gruesome little treat.

Higher and higher still we went. The path was difficult, and certainly not carved by anyone, but it was passable. If I'd still had a game leg, I would have been in all manner of difficulty, but such infirmities were a thing of the past. I started to become concerned, though, over my decision to leave the horses tied up behind. They would be helpless if some beast, such as the cat that had assaulted us, came upon them. We might indeed wind up walking back after all.

I also began to wonder what Beliquose had done with his horses. I could only come up with two possibilities. Either he'd found some sort of cave to hide them in, or else he had let them run wild. He could have done that in order to give the animals a better chance at survival, or perhaps intending to throw us off the scent by sending horse tracks off in another direction. Such an endeavor would not have worked with Bicce on his trail, of course. She was locked into following the man, not the beast upon which he rode.

Something else was occurring, though, that also vied for my attention.

The gem in my chest was beginning to burn.

It wasn't anything I couldn't live with, but it was constant and insistent as if the gem was demanding my attention. It was filling me with a sense of urgency that I couldn't ignore. The gem . . . wanted something from me. I had no clue what that might be, but for the first time I was having the sensation that the gem was more than simply some sort of mystic talisman, granting incredible powers to the person with whom it was fused. I was beginning to think that the damned thing had a mind of its own.

And even as I considered that, and the gem burned more intensely in my chest, I realized that the notion of that was truly frightening. Some . . . some living thing, attaching itself to me? With its own desires and agenda which might be completely unknown? The concept threw everything that I had done into question. How much was my doing? How much was the gem's? Everything that I had said and done made so much sense to me, but was that because it *did* make sense, or because the gem *desired* it to for its own purposes.

And as quickly as those notions came to my mind, they were discarded. *It's just a gem, that's all. You are in charge. You are the Peacelord. You are the god on earth. Do not let yourself be distracted or deterred. You are Apropos of Wuin. You are supreme.* All these thoughts and more went through my head, soothed my doubts and eased my worries.

Afternoon passed into evening. It was getting colder and colder, and even though the burning in my chest was steady, I still felt the chill in my bones. It did not frighten me, though, or put me ill at ease as it most certainly would have in the past. Instead it but fueled my anger. I was taking it rather personally that Beliquose was leading us on this chase instead of making himself available to be slaughtered, which would have been far more convenient for me.

We had no choice. Even trusting Bicce's senses to see us through, it was getting far too dark to proceed. We had actually gotten to the lower reaches of Mount Aerie itself and were starting to climb it. In the darkness one misstep could lead to a very long fall. I wasn't concerned for my personal safety, but I wasn't ecstatic about the notion of having to begin the climb all over again. And if That Guy or even Bicce fell, the consequences would be far more lethal.

We made a rudimentary camp under an outcropping which would provide minimal shelter. I instructed That Guy to take the first watch while I endeavored to get some sleep. Sleep, surprisingly, came easily. Rest did not. Perhaps it was the steady burning sensation radiating from the gem in my chest, but bizarre dreams raced through my head as if they were upon mounted horses and dashing against each other to deliver as much confusion to me as quickly as possible. Images flashed before me that I could not comprehend. I saw . . .

I saw . . .

. . . a second gem next to the first one, floating in blackness before me, and it seemed as if they were focused upon me, and within the center of each of them were small flames that gave them the appearance of burning eyes turned toward me, and suddenly I was burning as well from the inside out, and dark shadows were upon me, pulling me down, down into darkness, an infinite fall, and I reached out, desperate to stop the plunge, and someone grabbed me by the wrist, halted me, and I looked up and it was the Lady Kate, but she was laughing at me, laughing and sneering, and her eyes were now the two blazing gems, and then Beliquose fell past me on one side, and Sharee went by on the other, and they were falling and falling except they were in each other's arms and dancing as they fell in a lazy spiral, calling up to me, "We warned you, don't say we didn't warn you, tra la tra la," and then the Lady Kate laughed once more and said, "It's what she would have wanted!" and released me, and my arms waved about frantically as I fell and fell. . . .

I snapped awake and looked around frantically, convinced that I was going to wake up falling. That somehow I had tumbled off some previously unseen cliff and was even now plummeting to the ground far below. But no, I was right where I'd drifted off. I looked over toward That Guy.

He was dead, slain by Bicce.

I thought.

Except . . . I was wrong. He was on the ground, yes, and she was near him, but her hands were still tied harmlessly behind her. That Guy's chest was rising and falling steadily, and there was a gentle snoring coming from it. He had been leaning against a rock face, but apparently exhaustion had overtaken him, and he had slid down to his haunches, his head slumping over. And Bicce had curled up next to him and likewise gone to sleep. In fact, her breathing was in perfect synchronization with his. If one of them hadn't been a hardened warrior and slaughterer, and the other a crazed she-bitch, it might actually have looked rather charming.

I thought of waking That Guy and chiding him for falling asleep at his post. But then I reasoned, *No harm done, everything's fine, we're safe,* right before the gigantic flying form dropped down upon us with a screech that would have woken the damned, much less us.

"What the hell is that?!" I howled as the creature descended from on high, even as I yanked out my sword. I swung the blade and the creature, with a flap of its great wings, arced upward. Just for a moment I saw it backlit against the moon.

It looked like Mordant, except it was at least twenty feet from tip to tip of its wings, with a beak that looked as if it could bite any of us in half.

Oh, my God, Mordant's turned into a monster I thought frantically, and then I was instantly disabused of that notion as I saw Mordant himself, same size as before, descend screeching toward the giant drabit. For a heartbeat I thought that this was going to be resolved simply, with Mordant instructing his big brother, or whatever it was, to be off on its way. I should have known better. The huge drabit let out an ear-rattling bellow and, with a sweep of one of its massive wings, knocked Mordant aside. Mordant flipped tail over head, ricocheted off the side of a rock wall, and tumbled out of sight.

It descended again, but That Guy was ready for it. He swung his sword this way and that, attempting to create a sort of wall with his blade. The creature, however, was incredibly nimble considering its size. It bounded from one side to the other, avoiding That Guy's best attempts to cleave it into bits, and suddenly it flapped its wings with overwhelming ferocity. The result was a gust of wind that struck with the force of a battering ram, knocking That Guy flat onto his back. It was all the opening the beast required, and it descended upon Bicce in a heartbeat and snagged her in its talons.

Had Bicce's arms been free, she would have been more than capable of giving a good accounting of herself. But pinned as they were, she had no chance. She screamed defiance at the huge drabit and kicked furiously but impotently as the creature arched upward.

The trailing end of the leash dangled in the air, moving up fast, and That Guy did not hesitate. Scrambling to his feet, he leaped upward and snagged it. Obviously his hope was to haul the beast back down to the ground. In this, he was unsuccessful. Instead, such was the strength in the beast's wings that it was able to haul both the struggling Bicce and the frustrated That Guy into the air.

This was, of course, something of a setback for me. I wasn't concerned so much with the life of Bicce—I hadn't forgotten the damned creature tried to kill me, of course—and That Guy, well, he was capable enough, but I had no great emotional attachment to him. Nevertheless, I felt a certain possessory sense of frustration over the situation. They were mine. My lieutenant, my hairy creature. How dare this wretched beast make off with them as if it had any right to interfere with my affairs?

The creature was flying straight up. The rock face was treacherous, but scaleable. But I was going to need both hands. I yanked hard on either end of my walking staff, separating it into its two sections, and jammed each of the batons into either side of my belt. Then, taking a deep breath and trying not to lose sight of the beast, I started to climb.

In retrospect, it's amazing the amount of confidence I felt as I did so. Not once did I consider the possibility that I might lose my grip and fall. My servants had been stolen, and I was going to go get them. It was not much more involved than that.

The drabit had disappeared into the mists above, rising toward the uppermost reaches of the peak. Now I was recalling, rather belatedly it seemed, the comments as to why the place was called Mount Aerie, and the sorts of creatures that one might encounter there. As for Mordant, I had absolutely no idea whether he was all right. Unfortunately I didn't have the time to dwell on it too much.

Far above me I heard noises, and they were not pleasant ones. More of the drabit making deafening screeches, but even more disturbing . . . other drabit sounds that came across as smaller, thinner.

Instantly I realized what was going on overhead.

It was dinnertime. Dinnertime at the drabit household, and apparently hairy she-creature was on the menu. And That Guy had served himself up as an after dinner sweet.

I climbed faster, and the rock face gave way beneath my fingers. I started to slide, the rock tearing up my palms, and then I sought and found some toeholds and halted my abrupt descent. My palms healed instantly and with no less determination I started climbing once more. The screeches were louder and louder, and I couldn't tell whether they were the huge drabits, the offspring, or Bicce's, because they were all mingling together.

And then there was a high-pitched shriek, and I couldn't identify whose it was or what had happened. That was when something thick and bloody fell past me, and I barely had time to make it out before it vanished from sight. But I was just able to see it in time: It was a huge chunk of wing. The drabit's wing, if I wasn't mistaken, with part of its bony arm attached. Obviously That Guy was not about to just roll over and die at the mercy of a winged beast.

Then there was more screeching, more howling, and I was able to make out thick chopping noises as one would hear at a butcher's shop. More pieces of animal meat were falling past me, and I halted my climb by flattening against the wall. I had no choice; if I'd kept on going, there was a likelihood that a chunk of drabit would hit me sooner or later and knock me off my precarious perch.

It went on for several minutes, the hacking and screaming and more hacking and more screaming, and then slowly it began to taper off. The virtual rain of drabit parts began to slow, and then to stop. I paused there long seconds, and then I called up, *"I'm coming up! It's me! If you see a head protrude up in front of you, kindly do not attempt to lop it off as it would be disrespectful, plus I'm rather attached to it!"*

I made it up the rest of the way in short order and discovered a plateau some sixty feet wide. A thin layer of hoarfrost covered the ground and the nest. And damn, it was quite a nest, at least ten feet across and three feet deep.

But the frost upon the nest was steaming, because the hot blackish blood of the nest's former inhabitants was smeared all over the inside. The temperature of the blood was causing the frost to melt, and the former containers of the blood—namely the baby drabits—were strewn about in small pieces. Considering the amount of drabit meat that had been sent plummeting past me, I was somewhat amazed that there was anything of them left.

The grown drabit was there as well, also in sections.

And both That Guy and Bicce were, to my surprise, in one piece. That Guy was leaning against the edge of the nest, looking a bit weary but with a grim, pleased smile upon his face. Bicce was just shaking free of the cords that had bound her. Apparently when the drabit grabbed her, its talons had severely frayed the ropes, and now the hound was able to pull apart her restraints with minimal effort. But if I'd been expecting some sort of sudden attack on her part, I was much mistaken. Instead she was helping That Guy out of the nest with all the tenderness that he had offered her earlier when she had been shaken by the great cat. That Guy looked utterly exhausted. His armor was torn up, and there was blood all over him. I wasn't sure how much of it was his and how much had belonged to the drabits, but it was certainly evident that he'd been in a hell of a fight and that it had taken a lot out of him. And it was further obvious that his endeavors had had a huge impact on Bicce.

My, don't they look cozy, I thought with grim amusement as I hauled myself up onto the plateau some feet away from them.

Bicce was studying That Guy with such intensity that one would have thought she was about to devour him. But she made no hostile move toward him. Indeed, she seemed to be regarding him with reverence . . . or confusion . . . or regret . . . or possibly a mixture of all of them. She was standing several feet away from him, and to the right.

And that was when there was a *twang* in the ear that was so loud and so close, I immediately ducked even though I should have known that the huge arrow it portended would have done me no harm.

Bicce moved as well . . . but not down. Instead she leaped with all the animal intuition and agility that she possessed.

The arrow was huge. It would have been useless as a long-range weapon because it was simply too heavy to achieve any distance. But at close range—which this was—it was incredibly deadly and largely unstoppable.

Bicce tried to stop it anyway. The arrow took her square in the chest and kept going . . .

. . . and went straight into That Guy.

I cried out his Lack-of-Name and, to my surprise, her name as well. I have no idea whether they even heard me. The force of the arrow had driven Bicce right up against That Guy. The fletching of the arrow was visibly protruding from her chest; the arrowhead was sticking out That Guy's back. He coughed up blood and staggered back, back, and his arms were around Bicce's waist in what could only be called a loving embrace. She clutched his hands and sobbed.

To this day I've no idea how the bond that formed between them did so. It was bizarre, it was perverse, it was unnatural . . . and it was love in the purest form that I've ever seen. Of all the things I do not understand about the many things I've witnessed, it is that tragic, abortive relationship that I most wish I could comprehend . . . and most regret that I never will.

They tumbled back off the plateau and vanished without a sound.

From the mist just ahead of me, I saw the archer, nocking another arrow. I recognized him instantly; he was the one who had scored hits upon Sharee and myself and nearly killed us in the doing. I yanked my dagger from its place in my boot and screamed

"You son of a bitch!" and my arm snapped back and forward in a blur of motion. I hit the ground just as the arrow hissed over my head and then I heard another sort of hiss . . . the sound of air being expelled between gritted teeth. I looked up and saw my blade had penetrated the archer's forehead with perfect precision. His eyes rolled up into his head and he was dead before he hit the ground.

"ODD THAT YOU WOULD BE CALLING OTHERS SONS OF BITCHES!" came an all-too-familiar, and all-too-loud voice. "CONSIDERING WHO YOU ARE, AND WHAT YOU'VE DONE! SMITING OTHERS WITH IMPUNITY WHILE BASKING IN INVINCIBILITY!"

His voice was echoing all around me, reverberating off the rock walls. For an instant I feared an avalanche might be caused by the volume; I certainly had no desire to sprint out of the path of another one of those.

And then I saw him.

He was standing at the far end of the plateau, his sword in his hand, and I noticed that there was a huge spot of darkness behind him. It appeared to be a hole in the side of the mountain peak, large enough for a man to enter. Naturally I had no desire to do so. He took several steps forward, squinting in the darkness, and then slowly he nodded.

"SO . . . IT *IS* YOU. THE ONE WHO I KNEW AS POE. SOMEHOW I NEVER DOUBTED IT. COME THEN, APRO-POS . . . IF YOU BE A MAN. LET US SEE WHAT YOU'RE REALLY MADE OF."

And with that he disappeared into the darkness behind him.

At which point, my mind split.

It happened with such force that I almost staggered from the impact of it. Half of my mind screaming at me, *Get out of here! Run! This is madness! Do not enter that place! Keep away! Keep away!*

But at precisely the same time, the gem in my chest burned with such fury that, for the first time I cried out in pain. Even as my every base instinct told me to flee, my legs propelled me toward the hole in the side of the mountain, my body and blackened soul seeking something that my mind could not even begin to comprehend.

And with a final, strangled cry, I vanished into the blackness within.

Chapter 5

The Fissure King

I entered the darkness and I could see.

I had no idea how this was possible. There was no means of illu-mination that I could perceive. No torches lighting the way, no glowworms or lanterns. And yet there, in the darkness, I could see effortlessly. The only reason I knew it was pitch black within was because I comprehended intellectually that it had to be that way. It was night outside and so no sun's rays could filter through the opening. And it didn't matter, because in short order I had moved away from it entirely.

I found myself in a cramped grotto, ringed with stalagmites and stalactites. But not far ahead it seemed to open up wider, and from that area I heard, "THIS WAY, APROPOS. THIS WAY, PEACELORD. THE TIME FOR A RECKONING HAS COME."

I'll reckon you, you poxy bastard, I thought. I had my sword firmly in my hand as I crept forward. What surprised me was that

I was feeling waves of heat from ahead of me. Most caves I had encountered, from the small ones I'd hidden within to the chambers of Ba'da'boom which I'd thought I'd never leave, had always been very cool. Not this time. But the heat was dry, and for a moment I wondered if somehow I'd stumbled over some leftover lava flow from the Flaming Nether Regions.

I walked carefully and deliberately. Not only was I no longer feeling any of the trepidations in my mind that had actively been trying to prevent me from entering this place, but I had literally forgotten I'd had them in the first place. My jaw was set, my pulse was racing with anticipation of driving my sword deep into his gut, and the gem wanted . . .

I paused. *The gem wanted?* But as quickly as the notion came to me, it flittered away again, leaving me only with the vague thought that something important had occurred to me but had been forgotten. Mentally I shrugged and decided that if it was at all important, I'd probably remember it again later.

Alert to any sign of a trap, I eased my way through the narrowing passageway. I thought with grim amusement, *So this was what it was like being born,* and suddenly the area opened up in front of me.

It was gargantuan. A cavern as wide and vast as the largest of cathedrals.

In the middle . . . a death trap. A huge, black pit of a death trap. Stretching from side to side and all around, and only the narrowest of walkways surrounding it, a crevasse of such depths as I had never seen. And it was a fortunate thing that I noticed that first, and as a result had the requirement for caution impressed upon me with such intensity, for an instant later I became aware of the rest of my surroundings. And had I not known that to walk carelessly forward meant a very significant drop, I would have wandered forward into the nothingness without a thought, for all my concentration was upon that which surrounded me . . .

. . . gems. Glittering, sparkling, shimmering all around me, lining the walls of the vast grotto, gems of enough value to last a lifetime, to last a hundred lifetimes. None of them were as large or as perfect as the one which adorned my chest, but even so, each and every one of them was gorgeous.

This was it. That damnable little weaver, Sharee, had spoken truly. Through luck or fate or whatever one would call it, I had come upon a massive natural storehouse of riches beyond imagining. And how they could be twinkling in the darkness like a thousand stars, I had no idea. Well, perhaps it was indeed in the same manner that stars shone.

Or maybe . . .

. . . maybe it was . . . in response . . . to the gem that was upon me.

Without fully understanding why, I tore aside the fabric of my tunic, and there it was, the gem, glowing with an inner fire, and I could see why I was feeling such internal heat. I heard something, a sound, a glorious song, a chant that did not come from outside my ears, but from within, as if it and the others were singing to one another.

"Are they . . . alive . . . ?" I whispered. I had spoken to myself, and had not expected to receive an answer. Yet I got one anyway.

"IN A MANNER OF SPEAKING, BY CRUMM."

I turned quickly . . . so quickly that I almost lost my balance. The blackness below loomed before me, and at the last second I snagged a stalagmite and righted myself, letting out a slow breath of relief.

There was Beliquose, all right. He was about thirty feet away, just as brutish and barbaric as I'd remembered. He was also even harder to understand, because his bellowing echoed off the walls, making it almost impossible to comprehend him. If I'd been thinking with my right mind, properly analyzing the situation, I would have realized that he was seeing me in the darkness as easily as I was seeing him, and that should not have been the case. But I was too caught up in the intensity of the moment to comprehend that. Instead I snarled, "What do you mean, in a manner of speaking?"

"THE EARTH IS A LIVING ENTITY, APROPOS! EVERY PART OF IT, NO MATTER HOW INANIMATE IT SEEMS, HAS A SPARK OF LIFE TO IT! THESE GEMS ARE OF THE EARTH, AND HAVE A LIFE AND SPIRIT ALL THEIR OWN!" He took a step toward me, and I kept my sword up and at the ready, prepared for his charge. He appeared, however, to be in no hurry. "YOU HAVE COST ME DEARLY, BOY! MY MEN, DEAD! MY HOUND, MY BEAUTIFUL HOUND . . ."

"It was a trap all along," I said tightly, "wasn't it. You left her behind with instructions to lead us here."

He nodded. "YOU FIGURED IT OUT. YOU KNOW . . . I EXPECTED YOU MIGHT. I DID NOT EXPECT HER TO TURN, THOUGH. TO SACRIFICE HERSELF IN TRYING TO SAVE YOUR MAN. HOW UTTERLY POINTLESS."

"I'm not afraid of you!" I shouted. "In case you haven't figured it out yet . . . I happen to be invincible!"

"REALLY? JOIN THE CLUB."

And he tore away the great black leather frontpiece he wore . . . and there, embedded in his chest, just as in mine, was a gem. It was identical to mine in every way, with a glowing unearthly flame dancing within it.

My legs suddenly felt weak. It wasn't as if the frailty had returned to them; I was just startled to see someone who seemed to share the imperviousness I had. My bravado, my triumphs, had come entirely as a result of my conviction that I had an edge over all whom I faced. The notion of a level playing field was not one that I was especially fond of.

"I KNEW," he said, and he almost sounded a bit sad about it. "WHEN I SAW YOU BATTLE YOUR WAY OUT OF AN UNBEATABLE TRAP . . . WHEN I SAW SPEARS AND SWORDS DELIVER ENOUGH WOUNDS TO KILL A DOZEN PEACELORDS . . . I KNEW BEYOND ANY QUESTION THAT THE GEM HAD BONDED WITH YOU. JUST AS IT DID WITH ME. AND I FELT SORRY FOR YOU THEN, BECAUSE I WAS WILLING TO MAKE THE SACRI-

FICE ALONE. IT IS UNFORTUNATE THAT SOMEONE SHOULD HAVE TO SHARE IT."

"Sacrifice? What the hell are you talking about?" But then I knew. He took another step toward me, and I backed up, keeping my sword blade up between us. I knew that I couldn't stop him with it, any more than he could stop me, but it was reflex. "Oh, I understand now. You want to sacrifice the world to . . . to whatever craving for power these gems have. . . as Sharee warned me. You want to use it to—"

But he shook his head vehemently. "NO! NO, BY CRUMM'S BEARD! THE WEAVER MISUNDERSTOOD! SHE DID NOT KNOW! SHE BELIEVED ME TO BE A BARBARIAN BRUTE. SHE DID NOT COMPREHEND THE MISSION . . . THE PURPOSE! SHE KNEW THAT THE GEMS COULD SPELL DOOM FOR THE WORLD . . . AND THOUGHT THAT I WAS TO DELIVER THAT DOOM! BUT SHE THOUGHT WRONG! IT'S WHY I LURED YOU HERE, APROPOS . . . TO THIS PLACE! TO THE GREAT DIVIDE!" And he pointed at the huge fissure before us. "I BROUGHT US HERE . . . TO DO WHAT MUST BE DONE!"

"Done?! Done with what?" I tapped the gem with my free hand. *"What are these things, anyway?"*

"DO YOU NOT KNOW? DID THE WEAVER NEVER TELL YOU?" He looked both surprised and pitying at the same time. "CERTAINLY YOU HAVE HEARD THAT BEAUTY IS IN THE EYE OF THE BEHOLDER? BUT DID YOU NOT REALIZE THAT IS NOT SIMPLY AN OLD SAYING . . . BUT AN ANCIENT PROPHECY? A STATEMENT OF ABSOLUTE TRUTH?"

"No! How the hell would I know that? And how is that supposed to mean anything to—"

And then my voice trailed off, and he could see in my eyes that I understood, or at least was beginning to understand, for he said, "THESE ARE THE EYES OF THE BEHOLDERS! THE EYES OF THE GODS UPON THE EARTH! IT IS HOW THEY

WATCH US, HOW THEY AFFECT US. IT IS FROM THESE THAT ALL BEAUTY STEMS, YES . . . BUT ALSO ALL EVIL! YOU SEE, THEY ONCE SAT IN THE GATE OF HEAVEN, BUT WERE STOLEN FROM A—"

"No! Shut up! Don't start!" I howled, slamming my sword against a stalagmite for emphasis with such force that it rang throughout the gargantuan cavern. *"I see this coming! I see this coming a mile away! You're about to tell me that these . . . these things . . . have been the subject of a long and great quest, which you've gone on, and faced countless perils, and the fate of our entire sphere hangs upon what you do next! Right? Am I right?!"*

And Beliquose looked so startled, so taken aback by the vehemence of my response, that when he replied it was in the smallest and quietest voice I'd ever heard from him. In other words, it was a normal conversational tone.

"Well . . . yes," he admitted, looking a bit deflated.

Myself, I wasn't deflated. I was overblown with fury. *"Son of a bitch!"* I howled. ***"I'm in somebody else's adventure again! I'm another goddamn supporting character!*** *Shit! What do I have to do to be the center of attention around here?!"*

Beliquose looked utterly dumbfounded. He had no idea what I was ranting about.

How could he? How could I explain to him the situation, years ago, when I was confronted with the bravery and heroism that was epitomized in my former friend, Tacit? When I realized that in the annals of our world, Tacit was a hero of epic proportions, going through the paces of an equally epic adventure that was the kind of thing balladeers, poets, and storytellers loved to tell to rapt audiences? And there was I, Apropos, thinking that I was the center of my own life and world—which is how most people think of themselves. But in a raging epiphany, I had come to realize exactly what my station was: to be a supporting, even bit player in the true greatness that was the exploits of someone else. I was the throwaway, disposable side character.

And now here I was, thinking myself the epic conqueror of

nations, and it turned out that I was simply the last challenge for a damned barbarian hero to overcome so he could save the world.

"DO WE HAVE A PROBLEM HERE?" inquired Beliquose, back to his normal earsplitting volume.

"You bet your ass we have a problem here!" I shot back. "You want to be invincible, like me? Fine! Go be invincible someplace else! I was here *first!* I claim Wuin. Go destroy Isteria if you want. I've never had much use for the place anyway! As a matter of fact," I said with sudden inspiration, "it was written that I'm supposed to be here! Written that I would be involved in the Woad to Wuin! Was it written that you would be? I think not!"

"WELL . . . NOT THAT EXACTLY. BUT MY MISSION WAS WRITTEN, YES." He pulled out a rolled parchment, unrolled it, and held it up. "YOU PROBABLY WON'T UNDERSTAND IT. IT'S WRITTEN IN RUNIC. IT WAS GIVEN ME BY—"

More and more was becoming clear to me as I said hollowly, "By a smooth-headed, gray-bearded Visionary with a threadbare cloak."

He brightened. "SO THAT *WAS* HIM IN YOUR TAVERN THAT NIGHT. I *THOUGHT* HE SEEMED FAMILIAR. SMALL WORLD."

Beliquose rolled the parchment back up and tucked it in his boot as he said, with growing urgency, "APROPOS . . . YOU FEEL THE INCREASED BURNING IN THE EYE, DO YOU NOT? TIME IS RUNNING OUT. THE EYES SENSE WHAT I AM ABOUT TO DO, AND ARE TRYING TO OVERWHELM MY RESOLVE. MINE BONDED WITH ME BECAUSE IT READ THE DARKNESS ALREADY IN MY SOUL, JUST AS YOURS DID WITH YOU. BUT I'VE TRIUMPHED OVER IT, JUST AS YOU CAN. . . ."

"Right, because you're a loud annoying hero with delusions of grandeur! I'm a workingman! I don't need this grief!"

"THE WORLD DOESN'T NEED THE GRIEF! LISTEN TO ME . . ." He tried to walk toward me, but I backed up. We were circling the gaping hole he'd called the Great Divide as he continued, "THE EYES SHOULD NOT BE OF THIS WORLD. THEY SHOULD NEVER HAVE COME HERE. NOW THAT THEY ARE HERE, THEY REPRESENT INCALCULABLE POWER. AND THERE ARE DARK FORCES WHO HAVE LESS-THAN-GENTLE PLANS FOR THE WORLD. WHO WOULD USE THAT POWER TO REORDER THE WORLD TO THEIR LIKING. BUT YOU'RE NOT TOTALLY LOST TO THE EYE, APROPOS! I CAN SENSE IT. IT WANTS MORE FROM YOU. IT IS NOT YET SATED."

"Sated? Sated how?"

"PART OF YOU STILL BATTLES IT . . . AND YOU HAVE IT WITHIN YOU TO MAKE THE SACRIFICE THAT MUST BE MADE TO KEEP THE EYE FROM THE DARK FORCES WHO WOULD MISUSE IT. IN YOUR SACRIFICE, YOU CAN BE A MODERN PROMETHEUS, WIELDING THE FLAME OF KNOWLEDGE FOR HUMANITY. TRUE BRINGER OF ENLIGHTENMENT TO MANKIND. FLAME TO ILLUMINATE THE DARKNESS WHEREIN ALL IGNORANCE HIDES."

And suddenly he stooped and then stood, having grabbed something from behind a rock.

It was a torch, the flame upon it burning brightly.

I stepped back, alarmed. *"No! Get away!"*

He advanced upon me, bearing the torch toward me. I could feel the terror from the gem, more than matching my own. "GIVE UP YOUR INVINCIBILITY, APROPOS! TURN AWAY FROM THE PATH OF DARKNESS YOU'RE TREADING! IT IS THE ONLY WAY!"

"And go back to being what?" I cried out. I kept backing up, almost stumbling on the uneven surface. "To being nothing? I've *been* nothing! I won't return to that miserable, pathetic state! I won't!"

He thrust forward with the torch. I dodged behind a stalagmite, just avoiding the flame, and swung my sword as hard as I could. But my confidence was eroded, the fear made me clumsy, and the lunge was as bad as they come. Beliquose stepped sideways, avoiding the thrust effortlessly, and with casual ease he slapped the sword out of my hand. It clattered to the ground and he stepped around the stalagmite to get at me, but I backpedaled as fast as I could.

The pleading was gone from his face, replaced by impatience. "I HAVE MY DARKNESS, TOO, APROPOS! NOT AS RELENTLESSLY DARK AS YOURS, BUT IT'S THERE JUST THE SAME. I FEEL THE GEM CLAWING AT IT, TRYING TO EXPLOIT IT! BEFORE I LOSE MY RESOLVE, BEFORE THE EYES JOIN FORCES AT THE BEHEST OF THE DARK POWERS THAT CRAVE THEM, WE MUST PUT AN END TO THIS! THE EYES CANNOT BE DESTROYED BY ANY FORCE UPON THIS EARTH . . . SO THEY MUST BE HURLED INTO THE GREAT DIVIDE! THE ONLY TRUE BOTTOMLESS PIT IN EXISTENCE, SO THAT THEY WILL FOREVER BE BEYOND THE REACH OF GOD OR MAN! YOU WILL DO THIS WILLINGLY, OR OVER YOUR DEAD BODY! IT MAKES NO DIFFERENCE TO ME, BY CRUMM!"

I turned and ran.

I moved quickly across the rocky terrain, trying to run as fast as I could to stay ahead of him, but at the same time endeavoring not to slip lest I plunge into the yawning fissure to my immediate left. Beliquose was right after me, and his strides were much longer than mine. A desperate plan occurred to me then, and I picked up my speed, running with near recklessness. Behind me, Beliquose sped up. I could practically feel him breathing down my neck, and my mind raced, trying to figure out some way to beat that which was unbeatable.

"YOU SELFISH LITTLE BLACKGUARD!" he bellowed behind me. "TO THINK YOU'D PLACE YOUR OWN PETTY CONCERNS ABOVE THE WORLD! THAT YOU'D

EMBRACE THE UNNATURAL POWER GIVEN YOU BY A TALISMAN THAT COULD SEND THE EARTH SPI-RALLING INTO A PIT OF EVIL, ALL BECAUSE IN THE DARKNESS OF YOUR HEART YOU LUST FOR POWER! DAMN YOU! WHERE'S YOUR PRIDE?!"

And with a sudden, quick movement I yanked one of the halves of my staff from my belt, spun, and threw it between Beliquose's pumping legs. It snagged between his ankles, and he tripped over it, tried to untangle his feet from it, failed, and—waving his arms in futility to reacquire his balance—stumbled sideways . . .

. . . into the gaping fissure.

"My pride goes before your fall," I said icily.

It took him a second or two to realize that there was nothing around him save air, and then . . . well, if Beliquose's normal speaking voice was ear-shattering, that was as nothing compared to the scream he uncorked as he plummeted into oblivion.

"*AAAAAAAAAAHHHH!!!!*" Beliquose howled, and my teeth rattled and I staggered about and would likely have fallen in myself if I'd not thrown myself flat to the ground and just held on. The scream echoed and re-echoed for what seemed like for-ever, and to this day sometimes I wake up late at night, thinking that I can hear the last frustrated howl of a would-be barbarian hero, tumbling away into endless darkness with one half of the most infinitely potent source of power in the world holding on for the ride.

Leaving me, of course, with the other half.

And one half of infinity is still quite a lot to have at one's disposal.

This knowledge gave me great comfort as I picked up the other half of my staff, which lay on the ground where Beliquose had tripped over it. Then I connected the two halves, popped out the blade from the dragon's tongue on the one end, and proceeded to pry as many of the gems out of the wall as I could reasonably reach. I got quite a nice little collection, fashioning a sling from my cape so that I could carry them easily, and made my way out of the cavern.

I emerged from the cave some minutes later, blinking against the sun that was coming up over the horizon. The burning in my chest had subsided greatly. I could only conclude that it had been caused by the proximity of the one "eye" to the other, and with its mate gone, so, too, was the heat. I wondered what the result would have been if the one eye had joined with the other. Ultimate power for the holder? An explosion the likes of which had never before been seen in the world? I was glad I was never going to have to find out. And as for Beliquose . . .

Well, hell, it was entirely possible that everything he'd said to me had been a complete lie. That rather than dispose of the gems, he was instead going to use them for some nefarious purpose all his own. Yes, he'd talked a good game, certainly, but in the end . . .what does any of us really know about each other? I mean, really know?

These thoughts gave me great comfort as I prepared for my return home. Upon returning to where the horses had been tied, I was surprised to discover that not only were they still there, intact and untouched by predators, but Mordant was there as well. He was perched upon a rock nearby, and he flapped his wings slowly in greeting upon seeing me. He let out a caw that was much more restrained than his usual noise, which led me to believe that he was nursing an injury.

"Kept an eye on my ride, did you? Well done," I said approvingly. Mordant bobbed his head, but he was watching me with great curiosity. It was as if he was aware there was something different about me. And who knows, there might have been. At that moment, though, I was still not in the best of shape to give it any thought. I shoved the gems, wrapped up securely in my cape, into the saddlebag and then mounted up, my head still whirling with doubts.

But once I was under way, riding one of the horses while leading the other along by its reins, I had not only convinced myself that Beliquose was the greatest potential evil that the world had ever faced . . . but that I, in fact, had already saved all humanity from the insidious plans that he'd been cooking up.

Why? Because I was the hero, that was why. No damned supporting character or obstacle to someone else's epic tale was I.

Proving, I suppose, that with the capacity for infinite power comes also the capacity for infinite self-delusion.

Chapter 6

The Woad Not Taken

*I*t was odd. I had not remembered a fork in the path before.

The ride back to the Golden City had been fairly uneventful, which naturally was fine with me. I had already left thoughts of Beliquose far behind me; concerns and second-guessing were as dead to me as was Beliquose himself. I wondered idly if he was still falling, tumbling end over end and howling my name in fury. An ordinary man would not survive falling for any length of time, even if the landing never came. Twisting and turning in midair would cause the back or neck to snap before long, and it would be a lifeless sack of meat completing the plunge. But since Beliquose was, like me, invulnerable to harm, there was nothing to relieve him of the drop. Maybe he knew a few good, lengthy ballads to pass the time.

The sun was high in the sky, burning with intensity, and yet oddly I didn't feel the heat. I wondered why that was, even as I sat at the split in the road and wondered which way I should go.

I could not see the Golden City in the distance, so that was of no guide to me. The presence of the split bothered me. It was possible, I supposed, that in our hurry to pursue Beliquose we had simply ridden past it, joining up with the main road from the side path and just continuing along the way undistracted and uncaring. But still, it seemed . . . it seemed odd. Even unnatural in some way. I had no idea why that should be. It was just a split road, that was all, and I needed but determine which path I would travel.

I looked around for Mordant, to see if perhaps the little drabit might provide me with guidance. But he was nowhere to be seen. I whistled sharply and called his name, extending my forearm so that he could descend from the heavens and land upon it. But there was nothing. Nothing except the eerie sound of a breeze blowing across the barren landscape, and suddenly I had the uncanny feeling that I was alone in the world. The hairs on the back of my neck prickled, and I looked behind me and saw the same nothingness as was ahead of me. All landmarks had disappeared. Mount Aerie was not in sight, nor had the Golden City managed to appear magically. Yet magic this moment did stink of, and I did not like it in the least.

And then I saw two women approaching.

One was coming from the fork on the right, the other from the left. They were both wearing loose-fitting, sleeveless robes called *abas,* one of them blue, the other green. Their heads were veiled so that their faces were completely obscured. The one on the right was shorter than the one on the left, and even though I couldn't see their features, they both appeared familiar to me for some reason.

I was comfortable and unafraid, of course. Neither of them seemed to be wielding a torch or any source of flame, nor did it seem likely that they would suddenly produce a pit to throw me into. "Ho, there, good women!" I called to them as they neared. "I seek the Golden City! Would you be able to direct me?"

The shorter of the two of them, clad in green, was nearer, and she stopped and simply stood there. My horse moved around a bit uncertainly, as if it suddenly didn't like the company it was keeping and wanted to get out of there. I slowly became aware that something was wrong. I didn't want to risk panicking or losing the horse, but I didn't want to sit there and fight to keep the beast where it was; that would hardly be dignified. So I swung my leg over and dismounted adroitly. I didn't release the horse's reins, but I allowed it enough slack to permit the beast to back up a few paces. "How now?" I said slowly.

"Hail, Apropos," said the shorter of the women. "Hail, Peacelord of Wuin." And she raised a hand in greeting.

"Hail, Apropos," called the other woman, "slaughterer of thousands and destroyer of dreams."

It seemed most strange to me. Something wasn't quite right. "Why do I have the feeling there should be three of you?" I asked.

The two women looked at one another, and shrugged in unison. "Don't know," said the green one.

"Couldn't tell you," said the blue.

By that point I knew. The one in blue I still hadn't managed to place, although she seemed vaguely familiar, but the one in green I would have recognized anywhere. "All right, Sharee," I said sharply, "why the disguise? What's the game this time?"

"Sharee? Who's Sharee?" asked the green-clad one, trying to sound innocent.

"Fine, to hell with you, I'll figure out where I'm going on my own," I said brusquely and prepared to mount up.

The green-clad one took a step forward and pulled off her veil, and of course it was Sharee all right, looking well and truly annoyed. "All right, fine, it's me, happy?"

"Not especially, no. Are you and your associate going to try and kill me again? I doubt you'll have better luck than you did last time," I said carelessly, and placed my foot in the stirrup. To my surprise, however, the horse pulled away from me. My heel snagged and the animal dragged me along a few hopping paces before I could disentangle myself. "What are you about?" I demanded of the animal in annoyance.

"He knows it's not time for you to depart yet. He, at least, has horse sense," said Sharee. She was watching me very carefully, as if she thought I might somehow vanish into thin air at any moment. She came no closer, though, which was wise on her part. Considering the mood I was in at that moment, I wouldn't have held myself responsible for my actions.

"I'm getting tired of this, Sharee." I turned to face her, my arms akimbo. "Tired of your harassment. You're going to have to stop dwelling on the past."

"And you must start dwelling on your future," she replied. She pointed with either arm to each road. "You do not know which path to take because you have lost your way."

The woman was going to drive me insane. That had to be her plan. "Gods, Sharee, what are you doing here?"

"You summoned me," she replied. "Or at least, that small part of you that is not utterly bereft of hope did. Soon, though, that will be gone as well, and then you will truly be lost."

"If my being lost means that *you'll* never find me, I will happily embrace that option," I told her. I had to remind myself that she had no power over me save what I gave to her. That if I simply controlled myself, she could have no more impact upon me than could a passing breeze. "The simple fact, Sharee, is that I have found my destiny, and you can't stand that." I advanced on her, and she held her ground until I was almost nose to nose with her. "You can't stand that I'm no longer the poor, pathetic, crippled thing known far and wide as Apropos of Nothing, but instead a man of wealth and stature and power."

"That is what you are now," she said mildly, "but have you considered what is to come? For the sins you have committed, the next life you may return as some base animal, so that you can learn proper humility."

"There is no animal more base than humanity," I shot back,

"and all of the members of that species deserve whatever I choose to give them."

She shook her head and made "tsk" noises. "Such hatred. Such self-loathing . . ."

"No. No self-loathing. For the first time," and I thumped my chest, "I feel damned good about myself. So you and your less-chatty friend can go on your way, Sharee, if your plan was to make me feel guilty about what I've done. I've no reason to. In fact . . . I bow to the wisdom of others whose beliefs I once doubted," and I bowed mockingly to her. "I fully admit it: There is such thing as destiny. And to be the conqueror of Wuin, with woad upon my face and a thousand troops at my back, is mine. My mother end-lessly claimed that I had a great future to pursue, and I have done so. So save your disapproving looks and contemptuous tones, because if she were here, she would—"

The woman in blue stepped forward and pulled away her veil, and I looked in shock at the face of my mother.

The countenance of Madeline was just as I remembered it. Old beyond its years, careworn, her body sagging under the years of constant abuse that her steady stream of clients had put it through. Gray streaks in her hair, and infinite sadness in her eyes, but also hope for me and for my future.

I was rooted to the spot as she continued toward me, and when she was barely two paces away, she swung back her hand and brought it around in a blur. Her hand slapped across my face with such force that it rocked me on my heels. I didn't feel it, for all the blood had already drained from my face.

"How dare you," she said, her voice angry and brittle and unut-terably sad. "How dare you invoke my name after all you've done . . . as if that justifies it. As if I'd approve of it."

"You're . . . not here," I whispered. "You can't be here." I pinched myself, tried to wake myself in case it was some sort of dream. I felt no pain. Of course I felt no pain. I couldn't be hurt.

Madeline trembled a moment, as if seized with emotions so vio-lent that she couldn't figure out how to channel them, and then with an angry shriek she slapped at me again. What was I supposed to do? Punch her? Yank out my sword and carve her up? No matter the circumstances, no matter how bizarre and unreal what I was witnessing, this . . . this being . . . was my mother. I backed away, keeping my arms in front of my face to block her blows, but otherwise offered no defense.

"After everything I did for you!" she cried out. "All the sacrifices I made! The future I foresaw—!"

"Future! Future!?" I stopped retreating and instead shouted at her with wounded pride. "How many times did I have to listen to you spin fables about grand destinies and phoenixes—!"

"They weren't fables!" Madeline insisted, slapping at my chest. I stepped back, managing to avoid her altogether. "I saw a phoenix! A phoenix, rising from its own ashes in a glorious burst of flame!" She looked as if she were desperately trying to make me understand. "Flame is a symbol of purity! Of rebirth! Of knowledge! You recoil from flame because it's all anathema to the darkness within you! That's what you have to use against yourself—!"

"Against myself!? This is madness!" I pulled away my wrist as Madeline reached for it, and turned to face Sharee, who was watching all that was happening. "This is your doing!"

"Perhaps," said Sharee evenly. "Or perhaps it's your mother's. Or maybe it's even your own."

I lunged at her then. I have no idea what I would have done had I gotten my hands on her, but it didn't matter. One moment she was there, the next I was grasping at empty air. I stumbled and hit the ground, twisting around in place and looking up at the two of them. *"Why the hell can't you leave me alone! What do you want from me?"*

"We want you to achieve your destiny," they chorused.

"I did!"

"It's false," said Sharee, and Madeline chimed in, "It is not what it appears."

"The only thing that's not what it appears around here is you!" I said sharply. "I'm getting out of here!" I scrambled to my feet to

get to my horse, and stumbled back as I heard a deafening roar. What I saw nearly caused my eyes to leap out of my head.

A dragon and a lion were wrestling one another upon the ground. The carvings upon the head of my staff having come to life, they were struggling with the sort of ferocity that only truly wild beasts can summon. The dragon was on its back, trying to shove the lion away with its forelegs as the carnivore's slavering jaws sank closer and closer to the dragon's neck. Letting out a roar so fearsome that the ground beneath me shook, the dragon shoved the lion off, twisted around, and opened its mouth wide. With an explosive belch, a gargantuan fireball leaped out of its mouth . . . straight toward me.

I barely had time to unleash a terrified shriek and then the flame engulfed me. I went down, writhing upon the ground, trying to beat the flames away from me. Madeline and Sharee, standing nearby, watched impassively.

"If the gem is the Eye of the Beholder," Sharee intoned, as if I weren't dying right in front of her, "then it stands to reason that someone is watching through the eye."

And still there was no pain. There were small bits of smoldering flame upon me that I extinguished, but it took the last of my strength. I lay there upon the ground, staring up at the sun, unable to move, barely able to breathe. I couldn't lift my head to look at myself, but I was certain that the sight that would have greeted me would have been my body blistered and burned beyond recognition.

A great shadow began to move across the sun, blotting it out. It reminded me of the time I'd seen such a thing before, when I first awoke to my new life as "Peacelord." But this time it was moving far more quickly, as if anxious to devour the source of light and life that shone down upon our world.

And then my view of the sun was blotted out by the face of my mother. I tried to speak but once again found myself unable to do so, overwhelmed by emotion. My mother had woad upon her face, drawn in the same pattern that had adorned my own visage when I had gone into battle. She leaned forward and kissed me on the forehead. I didn't feel that, either, and tears began to run down my face because I'd never wanted to feel a kiss so much in my life as that gentle pressing of my dead mother's lips against my blackened skin.

She leaned back then and the sobbing in my throat turned into choked horror. It was no longer the blue mud of woad upon her. Instead her face was covered with darkened blood, dripping down. And it provided a stark and ghastly contrast to the softness of her voice as she whispered to me, "You've chosen the wrong path."

"But . . . but I did it for . . . for you. . . ."

Her bloodied features hardened while, behind her, Sharee rolled her eyes and shook her head. "Don't blame it on me," my mother said. "You did it for everyone *but* me. . . ."

"Meander," I said desperately. "King Meander. When I heard that he had returned, I knew I had to capture him, slay him . . . for you! For you!"

Mockingly, she feigned excitement. "For me? Truly? And how will slaying him bring me back?"

I paused. "It . . . it won't . . . but it will allow you to rest in peace. . . ."

"I rest, Apropos, with or without his death. It makes no difference to me. Only to you."

"But . . . but at least he'll harm no one else . . . he . . . he is the one who killed you . . . right? *Right?*"

The sun was almost completely gone. Madeline's face above me was beginning to fade, and she was shaking her head sadly.

And then, very slowly, very deliberately . . . she winked at me.

I cried out even louder, my voice rising. *"Right? Mother! Wait! Don't—!*

"—go!"

I sat upright suddenly, and Mordant let out a startled shriek. He had been staring at me with those glittering eyes, but my sudden movement had disconcerted him, and he squawked in protest.

I twisted about, gyrating in what must have been a most comical fashion to anyone who happened to be looking on. There was darkness around me, and for an instant I thought that the sun had been extinguished for all time and the world plunged into eternal gloom, before I realized and remembered that it was simply night-time. The horses were standing nearby, apparently having no trouble sleeping through my unexpected outburst. I got to my feet and turned all the way around. As before, I had no trouble seeing in the darkness, and it was clear to me that there was no split in the road ahead. Just one road leading to one destination.

It came flooding back to me. I had grown tired and made a crude camp for the night. I had relaxed on the side of the road, gone to sleep, leaving Mordant to watch out for me. But the drabit had not been able to protect me from the wandering thoughts and rogue dreams that wandered within my own troubled brain.

But . . . why troubled? I had everything.

Everything . . . except peace of mind.

"That will change," I said harshly to Mordant, who stared at me uncomprehending. "I'll return to the Golden City, dispose of Meander, and then . . . and then . . ."

I had no idea.

It seemed . . . that there was more. Much more. But it was as if a great wall had been erected before me, blocking my view of what was to come. More conquests, I supposed, more pillaging and plundering in my name, but something more . . . something more . . .

And then it faded, like a shadow as the first rays of daylight fall upon it, and was gone.

Chapter 7

Fools and Kings

*T*he sun had risen only a few hours before as I approached the main gate and saw the first—or perhaps it was the last—of the stragglers. Three, then five, then a dozen, and then more after that. They had haunted expressions, and when they saw me they cowered in fear. Old men and women, a couple of children hiding behind the legs of the adults.

I gazed down at them from my horse. For no reason other than that it seemed the thing to say, I inquired, *"Quo vadis?"*

They stared at me blankly.

"Where are you going?" I sighed.

"Oh," one of the old men said softly, and then he said, "Away. There is nothing left for us. The warriors of the Peacelord have had their way with the city. So we are leaving. Perhaps . . . we will return someday. I do not know. That is only known to . . ." And he shrugged and pointed heavenward.

An old woman, whom I took to be his mate, wrapped her arms

around his and said nervously, "Are you . . . one of the Peacelord's men?"

"No," I said in all honesty.

"Then . . ." She looked to her mate, who shrugged, and then back to me. "Then . . . *quo vadis?*"

I considered her question, and gave the second honest answer in a row.

"I haven't the faintest idea," I said.

The city was eerily quiet. I could even hear the steady clopping of the horses' hooves as we moved through it.

The air was still thick with the smell of burning—burning flesh, burning objects. But the laughter had faded, as had the screams. I saw none of the residents around, not even people stealing glances out through doorways. And I realized that the people I'd seen departing the city might well be the last of the city's residents.

That had never happened before.

Oh, we had gone through city after city leaving chaos in our wake. But our stay had never been extended. We had come through like a great sandstorm of violence, sweeping over all in our path, taking what we wished and who we wished, torching indiscriminately for no reason other than the pure joy of destruction, and then continuing on our way. We had taken prisoners, made them into slaves, yes, but we had also left plenty of residents behind. Why not? What interest were they to us?

In this instance, however, we had effectively set up base in the Golden City. It was not as if we were intending to govern it, though. I realized that my people must have continued their rampaging ways in my absence, for day upon day, to the point where the surviving populace had fled.

The result was a city which had been thriving and populous not all that long ago was now barren. A place where ghosts walked the streets in comfort because they did not need to concern themselves about running into the living.

I made my way through the lower city, seeing one burned-out

shell of a building after another. I couldn't help but think that the
entire thing seemed a massive waste somehow. I had no idea how
much time and effort had gone into building up the Golden City
into something great and impressive, but it certainly hadn't taken
us much time to reduce it to a hollow, bare semblance of its former
self.

*Well . . . they probably deserved it, because they were weak. They
depended upon others to fight their battles for them, and the others
failed, and now they deserve whatever they get.*

It was a remarkably pathetic rationalization, and yet for me it
was enough, and I took comfort in it and sat up a bit straighter
upon my horse. Mordant vaulted off my arm band and angled
away across the city's skies, no doubt doing some scavenging to see
what delights and treats he might be able to scrounge for himself.

There were sentries on the jagged wall that served to separate
the upper city from the lower, and at first they readied weapons to
hurl at me. But they allowed me to draw close enough—whether
to identify me or simply make a better target of me, I could not be
sure—and when they realized who I was, a joyous cry went up. It
was comforting to know that I'd been missed.

Within minutes I heard the clattering of hooves upon the road,
and here came riding up Boar Tooth and Slake. Their happiness to
see me was evident, but instantly they realized That Guy was not
with me. It was obvious to them that something tragic must have
occurred, and there on the streets outside the jagged wall I told
them of the strange final fate that had befallen their comrade in
arms.

"He felt . . . affection for that creature? And it for him?" asked
Slake when I finished. He clearly was having trouble grasping such
an absurd notion.

But Boar Tooth was simply nodding. "No, I can well believe it.
That Guy had a knack for the ladies and also a way with animals.
A creature who combines both attributes, well . . . I cannot say I'm
surprised that there would be some degree of attraction between
them. I am saddened, however, that it led to his demise. He must

truly have been distracted by her, else I have no doubt that he would have been able to evade the arrow that Beliquose's minion fired at him."

I wasn't altogether certain that was true, but it might have been. And if it gave comfort to his friends to believe it, who was I to gainsay them? "You are very likely correct," I said judiciously. "He died bravely; that is the important thing. The gods and goddesses welcome him into their bosom."

"If you say they do, Peacelord, then I am comforted since I assume you know whereof you speak," Slake said suavely and bowed his head. Boar Tooth followed suit.

"And speaking of goddesses," I continued with a smile and a bit of a leer, "does my own personal goddess fare well?"

"If you mean the Lady Kate—which ideally you do, lest most unfortunate circumstances befall you," Boar Tooth jested with me, "yes, she fares quite well. Indeed, she is the center of attention at this little home-away-from-stronghold that we have acquired. Every day she engages us in entertaining and witty banter; every evening she leads us in joyous songs and chants over the many victories that have brought us to this pass."

"All of which focus on you, Peacelord," said Slake quickly, with a glance at Boar Tooth.

Boar Tooth nodded very quickly and very unconvincingly. "Yes, Peacelord, all upon you."

It did not matter to me. Perhaps it should have, but it didn't. I was confident, secure enough in my greatness that I believed I need not concern myself about how much prominence my name held in ballads and songs. "She enjoys herself then, the Lady Kate?"

"I have never seen her more radiant," said Boar Tooth, and Slake's head bobbed in agreement.

"Well then," I said jovially, "I must go to her to see just how much she radiates. Oh . . . and gentlemen. How fares King Meander?"

The answer to that question seemed to bring the most pleasure to my lieutenants. They exchanged looks as if to silently decide who would be the one to tell me, and interestingly, without a word being stated, Boar Tooth was elected. He turned to me and announced, "He has emerged from his coma, Peacelord."

"And his faculties—?"

"As sharp as ever they were."

"Excellent!" I said. "I wish to have time to avail myself of the amenities offered by this glorious city. So we shall arrange for the disposition of the Keepless King to be held this very evening. The sun will set for a final time upon . . . upon . . ."

The sun setting.

My voice trailed off as I envisioned the sun . . . *the sun, covered by shadow, being consumed . . .*

"Peacelord?"

I shook it off and focused back on my men. "Apologies, gentlemen. I was . . . lost in thought."

Boar Tooth bowed slightly and said, "A god on earth need never apologize to mere mortals."

"Yes, that's true," I said serenely, and we rode off toward the mansion that was my temporary headquarters.

Somehow they must have managed to send word on ahead, or perhaps other sentinels saw me coming, for it was a true hero's welcome when I returned to the mansion. It was smaller scale, but reminded me of when I'd first arrived at Dreadnaught. I wondered how things were transpiring there, and was looking forward to being quit of this place as soon as possible.

I briefly toyed with the idea of hauling Meander with me back to Dreadnaught and having him executed there. It would get us out of the Golden City faster, and enable all the residents therein to share in the entertainment. I decided against it, though. I had no desire to take any risks with our prisoner. Who knew what sort of mishaps could occur between us and Dreadnaught? Unexpected natural disasters, attacking armies. Anything could happen, and if one such incident allowed Meander to escape in the confusion, I would never forgive myself.

Once I'd arrived, word quickly spread about the loss of That Guy. The general school of thought was that it was unfortunate, but he had died the way he would have preferred to die, namely in battle. And when I described the disposition of those who had stood against us—how I had cloven the skull of That Guy's killer, and then hurled Beliquose into a bottomless pit (which, let us be honest, sounds far more impressive than admitting that he tripped upon my staff while I was running from him)—there were many huzzahs and cries of appreciation from my men, and that made it almost worthwhile.

Mordant did not wander far from my side. He seemed a bit more clingy than he had been before, and he appeared to be regarding the men around us with a certain degree of suspicion. I did not, however, let it perturb me. I had other things to worry about.

"The Lady Kate is most anxious to see you," Boar Tooth informed me with a broad grin. And I was more than anxious to see her.

But then I saw, through a door and out in the main courtyard, a Crow's Cage suspended from an arch. A man was imprisoned in it, and I could see even from where I was that he was covered with the remains of overripe fruit and vegetables. People had been pelting him rather unmercifully, and I could only assume that the reason they weren't doing so at that point was because they'd run out of missiles.

I recognized him from behind. I was tempted to simply leave him there, for I had more delightful and delectable matters to attend to. But I couldn't pass this up.

The cage was narrow, as such things usually are, about five feet high which already required that he be, at the very least, bent over. In this instance, there were small holes at the bottom of the cage which were just large enough for him to slide this legs through so that he could sit. That's what he had chosen to do now. The cage was rocking back and forth softly with a faint creaking noise, and he was actually humming an aimless little tune. He paid me no mind as I approached him, and I gestured for my retainers to stay back so I could have some privacy with the bastard.

"Well well," I said as I approached him, walking around him and looking him up and down. He had not been given new clothes, and his warriors garb had been somewhat torn in the series of battles that had eventually brought him low. Visible through the rents in the fabric were assorted cuts, some of which I could tell hadn't healed properly, and hadeven become infected. My guess is that we were doing him a favor, since it was more than likely that—unless medical aids were able to work a miracle—he wasn't going to survive all that long. "King Meander, the Keepless King. Your Majesty," and I bowed mockingly low to him. "Not quite looking so majestic now, are we."

His hair was matted and unwashed, and his eyes seemed sunk deep into his head as he raised his head to look at me.

I was wrong. He still looked majestic. Wretched as he was in his fallen state, helpless within the Crow's Cage where he was deprived of food and water and would eventually become crow's food if left there . . . he still had a regal, even imperial look to him. It burned from within him in a glow that was no less intense than what I had seen ignited within the gem upon Beliquose's chest . . . or, for that matter, upon my own.

He did not glower at me, did not look in the least bit angry. He seemed utterly neutral, not at all perturbed by my presence. It was as if my being there didn't matter to him in the slightest . . . which, of course, was not how I wanted it to be at all.

I drew myself up, rallying my spirit as I said, sounding as regal as I could, "Where are your boasts now, highness?"

He actually seemed to give the question a good deal of thought. "Did I ever boast?" he asked quietly. That was not unusual. He said everything quietly. When King Meander spoke, one could almost hear the winds of the frozen north whirling about him, carrying away his words and leaving only the faintest whispers behind.

It was my turn to consider, and I realized that in point of fact, he never had. Meander might have been many things, but excessively prideful was not an attribute. I was hardly about to admit that, though. So instead I forced a smile and said, "You must have thought yourself fairly clever, did you not? Perched atop the wall, trying to lure me in."

"It worked," he said mildly.

"Aha!" I felt a moment of triumph and pointed at him. "So you remember it, then! You once told me you tended not to remember events from one day to the next! That you leave each one behind you so as not to burden yourself! Yet you remember your base trickery!"

"Well, yes." He pointed at bruises that lined his bare legs. "The men come along each day and beat me, and while they do so, they give a litany of my 'offenses.' That, apparently, was one of them." He smiled thinly. "Rather clever of me. I'm impressed I came up with it."

"You didn't," I said sourly. "I did. You got the idea from me."

"Did I? Hmmf. I thought it seemed vaguely familiar. That will happen to me sometimes. Ghosts of moments past come back to haunt me, and ridicule me with their familiarity." He glanced around his surroundings. "Considering how it's all turned out for me, it must not have been one of your better strategies."

"It worked when I did it," I told him . . . which wasn't exactly true. The truth was that Meander had seen through the bluff, but had instead elected—thanks to one of his legendarily capricious whims—to do nothing about it. But if you can't exaggerate your successes to someone who has no recollection of them, to whom *can* you exaggerate them?

It seemed that a wave of . . . of something passed over his face, and then he fixed a gaze upon me that seemed to bore through my head. "Is this," he said quietly, "how you treat a king?"

And I suddenly thought, *My gods, I have a king locked up in a Crow's Cage like a common thief. What in the hell have I done?* I felt an immediate impulse to go to the cage, break the door open, free him, and grovel at his feet begging forgiveness.

Fortunately for all concerned, I overcame that instantly. I forced myself to remember that, no, he was just a man. "You may call yourself what you wish," I said to him, drawing myself up and squaring my shoulders. "But the truth is that you gave up your claim to being a king long ago, when you walked away from your kingdom. You cannot simply and arbitrarily declare, as you have, the entirety of the world to be your kingdom."

"I never have," he replied evenly. "I have merely said that my kingdom is wherever I am. You do not understand, Apropos. Kingship does not come from out there. It comes," and he tapped his chest, "from in here."

"You know my name!" I said triumphantly. "You remember that, then!"

"Your men have repeatedly mentioned the name of the lord of this place. I simply surmised it was you." Grim amusement played upon his lips. "No one else has bothered to converse with me. They simply beat me . . . on your behalf . . . while shouting at me. Or are you intending to join in those festivities? That staff you're carrying seems more than up to the job." He paused and, when I made no move, said mildly, "Well?"

"I should," I said, my body trembling with barely suppressed rage. "I should. And do you know why I should?"

"No, but I suspect you will tell me."

I took a step toward him, my hands tightening on my walking staff, and at that moment it indeed was all I could do not to thrash him with it. "You once had scars on your cheek. They've faded almost to invisibility now, but they're still there. And they were placed there by my mother, when you brutalized her . . . and killed her."

His face darkened. "I did that? You saw?"

"No. But you bore her mark upon you, and when I asked you how you came by them, you said you did not recall."

"And that was proof?"

"Her assailant . . . her murderer . . . was identified as bearing the Journeyman colors . . . worn by your men, and, more significantly, by you yourself. Do you deny you assaulted her?"

"No," he said.

And then he hung there. The cage had stopped swinging. Like a child, he moved his legs slightly and got it rocking again.

"That's it? That's all? 'No'? I speak to you of a crime and you do not deny it?"

"What would be the point?" he shrugged. "I do not recall doing such a thing. It does not sound like something I would do . . . but, then again, people are . . ." He stopped, and then his gaze seemed to go inward, and very far away, and there was pain and mourning and the coldness of the icy realm he'd left behind, all visible in those steely and tragic eyes. "People are capable," he said softly, "of doing . . . very unexpected things. Things they never would have thought possible. So I do not rule out anything. Besides . . . if I denied it . . . what use would it be to you?"

"Use?" I didn't understand.

With what seemed a visible effort, Meander focused upon me once more, and I had never seen such pity turned in my direction. "You have so much hatred within you. So much . . . from so many different sources. A blind man could see as much, and I am many things, but blind I am not. And you must put your hatred somewhere. You cannot put it upon yourself, for that would be too much for you to bear. Put it on me, then. My shoulders are both broad and stooped enough to sustain it. Put your hatred upon me . . . and be done with it. It matters not to me."

My fury bubbled over, and I charged his cage and shook it violently. Astoundingly, he didn't even seem to notice. *"Do not dare speak so patronizingly to me!"* I bellowed. "You are a captured prisoner! Do not act as if you are a martyr, willing to lay down your life whether you are innocent or no, just to remove some sort of . . . of burden from me! *I won't have it! I won't!"*

"It is neither yours to have nor mine to give," he replied.

"Gaaaaahhh!!" I shouted inarticulately and shoved the bars away from myself. For an instant I felt as tired as he must have, my breath coming in ragged gasps, and then I pointed an angry and shaking finger at him. "You seek to make a mockery of my pain!"

"Grimmoir."

I stopped and stared at him. The word had come out of nowhere and at first made no sense to me. "Grimmoir?" I demanded.

"I seem to recall . . . vaguely, which is the way I recall anything at best," he said with a frown, "that Grimmoir bore marks such as you described."

Then I remembered. That had been the name of his second in command. The one whose head I had found littering the field. What a contemptible trick! "Foul creature," I sneered. "You would seek to escape your fate by blaming a dead man?"

"No man escapes his fate, by definition. Fate is what it is," he said mildly.

"Well, I looked full on Grimmoir's face, even at the time when the marks would have been fresh years ago," I informed him. "I saw nothing like that upon his cheeks."

"I never said they were upon his face. They were not. They were on the top of his head. Grimmoir was bald. Did you ever see the top of his head? Do you know for certain that the marks were left upon the assailant's face?"

I stopped, cast my mind back, and realized to my sinking horror that the answer to both questions was negative. I had only ever seen Grimmoir with his helmet on, even when his cranium had rested in the field of battle. And as for the way that my mother's assailant was described to me . . . I'd simply been told she marked him. No one had specified where, and I had always just assumed. But if a man had been atop my mother, his face burrowed in her bosom, she could have just as likely ripped up his scalp as anywhere else.

"It's a trick," I whispered. "A . . . pathetic trick . . . to confuse me. . . ."

"That was not my intention," replied Meander. "Very well, then. I shall make it simple for you. Yes, it was me. I am responsible. I did it. Or if I did not do it, then one of my men did and as his leader, his crime is mine."

"Stop it. . . ."

"Do as you will. You are, after all, the Peacelord. Your word is law. And all must abide by . . ."

"Stop it! Stop it! Stop it!"

I charged the Crow's Cage once more with the intention of shaking it as furiously as I could, and Meander's arm snaked out between the bars and slammed me in the chin. The impact sent me off my feet, and I hit the ground hard. I stared up at him, my chest heaving, and he wasn't even looking at me. He was simply dangling his feet once more, and once again singing that same damned aimless tune.

Slowly I hauled myself up, and in as fearsome a voice as I could muster considering how thoroughly unmanned I was feeling at the moment, I snarled, "You ambushed me and tried to kill me. That alone would warrant your execution. The rest . . . the vengeance that my mother's soul cries out for . . . that's simply a bonus. You die this very night. So if you have any gods that you believe in— gods of the north, gods from wherever—you'd best start praying to them for absolution. And before you think yourself so smug and so above me, let me remind you . . . you're the one who's hanging here in a cage."

I spun on my heel, started to walk away, and from behind me he said quite sadly, "There are all sorts of cages, boy . . . and all sorts of ways to be trapped within them."

I did not even deign to look back.

Chapter 8

Monsters and Gods

I walked quickly through the halls of the manor, my blood boiling, my mind in turmoil. That, of course, was what he had wanted. To confuse me, to make me feel less the man, less the conqueror. Well, to hell with him, and to hell with that strategy. I knew exactly who to go to and what to do with her in order to reestablish my manhood.

I threw open the doors to my chamber. Sure enough, Kate was waiting for me, sprawled upon the bed in a most alluring fashion. I couldn't believe it. "Radiant" was barely sufficient to describe her. She looked positively glorious, more vital, more alive than any creature on the planet had a right to be. She threw back the sheet and she was not nude beneath it, but instead clad it a shift so completely sheer that she might as well have been. She ran her tongue along the bottom of her top teeth and purred, "I was worried, my love. You were taking so long. I had almost given you up for lost."

"Lost? Me?" I strode forward, pulling off my tunic, feeling

excitement building below my waist, the frustration caused by Meander already fading into distant memory. "How could any man conceivably be lost when he has such as you to return to?"

"No mere man are you," she said, throwing wide her arms, and then I was upon her. She covered my face, my bare chest with hot kisses as she moaned beneath me, "You are more than man! You are my god put upon this sphere to please me!"

"Oh, is that my only purpose?" I laughed, propping myself up and gazing down at her hungrily.

She made a delightfully pouting face. "Yes. Yes, that's it. That's the only reason. You are here to please *me*. To service *me*. To sate *me*. To worship at the altar of my femininity." And she swung her hand down and between my legs, and grabbed with determination, causing me to gasp into her ear. "So get to it!"

I got to it. We moved against each other, and I wanted to be leisurely about it, but at the same time I was driven with overwhelming urgency. Ultimately I gave into it, tearing the shift from her, the rest of my own clothes piling atop it. I shoved into her quickly, harshly, and she gasped at the sudden entrance but didn't shrink away. With every thrust deeper into her, I felt I was pushing Meander that much farther away. I would not let him weaken me or my resolve. He deserved to die. The dreams about my mother were just that: fantasies spun from a mind that somehow could not believe I was finally going to lay that personal ghost of mine to rest. Once Meander died, I would be free. Free. The last bit of unfinished business would be disposed of, and finally—*finally*—I would be my own man.

Except . . . I was beginning to suspect I wasn't any closer to figuring out who the hell that might be than I'd ever been. The confusion was understandable. I had spent a lifetime with the only conviction I had being that I had no convictions.

I wanted to stop feeling confused.

My mind obliged.

Later, as I lay next to Kate, her head tucked serenely upon my shoulder, any doubts concerning Meander or his guilt faded away, and I was back to knowing that what I was going to do was good and right and true, and that was all. I glanced out the windows and saw the shadows lengthening. Night was rapidly approaching. Even now they would be preparing for Meander's execution. No death by hanging as was more fit for the common man would be Meander's end. No, his head would be lopped from his body. And as his conqueror, the duty would fall to me to carry out the sentence.

Then I remembered something, and I sat up. Kate, lying in bed, sleepily looked up at me. She looked . . .

"Younger," I said, doing so with some surprise as I realized it.

"What?"

"You look . . ." I laughed. "You look younger, that's all. I mean, I know I'm imagining it. . . ."

"No, you're not at all," she said, almost cooing as she spoke. "When I'm with you, I feel so exuberant, so alive as I've never been . . . naturally I'd seem younger to you."

"Oh!" I suddenly exclaimed. "I just remembered! I've brought something back for you!"

"Did you?"

"Yes." I got out of bed and drew on my robe. Lying in a corner of the room were the materials from my ride, including my saddlebag.

She bounced up in bed excitedly, letting the sheet fall to reveal her nakedness as I picked up the saddlebag. Walking quickly over to her, I opened it up and dropped the bound-up cloak onto the bedspread. Then I opened wide the cloak and the gems glittered up at her.

Kate let out a squeal of delight. "They're beautiful! They're . . . they're breathtaking! The men have been speaking of how you faced Beliquose in a cavern. Were these in the cavern, in the walls?"

"Good guess," I acknowledged.

She grabbed fistfuls of them, holding them to herself, and she moaned as if the gems were the greatest aphrodisiac ever created.

And who knew? Perhaps they were indeed. I stood there watching and grinning as she rubbed them against her skin, and her breath was coming in increasingly shorter gasps as if she were building to a climax just feeling them against herself. "Poor, pathetic Beliquose," she said. "I suppose after you sent him into the pit, he had no need of them."

I paused.

I was beginning . . . to feel a warning.

It had happened to me on occasion before. A vague sense of foreboding, and when I had ignored it, the results had always been . . . detrimental. I was feeling it now, with Kate. And I was further starting to realize . . . that I had been feeling it with her for quite some time. I had simply chosen to ignore it. I could have, should have, done it on this occasion, too. There was no reason to doubt her. She was who she'd always been, the Lady Kate, glorious and dedicated and perfect.

And what in this world . . . was ever perfect?

"You know of that?" I asked, sounding quite casual. "Of the pit?"

"Of course!" she said cheerfully. "Everyone knows of that! They're already writing songs about it! I told you, the men spoke of it."

"Of the pit."

"Yes."

"And Beliquose's demise."

"Yes, yes." She was beginning to sound impatient, even suspicious, and gods above, wasn't she the most glorious thing in the world? Too much glory, indeed, for the world to contain?

"And you heard this . . . while lying in the bed?"

"I was not here all this time," she said, and there was confusion in her expression, with an edge to it. "I was out and about . . . and I heard them . . ."

"Composing songs."

"Yes."

"About the battle."

"*Yes!* Apropos," she said with exasperation, "what is the difficulty here? You brought me these lovely gems, and yet seem bent upon not allowing me to enjoy them . . ."

"You heard about the battle."

"*Yes, gods above and below, my love, what—?!*"

"About how I tripped him."

"Yes, with the staff, now can we please . . . ?"

And she realized. A heartbeat after the words were out of her mouth, she realized what she'd said, and then she tried to leap free of the bed, free of me, but I was upon her fast as a jackal, faster than I'd ever been. I drove her back, shoving her head down and into the mattress, and she looked up at me with utter terror. She opened her mouth to scream, and I grabbed a pillow and shoved it over her face.

There was a brisk knock at the door, and I heard Boar Tooth's voice from the other side. "Peacelord," he called politely, "I do not wish to disturb you, but all will shortly be in readiness. Your presence is requested in the courtyard."

Kate was struggling fiercely beneath me, pounding at my hands, trying to shove me away. Small wonder: She couldn't breathe. She tried to bring her legs up to kick me, but I straddled her thighs and immobilized them. "I shall be along shortly," I called.

"Will the Lady Kate be joining you?"

"That is still open to debate," I said. "On your way, Boar Tooth. I shall be along."

I heard his footsteps move away, waited a few moments more, and then yanked the pillow off her face. As I knew would be the case, she wasn't able to let out a scream, because her first instinct was to suck in huge lungsful of air. Natural enough, considering I'd deprived her of the breath of life for nearly a minute. But her next breath would most assuredly be a scream, and though I feared no man under the roof, I was not inclined to answer a lot of questions at that moment.

I hauled the naked woman up with my hand clamped around her throat, cutting off her air again before she could raise her voice to try and summon help. Twisting around on the bed, I slammed her against the wall, and her eyes were wide with stark terror. She did not look especially young and vibrant at that moment; she looked frightened.

"Who are you?" I demanded.

Her voice was a hoarse, petrified whisper. "You're . . . you're mad. . . ."

"If you mean insane, no. Angry, however, I'll readily admit to. Who are you?"

"Kate! I'm Kate!" she practically sobbed in what was very convincing terror. "Apropos, my love, how could you not—?"

I pulled back my hand ever so slightly, then tightened it again and slammed her against the wall once more. Her naked breasts heaved back and forth, and unsurprisingly I wasn't finding it the least arousing. I leaned forward, my face practically in hers, and snarled, "I did not tell anyone that my staff tripped him, because I didn't consider it a heroic enough way to tell the story. No one else knew. This gem . . ." and with my free hand I pulled aside the robe to display the gem wedded to my chest, "is called the Eye of the Beholder. Did you know that? Yes, yes, I think you did," I continued, without bothering to wait for her answer. "And if the gem is the Eye of the Beholder, then it stands to reason that someone is watching through the eye. Someone saw the battle. That someone was you, wasn't it. *Wasn't it!*"

"My love, no, I—"

I drew back and slammed her against the wall a third time, and there was no trace of pity in my voice, no shred of mercy in my heart. "I am a liar, and have always been a liar," I said heatedly, "and if there's one thing I know, it's when someone else is lying to me. One more falsehood out of you, and I swear, Kate, I will kill you. Right here, right now. I will crush your throat like an eggshell. You were able to watch me through an Eye that was once within the province of the gods themselves. You become stronger and more vibrant with each triumph you witness, with each tribute given to you. You will tell me who and what you are, woman, and if you do not, then I swear if you are capable of seeing through this gem, *what you will witness is your own demise, now speak the truth or die,* **who and what are you?**"

And with both hands she lashed out, and suddenly she was gripping my throat with an intensity that made my own pale in comparison. Startled I released my hold on her and tried to pry her hands away. I did not come close to succeeding.

Her eyes seemed to flicker for a moment, and then orbs of emerald green were fixed upon me. Without the slightest effort she raised her arm and hoisted me off the bed. I desperately tried to kick free, but she was holding me at arm's length and I was helpless as a babe in her grasp. There was savagery in her expression that looked like some sort of perversion when adorning that beautiful face. And when she spoke, her words cut like knives.

"You should know," she whispered. "Your little bitch princess, Entipy, prayed to me on enough occasions."

As if hurling aside refuse, she shoved me away. She did not propel me in anything vaguely resembling a human manner. I must have landed a good ten feet away, and as I tried to catch my breath, she crossed the distance between us and gave me a solid kick in the ribs for good measure. Despite my imperviousness, it still hurt like hell, and I clutched at my chest as she presented her back and casually walked away from me. Normally a stark-naked woman strolling about in my presence commands my full attention, but at that moment my mind was very much elsewhere.

And as I lay there, in pain and confusion, it took long moments for the words to filter through my brain, for the full realization to settle upon me, to comprehend who and what I was facing. Meantime she yanked the sheet off the bed and draped it around herself. Slowly I sat up and then froze there, like a statue, hardly able to articulate the name that had emblazoned itself in my mind.

"Hecate?"

Casually she nodded, and damn, but the goddess looked insufferably pleased with herself. "So," she said, "at last we see each other true."

Honestly, I'd had no idea how she was going to respond when I'd threatened her with death. On some level I'd anticipated just more begging and pleading, or perhaps an admission of weaver skills of some sort. I thought she would allow that she was some kind of demon . . . a succubus, perhaps, draining away my very life force and incorporating it as her own. I certainly did not anticipate, however, being tossed about like a boneless baby and . . . and this . . .

. . . this . . .

"Hecate?" I said again.

"My, my, my," she said mockingly. With my fingers off her throat, with the revelation of her identity, she now seemed to have taken the upper hand. Truth to tell, I was too stunned at that point to try and wrest it from her. "Fancy the power the uttering of a single name has. Had I known it would command this degree of respect from you, I would have punted you about sooner." She displayed her perfect teeth in a grim smile.

I shook my head. "It's . . . it's impossible."

"There are those who would say that a warrior whose wounds instantly close up is likewise impossible. One never knows, does one." She stared at me, amusement seeming to bubble over.

I wanted to deny it, to continue to reject the notion out of hand. I clutched my chest and stayed where I was upon the floor, wanting to force myself to disbelieve, certain it was false, knowing it was true.

She nodded serenely. "Yes, Apropos," and she drew herself up. All she was clad in was a sheet, and yet it looked like majestic robes upon her. She did not speak so much as intone her identity. "Hecate. Mistress Ruler of all mankind, all-dreadful one, bursting out of the Earth. Hecate, of the first gods, spat out from the primordial soup of the universe, before any of the others crawled from the muck and mire of creation to claw out their own regions in the hearts and minds of humanity. Hecate, the far-darting one, she who works her will. Hecate, goddess of dark sorcery, and beloved of angry young girls with vengeance in their hearts . . . a description that certainly fit the Princess Entipy, did it not?"

"It did," I whispered hollowly.

"She has called upon me three times in her life . . . and three garners serious attention. The last time she did was several years ago, sitting in the window of her castle with a votive candle burning before her. She spoke of you in her prayers to me . . . spoke of you very prominently, and not very highly. Spoke of you with such fury, such ire . . . that she piqued my interest. Having experienced you now for a time, I admit I can see why she did. You certainly have a knack for provoking emotions, I'll credit you that much. So I decided to look into you . . . so to speak. See just what it was about you that prompted such combination of ire and frustrated love. Imagine my surprise when I liked what I saw."

She rubbed her throat as she walked toward me, and then eased herself onto the bed. She had a rueful smile as she said, "You gave me a bit of a scare there, though. I suppose I should, on some level, be grateful. It has been quite a few centuries since I've had any sort of scare whatsoever . . . and considering the darkness within which I dwell, you would think I, of all who walk the skies, would appreciate a good scare."

I wanted to flee. I wanted to run screaming into the night, to put as much distance between myself and this . . . this . . . whatever she was . . . as quickly as humanly possible. I felt my head swimming. I felt as if it were going to explode. I'd encountered phoenixes, unicorns, weavers . . . perhaps even ghosts, it seemed . . . all manner of beings and creatures in my life. But to find myself staring into the face of a goddess . . . to think that I had been the lover of such a being as that . . . it was overwhelming. It was getting hard to breathe, and I steadied myself, not wanting to give into the weakness of spirit which threatened to render me unconscious simply from having gotten the answer to the question I had so brutally pressed.

It's impossible . . . impossible. . . . My mind was screaming at me, trying to assure me that this was just some sort of grand jest.

"It . . . it . . ." My voice was scarcely above a whisper.

"It what?"

"It . . . makes no sense," I finally managed to get out. "You . . . say you're Hecate. A goddess. But you . . . you don't seem . . . god-like entirely . . . I mean, your strength . . . your strength was extraordinary, but I see . . ." I squinted. "Bruises . . . bruises upon your throat from my hands . . . they're already fading, but still . . . and you say you were scared. . . ."

"'Scared' may have been overstating it. Startled, I suppose, is more accurate." She examined her hands, her arms, as if she'd never seen them before, which of course was an affectation on her part. But I said nothing. I could think of nothing to say . . . a rarity in my life, I readily admit. Kate . . . no, Hecate, as I realized I should now be calling her . . . said, "You may have read myths describing gods walking abroad on earth. Well, they are just that, Apropos. Myths. Treading the world of man is not something we do lightly. Fashioning a body to inhabit is not an easy thing, and we expend great energy to maintain it."

"Great . . . energy . . . ?"

"Your little weaver friend . . . certainly she must have spoken to you of a loss of power? Something that has affected any weaver who draws upon the mystic threads of this world in order to work their magiks?" She shrugged. "That would be because of me."

"You?"

"Tragic, isn't it?" Obviously she was looking for some sort of commiseration. I managed a nod. "Gods and men . . . we're not truly meant to mix. When we walk the skies, our power is boundless, for we draw them from the stars in the heavens. But upon this sphere, we can only draw strength from the earth. Very, very limiting. And you know . . . that's the tragedy of it."

"Tragedy?" I echoed.

She strolled toward me, the sheet swishing about her, and then gathering the sheet around herself she sat next to me on the floor. She reached out to me, and I flinched automatically, but she simply draped her arm around me as if we were two old chums having a chat. "There is a great gulf between gods and men, Apropos, in case you haven't noticed. The fundamental difference in our natures, the risks entailed in our actually coming down to this sphere . . . these have only served to widen the distance. That . . . is why I am here."

"Is it?" I said feebly.

"Because I had to do something."

"You did?"

She sighed. "It's going to get worse."

"It is?"

She nodded. "I've seen it. Right now, Apropos, the world is filled with people who believe in us. Who trust in us. Who have faith that we're there. People who are—"

"Are terrified of you," I said, rallying some of the old insouciance, which was quite an accomplishment considering the churning of my guts within. "Who live in fear of offending you lest you strike them down or inflict some sort of . . . of horrible punishment on them. People who don't know how to live their own lives because they're waiting for you to live it for them."

Hecate shrugged her slim shoulders. "That's as may be," she said casually. "But it's a small price to pay for what we give them in return: a lush, clean world. A world with magic, and creatures of magic. A world of hope." Then she frowned, and when she spoke again it was with a mixture of dread and sadness. "But it's not going to stay that way. I, of all the gods, have foreseen that the most clearly."

"Why . . ." My voice choked a moment as I sought to overcome my trepidation over the notion of addressing a goddess in the copious flesh. "Why . . . won't it stay that way?"

"Do you know what entropy is, Apropos?"

"Entipy?"

She shook her head. "Entropy. No?" I shook my head. "Not surprising . . . the word doesn't exist yet. It is the tendency for systems to fall apart. It is what brings decay, death, and destruction to the world, and eventually sends it all spiraling into chaos."

"Sounds like Entipy to me," I said, trying to make a small joke when I wasn't feeling especially funny.

Hecate ignored it, although she did pat my shoulder in what seemed sympathy for my lame attempt at humor. "It starts with an abandonment of us, Apropos. It starts with humanity losing touch with the beings who were there at the beginning of it all. If the tree severs ties with its roots, then the tree itself will wither and die. Oh, it will begin slowly. First there will be a gradual loss of magic in the world. Unicorns, phoenixes, dragons and drabits, gryphons, manticores . . . all the creatures you've heard of, and creatures you've never heard of, will disappear. Magic lines upon the earth, so beloved by weavers, will become fewer and fewer and eventually disappear entirely. And humanity . . ." She hesitated.

"What?"

"Well . . . in the absence of magic, men will become even more aggressive in fighting in the belief of their gods. Religious wars will be fought, more and more barbaric, and hundreds upon thousands will die as different groups try to prove to the other that their god is the right one, the best one . . . all the time not realizing . . ." She took a deep breath, clearly about to say the hardest thing of all. "Not realizing . . . that the gods will be long gone. That no one is right, that you're all wrong, that there will be nothing out there, simply nothing, and the final death rattles of humanity as you all die in your own poisons of toxic hatred will be heard by nothing. You will live alone, and die alone, and that will be all. That, Apropos, is entropy. That is what you have to look forward to . . . or would have had . . . if not for me."

Slowly, as she spoke, I had gathered my scattered wits about me. I managed to stand up, attaining some minuscule amount of confidence and superiority by being taller than she. "You took them. You took the Eyes of the Beholder from the place of the gods, and you brought them here to earth."

She sighed heavily. "Yes. Brought them to this world, to the state of Isteria . . . but I was still weak, my body not fully up to strength. And at that point a sorcerer who . . ." Then she stopped, paused, and looked up at me. "You don't like to hear long, epic stories about heroics, adventures, and great feats of valor, do you?"

"Not as a rule, no," I said.

"Because I could tell you, but it would take a while."

"Not interested."

"As you wish," she said. "The point is, I had the Eyes, but then I lost them, others got them . . . and here you are, on the verge of greatness."

"On the verge? I thought I was already great."

She made a dismissive noise that I had to admit made me feel somewhat pathetic. "You're a conqueror, Apropos, but there are any number of those. There have been before you, long forgotten now, and there will be others after you when you yourself are a barely remembered footnote in history. But it need not be that way. Because the remaining Eye has chosen you, Apropos, for good or ill. And with my help, the Eye of the Beholder . . ."

"Can be used to reshape the world. Beliquose told me as much . . . and said that someone such as you had rather unpleasant plans."

"Beliquose was a fool," she said in annoyance, and I had to admit that it was an opinion I shared. "He had one of the Eyes in his possession and fought it. Fought the destiny to which it tried to guide him. In doing so, it made him insane. You, Apropos . . . you know better. Admittedly, you've had some help . . ."

"Help . . . ?"

There came a more insistent knocking on the door. "Peacelord," came Slake's voice, "we are all assembled! The men grow restless! The city holds no further pleasures for them, and they are anxious to dispose of Meander and return to Dreadnaught! What shall I tell them?"

"We will be there within moments!" Hecate informed him, and then turned her focus back to me even as she rose from the floor and crossed quickly to her wardrobe. "It's all been building to this, Apropos. It must be attended to. Even entropy tends to work on a sort of cosmic timetable, and once matters are set into motion, they must be resolved within a defined period or everything is put out of whack."

"What . . . do you want of me?" I had not yet started to dress. Noticing that, Hecate picked up my fallen clothing and tossed it at me. I caught it reflexively but still simply stood there.

"The people of this world are blind to what will happen if something is not done to salvage the situation," she said briskly. She pulled on her clothing with swift efficiency, which was consistent considering how expert she had been at removing them. "You have the opportunity to do so. The Eye of the Beholder comes from a realm of perfection, Apropos. For it to function to its full potential in this sphere, it must have perfection once again. It must have perfect darkness. I will be blunt, Apropos . . . you were not my first choice for this responsibility. But for a variety of reasons that I won't go into, because I know you *despise* lengthy discussions of that sort, you have been chosen to be the vehicle of perfect darkness."

"I'm . . . perfect darkness?"

"Not yet," she told me. Fully dressed in a gown of red crushed velvet, she saw that I was still standing there, unmoving. With a faint whistle of annoyance, she came over to me and started pulling my clothes on me. "There is one aspect left unfinished. You should have figured out by now what that is."

Frighteningly enough, I had. "Meander."

"Yes."

"I need to kill him."

"Yes, you do." She fastened the tunic around me. "To be a vessel of perfect darkness, there must be no uncertainty within you. No hesitation. No . . . unfinished business, as it were, that will connect you to the life you once knew. By disposing of Meander, you will have put paid to the last remaining tie to your old life as Apropos of Nothing."

"Would I? What of Entipy? What of her?"

"What of her?" asked Hecate. "Do you have anything left to say to her? To do with her?"

I racked my brains on that one, and realized that the answer to that was no. Everything that could be said, had been said. When I thought of Entipy, there was simply emptiness within me. A distant emptiness, as if I was aware that there should be something there in the cavity left in my soul, but I had no idea what it was and even less interest in filling it.

Hecate seemed to know the response even though I didn't articulate it, because she just nodded in approval. She picked up my sword and said, "Here. Hopefully I need not do everything for you."

I took my sword from her . . .

. . . and suddenly there was a stabbing pain in my chest from the gem.

I gasped, staggered, and barely caught myself on the edge of the bed, narrowly avoiding tumbling to the floor. The burning of the gem had returned, and if possible it was stronger than before. "Wh . . . what . . . ?" I managed to gasp out.

"Beliquose just hit bottom," said Hecate without hesitation, but with obvious regret.

"But . . . it was supposed . . . to be bottomless. . . ."

"It wasn't. Sooner or later, one hits a molten core . . . even in a bottomless pit. The gem still exists . . . nothing can destroy it . . . but the core dispatched its vessel quickly enough. Beliquose is no more . . . and the Eye upon you now demands satisfaction. You must provide it, Apropos. You must give yourself over to it completely . . . and, frankly, that should not be difficult for you. Disposing of Meander is but a small matter, and once that's done, the Eye of the Beholder will be fully empowered. Then you and I can use it to make certain that magic, that the supernatural, that the gods themselves, will never vanish from this sphere. All will be well. You can save the world, Apropos . . . and then have it all for yourself."

"You mean for you," I said tightly, gritting my teeth against the pain.

Again she shrugged. "For us, then."

"And if I don't?"

"Don't what?" She seemed puzzled over the question as she picked up the fallen sword, still in its scabbard, and handed it to me once more.

"Don't kill Meander."

Hecate laughed at that, as if the very notion was utterly absurd. "Why, then . . . the Eye of the Beholder will consume you. It will eat your soul; you will become trapped within it, howling defiance and frustration and surrounded by eternal darkness, while the world is left to spiral into mundanity. Why on earth would you wish for that to happen?"

Slowly I stood, and strapped my sword across my back. But my glare upon her was pure fury. "Because perhaps a world without gods . . . would be preferable . . . to what we've got now."

"Don't be ridiculous. A world of cynicism and lost faith? Of pain and misery and no magic? What sort of world would that be?"

"The kind I live in every day."

"Oh, don't be so melodramatic," she told me. "There's no choice here, Apropos. You saw what Beliquose was prepared to do . . . and did. Are you prepared to sacrifice yourself for some . . . some ephemeral ideal? For that matter, are you prepared to sacrifice yourself in *any* circumstance?" Once again she did not need for me to reply. "No. No, I thought not. Now come. Dispose of Meander, fulfill your destiny, and claim your power . . ." And she spread wide her arms enticingly, ". . . and your prize . . . once and for all."

"Why not both eyes?" I said suddenly.

She looked at me blankly. "What?"

"Why did you not require both eyes to accomplish your task."

"Oh. Well . . . both would certainly have been preferable. Easier. Less strain. But it does not matter. As I told you before, this is the kingdom of the blind . . . and in it, the man who has even one eye," and she tapped my chest, "is still king. Now let us go . . . and attend your coronation."

Chapter 9

Small Sacrifices

*T*here was quite a crowd waiting to see the death of King Meander.

There was no moon that night. Instead there was just the barest hints of it, if one looked very, very carefully. It was a new moon . . . a black moon. A black moon had risen, and I couldn't help but wonder what that might portend. Since there was no natural light being provided us, the courtyard was illuminated by torches set in holders upon the walls.

Hecate—the goddess who walked like a woman—and I stepped into the main courtyard where the execution was to take place. The moment we drew within sight, there was a deafening roar. The place was packed with my men, and they in turn were festooned with clothes, ornaments, and trinkets they had taken from throughout the city.

"*Peacelord! Peacelord! Peacelord!*" they shouted over and over. I raised my hands, trying to quiet them, but Hecate encouraged it.

She even thrived on it. Well, of course. She was a goddess, after all. Who else would most delight in the adulation of worshippers? I, who had worshipped at her altar, so to speak, knew this better than any.

Meander was waiting for me, not voluntarily; he had been removed from the Crow's Cage and instead was standing there, hands bound behind him. He did not seem the least bit concerned over what was to happen. For all I knew, he wasn't even aware of where he was, despite the seeming lucidity he'd displayed during our earlier "chat." Mordant was perched atop the now-empty Crow's Cage, watching the proceedings with obvious interest. Perhaps he was hoping that he would be able to snag a tasty treat once the business was done.

Boar Tooth was standing there at the ready, and Slake was doing his usual technique of getting the crowd even more agitated than they already were. He pumped the air with his fists, he jumped about, and he would shout things such as, *"Is that all the noise you can make?"* Which, of course, it wasn't, as the men were more than happy to prove.

There was no viewing box or place of honor for Hecate and me to go to, since this had once simply been a private mansion belonging to wealthy people, and not a place for nobility to oversee festive gatherings and executions. Besides, Hecate wouldn't have wanted to remain a reserved distance even if she'd had the opportunity. No, she wanted to be as close as possible; I could barely restrain her as she walked forward, almost pulling away from me in her eagerness.

Not that I had any incentive to wait. The gem was as eager as Hecate. It throbbed and pulsed with heat against my chest as a thing alive, as if ever so anxious to get to the business that Hecate had prepared for it.

Reshaping the world.

Reshaping the world.

Well . . .

. . . was that such a terrible thing, really?

Surrounded as I was by cheers, and with the steady burning of power waiting to be unleashed upon my chest, I felt alone as I pondered the question.

Was it so terrible? Really? After all . . . we live in a world that could produce someone like me. How good a world is that, really? And a world without magic, without wonder, a world of cynicism . . . as I said to Hecate, that's my world. Why should I wish to inflict that upon humanity? Doom everyone to such a . . . a lifeless and hopeless way to live?

Do it. Do it. Slay Meander. Take that final step, close that last door while opening another one that you can step through into the great and glorious destiny that you've always deserved. And besides, as she said . . . what choice have you? To sacrifice yourself? For humanity? To hell with that. What has humanity ever done for you?

My mind was made up. One choice, in the end, was no choice.

Slowly I approached Meander. I drew my sword, and the sound of the metal scraping from the sheathe was enough to get another round of cheers and howls. I stood about three feet away from him and pointed the sword imperiously. "Meander!" I called out, loudly enough for my voice to resound throughout the courtyard. "You stand accused of crimes against me . . . against my family . . . and against my men. What say you?"

He simply smiled at me.

"What say you?" I repeated more loudly.

Meander seemed to give the matter a good deal of thought, and then he simply shrugged and said, "It matters not."

"He chooses not to plead for his life because he knows he is guilty!" Hecate called out, once again stoking the crowd.

And then, despite the heat of our surroundings, despite the lack of rain, despite the fact that we were more or less surrounded by desert . . . despite all that, I felt a wintry breeze rolling in.

"Life . . . is not to be pled for," King Meander in that whispery soft voice of his, speaking so quietly that everyone there had to strain to hear, which was no doubt what he desired. "Life is to be lived. And then it is over. And that is all." The way that Meander regarded me, one would have thought that he was the one with the sword in his hand, that my life was at his mercy, rather than the other way round. "I am Meander of the frozen North. I am Meander, the Keepless King who has nevertheless kept his kingdom with him wherever he has gone in his travels. My soul is a frozen and shriveled thing, and its release will only benefit it. And yet, for all that," and he stared at me pityingly, "I would not trade places with you for all the power, all the privilege . . ." and then he looked straight at Hecate, ". . . or all the gods and goddesses fighting for their own, miserable survival in the world."

My blood ran cold, and I looked from Hecate to him and back again. She said nothing, just stood there looking regal and angry and utterly disdainful of the man before her.

"Peacelord, the men are waiting." It was Boar Tooth's voice. He was standing quite near me, speaking softly near my ear, and I realized that long seconds had passed as I stood there, immobile.

And the gem . . . gods, the gem burned. It was almost incandescent, except that none but I could see it or sense it, and the heat flowed through my veins, through my arms and legs and all of my body, building and building as if demanding release that was almost sexual in its cravings and longing.

I turned, looked at Hecate, and whispered, "You wanted Meander. *He* was first choice."

And Meander heard me. None else did, but he did, and he laughed with royal scorn and said, "I knew better. Why didn't you?"

There was confused murmuring from the men who had no clue as to the dynamics of what was occurring, but instead saw only their Peacelord hesitating. And as I noted earlier, there is nothing that is a surer death to leadership than even the hint of uncertainty. *Do what needs to be done, and do it quickly!* The voice in my head urged me on, even egged me on, crying out, *Coward! Fool! Hurry! Your enemy is helpless before you! Do what must be done lest your army realizes that you are but a poltroon, a sham, a shadow of a leader!*

It was no good. I was paralyzed by indecision, and then realized with growing dread that the consequences of that could be catastrophic. The relentless *need* of the gem for release was inexorable, building in wave upon relentless wave battering against the shoals of my resistance, and I had spent year upon year trusting my instincts, except every instinct was telling me to slay the helpless man who stood before me, and Hecate was telling me, and Boar Tooth was telling me, and the fact that every single damned person or entity was telling me to do one thing activated the fundamental perversity of my nature which insisted that I should do anything *but* what they were telling me to do.

And I suddenly realized there was one creature in the place that had never lied to me . . . never betrayed me . . . never led me astray in any manner . . .

My head snapped around.

I looked at Mordant, indecision and fear and uncertainty warring within me.

He stared straight at me and then very slowly, in an almost leisurely manner . . .

. . . he winked at me.

Just as my mother had winked at me.

And suddenly the sword felt so light in my hand, and the power from the gem was completely focused within me as my indecision melted away, my resolve suddenly honed and shaped. The intensity of the gem burning in my chest was almost beyond my ability to bear, and somehow Hecate sensed it, because she fairly cried out, "Hurry! Hurry! *Do it now! You know you must! You're not that damned fool Beliquose! You're not Meander! You're Apropos! You know better than to sacrifice yourself!*"

"You're right," I said, and I whipped the sword around, and it struck home, carving through flesh and bone, blood flying, and stunned cries being ripped from the throats of everyone who was watching.

Hecate gaped in utter bewilderment, staring uncomprehendingly at my blade which had run her through, front to back.

"On the other hand," I said coldly, "I have no trouble with the thought of sacrificing you."

Black liquid began to soak the front of her gown. Confused, horrified, terrified, she beat at the sword with her fists. And she screamed, *"No! No no no no—!!"*

I shoved her back with the sword, the men around me stunned into immobility. "You didn't overstate it at all, did you? You were indeed 'scared.' Scared because it's more than just a matter of you being weaker in this form. You're actually mortal. You can be killed . . . like this. . . ." And I twisted the sword in her chest and ohhhh, then did the howling reach a new level.

Pain exploded behind my eyes, then, blazing agony from the gem, expressing its fury over what was occurring, and with an instinct that was not my own, battling my very body, I placed my foot against Hecate's stomach and thrust as hard as I could. She slid off the sword, clutching at her chest, almost comically trying to shove the blood and guts back in where they came from.

I turned and shouted to the men, who were standing there stunned and appalled, "My soldiers! My servants! This creature, the Lady Kate, is not what she appears to be!"

Boar Tooth stepped forward, no less shocked than any of the others. "She appears to be a woman dying of a sword thrust to the chest!"

I glanced back at her. "All right, yes, that part is indeed more or less what it appears to be. . . ."

And then I cried out, cried out so loudly that my throat ached from the intensity of it, and images slammed through my mind. Images of . . . of . . .

 . . . a future, a great and glorious future, and there was Hecate with her arms draped around me, and me standing upon a reviewing stand and holding my sword on high while thousands of troops marched past me in perfect uniformity, and my power had surpassed anything that I had ever dreamt of, anything that anyone would have thought possible, and my eyes, I could see my eyes, and they were solid black, inhuman, but gods, the power that I was wielding, the majesty,

the invincibility, it was mine, all mine, all it had required was my
soul, and what a small sacrifice that would have been, because really, I
wasn't doing much of anything with the damned thing anyway. . . .

And then, like a mirror struck by a rock, the image shattered,
fell away, and I could almost hear the tinkling of glass as it did so.

I fell to my knees, gasping, the pain in the gem overwhelming,
and Hecate was looking at me with such despair as the ground
grew thick with her blood. Slake was at her side, trying to stanch
the wound, uncomprehending but acting on instinct. He was
looking at me with utter confusion, wanting to believe in his
Peacelord, in his god on earth, not realizing that the true earthbound deity was dying in his arms.

"Apropos . . ." Hecate managed to get out, blood bubbling up
in her throat. "I . . . I loved you. . . ."

Despite the agony that seared every part of my body, I was still
able to grunt, "You didn't love me. You loved . . . a shadow of
yourself."

She rallied, insanely trying to sit up, which made the blood spill
even faster. Slake looked helplessly at her, tried to call for a healer,
but with the dregs of the remarkable strength she still possessed,
she shoved him away. Onto her hands and knees she went, crawling toward me, her voice fading fast with every hoarsely whispered
phrase. "But that's all . . . humans *are* . . . we were going to change
that . . . bring you into your own . . . you could have been a god
on earth . . . instead . . . you've . . . you've condemned the world to
mundanity . . . guaranteed the eventual end of magic . . . you have
no idea what you've done. . . ."

"Nor do I care," I growled, and then once more I screamed as
the pain lanced through me.

And incredibly, the pupils actually faded from Hecate's eyes as
she breathed, "You will . . . *you will.* . . ."

I've heard people die before. In the past, there was always a
gravely death rattle, and then they keeled over.

Not this time. There was nothing soft or gravely or even subtle
in what happened next. Instead Hecate unleashed a screech that

was far more than a panicked reaction; it was a hopeless and frustrated protest against the injustice that had been done her. Her head pitched back, her eyes opened wide, and something . . . some *thing* . . . leaped out of her. Call it an incarnation of her power, call it her godhood, call it her essence or even her soul, call it what you will. To me it looked like a black cloud of hatred and distilled fury, pouring out of her mouth, her nose, her dead eyes, and from the gaping wound I'd left in her.

Then it hurtled toward me, and for a heartbeat I thought it was attacking me. But then I realized . . . sensed . . . that it was not coming at me. No . . . I was drawing it to me. Or rather, the gem was. Literally burning with the desire, the gem reached out with power that I could not even begin to comprehend and yanked Hecate's soul toward it like a spider drawing in a helpless victim.

And victim it most certainly was. I saw the blackness that had been Hecate struggle for an instant, try to pull away, try to tear itself apart rather than submit to the demands of the gem, but it was too late. All the pain that the gem had inflicted upon me up until that moment had been as nothing compared to the excruciating torture that hammered through me as the gem latched on to the essence of Hecate and drew it in.

I felt as if my skin was crisping and burning from within, as if I was being incinerated from the inside out. I had no idea what Slake or Boar Tooth or any of the others were doing at that moment. For all that I was aware of them, they might just as well not have been there at all.

It wants my soul . . . **it wants my soul . . . we want your soul, we deserve it, you took from us, we want it back, WE WE . . .**

The image of the gems sprang to my mind, light bending through them and splintering off in a thousand different directions, and that was how I felt just then. As if the light of my mind, of my spirit, was fractured and hurtling off down infinite paths. I felt the voices within me, each crying out for dominance, empowered by the dark essence that had been Hecate, pulling away from one another so emboldened, so strong by the influx of new and greater power, that they couldn't wait to be quit of one another, even as the still-audible screams of Hecate resounded within my head. And I, Apropos, had a part of me invested in each and every one of them, and knew beyond any doubt at that moment that something horrible was about to happen, and that I was going to be spiritually ripped into a hundred pieces. I would be everywhere and nowhere all at the same time, and I couldn't begin to fully comprehend it, but I knew I sure as hell needed to prevent it.

The men had snapped from their paralysis, and there was confused shouting and questions being hurled all about as I staggered to my feet and looked around desperately for some clue as to what I could possibly do. And then I saw it. It seemed to be calling to me, drawing it to me like an insect, which was perfectly appropriate since it was a flame. The torches on the wall were summoning me, and I lurched toward the nearest one, formulating a desperate plan. My head, my body, felt as if there was some massive force within them that was about to burst out, and I had no desire to be around when they did.

The world was blurring before me, and suddenly one of the biggest blurs was directly in my path. "You bastard!" came Boar Tooth's voice, bellowing at me from the haze that was growing before me. "You cut down a helpless woman!"

He must have been relatively incensed at the deed, considering he must have forgotten I was invulnerable when he attacked. Nevertheless I brought my sword up, still thick with the blood— or whatever it was—of Hecate's that adorned it. The two blades slammed into one another. I deflected his easily and shouted, "You speak to me of killing helpless women?" even as I slammed him aside.

And then I knew I was out of time, my body preparing to burst under the stress of whatever forces were being channeled through it, and the part of me that was still Apropos—whatever that was— cried out, *Get it out of us! Get it out get it out get it out . . . !*

I grabbed the torch from its place, felt the heat pouring off it, and something dark and sinister within me cringed back, howled a warning mixed with defiance, tried to stop me from doing what desperation had driven me to do. Uttering a quick prayer for strength without the slightest idea of to whom I might be addressing it, I reversed the torch, braced myself, promised myself I would not scream, and then broke that promise in spades as I jammed the torch against my chest.

There were outcries from everyone around me, who must have been utterly convinced by that point that their beloved Peacelord, their god upon earth, had gone completely out of his mind. Their opinions were of no consequence to me at that point. All that mattered to me was the excruciating agony of the flame against my chest. There is no more horrific smell than the aroma of burning meat when you know that what you're smelling is you.

And yet I kept it there. I was becoming effectively blind, all the world now one great fog, bodies moving this way and that with no pattern or logic. A haze of red had descended upon me, and still I kept the flame where it was, ruthlessly blackening and blistering the skin all around the Eye of the Beholder. *"Bastard!"* I heard again, which told me that Boar Tooth was coming up behind me, and I collapsed just in time to hear the hiss of his sword as it passed in a brutal arc above my head. Crumbling to the ground wasn't much of a challenge; it was miraculous that I had managed to stand for as long as I had.

The others started screaming at me as well. All those men who had cried such huzzahs in my name were now shouting out that same name in rage. How could I have done such a thing, they demanded. How could I simply have cut down my beloved consort right there, like . . . like a barbarian . . .

Hypocrites . . . stupid, hypocritical sacks of shit . . . That refrain kept going through my mind. The pack of bastards, voicing dismay at my actions, when their casual brutalities had been far more numerous, and for far less reason. Kate . . . Hecate . . . she hadn't even been human. She'd been a . . . a thing . . . masquerading as a female. But these men who condemned me now with such vituperation had assaulted men, women, and children with equal abandon and utter joy, and with no regard for rightness or morality or anything except filling their own purses and indulging their own lusts. And all in my name, in the name that they now cursed.

I saw them for what they were more clearly than ever I had seen before, and that awareness fanned the flames of my own hatred, for them . . . and for myself in indulging their activities and . . .

Flames . . .

. . . flames, the opposite of ignorance. Within flames lay knowledge, and purity, and cleansing. Shadows flee from flames, darkness runs scurrying under rocks and into crannies as the light generated by fire comes for it. All these things that I had been told, or variations of them, flooded through me, and even though I was biting upon my lip so hard that I nearly bit it in two, still I kept the flame pressed against the Eye of the Beholder.

And it was gone.

Just like that, the Eye of the Beholder fell from my chest, the tentacles of skin that had entwined themselves around it sundered by the flame. The Eye clattered to the ground . . .

. . . and shattered.

Shattered.

I stared at it, even though I could barely see straight. It was impossible. I'd been told by everyone concerned that the damned thing could not be destroyed, and yet a simple fall had caused it to splinter into a hundred fragments. I had been lied to. But then, what else was new in my life?

Well, the damage my chest had sustained was certainly new. I was a mess. There was a gaping hole where the fire had burned through my tunic, and the material itself was now on fire. Frantically I tore the tunic from me, ripping it apart and throwing the fiery tatters to the ground. My vision started to clear, and I looked down in dismay at the charred hole in my chest that the gem had once occupied. The hole did not go entirely through my chest, fortunately. It was more like a deep, blackened crater. It still hurt like hell, though.

And other things began to come clear as well. The veil upon my mind, that which had seemed to separate one part of my brain from another, was lifted. Suddenly the man that I was, and the man that I had become, were reconciled, and I fully comprehended for the first time in months what had truly happened to me. And the knowledge shook me to the core.

And that was when Boar Tooth, about whom I had completely forgotten, howled in fury and swung his sword at me.

I backstepped . . . and the only thing that saved me was my complete and utter collapse. My right leg totally gave way beneath the sudden shift, and I was on the ground, looking up in utter bewilderment.

Boar Tooth advanced on me, swinging his sword back and around, and at that moment I knew beyond question that my invulnerability was gone. And that instant, with death only a heartbeat away, I heard a high-pitched, angry shriek, and suddenly Mordant was upon Boar Tooth's face, clawing and screeching. Boar Tooth no doubt screamed, but the outcry was muffled by the drabit's body.

My sword lay barely a foot away. I threw myself forward, grabbed it up, and swung it with all my strength. It was a cheap and rather pathetic blow, but it was nevertheless an effective one, for I struck him in the tendon just behind the right ankle and severed it. Boar Tooth was busy struggling with the drabit and didn't realize until too late what had happened, and then he too was upon the ground, writhing in pain. Mordant had vaulted off him just before he'd fallen, and then I was upon Boar Tooth in a flash. Crippled I once again might have been, but the strength in my arms was still undiminished, and I slammed Boar Tooth's head up and down repeatedly against the ground, bellowing, *"You speak to me of killing helpless women!? This is for her! This is for that woman whose only crime was mourning her husband! Did you think I'd forgotten that? Monster! Brute!"*

The reality of the world around me spun away, and then strong hands were lifting me off the battered and confused Boar Tooth. I struggled the best I could in the grip of those who had once been my loyal men, but it was a struggle just not to pass out from the pain that was screaming within me.

And then terrified cries of *"Look!"* and *"Impossible!"* and *"Gods save us!"* erupted from throats all around me, and I looked at what was prompting them to cry out. With my newfound knowledge, with my awareness of just what had transpired during the time that the Eye of the Beholder had kept me in its grip, I somehow knew what to expect. And even so, when I witnessed it, it was still heartstopping.

From each of the fractured shards of the Eye, a single shadowy being was emerging. Each was of darkest ebony, with a twisted smile upon its face and a shimmering sword in its hand. Within moments a hundred of them were there, standing in the courtyard, looking around with that very familiar sneer.

Familiar . . . because it was mine.

Chapter 10

Shadow Dance

*I*t wasn't me.

That was the realization I had come to, the understanding that had flooded into me. It was not, and never had been, me.

All right . . . that was not entirely true. It was me in the sense that my darkness, my frustration and anger, my fundamental loathing for the world helped to propel the events and the things that had occurred. That part was me.

The rest had been the Eye of the Beholder . . .

. . . and the Rockmunchers.

The fury that had driven me, the thirst for vengeance and conquest, had been at the behest of trolls who had been unfairly and prematurely deprived of their lives by invaders. They had been a vanquished race as their conquerors had stormed through the caverns known as Ba'da'boom in a quest to deprive them of their fortunes and their lives. The quest had been successful, and the Rockmunchers had died beneath the fearsome weapons of the invaders. They had not, however, gone quietly.

In point of fact . . . they had not gone at all.

Sharee had been right. Their fearsome shades had continued to reside in Ba'da'boom, gaining strength from their eternal darkness and even more eternal resentment against the beings from above who had stormed them and annihilated them. And when I had passed through their caverns, when I had been assaulted by them . . . they had sensed in me a kindred spirit. One who harbored as much anger and resentment toward humanity as they themselves had.

And more . . . apparently, they sensed the power of the gem that I had upon me, even though we were not yet bonded. They sensed what the gem was seeking, and were more than happy to provide it. So they . . . they inhabited me. Set up shop within me. I, who had been an innkeeper, had become a living inn. More . . . I had become, just as foreseen, a shadow of myself.

There, in the desert, when I was on the verge of death, my life force at its weakest, my soul exhausted and ready to provide no resistance . . . that was when the vengeful essence of the Rockmunchers took full control of me. That was when the Eye of the Beholder knew that it had found its ideal mate and merged itself into my body, so as to take possession of the soul as well.

But the shades of the Rockmunchers required the darkness to survive, for they had spent centuries in that environment, both living and dead, and daylight was anathema to them. Thus did Apropos the Peacelord become known, at first, as the creature who came in the night. Stalking innocent and helpless victims, acquiring followers and then a following. Perhaps the preference for the night added to the mysteriousness that was the Peacelord. Whatever the reason, the night raids of Apropos of Wuin began to become legendary, and that was when the ranks of the followers began to swell. The more powerful and popular "I" became, the more formidable a force I was able to amass. Soon daylight raids were no longer a burden . . . except that the Rockmunchers in possession of my mind and body preferred to remain inside at such times. They feared the light of truth, the flame of knowledge. All they knew was instinct which told them to hide themselves while scheming and planning new assaults and terrors.

But finally, by purest happenstance, their instincts betrayed them. During the battle of Jaifa, as bizarre fortune would have it, the sun was blotted out by shadow. Day turned into night, and in his tent Apropos the Peacelord awoke from his daytime slumber and leaped to the erroneous conclusion that night had fallen. This obscuring of the sun and premature evening fall was caused by that rare phenomena generally referred to as an "occultation". . . or, as some call it, an "eclipse." Rockmunchers, even dead ones in possession of my body, knew nothing of such things. All they knew was day and night, and when night came upon them, they erroneously leaped to the conclusion that it was time to indulge in some mayhem.

And so they had, leaping out of the tent and into battle. A most zealous display did they put on, employing my body as they had before to hack and slash and attack all comers. But then they were startled by something most unexpected: The return of the sun. Faced with the advent of their most reviled enemy, the Rockmuncher's control of my heart and mind was shattered, and they slipped far, far back into the recesses of my mind as my own awareness finally took hold of myself after a lengthy "sleep."

Thus it was that I came to my senses standing over a slain foe and wondering how in the world I had arrived at this pass.

With my own personality, albeit befuddled, nevertheless back in control, the Rockmunchers could do nothing. Nothing except wait with the infinite patience that only the deceased can display. Wait for the last, few bright areas in my own soul to be totally devoured by the Eye of the Beholder so that they could reassert themselves and establish dominance over my mind and body once and for all. They had temporarily regained control during my berserker rage in fighting Meander's men. And now they had been anticipating becoming fully in charge and, with my own soul joining theirs permanently in hatred, never fearing light again.

I had thwarted that plan.

They weren't taking it well.

For a moment that might have been carved from the great gla-
cier of passing time, all stood frozen. No one knew what to make
of this new development. And really . . . how to explain it? How to
say that the mystic, caliginous spirit of the witch goddess Hecate
had been, in its dying throes, drawn into a gem of such incredible
power that it was called the Eye of the Beholder—the "Beholders"
being gods—and that the incredible potency of that soul had provided a final catalyst that enabled the long imprisoned, vengeful
shades of dead Rock trolls to utilize the Eye and manifest themselves in my shape.

"Run," whispered Slake to the assemblage, and really, that more
or less seemed to be all that was needed.

A storm of terror ripped through the men, and they had no
interest whatsoever in trying to trade blows with creatures who had
sprung fully formed from shattered shards of a gem. They knew
sorcery or matters of an eldritch nature when they saw it, and
none of them wanted any part of it. The shades of the Rockmunchers in the shape of Apropos, however, wanted a part of the
assembled soldiers. They saw, in the beings who surrounded them,
incarnations of the merciless monsters who had deprived them of
their futures. That my soldiers had had nothing to do with the
deaths of the Rockmunchers didn't really enter into it. They
wanted vengeance, my men were at hand, the power of Hecate had
emboldened them, and all the cries of "Run!" weren't going to do
one bit of good.

I had been wondering, even as I stood there paralyzed with fear,
whether they were capable of articulating any sort of noise. The
answer to that was a most resounding "Yea," as with one voice the
assembled shades of the Rockmunchers of Ba'da'boom cried out
their chants of longing and damnation, and then they ran in all
directions and began their attack.

My men tried to run. It did them very little good. The alternate "me's" were upon them in a flash, and my men would punch and claw at them to no affect at all. But my ghostly incarnations would then bring their own shadow blades down upon their victims, and each cut was deep and true and lethal.

It was also obvious to me that the . . . creatures . . . shared whatever anger happened to be upon me at that moment. Whilst the others scattered, wreaking havoc wherever they could, four of them concentrated on Boar Tooth. Apparently the resentment I'd carried toward Boar Tooth ever since I encountered his first act of brutality had been present within me but rather repressed. Well, there was no repression anymore. The four of "me" who had singled out Boar Tooth each grabbed an arm and a leg of his respectively, and he realized what was about to happen and alternately screamed curses and begged for his miserable life. Each was equally effective, which is to say, not at all. With only the slightest hesitation—more, I think, to hear what he had to say so they could laugh at it, rather than out of genuine interest in complying—the Shades-Who-Walked-Like-Me yanked in four different directions. They could not have gotten a more immediate, or gore-filled result from their efforts.

It was utter chaos, which of course was exactly what they wanted. It was amazing how quickly things could change; one moment I was the center of attention, and the next I was completely forgotten as the troops endeavored to fight back. They outnumbered my dark duplicates, but it didn't seem to matter. Remember, after all, how many soldiers I had been able to take down when it had been just me in berserker mode. Well, that was as nothing compared to these shades as they descended upon my men, hacking and slashing and drinking deep from the cup of revenge. They were fueled by their own resentment over the genocide of their race, my own fundamental hatred for humanity as a whole, and the fearsome power that had been Hecate. It was a potent combination . . . and one that I had no desire to be anywhere near.

I had a brief glimpse, in the midst of it all, of Meander.

Somehow he had managed to get his hands free, even though they'd been tied behind him. I suspected that he'd always had enough sheer strength to break his bonds. He had simply gone along with all of this in his odd, detached manner, possibly to see how it all turned out. He certainly seemed to be enjoying it now, for he had gotten a sword in his hands, and he was slicing this way and that at the various shades. Physically, he was having no effect on them. Yet I found it morbidly curious that, despite the lack of impact he was having, the shades were loathe to try and finish him. Several gathered near him, feinted, but did not yet press the attack. I had no idea why.

Nor did I choose to dwell on it, for at that moment my only concern was getting out of there. I had no reason to assume that the shades would spare me their wrath. Indeed, I'd probably be a prime target. For as enraged as I had been with the men who had sworn loyalty to me, I was just as infuriated with myself for having empowered them to indulge in such horrid activities. And that self-loathing would certainly translate into serious trouble at the hands—or blades, or whatever—of the creatures who bore my shape.

The important thing was not to run out of there in a panic. That's what virtually everyone else was trying to do, and it wasn't going well for them. The courtyard was already slick with blood, and my shades were having a grand old time in the midst of the slaughter.

I had already slid my sword back into my scabbard, and now with my staff firmly in hand, my back against the wall, I started to make my way out of the courtyard. I knew I had to get to the stables, grab a horse, and bolt out of there. I only wished that the marvelous Entipy had still been alive, since I had not yet found a horse that was her equal. But I was hardly in a position to be choosy; presuming I made it to the stables, I'd take whatever I could get.

Slake was trying to rally the troops, waving his sword over his head and screaming defiance. But his screams were laced with fear, and that drew the shades to him like a great beacon of darkness.

I was almost out the far gate when suddenly I skidded to a halt. One of my shades was blocking my way. It stared straight at me, and its eyes were burning with a black flame that generated no heat, but only cold. I felt my knees buckling under me, fear overwhelming me. It grinned from ear to nonexistent ear and advanced upon me.

"No . . . please, no . . ." My voice trembled, and I would have backed up if I could have commanded my body to do something other than quake. At that moment there was a warning screech, and the shade looked up just in time to see Mordant swooping down toward it.

The shade fell back, swinging its sword in anger and confusion at the rapidly darting beast, and not coming close to touching it. I realized that the drabit was serving as a distraction, and I did not hesitate to take full advantage of it. I quickly made my way out the gate as the shade, apparently having totally forgotten me, kept trying to pick the swift-moving beast out of the air and failing utterly.

I heard the cries and shrieks of pain and death behind me as I hobbled to the stable as quickly as my lame leg would permit me. I thought about how many times I had heard those sounds in other cities, other towns, and how it had never seemed to matter. After all, those were just the fortunes of war, correct? Oddly enough, hearing the death throes of my army, the agonies of men who had—until recently—sworn utter fealty to my name . . . it mattered even less than any of the cries I'd heard from our victims.

The horses were mad with fear in the stables, bucking about, knowing that death was hurtling about on raven-black wings, and unable to get away from it. Had they not each been tied to posts, they would easily have smashed down the walls in their crazed endeavors to get away. I picked one that I recognized from my expedition in pursuit of Beliquose. Moving as quickly as I could, considering my hands were trembling, I fastened the bridle on while the horse tried to buck away from me. I held it fast as I yanked the reins back around it, and didn't take the time to attach a saddle. I clambered onto the horse's back, and it certainly wasn't one of my more graceful moves, but I managed to get myself up there just the same. Once again for convenience' sake, I twisted my walking staff apart, shoved the two halves into my belt, and then yanked out my sword. I cut the horse's ties to the hitching post, and the great creature wasted no time at all in darting out of the stable, as anxious to leave this evil place behind as I was. The other horses whinnied and neighed in supplication, and I must tell you that I have always preferred horses to people, and been far more concerned about the fate of the former than the latter.

I drew the reins tight, snapped the horse around. With quick, efficient movements I sliced through the tethers that were keeping the horses in place. At first my horse resisted, anxious only to leave this place of uncanny death behind, but I think the beast realized what I was doing after I'd freed the first couple of its fellows. From that point on it stopped fighting me, and then it was only a matter of a minute to liberate the lot of them.

I could do nothing further for them; there was no time. It sounded to me as if the noises of battle and blood and death were drawing closer. I slammed my knees into the horse's side, cried out, *"Yaaahhh!!"* and urged the horse forward. Frankly, it needed no urging. The horse fairly leaped forward, and it was all I could do to hold on as it galloped out onto one of the main roads and headed for the front gates.

I was in the way.

That is to say, the shades of me. Several of them, blocking the path. I muttered an oath as the horse reared up, whinnying in terror, and the shades converged upon me. The horse needed no guidance from me. It darted to the right, and the shades moved to intercept, but the beast was too quick. It went as far to the right as possible, and my right leg slammed into the front of a small building. Fortunately there wasn't a great deal of damage to do to that particular limb, and then we were past our pursuers, pounding past the jagged wall and through the lower part of the city.

I heard angry howling behind us, and risked a glance. I saw

them, the shades, an assortment of them upon the low wall that divided the two sections of the city. They were pointing at me, and laughing and howling and screaming all with one voice. It was a formidable, and most terrifying, combination.

And then we were out the front gate, which had been left wide open. The horse's hooves moved with phenomenal speed as we thundered down the main highway, bound and determined to put as much distance between ourselves and the fallen Golden City as we possibly could.

The darkness was a formidable opponent as I rode, and I forced the horse to slow up lest we trip over something along the way. Since we had put some distance between ourselves and the slaughter, though, the horse seemed to be a bit calmer about the entire situation. I wondered where Mordant was, and how Meander had fared against his otherworldly opponents. I wondered if Meander even knew they were otherworldly, or if he had just been pleased to have the opportunity to go down fighting.

I had absolutely no idea where to go to. Returning to Dreadnaught seemed out of the question. The ruler of that place had been the bloodthirsty, invincible Apropos . . . not the lame of leg, doubt-ridden creature into which I had reverted. The path of my future was as impenetrable to me as the road I was traveling. I had only recently come to a full understanding of where I had been, and hadn't the slightest clue of where I was going to go.

Suddenly the horse started making noises of concern, and began to buck against the casual pace I had set. I wondered just what might be bothering the animal . . . and then I felt it before I actually saw it. The road beneath us was starting to vibrate, as if something huge was in pursuit of us.

I wheeled my mount around and tried to get a visual feel for what it was that was after us. "What in—?" I gasped, and then my breath caught in my throat as I saw, dimly, what was coming.

It was the shades. All of them, near as I could tell, and they appeared to be on horseback. But it was not horses of our world; instead they were great, black shadow beasts, as unnatural as the riders themselves and just as effective in terms of pursuit.

My horse let out a panicked cry. I did as well. I guided the horse in a turn, but that was certainly no effort because my ride was more than anxious to get the hell out of there. Despite the difficulty in seeing, I did not hold us back at all as the horse barreled down the road, giving it everything it had.

Panic surged through my veins as I desperately held on. *It's not fair, it's not fair, it's enough already* kept going through my mind as I did everything I could to distance us from our pursuers. It seemed, though, that everything wasn't going to be nearly enough. I had no idea how long I rode. All I knew was two things: that I was trying to get away from them, and that I was failing utterly. They were drawing closer and closer to us, and the same panicked thoughts speared through my mind: *I'm going to die, after all this, I'm going to die, please, no, gods, no* . . .

Praying. Praying to gods who had ill considerations toward us. Praying to avoid death that had come to so many save me . . . and I, who had killed so many and would have seemed therefore a logical target for retribution.

And running, running . . . always running. Because of the gap in my memory, my fleeing at Sharee's side from Lord Beliquose—across the Finger and into the Tragic Waste—seemed extremely recent, rather than months ago.

Foam was flecking my beast's mouth. The poor thing was terrified beyond imagining, its great heart thudding against its chest with such ferocity I thought it would explode. Its legs scissored beneath it, chewing up dirt, and suddenly, incredibly, the shades were coming from the other direction. I had no idea how they managed to get around, although I should not have been surprised. After all, we were talking about manifestations of other-worldly creatures. Certainly they were not bound by trivialities such as the laws of nature.

My horse veered off the main road, and we kept going, riding as hard and fast as I could. It seemed as if I had been pursued forever, that this was some sort of eternal punishment inflicted upon me for my many crimes. Behind me the shades were laughing, howling their contempt and scorn and loathing for me . . . which was, ultimately, loathing for myself.

And my horse went down.

I never knew for sure what it was that had caused it to take a spill. Whether there had been some sort of hole in the ground, or it had tripped over its own feet, or what. All I knew was that one moment we were riding along, and the next the horse was tumbling forward. And unlike when I'd been astride Entipy and that great beast had been cut down, this time I was not invulnerable to harm. If the horse landed atop me, I'd be crushed. *Not that it's going to matter; what difference does it make whether or not you're intact when the shadow creatures tear you to shreds?*

When I hit the ground, the natural momentum from the fall kept me rolling, and all I had to do was go along with it to be carried out of immediate danger. My horse stumbled about for a moment . . .

. . . and then righted itself. It shook its head violently as if clearing its mind, and then it took one look at me . . . and bolted.

"Get back here!" I shouted, but it did no good. It wasn't as if the animal had any particular loyalty to me. Desperately I added, *"I freed your friends! Doesn't that count for something?!"*

Apparently it did not, for without the slightest hesitation the horse turned and ran, leaving me alone in the desert. Well . . . as alone as someone who had about a hundred or so ghosts bearing down on him could possibly be.

Chapter 11

Fearsome Things

I was dead. That was all there was to it. I was dead.

They couldn't have been more than a mile or two behind me. The ground was continuing to shake as they drew closer, ever closer across the vast plains, and I . . .

I looked around.

I was standing there on a wide, empty plain, as flat and uninviting and unappealing as any I'd been on. I was not in the Tragic Waste, I was reasonably sure of that. But it was as flat as that distasteful place, and although there was no moon, there was enough starlight for me to get a feel for what the area was like. So wide open, so . . . so replete with nothingness was this nameless desert. Well, it probably had a name, but I had gotten myself very well and truly lost, and therefore didn't know what it might be.

The thing was, my awareness of how much time has passed was so battered, that it seemed like only yesterday that I had been utterly paralyzed by the desert. I had looked around me and been frozen by the wide-open surroundings. I had literally been scared . . . of nothing.

Now I found myself looking at my environs and feeling as if I was truly seeing them for the first time. There was . . . there was a beauty to it. A sort of natural wonder that I had not remotely appreciated when I had first seen it. Instead I had shrunk away in terror, allowed myself to be overwhelmed by it. It seemed patently absurd that I had done so. It might well have been that it was no longer having the same impact upon me simply because of everything that I had seen and been exposed to since then. Ultimately, it didn't matter. All it did manage to do was put my fears into their proper perspective.

How many things had I been afraid of in my life . . . really? How many things had held me in coils of mortal terror, and had driven me in directions that I might not necessarily have gone if left to my own devices?

How much had I let it rule me?

I mean, here I had spent such an inordinate amount of time allowing concerns over destiny and the intents of the gods to motivate me, without realizing that so much of what I had done had stemmed from sheer, stinking fear. Then again, it might be argued that fear was how the gods kept us in line. That fear was the direct opposition to free will. All things have two sides, after all. So on the one hand we had free will to allow us to do as we wished . . . and fear of the consequences serving to immobilize us.

It seemed a rather dreary way to live, really.

And yet that was how I had lived it. Fear, and anger, and resentment.

Was it worth it?

I didn't know.

I, who had never doubted the efficacy of the resentment I bore for the world, had no idea whether I had made a single worthwhile decision in my life. Not if it all stemmed from fear, certainly. Fear of . . . of nothing. Just like the desert. Nothing.   °

I hadn't moved from the spot when the shades arrived. I was just sitting there, staring out at the nothingness while holding my walking staff. The shades looked most puzzled at my lack of reaction. It was understandable that they would be bemused. They, after all, were me. They knew my weaknesses, knew my fears. Knew that I would unquestionably be as terrified of them as anyone else had been; perhaps even more so. Knew that at this point I should be begging for my life, or trying to fight a final, desperate battle while sobbing the entire time because I knew it was hopeless.

Meander . . . he hadn't been afraid. Of all the people in that courtyard, he had been the only one utterly unfazed by the situation in which he'd found himself . . . and the shades, why, they hadn't known what to do with him.

They began to surround me, riding their great ghost horses, but when some of them started to move around front of me, I said sharply, "Stop right there. You're blocking the view."

They stopped where they were. They looked at each other, their bewilderment increasing. Clearly they were waiting for one of their number to make the first move. But since they were all of a kind, nobody was the natural leader.

I stared at them disdainfully. "You don't even know where you are, do you. Look around. Look around and see the nothingness that surrounds you."

The shades resolutely stared at one another, no one wanting to lift their eyes from me. They had been so focused upon the chase that they had paid no attention at all to where it had brought them.

"Look!" I shouted with such command in my voice that they could not help but comply.

They stared around at the nothingness of the desert, the empty openness, and the horses bucked slightly under them. Clearly the beasts were influenced by the concerns of their masters.

On every level, what they were seeing was daunting to them. To the Rockmunchers, it was an endless vista of above-ground, which was certainly terrifying to beings who had lived their lives in even more closed an environment than I ever had. To the pathetic wretch known as Apropos, whose bitter dreams and frustrations comprised a part of their essence, the sheer vastness of what was before them still had enough terror packed into it to take him aback. And to the dark cloud of pure power that was Hecate, well . . . the pure force of her essence might have been energizing them, but I didn't think her perceptions had all that much to do with them.

And when I saw the fear reflected in their faces, all I could think about was how I must have appeared. I was filled with utter humiliation over how I must have seemed to Sharee, and how I had allowed myself to be so shaken. Long had I known the sting of self-loathing, but never had I felt such abiding contempt for my limitations. It was as if I was truly seeing myself for the first time, and I have to say, I was not impressed by the spectacle.

Abruptly I pointed to the east. "And over there!" I called out to them. "In that direction! The sun will be up before too long!" The horses reacted even more strongly to that, and now I rose and strode toward them. The horses stumbled back, and the shades held on tightly, looking as if they were worried they'd be thrown off.

"Yes, that's right! The sun! You don't like the sun, do you, you bastards! You don't like the pure light that shines upon you and reveals you for the shallow, wretched things you are! Can you feel it? Look!" and I indicated the horizon. "Look, the rays will be creeping across the distant plain just about any time! But you don't like the plains any more than the sun! Because you detest openness since you yourself are so secretive and petty and closed! You detest light because it shines upon the darkest reaches of your con- temptible schemes! You detest heat because you are so cold and heartless! Am I supposed to be afraid of you? Is that it?!" I limped forward determinedly and slapped at the nearest horse. It bobbed away from me. *"Look at you! You're useless and pathetic! You induce fear in others because you're hoping their screams will drown out the*

howls of fear in your own miserable little souls! Well, you don't fool me!
You can't fool me! I'm the one creature who walks this earth who
knows you for what you are, you worms! You nothings! Come! Let us
face the sun together! Let us have the heat and light wash over us, let
the vast plains upon which we stand be fully illuminated! You want to
prove to me that you have the slightest worth? Stand here and do what
every creature, from the greatest to the smallest, of this world does
every single day! Greet the sun! **Greet it, I say!**"

The shades screamed in a voice that was startlingly, depressingly
familiar, and backed farther off, totally disconcerted. I yanked out
my sword and shouted, "***Come on, pitiful bullying fools! Let's see***
what you're made of!"

And as if they were one great black wave, they swung their
steeds about and galloped off. I stood there and watched them go
as they turned tail and ran, ran back in the direction of the Golden
City. Watched them until they were no more than specks in the
distance.

Then I sank to the ground, and started to laugh, and then the
laughter mixed with tears until I felt utterly spent.

The sun did not come up immediately, which didn't surprise
me. I knew that I had been riding a while, but I didn't think it was
all night. It didn't matter, though. The shades had no idea when
the sun would rise, but they were so terrified of the notion that
they had opted to make themselves scarce before the great burning
orb made its daily appearance. I just sat there, facing the east, and
waiting. I realized that east was the direction of the Golden City,
and for no particular reason I found that vaguely amusing.

I remained where I was, and after a time I saw the first begin-
nings of the sunrise creeping up over the horizon. I also became
aware that someone was coming up behind me. I was alerted by
the steady *clip-clop* of horse's hooves, but it was a different tread
than any of the beasts ridden by the shades. This had weight and
substance to it. This was real.

I glanced behind myself and saw a rider approaching upon a
pale horse. The rider sported a dark cloak draped around it, and its

hood was pulled up. It drew closer and closer, and I tilted my head slightly, watching it get near. "Hello?" I said finally.

The rider brought the horse to a halt several feet away, and then swung one leg off and dismounted expertly. Oddly enough, I knew who it was the moment she got off the horse.

"Oh. It's you," I commented.

The hood fell back to reveal the face and piercing eyes of Sharee. She stared at me, and I studied her critically.

"Are you quite all right?" I asked. "You look a bit glassy-eyed."

"No. No, I'm not all right," she said. "You've no clue what I've been through. None at all. Ohhhh," and her voice broke in a slight cackle, "you're going to find out. Oh, yes . . . you're going to find out."

"Am I?" I asked mildly.

She nodded and, reaching into the folds of her cloak, she withdrew a dagger. It was, I have to say, a formidable-looking weapon. The hilt was a rather unique carving of a skeleton warrior, molded from what appeared to be genuine bone (although whether it was human bone, I could not have said). The blade was long, tapering, and curved, and there appeared to be runic lettering along the edge. "Do you know what this is?" she demanded, and I noticed that her voice sounded rather raspy.

I hazarded a guess. "A knife?"

"Not just any knife," she said with a sort of demented pride. "This . . . this is the dagger of Vishina. It is the only weapon in existence which can kill that which is unkillable." She turned it around, allowing the blade to glint in the early morning light. The sun had not yet fully risen, though. "Ohhhh, I admit," she continued, "you fooled me at first. When I speared you, and you yet lived. I couldn't believe it. And then, to display your contempt for me, you released me . . ."

"That wasn't to show contempt," I started to say.

"*Quiet!*" she bellowed, and I fell contritely silent. There was delirious joy in her eyes now. "But then . . . then I learned of the dagger of Vishina. And I knew that it could be mine . . . if I was willing to embark upon a dangerous and treacherous quest. Oh," she said sarcastically, "but I don't suppose you'd want to hear about it."

I gave it some thought.

"Yes," I said finally. "Yes, I would."

She blinked in surprise. "Wh-what?"

"I'd like you to tell me about it."

She licked her dry lips, steadied herself. Truthfully, she looked as if she was going to fall over. "I get it. This is a trick. A stunt to try and forestall your doom."

"No." I thought I was sounding perfectly reasonable. "I'm genuinely interested. I mean, if you really went to all that trouble just to try and kill me, I think the very least I can do is attend to how you went about it."

"But . . ." She stammered. "But . . . you never want to hear about such tales!"

"They're never about me. This one is."

Sharee swayed slightly where she was standing, and then slowly walked toward me. She dropped down to the ground next to me, still clutching the knife tightly and watching me with care, obviously wanting to make certain that I wasn't going to try and snatch the weapon from her.

This, of course, I had no intention of doing. It was far too nice a day to engage in such shenanigans.

And she proceeded to lay out in detail everything that had happened to her in her lengthy, and considerably perilous, quest to find the dagger she was holding. Every so often I interjected a question, and she answered it with reasonable patience. Indeed, she seemed pleased, since my questions were evidence that I was genuinely paying attention. She only interrupted her narrative at one point, at my request, when the sun truly began to encroach upon the horizon. We sat there in silence, watching it go up, up, its rays stealing across the plains and caressing them like a tentative lover. The ground was parched and cracked, and I said idly, "You know . . . your puissance should be returning to you about now.

You may want to think about utilizing your weaving skills to bring some rain to this territory. They could certainly use it."

Slowly she nodded. "I was noticing the regeneration of the threads."

I envied her that: The weaver's skill to see dangling in the air the threads of power that were part and parcel of nature. If I were to believe what Hecate said . . . and I had no reason to assume she was wrong . . . they would not always be there. Slowly, over time—decades, centuries, whatever—those threads would dissipate. The ability to manipulate the forces of nature, and all other weaver skills, would fade away, become obsolete. Those who practiced magiks would be reduced to offering up hopeful prayers to an assortment of uncaring gods, including one whom I very well might have dispatched to her final reward . . . whatever such a thing might be for a god.

I thought of telling Sharee all this . . . and found, a bit to my surprise, that I couldn't. Once upon a time I would have taken cruel joy in informing her that her trade was destined to be obsolete, and that her or her children or her children's children would one day be unable to summon so much as a stray zephyr, much less a lightning bolt to hurl at someone who had irked them. But now . . . now I couldn't find it within myself to do so. Perhaps I felt a bit sorry for her . . . or perhaps, more likely, there was just the smug notion of my knowing more about her destiny than she did herself.

"So . . . you were saying?" I prompted as the sun fully cleared the horizon, great and glowing and ushering in a new day. "You were suspended over the Cavern of Keeyops, the rope you were clutching was burning through, and angry acolytes were on either side firing arrows at you. . . ."

"Right, right," she said, and resumed her narrative.

By the time she finally finished her adventures, it was at least an hour later and I was feeling somewhat parched. "And that," she said dramatically, holding up the knife, "is how I came to possess the dagger of Vishina. Finding you, of course, was no difficulty. I simply followed the trail of carnage. Sooner or later I knew it would lead to you."

"Do you have anything to drink?" I said abruptly.

She looked disconcerted at the question. "Being thirsty is the least of your problems at the moment, don't you think?"

"No, I'd actually rank it much higher. Well? Do you?"

Sharee shook her head and sighed even as she pulled a water skin from beneath her cloak and extended it to me with her face carefully neutral. I took a quick drink from it, just to take the edge off my parched state, and then handed it back to her. "You look like you could use some yourself. That's quite a story you told. You must be dry after it."

"I am," she admitted, and knocked back a swig herself. Then she capped it and reattached it to her belt.

"You told it very well."

"Really?" She seemed surprised at the compliment. "I've no bard skills. . . ."

"Do not sell yourself short."

"So . . ." She suddenly held the dagger in her hand and then flipped it from one to the other like an experienced knife fighter. "Are you prepared to die at the hands of the one blade that could kill you?"

"Three things to say before that happens. First," I said patiently, making no move to defend myself, "you're mixing your metaphors. Blades don't have hands."

She paused, considered that, and then said impatiently, "Fine. Die at my hands, then, with the one blade that—"

"The second thing is . . . you went to a lot of trouble for nothing. I'm mortal again. You could probably kill me with a decent-sized rock."

"What?" She paled. *"What? Are you jesting with me . . . ?"*

"I'm afraid not," I told her apologetically. "I have no reason to lie. If you stab me with that dagger, it would dispatch me whether I was god or man, so if that's your weapon of choice, it really doesn't matter. But I thought you might appreciate the irony that your whole adventure was for nothing. I'd . . . rather not go into the details as to how I came to this pass, if that's all right with you. For one thing, it's not remotely as exciting as your escapades, and for another—"

She wasn't listening. Instead she was stamping about in a small circle, her frustration bursting from the seams. "That is so typical of you! The lack of consideration! I risk life and limb to obtain this weapon as a means of killing you, and you go and lose the ability to not be killed! I could have just waited and thumped an arrow into you at my leisure!"

"If it'd been a flaming arrow, it would have dispatched me at any time, actually," I offered. "Turns out I was always vulnerable to flame."

This new piece of information froze her in place. I thought she was going to have a bout of apoplexy. "You had a vulnerability? *And you didn't tell me?*"

"I didn't know at the time. Sorry." Then I frowned. "Why am I apologizing? It's not as if you had my best interests at heart."

"Well, it's just damned inconsiderate." She raised the knife, cold fury in her face. "Just one more reason to kill you, Apropos . . . as if everything you've done isn't already excuse enough."

The entire outward display of my concern was a single raised eyebrow. "You'd kill me even though I'm not what I was?"

"I'd kill you because of what you've always been, and for what you once were, and what you might yet become. That's *my* three reasons," she said tightly. She paused a step away from me, knife cocked, ready to slash down at me or to try and drive the blade into my heart. My sword remained in its scabbard on my back; my staff was in two pieces in my belt. I could have yanked out either one to try and beat back her attack. I did neither. I just stood there. "You," she continued, "said you had three things to say. You've spoken two. Utter the third so they can be your last words."

"Actually," I said calmly, "they're your words . . . specifically, that names have power."

She stared at me. "So?"

The fact that I'd been up all night, and on the run, was beginning to catch up with me. So, very tiredly, I told her, "So put down that damned knife, let's return to the Golden City and see if there's anyone left alive there—which I suspect there's not—and if there's any food to be had—which I suspect there is—and we can just put aside these foolish notions of you killing me, okay, Denyys?"

She froze, and a dozen emotions played across her face as she heard the name uttered by a dying Visionary in what seemed a lifetime ago.

"'kay," said Sharee, a.k.a. Denyys, and she lowered her knife. She shook her head and stared at me wonderingly. "I should have known," she murmured. "I should have known."

"Known what?"

She reached into her cloak once more. It was the most ubiquitous garment I had ever seen; I was beginning to think she had a small army hidden within. She produced a parchment and held it up. "It was right here. 'And will come a man who knows your name, and he will go on to . . . ' Just as he said."

I recognized the handwriting instantly. "Oh, gods, no . . . is that . . . ?"

She nodded, her eyes shining with excitement. "Yes. Produced by the Visionary who died in your inn. That's where I knew him from. We were in a card game, and he lost a considerable amount to me, and did this casting in exchange for money. You can't read it. It's—"

"Written in runic, yes, I know," I moaned. "Is . . . is that why you—?"

"Stole the gems from Beliquose, yes. Or at least the one. It's why I did most of the things I did."

"Because it was on a piece of parchment?"

"It was written," she said stubbornly. "That means it had to be so. No one takes the time to write things down if they're not true. So all these other things about the man who knows my name . . .

those are all about you. Look, here," and she pointed, "it says that you'll . . ."

I grabbed it from her hands and, before her horrified face, ripped the parchment to pieces. Then I threw them down, stomped upon them, and kicked the remaining shreds around. I did this for some time and then just stood there, huffing and puffing, and glowered at her. "All right?" I demanded.

She held up her hands in a nonconfrontational manner. "Fine."

"Good. Now let's get out of here. Me, you, and the horse you rode in on."

We mounted the horse, which seemed a sturdy enough beast and bore both our weights well enough. Sharee . . . I feel odd referring to her as "Denyys". . . swung the horse around, and we set off at a brisk trot for the Golden City. Seated behind her, I kept my arms about her waist, which felt surprisingly better than I would have thought. "I cannot believe," I told her, "that you tried to kill me just because it told you to in some parchment."

"Oh, that wasn't in the parchment," she said cheerfully. "I came up with that part myself."

"Ah. Very . . . resourceful of you."

There was absolute quiet for a time after that, and then I said very tentatively, "Sharee, there are . . . things that need to be said. Things about . . . what happened between us . . . earlier . . . a while ago. . . ."

"You don't have to dance around it," she replied, her voice firm and even. "I know to what you're referring. But you're under a misimpression."

"Am I?"

She glanced over her shoulder at me and said, "There is no 'us,' Apropos . . . at least, not in the sense that you mean. I don't think you've realized that yet. There is you . . . and there is me . . . and there are the forces which act upon us that have us do things to each other. That take control of our lives and bodies and smash us together like waves upon the Middle Finger. The only way I've managed to recover from . . . that event . . ."

"You mean with the ring . . ."

"Yes," she snapped, obviously more angrily than she wanted. Then she pulled herself together and continued, "It wasn't me . . . and it wasn't you . . . neither of us had any say or influence or—"

"I wanted to," I blurted out.

She stopped the horse, who snuffed a bit at her in annoyance, and she turned around to look me in the eyes questioningly, and with raw and naked hurt in her face. "You . . . *wanted* to . . . ? How . . . how could you—?"

"Not *that* way," I quickly amended. "Gods, not in that manner. But I . . . I had thought about taking you that way . . . because I knew you'd never willingly . . . but I never would have. But from time to time . . . it crossed my mind . . . and I just . . . I mean, I know technically you were the one who assaulted me, but it would never have happened if . . ."

"Are you trying to apologize?"

I went stone silent and looked away. I couldn't get the words out.

And without lowering her gaze at all when she spoke, she said, "It was my first time."

I blinked in surprise. "What?"

"It. You. That time, and all those subsequent times . . . it was my first . . . well, obviously, not the times after that weren't first, but . . ." Her chin quivered ever so slightly, and I think I truly realized for the first time just how young she was. Younger than I by a couple of years, at least. How young and how truly vulnerable. "I'm not a fool. I'm not . . . a romantic nitwit," she said, and it was obviously great labor for her to keep herself together. "I know the way of the world, and the realities. I had no fatuous fantasies over what the first time would be like . . . but I . . ." She shook her head. "I never envisioned it like that. At least, though, you'll be relieved to know that even if you did say you were sorry . . . it wouldn't help."

"Oh."

We sat there for a long moment, and then I said very softly, "I am, though. Sorry, I mean. And I'm even sorrier . . . that it doesn't help."

"Yes, well . . ." She turned around and snapped the reins, urging the horse forward again. "You can't trust anything weavers and wizards say."

I frowned in confusion. "Meaning?"

"I said it wouldn't help. Well . . ." She shrugged. "I may have been less than honest about that."

I started to laugh.

"Don't laugh," she said sharply. "It's not a laughing moment."

I stopped, and we rode the rest of the way in silence.

As deathly quiet as the Golden City had been upon my previous entry to it, this time it was a different sort of deathly quiet . . . namely the sort of quiet that fell upon an area when death had been there in abundance.

Sharee's horse had no desire to enter the place. I couldn't entirely blame it. Animal's senses are far more attuned to the way of things than ours, and even I could sense that death hung heavy about the place. If I'd had any brains, I wouldn't have entered the city, but I was prompted by morbid curiosity to look upon the aftermath. And so Sharee and I left the animal tethered to some brush outside the wall and entered.

We said nothing to each other for much of the walk through the paths toward the upper city. At first Sharee was looking around intently at all the damage that had been inflicted, but after a while she just forced herself to look resolutely straight ahead. Perhaps she was concerned that, if she dwelt too much upon the hardship and strife that had been brought to the former residents of the city, she might feel inclined to go against predictions, destiny or what-have-you, and lodge that hard-fought-for knife between my ribs.

We approached the low wall, and I studied it for some sign of the shadows of me, perched upon it and waving their phantom blades. But there was nothing. Of course there was nothing; it was broad daylight. Nevertheless, I shuddered inwardly at the recollection as we passed through and kept going.

Then I stopped, and Sharee halted beside me, looking at me questioningly. "Do you hear them?" I asked softly.

She paused, pricking up her ears, and then she heard it as well.

A distant buzzing.

"Flies?" she said uncomprehendingly . . . but then she understood when she saw my grim nod. "Oh. Flies."

"Yes. They do seem to come from nowhere when the feast is available, don't they," I observed. "You may want to hang back; this isn't likely to be pretty."

"I can endure whatever you can," replied Sharee.

I shrugged. "As you wish." We resumed walking as I commented, "I suspect within a day or so, we wouldn't be needing the buzzing of flies to alert us to the whereabouts of the fallen. The odor should be pungent enough to draw predators, and keep people away, for miles around."

We arrived at the great house, and I saw the first of the bodies lying upon the steps. It was Gavin, the young man who had been so determined to emulate me. He lay with his head angled downward, his arms splayed, a quizzical look upon his face and blood upon his chest. Sharee gasped when she saw him. "A boy. He's just a boy," she murmured.

"He was," was all I said, not bothering to tell her about his aspirations to be one who ravished and pillaged . . . just like his idol, me. We stepped gingerly around him and made our way into the house.

There was blood everywhere. Blood upon the walls, on the floors. Insects were crawling all over, feasting, and I heard the distant fluttering of wings that told me airborne scavengers had become alerted to the waiting banquet. Out into the main courtyard, and that was where the majority of the damage had been done. The place was thick with flies, but the insects paid us no mind, attending to their own interests. Every so often one of them would buzz near us in curiosity, and I would slap the little bastards away from me. I glanced over at Sharee. She was slightly pale, but appeared to be holding up in the face of such unrestrained butchery.

I had seen so many battlefields littered with the bodies of warriors, and overseen so many pyres as we had burned the remains lest the vermin come. Over in one area I thought I saw pieces of what might have been Slake. *Who would have thought that That Guy would turn out to have been the lucky one,* I thought. "We should . . ." I said slowly, "we should torch the place. Not leave them like this."

"Yes," Sharee nodded, staring fixedly at the bodies all around. "Yes . . . we should."

I saw something then, over toward one corner of the arena of slaughter that had once been my army. It was a piece of parchment, stuck in the midst of a pool of blood. And I realized that it had been the place that I'd seen Meander making his last stand. "What is it?" Sharee called after me as I walked quickly over to it, delicately picked up the parchment, and smoothed it out so that the words upon it were clear. "What is it?" she repeated.

I felt my throat closing up, and a distant pounding in the back of my head. "It's a note. It's to me."

"A note? From whom?" she asked, coming closer and trying to peer over my shoulder to see it.

I took a deep breath and read . . .

My dear Apropos. I suspect you will survive to read this. I suspect you could survive if the sun itself were extinguished. In the event that I am correct, which I usually am, I wish to do you a service, one leader of men to another. I wish to tell you that I have lied to you almost consistently. I remember every moment of every day of my life that I have ever lived. And I remember killing your mother quite clearly. The last thing she cried out before I did so was "I forgive you." I never knew whether she intended that for me or for you. In any case, I was concerned that, as a result of the events which I have borne witness to, you might somehow lose your capacity for hatred. That would be a tragic waste of material, for I believe your hatred will take you very, very far. It is your greatest weapon. Do not let it go. So hate me. Yours in elusiveness . . .

King Meander

She stared at it for a good long time, and then she said softly, "He's quite mad, you know. There's no reason to believe this to be any more true than anything else he's said."

"I know," I said very quietly, and then deliberately tore the note to pieces, just as I had done with the document that I'd snatched from Sharee's hands. "He wishes to write my future for me."

"You're not going to let him, ar—"

A loud screech filled the air. We both turned and there, somehow as I knew he would be, was Mordant. Something was glittering in his talons as he angled downward, and then he released it and it thudded to the ground next to us.

We stared at it in amazement.

It was the Eye of the Beholder . . . intact. Ribboned through it were what appeared to be over a hundred fractures . . . but nevertheless, the gem had fused into a whole once again. It glinted at me in the light of day, and instinctively I backed up. To my surprise, Sharee did as well. She seemed no more anxious to be near the thing than was I.

"Is that . . . ?" she inquired.

Slowly I nodded. "I saw the damned thing shatter into shards, but there it is again," I said wonderingly. "I wouldn't have thought it possible. But considering all that I've experienced, I'm beginning to think nothing is impossible." I had told Sharee some of what had transpired: of everything that I'd learned of the Eye, of the true identity of my consort. I continued not to tell her about the notion that I'd condemned the world to eventual mundanity. It was hardly something I was anxious to boast about. "So . . . what do we do with it? I mean . . . we can't just leave it here."

"No, it's too potent," she agreed. "We have to dispose of it."

"Right, yes. Absolutely."

Sharee looked slightly agitated as she continued, "I mean, that . . . that thing . . . it's an icon of pure chaos. Whoever remains in continued contact with it, well . . . it's obvious that horrible things will happen as a result. It will cause discord and strife and war and . . . and all manner of horrible things . . ."

"Frequently in the names of gods," I added.

"Yes, correct. Right. Well," and she took a deep breath, "I'll just . . . I'll just go and get it, then." She took a step toward it, and I immediately clamped a hand on her shoulder.

"You?" I said softly. "Why should you get it? I should get it. I was bonded with it, after all. I know how to handle it."

"Oh, and didn't you just do a fine job of handling it thus far," she said, pointing around the courtyard at the assortment of corpses. "I, on the other hand, never was corrupted by it. . . ."

"It was more likely deciding which of the two of us to go after. It might well settle for you since I fought it off," I replied. "I should carry it."

"I should!" snarled Sharee, and she started to reach around for her knife. I, meantime, swung my now-intact walking staff around and snapped the blade out of the dragon's mouth, ready for her to make a move.

The loud screech from Mordant jolted us out of the moment, and we stood there and stared at each other sheepishly. "It would appear," she said softly, "that neither of us should be in possession of it. So . . . now what?"

"We find some shovels," I said.

We were able to turn up a couple before long, and we began to dig. As we did so, I thought briefly about the assortment of gems currently sitting in the mansion. The generous present that I had brought from deep within Mount Aerie as a gift for my beloved consort. I toyed with the notion of going back for them, but painfully decided against it. I might have been imagining it, but I couldn't help but worry that there was some sort of connection between those gems and the frightening large one that lay on the ground next to the deepening hole Sharee and I were digging.

Besides, the fewer remembrances I took along with me of this entire madness, the better I would like it.

We dug for much of the rest of the day, feeling that there wasn't a hole deep enough to bury this thing in. We had a small bit to eat, but I can assure you that being surrounded by corpses is a superb way to lose one's appetite. As the day wore on, the bodies began to become more pungent, but Sharee reached out and gently tugged some of the threads. Soon stiff breezes were rolling in, pushing the aroma substantially away from us. I was extremely grateful for that, and told Sharee as much. She shrugged it off.

Finally the hole was deep enough to satisfy us both. I tapped the gem into the hole with the flat of my shovel, and it tumbled in without a sound. "Let's put a couple of bodies atop it," suggested Sharee, "so if anyone happens to realize there's turned up earth and they begin digging, they'll come across a corpse and stop."

"Excellent idea. And I know just the corpses."

I went out to the front steps, brushed the flies away from Gavin, slung him over my shoulder and brought him back to the hole, tossing him in. On top of him, I lay Hecate's body as well. It felt impossibly light; perhaps the only thing that had given her any weight at all was her hatred. I wondered briefly how much my own hatred was weighing upon me, and then dismissed the notion as being excessively profound.

Sharee stared down at her. "I've never seen a god before," she said.

"What do you think?"

"I thought she'd be taller."

And we proceeded to shovel the dirt back onto them. The dirt certainly went down much faster than it came up. We were covered with grime and sweat by the time we were through, and the sun was setting. It had certainly been a hell of a way to spend the day: in a city where the only sounds were the buzzing of insects and the scraping of shovels.

Once we were done, I went back into the house and returned several minutes later with tins of oil. I started spreading them everywhere while Sharee looked on. "You seem pensive," I ventured as I emptied the last of the containers on the bodies.

"It's nothing," she said dismissively, and ignored any attempts of mine to press the matter.

Several minutes and a couple of well-placed torches later, the courtyard was burning. The flies were no doubt rather upset about the development as the flames licked hungrily at the corpses of men whose main sin in life had been following me. *Well . . . they should have known better* was all I could think.

By the time the flames were really high, we were already out of town. I had made only one, brief stop during our exit: I had passed a shrine dedicated to me. One of many, I was given to understand, that dotted the city. It had originally been dedicated to some other god, but there were crude portraits of me now placed all around it, and a few sacrificed animals strewn about. I stared at it for a long moment, ignoring Sharee's urgings to depart, and then I knelt before it and whispered something softly. I returned to her then and she said impatiently, "What did you just do?"

"Prayed for myself," I replied. "If I can't pray to myself for myself, to whom can I pray?"

We stood outside the walls of the Golden City and watched the flames licking the sky, smoke spiraling upward in great thick black clouds. Mordant was perched upon my outstretched arm. I could see that same thoughtful look in Sharee's eyes as the flames continued their cleansing work. "What is it?" I demanded. "You wouldn't tell me before. Reticence has never been your strength. So out with it."

"Well,"—she sighed—"I'm just thinking that we've likely doomed this city, that's all. As I said to you before: That gem is a focal point for discord and strife. It may be that, in time, it becomes more and more powerful, which means that anyone who resides within those walls could eventually fall prey to the chaotic energies the gem gives off. Perhaps we should have found a way to dispose of it in some other manner . . ."

"No, we did the right thing," I said firmly. "First, the chances are that no one is ever going to try and take up residence in that city again. And *if* they do, and *if* they start fighting over it, well . . . how long can they keep it up? Eventually they'll have to come to peaceful terms, lest they kill each other off wholesale. Either way, it won't be our concern. Isn't that right, Mordant?" I added affectionately.

She looked at the drabit with distaste as we started walking, with Sharee holding her horse's reins and guiding it along the road. "How you can dote on that hideous-looking beast, I've no idea."

"This isn't just any beast. This," and I jostled Mordant slightly, "is my mother, reborn again into this lower creature and keeping an eye upon me."

Sharee looked well and truly appalled at the notion. "Where the hell did you get that idea?"

"From a dream I had. You were in it, as a matter of fact. Or are you going to deny you sent me this dream, as you've denied it in the past?"

"Bloody well right I'll deny it. You've got to start thinking for yourself, and stop ascribing everything in your life to me."

"Do I have to do that, Mordant?" I inquired.

"Absolutely," said Mordant.

And as we both stopped dead and stared at the creature who had just spoken to us with perfect articulation, the Golden City—known by many other names, but most commonly called "Yerushalem" by the natives—continued to burn brightly against the rapidly darkening skies.